"Hold-your-breath romantic suspense with one of the most chillingly evil villains I've ever read. *Fade to Black* crackles with dark, edgy danger."

—JoAnn Ross, *New York Times* bestselling author of *Shattered*

NO TURNING BACK

Unable to keep the smile from his face as he drove, Dean had to acknowledge that for the first time in months, he felt genuinely good about something that did not involve his son.

Surprised by that self-realization, Dean almost drove right by Stacey's house as he turned into her neighborhood. Spying the number on the mailbox, he swung into the driveway, parking right behind her dusty cruiser.

He sat there for a moment, wondering whether he was losing it. Maybe. Maybe not. Either way, he was looking forward to seeing just what else he figured out about himself and about Sheriff Stacey Rhodes. Starting tonight.

Smiling in anticipation, he grabbed the beer and walked toward the house, up the curving sidewalk lined by tall, ragged hedges. He came around the corner, intent on avoiding the sharp thorns on the holly bushes. So intent, he didn't at first notice what was happening just a few feet in front of him.

Then he saw it: the front porch stained red. The woman kneeling on it.

The woman covered in blood.

And he stopped smiling.

Fade to Black
A Black CATs Novel

Leslie Parrish

A SIGNET ECLIPSE BOOK

SIGNET ECLIPSE
Published by New American Library, a division of
Penguin Group (USA) Inc., 375 Hudson Street,
New York, New York 10014, USA
Penguin Group (Canada), 90 Eglinton Avenue East, Suite 700, Toronto,
Ontario M4P 2Y3, Canada (a division of Pearson Penguin Canada Inc.)
Penguin Books Ltd., 80 Strand, London WC2R 0RL, England
Penguin Ireland, 25 St. Stephen's Green, Dublin 2,
Ireland (a division of Penguin Books Ltd.)
Penguin Group (Australia), 250 Camberwell Road, Camberwell, Victoria 3124,
Australia (a division of Pearson Australia Group Pty. Ltd.)
Penguin Books India Pvt. Ltd., 11 Community Centre, Panchsheel Park,
New Delhi - 110 017, India
Penguin Group (NZ), 67 Apollo Drive, Rosedale, North Shore 0632,
New Zealand (a division of Pearson New Zealand Ltd.)
Penguin Books (South Africa) (Pty.) Ltd., 24 Sturdee Avenue,
Rosebank, Johannesburg 2196, South Africa

Penguin Books Ltd., Registered Offices:
80 Strand, London WC2R 0RL, England

First published by Signet Eclipse, an imprint of New American Library,
a division of Penguin Group (USA) Inc.

First Printing, July 2009
10 9 8 7 6 5 4 3 2 1

To Bruce.
You've been by my side for every step
of this long journey, pushing me on, sometimes pulling me,
and always lifting me when I fell.

I cannot imagine walking through my life
without you right there by my side.

Acknowledgments

I must extend sincere thanks to several people who helped me with this project from start to finish.

To Janelle Denison, Julie Leto, and Carly Phillips—aka the Plotmonkeys—thank you so much for supporting me from the very minute I said I wanted to try writing something dark and thrilling.

To my agent, Pamela Harty. Thanks for looking at a romantic comedy writer and seeing the potential for blood and gore. I so appreciate your standing by me.

To my editor, Laura Cifelli . . . you won't regret giving me this shot. I promise.

Sincere thanks also to Leo A. Notenboom (www.ask-leo.com) for the technical advice and consultation. All the computer expertise is his . . . any errors are entirely my own.

Prologue

In the final moments of her life Lisa Zimmerman realized she knew her killer. With his black-cloaked form illuminated by moonlight, it took just one particular whispered expression to send the truth flooding into her pain-numbed consciousness.

Her slowing brain cells jolted back into awareness. *"You?"* It hurt to push the whispered word across her swollen lips, which were caked with blood and dirt and flecked with bits of dug-in gravel. Despite the pain, she added, "Can't be."

But it was true.

She knew who had tied her to this tree, her arms stretched painfully above her head, leaving her to dangle from wrenched shoulders and balance on the tips of her bare toes. Knew who had viciously slashed the blade across her abdomen until she'd felt warm, sticky blood spill down her legs onto her feet. Knew who watched her from behind the black hood, his dull eyes reflecting no emotion, as if her agony didn't exist.

Knew him.

Until this moment, she'd been floating, dazed and nearly disappearing into a world she'd created in her own head, one in which this was happening to someone else, and she was merely an observer. Now, though, shock sent her blood-deprived, slowing heart back into overdrive, until it thudded in a hard, desperate rhythm. Her shallow breaths, each of which caused a strange whistling sound in her chest, grew more rapid.

Knowing made it worse. That *he* could do such a thing . . .

Knowing didn't, however, ease the pain that had begun with the first sweep of the knife. She'd tried to escape it by giving in to the slow lethargy of blood loss. Now the terror she'd felt when she'd realized she was being kidnapped came rushing back like a bullet hitting her heart dead center.

Feeling capable of moving again, she expended what little energy she had left in a vain effort to pull back and evade the next slow, deliberate stroke, meant to torment more than wound. He'd wounded her deeply enough the first time. Now he was just playing.

I've known you most of my life. How could *you?*

His identity offered no glimmer of salvation. Sent no ideas of how to escape through her half-dead brain, which seemed ready to shut down, with one final prayer that it would be over soon. It didn't give her courage or make her want to put up a fight, as she had when he'd grabbed her as she'd stumbled out of Dick's Tavern. That had been . . . days ago? Weeks? *Centuries?*

No. It might have seemed like an eternity, but it had probably been an hour or two since she'd left the crowded bar. She'd been so drunk that she had at first thought some guy who'd bought her a drink was hoping for some payback in the dark shadows of the gravel parking lot. Or that the one real friend she had left in this town had come to drag her home, safe and sound, whether she liked it or not. *Safe and sound . . . at home?*

The merciless crunch of his powerful fist on her

jaw had quickly killed those ideas. Her kidnapper had dragged her across the ground, half-conscious, unable to whimper, much less call for help. Not that anybody else had been outside to hear.

He had thrown her into the back of a covered pickup and driven her out here into the middle of nowhere, where she'd assumed she was going to be raped. But every minute since, he'd made it clear he didn't want to fuck her. He used to—*God, why did you laugh at him?*—but now he wanted only one thing: to watch her die.

The pain, so sharp at first, had dulled into a deep burning. She begged for mercy, knowing it wouldn't come. "Please let me go. I won't tell. I know how to keep secrets."

"Just stay quiet," he said. His words were a little choppy, as if, despite his still, calm demeanor, he felt some emotion about what he was doing to her.

Maybe ...

As quickly as it had arisen, the hope that he might actually have some glimmer of humanity that could be appealed to disappeared. Because through swollen, half-closed eyes, she saw him reach down and rub his crotch.

Yeah. Definitely feeling some emotion. "You sick motherfucker," she spat.

"Shut up, filthy slut!" He swung his arm back, but this time, instead of the blade, he used his fist to quiet her. He didn't want this to end too soon. There would be no goading him into killing her quickly. "You're dirty and you deserve what you get."

The blow flung her head back and she saw stars. Not the figurative kind, but a blanket of real ones filling the midnight blue sky above. So many they'd take a thousand nights to count, a lifetime to appreciate.

She had minutes, at most. Seconds if she was very lucky.

Trying to distance herself from it, she kept staring upward, focusing on the full moon, the heavens. "Daddy," she whispered, pleading for something she'd lost long ago.

How could the world still be turning and life continuing everywhere else when she was being tortured to death? Beneath all that light, that immenseness, she was entirely and completely alone with the monster who wanted her dead.

"I'm sorry." Tears oozed from the corners of her eyes to mingle with the blood and dirt on her cheeks. She didn't know whom she was talking to. Some God she'd long since stopped believing in? Herself for getting caught in this trap?

Maybe she was trying to say the one thing she'd never said to the one person who truly deserved to hear it. *This will break her heart.*

The vision of her sad, weary mother, who'd been so loving, yet so impossibly blind, brought her head forward. She again focused on her attacker.

He was no demon. Just a vicious, awful human being.

"Why?" A weak whisper was all she could manage. She had to have lost a lot of blood. It no longer gushed, but still dripped slowly down her front. Its warmth against her bare skin contrasted sharply with the cold air of the March night. *Not long now.*

"Because you're a whore and nobody will miss you," he said with a shrug.

How had nobody ever noticed he was insane?

"Wait here." As if she had any other choice.

He glanced to his right, shook his head, then strode to the edge of the small clearing in which he'd imprisoned her.

That was when she saw the video camera.

Standing on a tripod, it was pointed directly at her. A small red light pierced the darkness, indicating that the camera was on, recording this. He was capturing her pain, casting her final moments into a bloody sequence of two-dimensional images.

"You're gonna be famous," he claimed as he adjusted the thing.

He tilted it down a little. A whirring noise told her he'd zoomed in closer.

"Sick pig," she mumbled, though the words were so soft she barely even heard them. She wasn't able to breathe well, barely had the air to make any audible sounds.

"We're both gonna be famous."

Both famous. Lisa's eyes drifted closed. Her muscles unable to support her any longer, her legs slowly went limp. She hardly felt the agony of her shoulders pulling from their sockets under the full pressure of her body's near deadweight.

Famous.

The word zipped through her mind, making her suck in one last desperate breath of hope. Even as she heard the crunch of dried leaves beneath his feet as he returned to finish what he'd so brutally started, she couldn't help feeling a tiny moment of triumph.

He was on that tape with her. Disguised, yes, in a black cape and a hood. But she had recognized him. Somebody else would, too. Long after she was dead and gone, someone would see that video and catch him. Small comfort, but it was something.

The footsteps stopped. Lisa didn't have to open her eyes to know he was again beside her. The warmth of his breath emerging through the opening in his hood brushed her cheek. If she had any strength, she'd turn her head and sink her teeth into his throat. But strength had long abandoned her. As had dreams of escape. Justice, though—that fantasy hadn't disappeared yet.

"Ready for your close-up?" he whispered.

Close-up of you, too, bastard.

He touched her cheek with one black-gloved finger. "Don't be sad. Lots of people will see this. They'll love you, and they'll never know what a cheap whore you are."

The arm swung. A kiss of steely fire. And a few random thoughts before oblivion.

Why was he making this video?

Who would see it?

Don't let Mama see. . . .

Then blackness.

Cutting the thing that had once been a woman down from the tree, he couldn't help feeling surprised at his own calmness. There was no panic. No fear. No remorse. Nothing except an exhilarating sense of triumph that he'd done it.

"You shouldn't have laughed at me," he said as he dragged the body across the ground. "It could have been anyone, but it was *you* because you laughed."

Any other nasty, dirty female might have done, but this one had deserved it most of all because of the way she'd acted when he'd approached her, at the mercy of his own vile urges. He was tired of being laughed at. Sneered at.

He wouldn't be anymore. The lump he was rolling into a tarp and tying closed for burial proved that much. And soon, thanks to his video, which he would edit to make sure there was nothing in it to give him away, he'd be able to show the world.

At least, his world. The only one where he was understood. The only one that mattered to him anymore.

The only one where he belonged.

Chapter 1

Seventeen months later

During his five years working the roughest streets of Baltimore, and his seven in the FBI's Violent Criminal Apprehension Program, Special Agent Dean Taggert had seen firsthand just how vicious people could be.

He'd responded to shootings and gang hits. Had put his hands onto gushing wounds to try to save a victim waiting for an ambulance. He'd shot and had been shot at.

But this . . . God, he had never seen anything like this.

"It can't be real," he muttered. "This video is a fake. It's got to be."

He spoke more to himself than to IT specialist Brandon Cole, who had pulled him aside and asked him to take a look at something he'd stumbled across on the Internet. Cole, who'd been with the FBI's Cyber Division for less than a year, was a bit of a renegade, but the kid knew his stuff when it came to computers.

This time, though, he was wrong. He had to be wrong.

"It's real," Cole said.

He didn't elaborate, letting Dean see for himself, waiting for him to concede that something so far beyond his darkest nightmares could really have happened.

Waiting for him to accept it.

He didn't want to. Didn't want to even imagine that someone could do such a thing, and then upload it to the Web for others to see, as well. When the final moment came, however, when the poor woman on the screen died without the camera pulling away for a single second, he could no longer deny it.

"Okay. It's not a fake," he admitted, both to himself and to his coworker.

Nobody outside of Hollywood could pull off a scene as horrifically convincing as this one. And the video they were watching had been taken by an amateur, not a cinematographer with a multimillion-dollar budget for gory special effects.

The crime itself, however, was anything but amateur.

He'd thought leaving ViCAP for a new Cyber Action Team—CAT—would mean never having to work a case like this again. He'd wanted to get all that darkness and violence out of his life so he could be normal. Have fewer nightmares.

Be a better father.

Even in a new type of CAT devoted to solving Internet-related murders, he'd never imagined the hideous possibilities, picturing only money launderers who'd embezzled from the wrong guys or scumbags luring victims via online dating sites.

This? He'd never even conceived of it.

"I recognize that setup," he said, swallowing hard, trying to keep his breakfast down as the video faded to black. "It's a scene right out of that old movie *The Hitcher*, where the girl is chained to the back of a semi and then pulled apart."

"Yeah, I think so," Brandon said. He tapped a few keys to return the digital video file to the beginning, as well as enlarge the image. As if anybody would want a better view of that. Pausing on a close-up of the victim's face, he added, "I wouldn't have shown it to you if I hadn't been sure it was authentic and not some fake snuff film. To be certain, I did some digging on unusual unsolved murders and I found her."

Smart. Very smart.

"You might even remember the case. It made national news after her remains were found. She was a twenty-seven-year-old accountant, murdered five months ago. She left her office for lunch one afternoon and was found in pieces a week later in a wooded area outside a small Pennsylvania town."

"Yeah, I remember it. Sick."

Brandon nodded his agreement. "The victim's photo looked close enough to the woman in the video footage for me to contact the locals and get a copy of the autopsy report. It was like reading a script for what happened on the tape." Shrugging in self-deprecation, which was completely out of character for the young man, he added, "Not that I'm an expert on that type of thing, of course, but it seemed pretty irrefutable."

Brandon, with his obviously bleached blond hair, his brightly colored dress shirts worn beneath his trendy suits, and a damned cocky attitude, was smart enough to be an expert on just about anything. He'd probably never try it out in the field, but the twenty-five-year-old got away with a lot here in cyber crimes because he was pure magic when it came to computers. The FBI had been lucky to get him. Brandon could have made himself rich in the private sector. Or in the criminal one.

Finally, when the tension in Brandon's small office reached its breaking point, the younger man closed the video player window. At last able to look at something other than the victim's terrified face, Dean released the breath he didn't know he'd been holding.

"I figured it was time to bring somebody else in once I knew for sure."

"Next time, how about a warning before you show me a real-life slasher flick?"

"You're warned."

Damn. Something about the intensity in Brandon's voice, and the tense way his body hunched over his keyboard, told Dean there was more to this case. More than just one poor, pretty young accountant who'd met a human savage.

"Why'd you decide to show *me*?" Dean asked.

"With your violent crimes and Baltimore PD background, I figured you'd be the best bet. I didn't want to take it to Wyatt until I knew for sure."

Supervisory Special Agent Wyatt Blackstone was their leader, and though the new team had come together only a month ago, Dean already knew his boss was very good at what he did. Not everyone agreed with that, however—as evidenced by the fact that some called the new team the Black CATs, with both humor and a little malice.

The malice—spite, really—was all directed at Wyatt. And everybody knew why.

Exposing a case of internal corruption had taken guts and a desire for career suicide. Despite being highly respected by many, Blackstone was also hated by some. Especially those whose friends had been brought down in the scandal uncovered by Blackstone last year, a scandal that had gone all the way up to the deputy director's office. Dean didn't know everything, but he did know that a couple of convictions that had relied on evidence run through the FBI crime lab had been overturned after Blackstone had brought up the allegations of evidence tampering against several other agents.

"So what's the matter, Cole? You think Wyatt's not going to believe you?"

Brandon leaned back in his rolling chair. "He won't

doubt it once he sees all the evidence. But I want backup when I fight for the case."

"Fight for it?" Dean tensed, afraid he knew where Brandon was headed. The kid might be a computer genius, but he had joined the FBI because he wanted to catch bad guys. He actually sounded as though he thought their group would be investigating what he'd already admitted was a Pennsylvania murder case.

"You know nobody ever expected this team to really succeed, right?"

Dean simply stared. He'd had his suspicions that the new CAT had been set up for failure to punish Blackstone, but he'd never spoken about them.

"They'll try to take this case as soon as word gets out," Brandon added.

"You're right, but what does it matter? It's not ours; it's the local PD's. You should give them the file and let them do the investigating. If they want the bureau's help finding this sick bastard, they can ask the NCAVC like everybody else." He glanced at the screen again, noting the ferocity of the crime, doubting they were dealing with any kind of "normal" killer. "Or the BAU."

The way things went at the Behavioral Analysis Unit, however, they might not get help. That department was overworked, overbooked, and able to assist in only a fraction of the cases local jurisdictions asked them to come in on.

Brandon's chin jutted out in visible determination. "You're wrong, and I'm about to prove that. And then, together, we can make sure Wyatt has absolutely no doubt that it's legitimately ours to investigate."

Frowning, and not sure he wanted to know, Dean narrowed his eyes. A sudden fear that he understood made him say, "She's not the only victim."

When the other man shook his head, Dean felt his

legs weaken. He slumped onto an empty chair, figuring he'd need to sit for whatever Brandon had to tell him.

"There are more, spread across four states."

Damn.

"And every one of them has a Web connection."

Double damn.

Now he understood Cole's determination to keep the case, and why he feared they wouldn't be able to. Getting Wyatt Blackstone completely on board was the only way their group would not be steamrolled out of the investigation. The videos were aired on the Internet; some would say that didn't mean the Internet was actually involved. And that the NCAVC, which contained both ViCAP and the Behavioral Analysis Unit, was the better department to coordinate the investigation.

They might be right. Dean couldn't deny that he wouldn't mind if it played out that way. He hadn't clocked in for this. He'd left his secure job in ViCAP to join an experimental team, hoping for a little normalcy, some stability so he could go back into court and fight his ex-wife for more time with his seven-year-old son.

It wasn't that Dean didn't feel a stirring, deep inside the determined law enforcement core of him, that demanded the privilege of taking this bastard down. This transfer, however, had been about getting away from that dark shit so his ex could no longer use his position working violent crimes against him. It wouldn't work if his new job involved hunting down a serial killer who could teach Dahmer a thing or two about causing pain.

It's what you do. What you do best.

"How many?" he asked, needing to know.

"Eight, going back almost a year and a half. I'm pretty sure I've found them all."

Eight.

Eight victims. Eight people brutally murdered, their last painful moments captured on film. Had they all, Dean wondered, been tortured before their deaths and mutilated after them, as this victim appeared to have been?

A dull throb began to pound inside his skull, and his stomach churned. He closed his eyes, a series of faces appearing in his mind: his sister's, his parents', his son's. Each of them replaced the face of that woman on the video until he felt almost physically ill.

And finally, he simply couldn't stand it anymore.

"All right. Let's go find Wyatt."

An hour later, with the entire team crowded into their boss's cramped office, Dean watched his colleagues experience the videotaped horror.

Wyatt had reacted immediately to the information Dean and Brandon had brought him. After watching the video clip and asking a few pertinent questions, he'd called everyone together to get the details on the case all at once.

They'd started with the tape. Which, after a third viewing, was embedding itself frame by frame into Dean's mind.

"Anybody need to see this again?" Brandon asked as the screen of his oversize laptop faded to black.

"No way," said Special Agent Jackie Stokes. "Come on, Cole. It's fake, right?"

Stokes, a striking fortysomething African-American woman whose forensic skills were matched only by her talent with a keyboard, stood beside Dean, rigid with disbelief. Tension rolled off her lean, muscular form.

"It's not. And I also hate to say it, but this is just one of the videos I've found." Cole leaned back in the chair and crossed his arms, looking up at each person in the group, all clustered tightly around their boss's desk.

"There's more?" snapped Special Agent Kyle Mulrooney. "Tell me we're not gonna have to pop some popcorn and watch a whole afternoon of this filth."

Mulrooney, a barrel-chested agency man who'd been around since the Reagan years, shook his head in disgust. His usually smiling, round face held no hint of surprise—as if he'd long since lost his ability to be shocked by anything his fellow man could do.

Dean wasn't quite sure whether he was going to like working with Mulrooney yet. The older man was a little too jovial to work well with someone who'd often been accused of having no sense of humor at all.

Well, his ex-wife had accused him of that. And where she was concerned, he really didn't have much of a sense of humor. Who would?

"Sweet Jesus, just when you think the species can't go any lower," Mulrooney muttered, proving he and Dean were on the same page, at least today.

Wondering what their second IT specialist was thinking, Dean turned to gauge Lily Fletcher's reaction. What he saw didn't surprise him. Lily stared blankly at the screen, her blue eyes widened in horror and glassy with unshed tears. With more years on the job than Brandon, she was still untried, with no field experience. She was a computer geek, though a pretty one. And right now she looked ready to throw up.

Standing behind them all, arms crossed, face expressionless, stood Supervisory Special Agent Wyatt Blackstone. Their leader. The man who'd talked Dean into giving up a pretty good gig with a prestigious department for an experimental one here. One that was supposed to be a whole lot more normal and a whole lot less bloody.

Huh.

Even aside from the brutal case he might soon be working, the jury was still out on whether he'd made the right decision. The fact that all six of them were crowded into Wyatt's office, since they didn't even have a usable conference room, said a lot about how their team was regarded.

"We'll need to see the rest." Wyatt, as if sensing the tension in the room, added, "But let's talk for a while first. I need to hear why you think this case is ours, Brandon, and why I shouldn't pick up the phone and hand it over to NCAVC."

Brandon's eyes gleamed with confidence. "It's ours. Trust me."

The enigmatic team leader's expression revealed nothing. "Convince me."

Hearing the note of censure in his tone, Brandon nodded, getting the point. That was all it ever took with Wyatt. The man never raised his voice, never issued threats, never looked uncomfortable in his black suits or strangled by his dark, conservative ties. Never a hair out of place or a sheen of sweat on his brow. In fact, he never appeared affected by anything the job threw at him, not even getting ostracized as a whistle-blower.

"If you'll excuse me, I think I need to go splash bleach in my eyes before the second feature," Mulrooney said.

Nobody laughed. They all felt much the same.

Brandon closed the video player window on his powerful, state-of-the-art laptop, and swiveled in Wyatt's chair. "It's not a double feature. I've found eight so far."

Wyatt put a hand up, halting the conversation that erupted after Brandon's bald announcement. "Let's take five, then meet back here when we've all regained our focus."

Leaving the tight office, Dean finally felt capable of drawing a clean breath of air. Or at least as clean a breath as one could get in this stuffy, stifling old suite of crappy rooms at FBI headquarters.

Only the computer equipment was top-of-the-line. Everything else had been handed down to the team by other departments: desks, chairs, and worktables that had been gathering dust in their own storage rooms.

Wyatt's requisition for office equipment had been stalled. And their so-called conference room was stacked floor to ceiling with dusty boxes full of ancient files.

"What the hell did you get yourself into?" Dean asked himself aloud as he grabbed a bottle of water from a small fridge somebody had stuck in the hallway between two rickety bookcases. He took it into his office and sipped it slowly, savoring the clean, cool relief that seemed to wash away some of the ugliness of the morning. When he was finished, he headed back into the lion's den.

Entering his boss's office, Dean found the others already there. They were seated in folding chairs around a small worktable somebody had set up at the end of the desk. Wyatt sat behind it, Brandon to his right.

Brandon, suitably subdued, didn't volunteer any new information. He quietly waited for their boss to ask him for the exact details he wanted to know.

Blackstone picked up right where they'd left off. "Are all of them bad as the one you showed us?"

The young IT specialist shrugged. "Define *bad*. If getting buried alive is nicer than being ripped in half, I suppose some are worse than others. They're all pretty awful, by any definition."

Buried alive. God in heaven.

"How do you know they're connected?"

"The unsub himself. He's got a portfolio, I guess you'd call it."

"Hold up," Dean said, not willing to accept the brief answers a chastened Brandon Cole might offer. He wanted the whole story, start to finish. That might not be Wyatt's style, but the supervisory special agent wasn't a field guy; he hadn't been for a long time. He was used to running an office, being briefed along the way—succinctly and concisely.

Dean knew from experience, however, that succinct

and concise didn't cut it at the start of an investigation. They needed to know every detail, as ugly as those details might be. Learning the minutiae would allow all of them to watch for patterns, to hunt for mistakes. And bring them closer to nailing this sick bastard.

Besides, something this distasteful had to be built up to, not just gulped down in huge bites of information.

"Start at the beginning, Cole. Who the hell is this guy, and how'd you find him?"

"I got a tip from an old friend," Cole said. "He's a gamer. D and D, Second Life, Zanpo. Guy lives a virtual existence; I don't think he's seen the sun since 2006. He heard rumors about a very secretive site, an international one, where things don't just get realistic; they're downright bloody." Cole tilted back on the rear two legs of his chair, like some kid in science class. "It's called Satan's Playground, and from what my friend said, that's a pretty good name for the kinds of things going on there."

"Never heard of it," Dean said.

"Considering it's been around for a couple of years, you'd think there'd be more whispers about it among that circle, but the people who run the site are smart, and they're secretive. Nobody gets in without an invitation and five 'references.' The whole thing's hosted overseas, with members in probably two dozen countries. Redundant servers, constantly changing passwords, encryption, layer upon layer of security."

Dean might officially be part of the Cyber Division now, but he had only the most basic knowledge of computers, so he didn't even try to understand the technical details Brandon rattled off. Mulrooney, he already knew, was the same way.

That was another thing that made their CAT unique— having a good mix of experienced field agents and IT specialists. It was, of course, the only way a group formed to solve Internet-related murders could ever work. They needed both skill sets. Make that the best of both skill sets. Which was exactly what Blackstone had told Dean when he'd recruited him.

"Sounds sophisticated for a bunch of bored losers with no real lives," Lily said.

Brandon shook his head. "I don't think that's what we're looking at. Judging by the money involved, and some of the conversations I've seen, we're talking about normal people with careers, families, wealth. It's much more like a pervert's secret worldwide club than any gaming universe for teenagers with no social skills and no jobs. Accountants by day, cyber S and M masters by night."

"So, Brandon, how'd you break in?" Jackie Stokes asked, her tone challenging. Stokes was the unique one in the group, straddling both lines. She'd done forensic work in the field early in her career, but had started working cyber crimes several years ago when her kids were little. Now that they were older, she seemed itchy to get back out there, traveling, getting her hands dirty. Though Dean doubted she'd ever pictured them getting this dirty. "I don't suppose you got an invite. And if you did, I have serious questions about these friends of yours."

Brandon merely shrugged, a tiny smirk on his mouth. The guy was cocky. Maybe as cocky as Dean had been when he'd started with the Baltimore PD fresh out of college a lifetime ago.

"Let's just say I came in through the unattended back gate of the Playground." Then the young man focused his attention on Wyatt. "Satan's Playground doesn't exist anywhere but in cyberspace. Sounds to me like it's exactly our type of case."

Wyatt didn't reply, appearing to mull it over.

Wanting more, Dean prodded, "Okay, we've got the backstory. Tell us what you discovered when you actually made your way inside."

"I discovered that animated people can have all kinds of wild, nasty sex and can do the most violent, degrading things to each other." Brandon spoke quickly, as always, expecting everyone to keep up. "Rape, pedophilia, S and M, incest, whatever your kink, there's an area of the playground for you. Including a big hellhole under the sliding board for those who like to enact murder scenes, to the cheers and adulation of others."

"Virtual murders," Dean clarified.

"At first. But then, almost a year and a half ago, something changed. This new guy appeared on the scene. Calls himself the Reaper."

How original.

"His avatar is this black-cloaked dude with a skull face; a totally off-the-rack, Grim Reaper Halloween-costume look. And he invites people to join a new club within Satan's Playground. A club for those who want to see people really die."

Dean would like to think such a club would have very few members. But he knew better. After twelve years in law enforcement, God, did he know better.

Still needing to work off the nervous energy that always enveloped him, Brandon began to tap his pencil on the table, keeping an underlying staccato beat—a sense of urgency in the rhythm. "His first one was a freebie, just to show he could do it."

Dean wanted to be sure he had things straight. "Was that the one we just saw, with the woman pulled apart?"

"No. That came later. From what I can tell, the first was uploaded a year ago last April, and it showed a naked woman tied to a tree and slowly sliced to death. Like I said, a free sample, just to show he was for real. New videos have followed, one every two or three months, and after that freebie he started charging people."

Lily *tsk*ed in disgust. "For the privilege of watching?"

Brandon shook his head. "Not at first, though he's doing that now, too."

"So what was he charging for?" Mulrooney asked. He leaned back and crossed his big arms across his beefy chest. "Whether this vile crap's in color or black-and-white? Murder on demand? Kill-per-view?"

"That's closer to the mark." Brandon stopped tapping and glanced at every person there, as if to stress that they'd reached the most important part.

"He's holding auctions so other members of the club can participate in the kill. Within seventy-two hours of every auction, another 'feature' title goes up on the marquee of the drive-in theater."

"This playground has all the perks, huh?" asked Jackie.

"Right down to an ice-cream parlor where you can lure little kids." He quickly got back to his point. "The lucky members drive up in their stupid cyber cars and park in front of the screen. They chomp their fake hot dogs and popcorn, and then see a five-minute preview. If they pay the full price for their ticket, they get to stay for the full show. Only there's nothing cyber about it. It's all the real thing, just like you saw."

Mulrooney almost growled. "Lousy prick's probably getting rich as well as making himself infamous. And getting his personal kicks."

"Given the auction amounts and the ticket prices, I'd say that's likely."

Immediately zoning in on what Brandon hadn't told them, Dean asked, "So what's the purpose of the auction? How, exactly, is this thing audience participation?" Something occurred to him, which could make catching this guy easier. "Are you telling us people are buying the services of a virtual assassin to kill their real-life enemies, or unwanted spouses?" If they could nail a single customer, they could nail the Reaper.

Brandon shook his head. "Nothing that simple."

There wasn't anything simple about it, in Dean's view.

"He's not auctioning off the right to choose a victim. In fact, the auction winner has no say about who gets killed." Sighing heavily, disgust evident in the droop of his shoulders, the other man finally got to the bones of it. "He's auctioning off the right to choose the means of death."

A momentary silence fell as everyone absorbed the words. Then Wyatt slowly spoke. "So, anyone with a proclivity for a certain kind of death can, for a fee, have that type of execution carried out for his personal viewing pleasure. And the pleasure of others who will pay to watch."

"That about sums it up."

Dean swallowed, now definitely not looking forward to watching the remaining videos. The excesses of a bunch of deviant human minds given an outlet for their violent fantasies promised to be among the most disturbing things he'd ever seen. But the videos were the starting point in stopping the killing. There was no other choice.

He suddenly realized he was no longer wondering if he was going to work this case. Something deep inside him, something that rebelled against the very concept of what this Reaper was doing, demanded the right to work it. Jurisdiction didn't matter. The reason Blackstone's CAT had come together didn't matter.

More visitation time with his son still mattered. Yeah. That mattered. But right now, all he could think about was nailing the sick monster who was making this world a whole lot uglier for his child. For everybody's children.

Somewhere out there, the friends and families of at least eight women wanted to know what had happened to their murdered loved ones. Who had done it, and why.

And soon, hopefully, Dean and his new teammates might be able to give them some answers.

Chapter 2

In the small town of Hope Valley, Virginia, time didn't just move slowly; it sometimes seemed to meander off the rest of the world's clock before coming to a complete standstill. And then go into reverse.

Because aside from nothing ever changing—not the landscape, or the faces, or the businesses dotting the ten blocks that made up the entire downtown—some scenes seemed to be repeated over and over, like the replaying of a dream. Not a nightmare that might terrify you into sharp wakefulness, just a jumble of images about nothing of importance, notable only for their sheer blandness.

It was especially noticeable at this time of year. The blazing August sun sucked the very energy out of the air. Any occasional lapse into productivity was quickly quelled. Most folks around Hope Valley secretly wanted nothing more than a tall glass of iced tea and a nap. Too much effort was required to think of something to say to the people you'd seen every day of your life. Beyond "Good morning" or "Have a good one," what was there to say to the girl at the deli who made you the same turkey on wheat every day? Or the kid who delivered the paper, or the woman who brought the mail?

Sheriff Stacey Rhodes had once hated that sense of normalcy, the laid-back slowness the town wore as comfortably as an old coat. As a teenager, when she'd experienced none of the outside world and had considered anyplace better than this one, she'd imagined nothing worse than spending her life in Hope Valley.

Yet here she was.

The biggest surprise of all? She was okay with that. Compared to some of the things she'd seen, Hope Valley now seemed like the last sane place on earth. It was only on slow, hot days like this when she felt antsy. Like if something didn't happen to break the monotony, somebody was going to make something happen. And that something might be a whole lot worse than a little heat.

"Morning, Sheriff!"

Waving at the kid who delivered her paper, she called, "Have a good one."

Getting into her squad car and buckling up, she backed out of the driveway of her small two-bedroom house, passing the delivery boy a few doors down. The kid gleefully steered his bike through a hopelessly outgunned lawn sprinkler that was trying to force moisture into the still, uncooperative air, and greenness into a brown, parched landscape.

Water ban. No sprinkling sunrise to sunset. She noted the address, figuring she'd pass it along to the town secretary. Playing water cop wasn't exactly the county sheriff's job, but hell, it wasn't as though there was much else on the agenda for today. Or any day.

Though she trusted her ancient radio about as much as she trusted car salesmen, she flipped the thing on as she headed downtown. A burst of static erupted from the speakers; then, surprisingly, a voice came through. "Sheriff? You there? Over."

She reached for the handset, her interest rising. "Go ahead, Connie. Over."

"Can you stop at the Donut Shack and pick up a dozen? I didn't have time. Over."

A doughnut emergency. Call in the reinforcements. Smothering a sigh, she muttered, "Ten-four," and turned at the stop sign rather than going straight.

Doughnuts for deputies. If it weren't so sadly clichéd, it'd almost be funny.

But when she pulled into the Donut Shack's nearly empty parking lot and glanced through the window, things became a lot less funny. Because clearly visible inside was the owner's daughter, who worked as a waitress, looking nervous and frightened.

She was surrounded by three teenage boys.

Stacey put names to the faces in an instant. One was the crowned king of thugs at the local high school, the other two his football-playing cronies. The sidekicks she didn't worry about. In ten years, they'd be married with kids, working at the lumberyard, drinking hard on weekends as they scratched their beer guts and relived their glory days.

But their leader, Mike Flanagan, was a mean punk. He was too cocky to fear authority, and Stacey had hauled him in before. That one would end up in jail, or in the military, where he could legally injure others, which seemed to be his favorite thing to do.

What made this worse was that his older brother, Mitch, had straightened himself up, shaken off his roughneck family background, and gone in the opposite direction. He was now Stacey's chief deputy, and the best man she had.

Why did brothers have to be such a pain in the ass? Damn, she did not want to have to call Mitch and tell him she'd busted his troublemaking younger sibling. Again.

"You wanted something to happen," she reminded herself as she stepped out of the car, pushing her broad-brimmed tan hat onto her head.

Her boots crunching on the gravel parking lot and her fingertips resting on the short, blunt club at her hip, she walked with determination but not haste toward the entrance. Deliberate and thorough, she evaluated the situation with every stride. Through the windows running the entire width of the small building, she noted who was inside, and where. One customer sat at the counter, his back to the kids, completely oblivious to the situation. Or just a damn coward. No one else was in sight. The girl spotted her, the relief on her face saying a lot about how serious the situation was. Shoving the door open, Stacey watched the troublemakers swing around, unhappy with the interruption. Then they saw who had interrupted and paled.

"A little early to be out causing trouble, isn't it, boys?"

"No trouble here, Sheriff, ma'am." Flanagan. Arrogant little jerk actually shot off a crooked salute. "Just nice, wholesome teenagers. Right, guys?"

Mike's signature reply whenever he was up to no good. His two buddies had the sense to remain silent.

"Cara, are you okay?"

The girl glanced back and forth among the boys. Stacey could have predicted the words that would come out of her mouth, given that high school was brutal and paybacks a bitch. "I'm fine. My dad just ran to the bank; he'll be back in a minute."

Huh. She wondered if the opportunistic boys had seen the man leave and decided to have some mean-spirited fun. She wouldn't put it past Mike.

"See?" he said. "No problem. We just stopped by to eat on our way to practice."

Noting their gym clothes, she figured they really were on the way to the field. School started in a few weeks, and the coach was already working his players to death in the heat. Maybe it would sweat some of the aggression out of them. One could only hope.

She pointed at the two followers. "Go. But from now on, stop for breakfast somewhere else. Or better yet, stay home and let your mamas make it for you."

Mike took a step, too, but Stacey stopped him. "We're not done."

His jaw thrust out in pure testosterone-laden male belligerence. "I'll be late."

"You weren't worried about that before I came in, now, were you?"

The two other boys scuttled out sideways, as if they didn't want to turn their backs on her. Cara dashed toward the phone. The obviously deaf and blind customer remained hunched over the counter, ignoring the situation. Staying out of it.

What would the guy have done if things had really gotten rough? She hated to think that anybody here in Hope Valley would be so uncaring of a girl in need, but that bystander hadn't moved so much as a muscle since she'd pulled up.

"Nice job, mister," she snapped, unable to help herself.

He flinched, then turned his head to peer over his shoulder. When she recognized him, everything suddenly made sense. Because prissy, fussy insurance salesman Rob Monroe hadn't had a set of balls in the twenty years she'd known him. He still lived with his parents, never having moved away from Mommy the socialite and Daddy the ass of a mayor. It was all the more embarrassing since she'd actually gone out with him once in high school. To her consternation, he'd been trying to get her to repeat the experience ever since she'd returned to Hope Valley to serve out her dad's term as sheriff.

As if.

"Morning, Stacey," he mumbled. "Is there a problem? I was reading the paper...."

"Well, don't let me keep you from it."

He hopped off his stool. "What's wrong? Can I help you?"

"Not on your best day."

Their stares met and he had the audacity to look hurt. That why-can't-you-love-me crap might have worked when she was sixteen and felt sorry for him, since he was the target of a little teen maliciousness. But no more. When she didn't relent by so much as the softening of her frown, he slapped his paper down on the counter and stalked out.

Stacey immediately turned her attention back on Mike. "Let's go."

She grabbed him by the upper corner of his ear and squeezed. The kid was about her height, and probably had thirty pounds on her, but he yelped and followed her outside. "Hey, I didn't do nothin'!"

"The look on that girl's face said you did. Now, I can't haul you in for being a jackass, but if I hear you've been bothering her again, I will be visiting your house."

Absolutely the only thing the teen feared was his own hard-edged father, who, if the rumor mill was to be believed, lived by the spare-the-rod-and-spoil-the-child motto. So the threat worked the way a plea or a suggestion that he follow in his brother's footsteps would not have. He snapped an insincere apology. "Sorry."

"Tell it to Cara at school next month. Otherwise, stay away from her."

"Fine." His fuming eyes fried her where she stood. "Can I go, Sheriff?"

She waved him away without another word, watching him take off running down the road toward the high school. His last defiant gesture, flipping her the bird over his shoulder as he ran, came as no surprise. "Tomorrow," she reminded herself with a sigh once he was out of sight, "don't complain about nothing ever happening."

A half hour later, armed with doughnuts and stuffed from the two Boston creams she'd scarfed down while waiting for Cara's father to return, Stacey finally arrived at work. With things having started out so badly, the day could only get better.

When she parked in her reserved spot outside the station, however, she realized she might be wrong about that. Because before she'd even stepped out of her car, a snide voice called, "Running late this morning, Sheriff?"

She forced a tight smile and nodded at the older woman about to walk into the bank next door. Alice Covey was a hateful old harpy who tap-danced on her very last nerve even when Stacey was in a good mood. Which definitely didn't describe today. "Everything seems to move a little slower in this weather, Mrs. Covey."

God, how much would it be to ask to arrive at work a few minutes late and not have it publicly commented on?

You wanted this. You chose this.

Yeah. She had. About two years ago, when her father had retired midterm, his arthritic knees so bad he couldn't walk comfortably from his car into the station, she'd accepted the town's invitation to come back here to fill his shoes. The timing had been right, considering what she'd been going through, and she didn't regret it.

But, boy, her father had worn big shoes. They had been walked in not only by him, but by his own father, as well. A Rhodes had been sheriff in this county for forty years. The others, however, had been males, which some people around here, like the timekeeping town busybody in the bank and the blowhard mayor, never let her forget.

She doubted they would have said a word to her father, or to her older brother, who everyone had assumed would take over, at least until he'd joined the Marines and ruined their plans. "Maybe you'll get the right sheriff next time," she muttered, her jaw tightening. Because with Tim back home after twelve years in the service, some people thought she should be a nice sister and step aside for him during the next election, coming up in just a couple of months. Especially given his injuries.

Stacey had done well; even the most chauvinistic townies would concede that. But she was, after all, just a woman. And Tim, despite his lack of experience, versus Stacey's law enforcement degree and six years with the VSP in Roanoke, was obviously the better Rhodes for the job.

Because he had something between his legs and she didn't. At least, not often. Frowning over the thought, she entered the station.

"Hey, Stace." Connie, their receptionist/dispatcher/911 operator, sat behind the front desk, all smiles and big hair. "Brutal out there already, huh?"

"Uh-huh." Stacy placed the doughnuts on the edge of Connie's desk, not wanting to discuss what she'd gone through to get them. "Hope it doesn't last through the weekend. We'll get called out to Dick's Tavern every hour."

"And how would that be unlike just about every other weekend of the year?"

The woman had a point. "How's Dad doing this morning?"

"Oh, he's fine, staying inside in the air-conditioning." Connie looked down, busied her hands, and mumbled, "I stopped by and brought him something to eat on my way to work."

Sure. Stacey hid a smile, not wanting to embarrass the woman. Because Connie, at fifty-six, not only kept the sheriff's office organized and cheery; she also managed to do that for Stacey's father. She'd been dating him since the day he'd retired, both of them being too old-school to let anything happen between them while they worked together. Now that he was retired they seemed ready to move forward.

"Anything happening so far today?"

"Warren Lee threatened his neighbor's dog again."

She grunted. "When doesn't he?"

"What's he hiding on all that land, anyway?" Connie asked. "You'd think he'd sell it to one of those big-city developers, make a fortune, and go start his own army in some third-world country."

The former army sergeant lived just outside of town on a beautiful piece of property with views to rival any on the Skyline Drive. But his home was hidden by thick woods and encircled by a six-foot-tall fence topped with razor wire. The KEEP OUT and FORGET THE DOG, BEWARE THE OWNER! signs demanded privacy. And most people in these parts gave it to him, sensing he was a little off.

She supposed she should at least be thankful her brother had come home from the service moody and silent, not downright mean and hostile, like Mr. Lee.

"Anything else?"

"Mitch is out sick. He was fixing his roof after his shift yesterday afternoon. . . ."

Stacey's eyes widened. "In this heat?" It had to have been close to one hundred degrees yesterday, and probably hadn't dipped below eighty until well into the night.

Connie merely shrugged. "Men."

She had a point.

"Said he broke his arm."

"Oh, no."

Damn. Though maybe it wasn't such a bad thing. If Mitch were here, she'd have to tell him about the nasty antics his brother had been up to. Funny how different the brothers were. Mike was a punk, while Mitch was a good guy and a great deputy. He and nine others helped Stacey keep the town and the rest of the sparsely populated county safe without complaint.

"He swears he'll be back in a week, but he'll be in a cast for six. He said to tell you it's his left hand, though, so he can still shoot."

"The last time a local deputy discharged his weapon, it was when one of Dad's guys had to put down a poor, dying deer somebody had hit out on Blanchard Road." Stacey might wear a semiautomatic comfortably on her hip, but she'd never had to pull it out for anything other than cleaning or occasional practice at the shooting range.

She turned to walk away. But she hadn't gone two steps when Connie whispered, "Wait!"

Tensing, Stacey glanced back and saw someone at the front door. A familiar someone. "Oh, no. It's Wednesday."

How could she have forgotten? This weekly ritual had been going on for almost a year and a half. Every Wednesday. Talk about an unwelcome dream repeating itself and never having a better ending. Not for her and not for the woman whose heart she broke four times a month.

Stacey's eyes shifted toward the bulletin board hanging by the door. On it were handwritten notes, FBI Most Wanted lists, and statewide bulletins about bank robbers who didn't know places like Hope Valley existed. A copy of the weekly on-call schedule hung there, as well as a sign for an end-of-summer barbecue for all the deputies and their families.

There was also one section marked MISSING PERSONS.

In the past, that area might have been crowded with crayon-drawn flyers offering rewards for the return of Spot or Baxter or some other lost pet. In a town like this one, kids still felt free to ask for help finding a beloved puppy who'd last been seen chasing the ice-cream truck.

Not anymore, though. Now, out of respect to the woman walking into the station, that section of the board held just a single sheet of paper. Yellowed at the edges, curling at the corners, it was forlorn in its solidarity.

Much like Mrs. Winnie Freed.

"Mornin', Sheriff," said the woman as she pushed into the station. She brought a stifling blast of summer air in with her. And about a ton of sorrow.

Stacey noted the shapeless dress hanging off the woman's bony shoulders. Mrs. Freed, who was probably only about fifty, looked twenty years older. She'd been aged by decades of working as a maid at a chain hotel up in Front Royal. Bending over to strip and remake beds had curved her entire body into a human-size comma. Her thin, red hands told tales of endless buckets of hot water and cleaning chemicals. And the way she kept her head down and her eyes averted revealed a lifelong habit of staying nearly invisible to the customer, remaining unobtrusive, unnoticed.

The physically demanding job hadn't been entirely responsible for turning Mrs. Freed into the frail woman she was today. In the past seventeen months, she'd appeared to wither away. Anguish had gouged deep lines in her already weary and careworn face. Her graying hair hung loose and tangled around her shoulders, as if she lacked even the will to brush it on her day off. The eyes ... well, the glimmer of hope that drove her here every Wednesday was barely visible behind the sadness.

"I'm sorry, Mrs. Freed." Stacey reached out to take

the woman by the arm, almost afraid she'd fall down without support. "I have no news for you."

Winnie bit her lip. Beneath her hand, Stacey felt her body sway a little. Wondering if the woman's sorry excuse for a husband ever even made sure she had a decent meal, she murmured, "Why don't we go into my office and sit down?"

"I made coffee, and we have fresh doughnuts." Connie rose from her desk and hurried out from the receptionist's cubicle.

Stacey led Mrs. Freed down the hallway to her office, helping her sit in a visitor's chair. She tossed her jacket and hat onto a wall hook, then sat down. "Are you all right?"

The woman ignored the question. "You really haven't heard nothin' about Lisa?"

Stacey shook her head slowly.

"But you been lookin'?"

"I have. I promised you I wouldn't give up, and I meant it. I run Lisa's name all the time. I make sure to keep her missing persons report active and updated."

Not, in Stacey's opinion, that it was going to do any good. Lisa Zimmerman, Winnie's twenty-three-year-old daughter, had apparently dropped off the face of the earth. The way Stacey saw it, that was how the wild young woman wanted it. If she ever did get hold of the girl, she'd be sorely tempted to slap her.

Be fair. Breathing deeply, she forced the angry thoughts away, knowing they were inspired only by her sadness for Mrs. Freed. And because, once upon a time, Lisa had been a sweet child, and Stacey her favorite babysitter.

Difficult to believe the pretty, smart little blonde had gone so bad. And hard to reconcile that used-up druggie with the nice kid Stacey had once tucked into bed.

"She could be in a hospital in a coma, couldn't she?"

The woman's lips trembled. "I see that on the stories sometimes. People get in comas and their kin can't find 'em."

"I doubt that," she said, her tone gentle but firm. Mrs. Freed had been making excuses for her daughter's disappearance for months. She didn't need more false hope.

Nor, however, was Stacey cruel enough to be blunt. Telling the woman her daughter had probably skipped town with some dealer, not giving a damn about her mother's feelings, would be beyond mean. So she skirted as best she could, making the efforts Winnie asked her to, holding out no hope that they'd lead to anything. Lisa would come back when she was good and ready, probably when she was broke and desperate.

"But it's possible, right? She could be hurt somewhere, not knowin' who she is."

"Any hospital with a Jane Doe would be looking at missing persons cases."

Lisa's mother let out a long, slow sigh, almost visibly deflating, even though she'd gone through this before. It wouldn't have been the first time the young woman had run away and stayed out of contact. No, it had never gone on for this long, and she'd always at least left a note, but it was still the most likely story.

"Do you think if I could come up with a few hundred dollars for a reward . . . ?"

"No, Winnie. I don't think so."

Some said Lisa had been wild from the cradle. Stacey didn't remember her like that. In fact, she'd found her shy and affectionate on those summer days they'd spent together. Lisa had been so smart, inquisitive, bubbly.

Then, when Lisa was twelve, her father had died. Her mother had remarried and Lisa had changed. She'd met the wrong guy with the wrong needle, and the smart girl with the big dreams had turned into a bleary-eyed waif with track marks up her arms.

"Here you go, honey," Connie said as she entered the room. She placed a foam cup on the edge of the desk and handed Mrs. Freed a napkin-wrapped doughnut.

Winnie took the coffee and slipped the doughnut into her large handbag, squirreling it away as if wanting to hide it. Just like she hid these trips to the sheriff's office.

Stan Freed's feelings toward his stepdaughter weren't as charitable as Winnie's. The hard-eyed man had written Lisa off for good. Which was why Winnie came in on Wednesdays: the one day of the week when she was off work and her repairman husband was not.

"Thank you, Sheriff." Winnie slowly stood. "I appreciate your not giving up."

Stacey stood and extended her hand across the desk, feeling the frailty of the other woman's fingers. "You're welcome."

The woman lurched out, carrying the weight of the world on her bony back.

Sad. Most people had given up on Lisa long ago. Her mother never would. And, out of loyalty and because she was good at her job, neither would Stacey.

That thought was on her mind throughout the day. It was a quiet one, no calls, not even any speeders racing through downtown. She mostly stayed in her office doing paperwork and keeping her promise to Mrs. Freed.

Ignoring the futility of it, she once again checked online, updating Lisa's missing persons listing. She checked NCIC's latest crime reports, scanning for anything involving unidentified women of Lisa's description, particularly drug arrests. As usual, she found nothing. But at least a week from today, she'd be able to say she'd tried.

Late in the day she realized there was one more effort she could make on Winnie's behalf. Lisa's missing persons flyer had been on the board for a long time, and it showed. Printing off a new one seemed so minor, yet it was one small thing she could do to help.

Opening the electronic file, she glanced over the pertinent details, again feeling the single flash of confusion she'd had since Lisa had disappeared. Lisa had been driving her stepfather's company car that night, without permission. It had been found outside of Dick's Tavern. But why had she left without the fifty dollars that had been lying right on the console?

Stacey could guess why she hadn't brought the cash into Dick's. "You were saving it for a score," she told the woman whose haggard face appeared on the monitor. "You feared if you brought it inside, you'd get drunk and spend it."

But why leave town without it? For someone like Lisa, the money should have been the first thing she'd go for. Hell, given some of the characters she'd hooked up with over the years, and Lisa's well-known dislike of Stan Freed, it was a surprise she hadn't stolen her stepfather's car and sold it for whatever she could get.

Then again, the young woman wasn't stupid. The car was pretty damned distinctive, with that silly talking-laptop logo on the side of it. Still, leaving that fifty dollars didn't seem like something Lisa would do.

"Strange that you'd forget it," Stacey murmured, still staring at Lisa's photograph, trying to find the pretty girl in the strung-out woman before her.

Hearing a beep, she sent the document to the printer, then answered the intercom. "Yes, Connie?"

"Sheriff, there's a call for you on the private line."

The private line wasn't exactly private. It was merely the phone number they used in-house, and for the rest of the law enforcement world. They kept it from locals, who'd tie it up with complaints about the trash man being too late, or too early. "Who is it?"

"He says he's from the FBI! Special Agent Taggert."

An FBI special agent. Not exactly an alert-the-media moment, but it was something different. "Put him through."

While she waited for the call to ring in, she grabbed the single white sheet coming off the printer. It was in her hand when the phone trilled twice.

"Sheriff Rhodes."

After a split second's hesitation he introduced himself, adding, "I'm calling about a missing person you reported."

Stacey stiffened, glancing at the flyer still in her hand. The FBI was calling about Lisa Zimmerman. What kind of trouble had the young woman gotten herself into this time? "Do you have information about her?"

"You know who I'm calling about?" Surprise brought his deep voice up a notch.

"I've only filed one missing persons report in the two years I've held this job," she replied, her tone dry.

"I see." Some papers ruffled in the background, as if he were consulting his notes. "This young woman, Lisa Zimmerman, went missing in March of last year?"

"Yes, she did."

"And nobody's heard a word from her since?"

Stacey's breath slowed. Something in his tone, low and serious, tugged her thoughts in a different, darker direction. Everyone in this town was so used to Lisa causing trouble and victimizing others that it had almost never even occurred to Stacey to think of Lisa as a victim herself.

Oh, God, please, no. That little-girl face, the sweet smile, the soft blond hair flashed through her mind. So did the image of sad Winnie Freed trudging out of the office, already anticipating the day, one week hence, when she'd hear good news.

"Sheriff? Nobody's heard from her?"

"Not a word." Her throat tight with dread, she asked,

"Do you know where Lisa Zimmerman is, Special Agent Taggert?"

"No, I don't know where she is." There was another hesitation. "But I might be able to tell you what happened to her."

Chapter 3

Arriving in Hope Valley was like entering a 1950s TV show. Dean had heard of places like this; he just didn't know they still existed. He'd been raised on the mean streets of Baltimore and now lived in D.C. He had never experienced towns with ice-cream parlors, free on-street parking, and community centers complete with signs for dances and bake sales.

The main streets through downtown were lined with green trees that overhung the neatly swept sidewalks. Rather than antique shops and galleries designed to lure tourists on day-in-the-country outings, this place had normal businesses serving the people who lived here. A small grocery store was tucked between a bank and a pharmacy. A diner offered blue-plate lunch specials. Outside a barbershop stood an antique spinning pole that actually worked.

There was no major shopping center in sight. Since leaving Front Royal, they'd passed only one weary, dilapidated strip mall with a Family Dollar as its anchor. Hope Valley truly appeared to be a self-contained little town that wasn't merely an extension of some larger city's urban sprawl.

"Serial killer in a small town, much?" he muttered, talking more to himself than to Wyatt, who was driving the sedan.

Dean had thought Wyatt would send him out with Mulrooney, but their team leader had insisted on driving out here to Nowhere, Virginia, with Dean this afternoon. As if he suspected, as did everyone else, that this case could be the key to bringing down the Reaper, whose crimes were the stuff nightmares and slasher movies were made of.

"So you still believe the unsub's actually from this area?" Wyatt asked.

"Don't you?"

The man pulled into a parking place in front of a small, single-story building marked SHERIFF'S OFFICE. "If our theories are correct, that Lisa Zimmerman was his first victim, and that her killing might have been personal, then yes, I think it's likely."

"The details fit. The physical description, identifying marks. We know the timing of her disappearance works, since Fletcher was able to determine within days when the murder occurred, given the lack of buds on the tree the vic was tied to."

A ghost of a smile crossed Wyatt's mouth. They'd all been impressed by that one. Lily might be a quiet office type without much field experience, but she had a brain like a steel trap. Because even though Lisa Zimmerman had disappeared in early March, a month before the "freebie" video had gone up, that hadn't meant she'd died right away. But the bare, sullen trees hinted she'd met the cold, steely blade very close to that time.

"And," Dean concluded, "the missing persons photo looks just like the woman on the tape." To the untrained eye, it seemed irrefutable that Lisa Zimmerman had been their unidentified victim. Now they just had to get confirmation from someone who knew her.

Dean stared out the window, wondering how the locals would react. The idea that the Reaper lived here in their small-town heaven would probably send most of them running for their basements.

But it fit. If Lisa had, indeed, been the unsub's first victim, it made complete sense that her killer was from here. And Dean wanted him. Badly.

The murder had been hard to watch, but it hadn't gone on as long as the others. The young woman had been tied to a tree, naked, with her arms extended above her. While the killer had been free with his blade, Brandon had estimated that she'd died within twenty minutes of the first cut.

It had been brutal. But not quite as bad as some of the other victims, whose torture had lasted for *hours*. As Cole had said: There were different degrees of awful.

"You said you had the feeling the sheriff personally knew the missing woman?"

"Yeah." Dean again looked around the town, all twelve inches of it. "I think so."

Sheriff Rhodes, whose young, strong-yet-feminine voice had surprised him for a moment on the phone yesterday, hadn't given him any details about her relationship with Lisa Zimmerman, but he'd lay odds she'd had one.

"Good thing we had Brandon capture some still frames," Wyatt said. "I'd hate for anyone who knew Miss Zimmerman to have to actually watch that entire video."

"It's hard enough to see it happen to a stranger."

"Fortunate that we didn't have to get family members to ID any of the others. Or to make the pictures public in order to identify the victims," Wyatt replied.

"No kidding. Tipping off those Satan's Playground bastards would have been suicide for the entire case. The unsub would have taken a deep dive straight into cyber hell and might never be found again."

They hadn't needed personal identifications to determine who seven of the eight victims had been. There had been autopsy reports and police investigations to go on. Brandon had found the first; then they'd put names to six more. They had scoured reports and databases, matching unsolved murders to the videos. And in every other case, except the woman in the free preview, the victims' bodies had already been found and ID'd.

"Let's hope this sheriff is as cooperative as the other agencies have been," he said. Each murder had been stymieing the local police, so, for a change, none of them had minded the FBI's intrusion. The cases were growing cold, some stretching back more than a year. Plus, they were unlike anything the small-town authorities had ever seen.

If anybody had ever connected the killings, the FBI would likely have gotten involved long before now. But nobody had. The Reaper's gimmick, auctioning off "means" but not victim, had helped him escape detection. There had been no common signature for anybody to stumble over. No similarity in the crimes, except that they were all unusually brutal. Or even in the victims, aside from the fact that they were all female and Caucasian. They ranged in age from seventeen to forty. Two were married, with kids, and three were young college students. A few had been sexually violated though not raped. Bodies had been dumped in wooded areas, a landfill, one in the bathroom of a rest stop. The crimes had been spread across four states, the only string tying them all together being a cyber one.

Chilling to think the cases might never have been connected at all had Brandon Cole not stumbled into Satan's Playground.

"So, if the sheriff identifies Lisa Zimmerman as the Reaper's first victim . . . ?"

Wyatt cut the engine, and heat invaded the interior

of the sedan so fast it might have been piped in. "Then you'll be sticking around Hope Valley for a while."

Exiting the car, Dean waited for a rusty Ford to wind its way down Main Street; then he crossed, Wyatt behind him. He entered the sheriff's office, no being buzzed in, no metal detector, and glanced around. A trio of folding metal chairs stood in the empty waiting area.

"Notice something strange?" Wyatt asked, sounding bemused.

Dean nodded. Not only was there no security; there was nobody, period. The lobby was silent as a church during confession. And the glassed-in receptionist's cubicle stood empty, the rolling chair pushed far away from the desk and turned, as if its occupant had hopped from it midslide.

"Afternoon siesta?" he mumbled.

As he began to wonder if they were going to have to go on a sheriff hunt, Dean suddenly heard raised voices coming from somewhere down a hallway marked, PRIVATE.

"God damn it, Stacey, if you can't use your job, give it to someone who will!"

He and Wyatt exchanged a quick look. Both went on alert, as anyone would when it sounded as though a fellow law enforcement officer was being threatened.

"When did it become my job to get you out of your own messes? It's not my responsibility to keep you from getting fired," a woman snapped back, crisp and in control. Her voice sounded calm, betraying none of the throbbing anger of the male one that had preceded it. "You don't want to lose your job? Then convince your boss you didn't have anything to do with the cash shortage. Kiss his ass, whatever you have to do."

Listening, Dean realized he knew the voice of the woman. That confidence had impressed him yesterday on the phone, especially since the strong, authoritative tone did not entirely disguise a slightly husky, sexy quality. Sheriff Rhodes, he had already decided, was one cool customer. Which was probably a good thing, if this morning's argument was anything to go by. She apparently faced some crazy demands in her job.

"You can go talk to him; Dad would have. Threaten him, tell him you'll start enforcing the no-parking zone behind the dealership. Damn it, you're my sister; isn't that supposed to be good for something?"

Ahh. He got the picture. This wasn't some random townie making demands. It was a loudmouthed brother trying to browbeat his sister. He waited, wondering how she'd handle it, knowing he would already have thrown that sorry-ass sibling out.

"Get out of my office." *Good.*

"I've been patient, Tim. We all have. But everybody's getting a little tired of your bullshit. All you've been doing is getting drunk and getting into trouble with Randy like you're still a couple of teenagers. It's time to grow up." Her temper was building; he could hear the sharpness of it, strung tight like a wire. If he knew what was good for him, the brother really ought to get out while he still could. He sensed the sheriff would be a formidable opponent.

"Go home, stop feeling sorry for yourself, and try to make this right."

The brother said something else, in a voice too low to hear, but the sheriff's response was fully audible. With words as sharp and hard as chips of ice, she again ordered her brother out, adding, "Or else you'll find out what a bitch I can be."

Ouch. If Dean ever called his own sister such a name, she'd bash him in the head.

The sharp slam of an inside door was followed by two sets of footsteps. The first was the hurried click of shoes belonging to the missing receptionist, who raced into her oversize fish-bowl cubicle. She threw herself into her chair, as if to avoid being spotted by the man who'd been arguing with her boss. Dean had a sudden visual of the big-haired woman with her ear pressed to the keyhole. Not that it would need to be—that argument could have been heard on the street.

The next footsteps, heavier and hard, belonged to a lean guy, probably in his mid-thirties, around Dean's age, wearing ragged jeans and a T-shirt. His deep scowl was matched by angry red scars that ran from his neck all the way up his cheek and into his hairline.

"The fuck you lookin' at?" he snarled as he strode past Dean and Wyatt. He shoved the handle and pushed the door open, stalking outside without another word.

The whole scene had taken less than a minute, but it left an aura of unease in the office. Wyatt straightened his tie, shifted his jacket, and finally cleared his throat.

"Oh, my, I didn't see you standing there," the receptionist said. She must have thought Mr. Friendly's parting remark had been addressed to her. "I'll go get the sheriff."

Another female voice intruded. "No need."

Even before she introduced herself, Dean knew they were being greeted by Sheriff Rhodes. He'd been curious about her since they'd spoken yesterday afternoon, wondering how she would hold up if the team's speculations were correct and a serial killer was living in her jurisdiction. Hearing her fight with her brother, he suspected the woman could seriously hold her own.

Seeing her confirmed it.

"Thanks for meeting with us. I'm Supervisory Special Agent Wyatt Blackstone," Wyatt said as he showed the woman his badge. "This is Special Agent Dean Taggert."

While she checked out their IDs, Dean made a quick visual assessment of the sheriff.

Probably in her early thirties, Stacey Rhodes didn't come across as too young for her job. In fact, she wore her uniform as if she'd been born in it. She was tall, close to his six feet, with shoulders squared and posture military-straight. Her chin was up, her green eyes assessing, though not cold. Her reddish blond hair was pulled back too tightly to determine its length, but the style emphasized the determined jut of her jaw and the sculpted lines of her face. She exuded competence.

Thank God. Before he'd picked up the phone to call here yesterday, he'd envisioned a turf battle with a blustering, small-minded, small-town bureaucrat who'd like the spotlight of an FBI investigation, but not the down-in-the-dirt work of one. Since Lisa Zimmerman was still officially a missing person, they could have encountered trouble. But he already suspected they wouldn't. Nothing about Sheriff Rhodes indicated that she was someone who'd get belligerent or territorial at the expense of a murder investigation.

"Special Agent Taggert." The woman extended her hand after she'd shaken Wyatt's. "We spoke yesterday?"

"Yes, we did." Clasping her hand in his for a brief shake, Dean noted the strength, expected, but also the softness of her skin. That was definitely unexpected.

As was his sudden reaction to it, which came completely out of nowhere.

Because while he'd been visually running down her qualifications for the job, he had obviously mentally processed something else—that she was very attractive. The brush of his hand against hers brought that realization home with a sharp jolt deep in his gut.

Her fitted uniform appeared as uncomfortable for this weather as Dean's suit, but she wore it well. Incredibly well. Damn, no wonder the woman carried herself with such professional dignity. Her attitude was sure to provide at least a momentary distraction from the tall, lithe body, with the full hips and slim waist emphasized by the khaki pants. Not to mention the prominent curves beneath her long-sleeved, button-up shirt.

He wasn't distracted anymore, though.

Suddenly feeling the heat of the day even more than he had outside, Dean forced himself to ignore the soft, feminine form trying to hide beneath the stiff, starched clothes. He put his focus back where it belonged: strictly above her shoulders.

That didn't help much. Because despite the lack of a smile, her mouth was just a little too wide, her lips a little too lush for someone oozing such authority.

So this is what instant attraction feels like.

He hadn't experienced it before, this sudden, heated awareness that made him incapable of putting two thoughts together. And frankly, he didn't like it. Distractions caused problems and mistakes.

Neither of which he could afford right now. Not when he was so busy trying to keep all the balls of his life up in the air. A new job on a probationary team, a new apartment courtesy of a lopsided divorce agreement . . . a new man being called Dad by his own son. Hell, he had so much on his plate he might as well call his life a Denny's breakfast special.

He nodded coolly and kept his expression impassive when the sheriff invited them to her office. And he kept his eyes glued to the back of her head rather than even considering watching the sway of her hips and the curve of her ass as she led them there.

"Please have a seat," Sheriff Rhodes said, gesturing toward two empty chairs opposite her desk. The office was neat, and despite the age of the furnishings, it was equipped with new-looking computer equipment. Not nearly up to CAT standards, but better than he'd have expected, given the fact that the sheriff's department was housed in a building smaller than an average fast-food joint. "Would you like some coffee? Or something cold to drink?"

"No, thank you," Wyatt said, as Dean shook his head in refusal.

"Okay." The sheriff crossed her arms and eyed them both.

For a second, he wondered if she would comment on the fight they'd heard—she had to have known they were there. But she didn't, choosing to ignore it. "Tell me what you know about Lisa Zimmerman." Her full mouth tightened. "Special Agent Taggert was a bit cryptic on the phone yesterday."

Not used to being thwarted, this one. The instant realization, the way her personality was revealing itself in her every gesture and word, almost made him smile. But Dean squelched the reaction. "Sorry. I didn't want to tell you what we think happened to Lisa without giving you a chance to look at some photographs. We don't know the identity of the woman in the pictures, or when or where they were taken. So it's best for you to just look at them cold."

"Ever heard of e-mail attachments?"

"These need to be seen in person," he explained, taking no offense. He'd have been annoyed at the stalling, too. "Preferably by someone who has met Lisa."

She stiffened, preparing herself. "I've known her since she was a kid."

Damn. Good news for them, but it would make it harder for her if she'd known the victim for so long.

Reaching into his briefcase, Dean drew out a few stills Brandon had isolated from the digital recording. The images weren't the best, taken at night with an average-quality video camera. But that night had been a clear one, and the killer had been using some type of artificial lighting. He'd also zoomed in on his victim's face, nice and tight, as well as pulling back to present the whole scene.

The killer had wasted no effort in making his show more enjoyable for his audience. And he'd turned his camera away from absolutely nothing.

Starting with the ones from the earliest part of the torture session, Dean spread three photos on the desk, turning them to face the sheriff. The victim's eyes were closed in the first, her head slumped, her chin touching her chest. She'd been unconscious for the first few minutes of the film. Judging by the trickle of blood coming from the corner of her mouth, she'd been made that way by one or more sharp blows to the face and head.

The next shot was more disturbing. The victim's eyes were open, confusion and pain warring with terror in her expression. Seeing what she'd been seeing—the hooded figure, the moonlight glittering on the knife—anyone would have been the same.

Anyone.

He positioned the third picture, hoping this would be the last he'd have to show the woman sitting so stiffly, her posture revealing nothing, though every ounce of color had fallen from her cheeks. This was a full-length shot, showing the naked victim, conscious and aware, her face bleeding but her body still unblemished by the blade that was about to be visited upon her with such excruciating ferocity.

Watching the sheriff's reaction, he knew when her eyelids fluttered down and she sucked her bottom lip into her mouth that they'd identified their victim. The sheen of moisture in her eyes when she reopened them confirmed it, but also made him feel like crap for having to put her through this.

Bad enough for anyone in law enforcement looking at the final, agonizing moments of a stranger. But to see someone she'd known since childhood? *Hell.* "Sheriff

Rhodes?" he asked, his tone gentle. "Can you identify the woman in the photographs?"

She swallowed visibly, then nodded once. "It's Lisa Zimmerman."

"You're sure?"

"Even if I didn't recognize her face immediately, I'd know her by that bumblebee tattoo on her shoulder. She was a finalist in a statewide spelling bee in elementary school. She had that put on a couple of years ago, I guess to remind herself that she'd once accomplished something." She pushed the pictures away, the tips of her nails touching the very edges, as if she couldn't bear any more contact with them. "So she's dead?"

"We haven't found her body," Wyatt explained. The man sounded coolly professional, as always, but also quietly subdued in respect for the sheriff's obvious dismay. "But yes, there seems to be no doubt the woman in these pictures is dead."

Silence descended in the office for a long moment, broken only by the hiss of the air-conditioning unit in the window. The stream of cold air ruffled some papers on the sheriff's desk, and lifted a finger-size strawberry blond curl that had escaped the bun at her nape. The skin it rested against looked slick, damp with the kind of sweat that could never be chased away on a day this hot.

That soft, fragile strand of hair was the only part of her that moved during the full minute it took her to process the situation. The rest of her remained frozen in place, unmoving, unblinking, almost not even breathing.

She was the picture of a professional—dealing with an awful crime that touched her personally. Yet already detaching herself from it in order to do her job.

He'd have expected nothing less. Dean watched closely, wondering why he understood her so well after such a brief acquaintance. But he didn't have to wonder for long before the truth washed over him with sudden clarity.

She was like him. Stacey Rhodes compartmentalized her reactions. She put the tough ones aside to be dealt with later, at a more expedient time, in a more appropriate place. He could almost see the way her brain churned behind those green eyes, putting up walls and barriers to separate facts from emotion.

With Dean, it was usually his anger that he thrust away, shoving it aside to focus on getting the job done. When the release came, it was often quick and ruthless, exploding out of him blow by blow against a punching bag at the gym or with a brutal workout that left him free of any feeling at all.

With Sheriff Rhodes, it was her sadness she was tucking away out of sight, boxing up, hammering it closed with tenpenny nails. She would eventually release it in the privacy of her home, with a few tears, perhaps. At least he hoped so, because, God, holding on to that kind of grief for too long could crush a person.

He knew that from experience. They had different emotions. Different reactions. But the same basic method of dealing with them.

Finally, she cleared her throat and her chin went up. That curl remained beside her soft neck, but every other inch of her was sharp. "I assume there are more pictures?"

Dean's hands closed tightly around the folder containing the additional shots of Lisa Zimmerman's final moments. He kept it in his lap, not willing to show her the rest. He didn't know if her mind had enough safe rooms to deal with them all.

"Yes, there are," Wyatt said.

"They don't look like typical photographs." She tented her hands on the top of her desk and matter-of-factly surmised, "Screen shots?"

Dean nodded. "Yes."

"So there's a video."

A frisson of concern rising up his spine, Dean felt his fingers tighten on the folder, and this nod was slower in coming. "A digital video file. It came to our attention recently, though it was originally uploaded to the Internet in April of last year, a month after Lisa disappeared."

She blanched at the *uploaded to the Internet* part. "I need to see it."

He had no idea what Wyatt was going to say when he opened his mouth, and he didn't care. Dean immediately answered, "Out of the question."

"I have to see it, especially if you want my help."

"Of course we want your help," Wyatt murmured, "and of course you can see it. If you're really sure you want to."

"No, I don't want to," she admitted. She swallowed, her slender throat working with the effort, as if she'd scooped a handful of sand into her mouth. "I need to."

Dean continued to shake his head. "No."

She leaned over her desk, tension and heat rolling off her in waves, as if the mental barriers holding back her fury and anguish over Lisa's murder would burst if she were pushed too hard. "What's the matter? Afraid a small-town sheriff, a female one, can't handle it? You should know I—"

He interrupted her, putting one hand up, palm out. "That's not it. To be frank, Sheriff Rhodes, that video is something nobody who actually knew Lisa Zimmerman should ever see if they can help it."

They stared at each other for a moment, and he saw the indignation leave her. He understood the reaction. She probably dealt with sexism on a daily basis. It was unfortunately commonplace in law enforcement.

She remained silent, mollified. The tense hands unclenched and she sat back in her chair. She nodded slowly, conceding the point, acknowledging her rush to judgment.

Calm and levelheaded, reasonable and intelligent. And incredibly sexy. God, where had this woman been all his life?

Forcing that insane thought away, he muttered, "We've got more screen shots, if you need more verification."

"Agent Taggert, please listen."

Her serious tone told him she wasn't just playing I-can-keep-up-with-the-boys-in-the-schoolyard, as if he'd ever for a moment thought she would. She offered him a small, rueful smile. Her expression held warmth for the first time since she'd greeted him in the lobby. Knowing how those tightly sealed boxes of emotion had to be screaming for release behind those green eyes, he could only do as she asked.

"I appreciate your concern, and believe me, if it weren't important, I wouldn't press the issue. I can think of a thousand things I'd rather do than sit through what I suspect is probably going to be the worst thing I've ever seen in my life."

Giving up had never been one of Dean's strong suits, so he couldn't help saying, "No *probably* about it. It'll be worse than your darkest nightmare. This unsub— unknown subject—is among the sickest, most perverse killers I've ever seen. Why put yourself through this? Are you having second thoughts that it's her?"

"It's her."

"Then why?" She sure wasn't the type to get off on voyeuristic violence. If he was wrong about that, then he'd learned nothing in his twelve years in law enforcement.

Her answer took Dean completely by surprise. He'd been prepared for protestations that she had to be sure, for the family's sake. That it was her job. What he didn't expect was the answer he got.

"I have to watch the film, Agent Taggert, because I

think I might be able to tell you where Lisa Zimmerman died."

Stacey could probably have told the FBI agents sitting in her office where she thought Lisa had been killed without watching that horrific home movie of the slaughter. Considering she was now leaning over the bathroom sink, having puked her guts out one minute after the clip had ended, she almost wished she had.

Almost.

Her only solace was that there had been no audio accompaniment. If she'd had to hear Lisa's anguished screams, she doubted she'd ever get their echoes out of her ears.

But she'd needed to see it. Having a hunch based on the shimmer of something in the background of one of the original three pictures wasn't enough. Not for a case like this. Not when Stacey was going to have to go tell Winnie Freed her daughter was dead.

Another parent mourning another child. It was too much. She'd come here, back to Hope Valley, specifically because she never wanted to see such anguish again. Never wanted to witness the pain she'd seen in her last days as a state cop, when parent after parent had cried their grief for the children they'd sent off to school and never seen again.

God, how could they possibly bear it? How would Winnie bear it?

"Sheriff?" Someone knocked on the closed bathroom door. Fortunately, it wasn't one of the two agents. The voice was female.

"I'm okay, Connie." She wet a paper towel, holding it to her forehead and her cheeks, trying desperately to get her heart to stop racing and her stomach to stop heaving.

Finally, either because she'd gotten herself under control or because there was nothing left inside her to spew out in protest of what had been done to Lisa, Stacey rinsed her mouth out and left the bathroom. Reentering her office, she found the two men sitting where she'd left them.

The agents looked up at her return, but didn't rise to their feet in some antiquated show of courtesy. "I apologize for the interruption, gentlemen," she murmured, returning to her seat.

"We quite understand," the supervisory special agent, Blackstone, said. "It's not something any normal person would ever want to see."

He was stiff, dispassionate, his black suit starched and crisp despite the heat and humidity. Probably in his early forties, the man was almost too elegant to be in law enforcement. She suspected he kept a wall of formality and coolness around himself at all times. Even the way he sat, one leg crossed over the other, hands folded in his lap, displayed an almost visible disdain for any macho law enforcement posturing. Yet he was so intense and focused, she dared anyone to think the pose was at all feminine.

"Are you all right?" a gruff voice asked. That was the other one—Special Agent Dean Taggert. And he was not stiff, dispassionate, and aloof. Definitely not cold, either. Not one tiny bit.

"I'm fine."

From the moment they'd shaken hands in the vestibule, Stacey had been unable to help noticing the coiled strength of the man. While Blackstone was all calm, controlled professionalism, Taggert appeared tense and hard, wary and maybe even belligerent. Blackstone's grip had been cool and smooth, Taggert's powerful and rough. The older agent never looked around, appearing completely at ease and comfortable with his surroundings. The younger one never stopped checking things out, eyeing entrances and egresses, always on alert, edgy and ready for action. With his thick dark hair, flashing eyes so deep brown they were almost black, and strong-boned face, he looked almost too streetwise to be in the eminently professional FBI.

The senior agent emanated authority. The junior one, pure physical excitement.

"Here," Taggert muttered, tossing a pack of mint-flavored gum toward her.

Stacey caught it in midair.

"Believe it or not, it helps get the taste of imaginary blood out of your mouth."

Perfect description. Watching Lisa's final moments, she'd felt as if she were swallowing the horror whole. "Thanks."

She took a piece, hoping her stomach could handle the simple act of chewing, then pushed the pack across the desk toward its owner, watching him pocket it.

"Want some water or something, too?" he asked, displaying concern that completely surprised her.

"No, really, I'm okay."

Though as polite as his colleague, Special Agent Taggert's gravelly voice, tight tone, the tension in his body, and the fire in his eyes told her the man wasn't used to playing nice, to asking courteously and talking quietly.

Right now, he watched her with an assessing stare. But there was also a hint of warm compassion. Understanding. It was as unexpected as it was genuine, just like the offer of the gum. Stacey found herself staring back at him for a brief moment, their eyes locking as they took silent measure of each other.

"Did you find what you were looking for in the footage?" Blackstone asked, sounding courteous, yet not quite so . . . What was that tone in his colleague's voice? Protectiveness, maybe. Yes, when she thought about it, the near-stranger had seemed almost protective of her.

Such a novel thing. Nobody had tried to protect her in years. She did a damn fine job of it herself, and part of her should have been offended.

She wasn't. She'd evaluate why later, when she didn't have to look across her desk at those deep brown eyes.

"Sheriff?" Blackstone prodded.

Determined to get past the awkward moment of her sickness, she nodded and reached for her notepad. She'd jotted down specific moments of interest in the film. "You said this video was made public last April? About a month after she disappeared?"

The senior agent nodded. "But we believe it had been made sometime prior to that, given the wintry appearance of the background location."

She thought about the scene, the stark, skeletal bareness of the trees. Then she recalled the early spring they'd enjoyed last year; her pollen allergies had been in high gear by the first week of April. The timing definitely fit. "I noticed that, too."

Blackstone folded his hands in his lap, saying nothing.

"She left Dick's Tavern, a hangout two miles outside of town, a little before two a.m. That night was the last full moon of the cycle. I remember because we'd had a really bad week, calls out to Dick's every night. Around here the general consensus is that the crazies come out during the full moon, and they all end up at Dick's. Most folks think Lisa ran off with one of them."

"Maybe she did," Taggert muttered.

"Maybe. But if so, she didn't get far. Because she died within hours."

Both FBI agents watched her closely. Neither appeared surprised. Just interested.

"There's one moment when she's looking directly up, when the camera panned up, too," she explained, suddenly feeling weary. "Maybe the bastard wanted to see if there really was a God up there listening to her prayers.

It's only a split second, but I'm nearly certain the moon was full."

"Yes, we saw that," Blackstone admitted. "We sent the tape for evaluation beyond what our office could handle, and I imagine they'll verify it. But the fact that you caught something that appeared so briefly says a lot about your powers of observation."

Under other circumstances, she might feel pleased by the compliment. Now, though, her mind still awash with the visions of Lisa's final moments, there was no room for anything positive.

"To recap . . ." She ticked off the obvious points on her fingers. "We know she was last seen at close to two a.m. on the final night of the full moon in March. We know she was killed under a full moon. We know there were no buds on the trees, while if it had happened at the next full moon, there would have been. And we know the video went public in April." It was simple deduction, really. "She had to have been killed the night she disappeared. It had to have happened somewhere close to here, since there would have been only a few hours between when she left the tavern and dawn, and there was no sign of morning on that video. With the time it took to grab her, get her somewhere entirely secluded, and do what he did, there wouldn't have been time to drive too far out of the area."

Agent Taggert leaned forward in his chair. "You said you might know where she died, meaning you saw something else."

"Yes, I did."

They waited.

"During the segments when your suspect zoomed out and panned the clearing, you can see a glint of silver through the branches of some of the trees, to Lisa's left. I first spotted it in the third picture you showed me. You can see it better in the video."

Taggert opened the folder, glanced at it, then offered it to his colleague.

"Brandon Cole, our IT specialist who's been working on this, spotted the same glimmer," said Blackstone. "But he couldn't isolate it enough to identify it. It was too far away and too small. It could be a flash from the spotlights, a smudge on the cheap camera lens. Maybe even a reflection from one of the blades the perpetrator used." He put the picture down. "It's not a headlight or something, if that's what you're thinking. We considered that, but the height and dimensions don't work. We're hoping the final analysis of the footage will give us more to go on."

She wasn't thinking vehicle. And the other explanations could be correct. But the first impression Stacey had had when she'd spotted it hadn't been of any of those things; it had been of wire. Very thin, very sharp wire, looping on itself.

Intuition. But she trusted her own intuition. She always had.

"I think it might be razor wire. If you use Lisa's position to gauge it, the image is about level with the tops of her hands."

She stood, demonstrating, raising her arms above her head, thrusting away the thought of Lisa being tied in this position. Actually, she needed to thrust away the thought of the Lisa she'd known, period, if she was going to be of any help in this investigation. She needed to think of her as only another victim. Nothing else.

"I'm five-ten. Li— The victim was a good six inches shorter. The level of her hands would be right about the same height as the wire running across the top of a steel fence."

Blackstone immediately reopened the folder, and the two agents looked down to test her theory against the eight-by-tens. Stacey lowered her hands, tucked her shirt, which had slid up over her middle, back into her khakis, and returned to her seat. Why the hell she'd had to play Miss Show-and-Tell, she had no idea. Far from being eminently professional, she'd probably looked like some amateur detective solving bloodless murders on an old, pre-*CSI* TV show.

"Damn, I think she's right," Taggert said. He looked up, caught her eye, and immediately leaped to the next conclusion. "Not many places need that kind of security. You know of a fence like this in the area?"

Still not quite believing that Lisa could have been killed at a place she drove by practically every day, Stacey nodded. "I do. One of the locals, Warren Lee, has a farm outside of town. He's a bit of a character."

Taggert stiffened. "Violent?"

She considered it. "Possibly. He's a survivalist type; I suspect he's armed to the teeth out there." Realizing why he'd asked, she almost immediately ruled out the agent's unspoken supposition. She knew Warren well enough to fear that when he snapped he'd go out guns blazing. He didn't have the patience, the calmness she'd seen in the video.

"I don't believe that was him on the tape, but it could have happened near his place. He has a huge spread. It's fenced in, with razor wire across the top."

Agent Taggert immediately swung to face his boss. "Can we get a warrant?"

Blackstone shook his head. "We've got nothing to justify one."

Stacey cleared her throat. "I didn't mean I thought the crime occurred on Warren's property. The way he guards his place, the only way it could have is if he did it, and I tell you, everything I know about the man says he didn't. I think it's more likely this happened on the other side of his fence. In which case, you can easily look around."

They both waited in tangible expectation.

"Most of Warren's land skirts along part of the Shenandoah National Park."

A quick grin appeared on Taggert's face, as if he'd heard his first good news in days. "Federal property."

"Exactly," she replied, thinking for a fleeting moment how much younger the man looked when he smiled. "No warrant required."

Chapter 4

You're ugly. You're damaged. Who would want you?

"Shut up," he whispered, not even looking away from his computer screen. He'd heard the words too many times to feel anger or fear, and merely brushed them away like he would have a pesky fly.

But the voice wouldn't shut up. The voice never shut up. Awake or in his dreams, it taunted, it ridiculed, it bit with teeth as sharp as the incisors of a hound from hell. Only . . . he no longer felt the bite.

Hideous. Evil. Nasty.

"Go away; I'm busy."

It didn't go away, so he reached for the volume button on the front of his laptop. He jabbed at it ruthlessly, until his index finger bent backward and almost snapped. That might have been interesting, just to see how it would feel and how he handled the sensation. Better than most, he suspected. Better than any woman, that was for certain.

Pain had interested him for a long time. How to take it, how to deliver it. He'd done some experimenting over the years—starting small, with rats or strays that wouldn't be missed. And he'd found that when a creature was frightened enough, it almost didn't even seem to notice when it was dying. Or maybe it was merely grateful for the release.

Much like Lisa. And all the others.

He himself hadn't been tested that far yet, but he'd certainly experienced the acrid bitterness of terror and the cloying taste of physical agony. So he understood how some pain simply ceased to exist when a mind drifted to other places in the sheer, primal need for escape.

Would it do so if the pain were self-inflicted? He'd often wondered.

He pushed his finger against the button again. Hard, until the metal bit into his skin and left an indentation. The joint bent backward, the tip turning bright red, the knuckles ghostly white.

He could snap it. Easily.

"Not now," he whispered. He was busy now. He could test that another time, as he'd tested the feel of fire licking the soles of his feet or blades scraping across his belly.

Now there was only this. The sounds emerging from the fully enabled speakers grew louder, filling the room, filling his ears, filling his brain.

Filling his soul.

He relaxed in his chair, one world falling away, another spreading out before him, full of unexplored places and exciting opportunities.

No hateful voices greeted him, and none followed. Just friends speaking their cyber chatter. Some people would listen and hear only gibberish. But he understood it perfectly, even without reading the flood of text messages that appeared the moment he arrived in the playground. *Welcome, where have you been? Come see my latest project. Take me. Choose me. Hurt me.*

We've missed you.

His friends were all here, waiting for him in the only world he wanted to inhabit. Here he was somebody.

Here he was never called useless or ugly. Here they respected him, were in awe of him. Feared him.

Because here, everyone knew who he really was. And what he was capable of.

When? someone asked. More took up the cry. *When will you show us more?*

He checked the date—nearly five weeks since his last premiere. And then he considered his finances—very low. How he'd managed only one auction every couple of months at the start was beyond him.

It was time. He had things he wanted to buy, places he wanted to visit, and he didn't have the means to do it.

Besides, his palms were beginning to itch. Right hand meant money coming in, left meant money going out, according to the old saying. But to the Reaper, both meant only one thing.

Time to kill someone.

Dean wanted to get right to work on the search for the murder site. Though they suspected it had been a long time since Lisa had died, and the odds of their finding anything were minimal, this was the first real break they'd had in the case. All the other bodies had been found in dump sites, the original location of the killings unknown.

That the lead came courtesy of the sharp eyes of a small-town sheriff with a great ass did not escape him.

"Enough of that," he muttered, not even wanting to go there in his head when it came to Stacey Rhodes. No matter how attractive she was—physically and mentally.

"What?"

"Nothing," he told Wyatt. "Just wishing we could get right on the search."

But they couldn't. They'd spent the past two hours with the sheriff, laying out a search grid and making plans to start first thing tomorrow. Not only because it was late in the day, but also because they lacked the manpower. Even with the help of the sheriff and her deputies, there weren't enough of them to search hundreds of acres of woods.

Besides, neither he nor Wyatt knew a thing about the deputies on her staff. For all they knew, the guys who worked for her could be small-town old-timers who'd been in their jobs for decades. Given the emptiness of the sheriff's office, and the casual, laid-back atmosphere inside, they weren't expecting a top-notch crew.

Stacey Rhodes was top-notch enough all on her own.

"Rather a remarkable woman, Sheriff Rhodes, wouldn't you say?" Wyatt asked as he drove them down the main street, in search of the town's only hotel.

Dean flinched, wondering if he'd been wearing an I'm-thinking-of-a-hot-female expression. Then again, any man with an ounce of blood below the waist and a brain cell in his head would be thinking about the woman whose office they'd just left. "Oh, yeah."

"Good of her to arrange for us to get a block of rooms on such short notice."

The sheriff had called the owner of the inn, getting him to offer government rates on their rooms. Dean and Wyatt were alone now, but Mulrooney and Stokes would show up tonight, Fletcher and Cole in the morning. With all of them, as well as Stacey and the deputies she vouched for, they could begin the search for the scene of the crime tomorrow. Jackie Stokes was bringing all her forensics gear, and they'd have the state police on standby with a cadaver-sniffing dog, just in case they got lucky.

Dean doubted they'd get that lucky. Finding the site would be enough of a stretch. They knew the Reaper dumped his bodies far from his kill zones, so they almost certainly wouldn't find remains. If they could find where he'd killed her, though, there might be some surviving evidence. Doubtful after more than a year's worth of weather and animals and natural decay, but it was more than they'd had twenty-four hours ago.

"If we find the crime took place on federal land, it'll make things easier. But even barring that, I get the feeling the sheriff will be highly cooperative," Wyatt said.

Dean was about to respond when he saw Wyatt flip on the blinker and turn into a small, gravel parking lot. "God, I didn't even see the place," he said, gawking out the window at the rambling, single-story building before them.

It was an inn only by the loosest definition of the word. A long, low strip of rooms with a sagging roof and paint-stripped doors that ended an inch above the jamb, the Hope Inn was in serious need of renovation, or a few gallons of gasoline and a match. "Think this is really the only option? What about Front Royal?"

"Too far away." Wyatt shrugged. "When in Rome . . ."

"But you're not the one who's probably going to be stuck here for days." His boss was heading back to D.C. tomorrow, once the rest of the team was in place.

"Getting stuck here for several days would be a good thing," Wyatt reminded him, his voice quiet, getting his point across immediately. Because having to stick around would mean there was something to stick around for. Like evidence, or definite leads.

"I know. I just wish I'd packed a few more things. A tent and a sleeping bag, for starters." Dean had brought an overnight bag, just in case, but he wasn't used to sleeping in anything but his skin. And he had the feeling he wasn't going to want that skin coming into contact with anything in one of those rooms: bed, sheets, shower, nothing.

"I have some calls to make." Wyatt parked outside the small, dingy office. "Why don't I check us both in, take care of my calls, and you can go scout around, see if there's anyplace decent to grab a bite for dinner."

Sensing that Wyatt generally ate four-star, he didn't even want to imagine the man sitting in the local diner ordering the meat loaf special. But he didn't argue. Obviously Wyatt wanted privacy for his calls. "Not a problem."

Knowing his boss wasn't just calling back to the office to update the team, he took no offense. Wyatt had other fires to control. The powers that be had him on a tight leash and a choker collar. He was always second-guessed, having to explain himself the way no other supervisory special agent in his position *ever* had to. Superiors continually asked questions, many of them because they wanted the wrong answers. Any excuse, any chance to mess with Wyatt, who'd brought down one of their own, and they'd use it.

It had taken balls of steel for Blackstone to expose the man who'd been the deputy director's right-hand man for the lying, crooked scumbag he really was. Especially since the lying, crooked scumbag had once been Wyatt's mentor.

And, man, had Wyatt paid for it. Officially, they'd given him a commendation. Unofficially . . . a lot of people would like to give the whistle-blower his ass on a plate.

"You can take the car if you need it," Wyatt said, "then come back for me. Though I don't imagine driving is going to improve the selection."

"Probably not," he agreed as they exited the car. No need to drive in a town no bigger than his fist. "I'll walk. If I'm not back by the time you're done, give me a call."

Before he left, Dean glanced at his watch. Five thirty. *Screw it.* He loosened his tie, tugged it free, and tossed it into the car, then unbuttoned the top few buttons of his shirt. He'd lose the jacket, too, if he didn't have his sidearm strapped to his hip.

Wyatt did not follow suit, which didn't surprise Dean.

Wyatt would wear the whole damn FBI ensemble, head to toe, until he closed the door of his hotel room for the night.

Not Dean. Despite the hour, the heat remained monstrous, and he was ready for relief. He even found himself wondering if the no-tell motel had a pool. And if there was any chance in hell that pool didn't contain rare, disease-causing bacteria.

Heading across the street toward the center of town, he noted the quickest way into and out of the parking lot, the access to it from the woods beyond. He estimated the distance to the sheriff's office, and the number of intersections along the way. He might have been half joking with that serial-killer-in-a-small-town crack, but the thought had been in the back of his mind from the moment the sheriff had ID'd the victim.

The two-inch-wide strip of creamy, soft skin around the sheriff's middle had been on his mind, too.

Ever since she'd stood and stretched her arms above her head back in her office, he'd been unable to shake Stacey Rhodes's image from his brain. God knew the scenario had been all wrong to think about how attractive she was. Yet even the reason for his presence here hadn't been enough to stop him from appreciating that combination of strength and softness evident in every move she made. He found the stubborn jut of her jaw as attractive as the femininity of that loose strand of hair. He'd wanted to see her handle the Glock she wore so comfortably on her hip as much as he'd wanted to taste the slight sheen of sweat shining on her throat in her hot office.

"Man, you need to get laid," he muttered as he turned a corner and headed down the block. Going without sex since his divorce had been a bad idea. Celibacy was making women he had no business thinking about look way too good to him.

He needed the kind of woman who wouldn't care about his last name the next morning, nor he about hers. A bar hookup was the required response for any recently divorced guy whose wife had remarried. At least, so his twice-divorced brother said.

Stacey Rhodes was no bar tramp. The prickly yet soft small-town woman probably knew not only any potential lover's last name, but the names of his parents and grandparents, too.

Tugging his thoughts off the sheriff and back onto his job, where they belonged, he continued to scope out Hope Valley. It took ten minutes to traverse the ten or so square blocks of it. On foot. Meaning if someone were driving through and looked down to squirt ketchup on a carryout burger, they'd probably miss it.

The town had a few small restaurants—bars serving burgers, and an Internet café. But he opted for the diner. He didn't choose the place because of its proximity to the sheriff's office, or his curiosity about whether she ever stopped in for a bite after her shift ended. At least, that was what he told himself.

Once he stepped inside, however, his gaze shifted to the right, and his stare locked on the woman sitting at the first booth. The strawberry blond woman with the moist lips and the moist throat, and the look of almost guilty surprise on her face. And he knew that even if their hotel had been four-star, with room service, he would have come here, on the off chance that she would, too.

"Sheriff Rhodes," he said, his voice low, for his ears only.

She heard anyway. "Special Agent Taggert."

She'd come here on purpose. He wasn't a profiler, didn't do any behavioral analysis stuff. But he knew that as surely as he knew the sound of his son's voice.

"I've been wondering when you'd show up," she said, admitting as much.

Any other woman he knew would have danced
around that admission all night. Or avoided making it
altogether. Not this one. She was in-your-face truth and
nothing but. He shouldn't have expected anything else.

Knowing the empty seat opposite her was for him, he
took it without an invitation. "If we're going to do this,
you might as well call me Dean."

She nibbled her lip, that full lower lip that had trembled the tiniest bit earlier today when she'd first seen
those pictures. "Going to do what?"

Any number of possibilities flashed across his brain,
but he settled for the most basic. "Have a drink together.
Work together." *Do anything else two unattached adults
who are attracted to each other do together.*

Suddenly realizing he'd made a huge assumption, he
cast a quick glance toward her left hand. Because he had
no idea whether Sheriff Rhodes was unattached or not.
He'd just wanted her to be, so he hadn't even considered
the alternative.

He saw no ring. And suddenly his heart started beating again. Dean might be a lot of things, but a home
wrecker he wasn't.

"Okay. And I'm Stacey." She glanced past him.
"Where's your boss?"

"Making some calls back at the hotel."

"You get settled in okay?"

He grunted. "I didn't stop to introduce myself to the
bedbugs."

Her lips might have twitched the tiniest bit. "Sorry.
The closest chain hotel is several miles away. There is
a very nice B and B a mile outside of town, but I know
they have a wedding scheduled there for this weekend
and every room is booked."

"Think I could pass for the best man?"

"Unlike your boss, you don't look like the tux type."
She actually smiled, visibly relaxing for the first time

since they'd met. Her wide mouth seemed made for
smiling, and her green eyes twinkled, negating the tiny
lines of worry on her brow.

She'd been incredibly attractive before. Now she was
damn near beautiful.

"You're right," he admitted. "Wyatt's the Dom Péri-
gnon of our team. I guess I'm the Mad Dog 20/20."

Laughter spilled across her lips, husky and soft all at
once, so natural it could never have been forced. Hearing it gave Dean the first real flash of pleasure he'd had
all day.

"I know the inn looks bad from the outside, but I
promise the place is very clean. The owners can't afford to renovate, but they make sure the rooms are
spick-and-span."

His hopes rose. But he still intended to reserve judgment until he actually had a chance to check out the
inside of his room for himself.

About to tell her that, he was startled by the sound of
glass breaking nearby. He and Stacey both jerked their
heads reflexively, though he imagined they'd see nothing more than a waitress standing in the middle of diner
plate wreckage.

Instead, he saw a man, pale and wiry, standing in the
midst of the broken dishes on the floor. No waitress was
in sight, and the glass and plate, complete with half-eaten
sandwich, seemed to have slipped off his own table.

"Oh, great," Stacey muttered, her voice soaked in
dislike.

That tone, accompanied by the flash of anger that appeared in the stranger's eyes when he met Dean's, made
him wonder if the dishes had slipped after all. When the
man cast a glare of barely disguised anger at Stacey, he
wondered even more. "Problem?"

"Not on my part."

Dean sat up straighter, assessing the dish-killing stranger. With curly, dingy brown hair, and his tall, skinny, pale form, he most resembled a used Q-tip. The man, realizing Dean was staring, finally tugged his attention off Stacey. Grabbing some cash out of his pocket, he thrust it at the waitress, who'd come running to clean up. Then he stalked across the broken glass, beelining toward the door, not casting another look in their direction.

"Please don't tell me he's your ex," Dean murmured, knowing the unusual exchange had been a personal, not a professional, one.

"He'd like to have been," she acknowledged. "His name's Rob Monroe. I had to let him down hard when he didn't take the hint that I wasn't interested."

"Gee, can't imagine what's not to like."

She snickered a little. A cute snicker. "Aside from the fact that I think his mommy still makes his bed and his daddy the mayor tells him what time to be home every night? I can't imagine."

Dean groaned at the very thought, even while tempted to ask her what did interest her. He was so not the smooth type who played those kinds of games with women, however, and didn't know the language. He had no clue how to find out if she was feeling the intrinsic pull that he had since the moment they'd met. He only knew that when she'd laughed a few moments ago and her eyes had twinkled with genuine good humor, his heart had skipped a beat. Or ten.

"I saw you scoping out the town."

Back to business. She obviously didn't want to talk about her unwanted admirer, ignoring him just as she'd ignored the altercation with her brother earlier.

He wondered how a man might react to being so easily put out of this beautiful woman's mind. And suddenly he felt the tiniest hint of sympathy for the angry Mr. Monroe.

"Didn't take long to explore all of Hope Valley, did it?" she asked.

"No."

"Two-stoplight heaven—that's us." She lifted her glass and sipped what appeared to be strong iced tea. Not exactly the beer he'd like to have at the end of a long, shitty day, but it looked refreshing.

A polyester-uniformed waitress approached and mumbled, "Getcha somethin'?" After Dean pointed to Stacey's glass and asked for the same, she stuck her pencil behind her ear and ambled away.

Once they were again alone, Stacey continued. "I watched you from my office window. It's dinnertime, and I figured if you were looking for a place to eat, you'd eventually end up here. There are a few restaurants on the outskirts—a pretty good steak place and a Waffle House. But they're not walkable, and this is." She shrugged and sipped again. "So I decided to come over here and wait for you to show up."

He glanced at his watch. Dinnertime at six o'clock? Only in small-town USA. Most nights, like every other worker in D.C., he didn't get home before seven. "I was just taking stock, picking someplace to eat while Wyatt makes his calls."

"Whatever the reason, I'm glad you came."

Her tone told him she had more to say, and that it wasn't personal. While Dean had seen the guarded looks she'd sent his way earlier, and knew his interest in her was returned, he also knew she wanted to talk business. She might have loosened her uniform jacket and taken her hair out of its bun to hang down her back in a long ponytail, but she was still on the job. He doubted there was ever a time somebody in her position *wasn't*.

"I've been doing some thinking."

"I'm not surprised." In the brief time since he and Wyatt had left her office, he imagined a whole slew of

questions had entered her thoughts. Earlier, hit with
such shocking news, she'd gone along with them, had let
them take the lead. She hadn't had a chance to think of
the ramifications.

Now she'd thought about them.

He imagined the vivid pictures in her head would
haunt her for a long time, each one raising a thousand
questions. They certainly did for him.

How such things could happen, how he could watch
such things happening on the same day he could find
himself warmed by the laughter of a near-stranger, was
beyond him. But he thanked God for the laughter, for
the simple pleasure of bidding his son good night, arguing baseball with his brother, or hearing the latest news
about his sister's kids. Simple pleasures were the only
things that kept anyone in his line of work sane.

"This case is a lot bigger than what you've let on so
far."

Oh, she had most definitely been thinking. "Yes."

"How much haven't you told me?"

Mindful of the chattering customers all around them,
Dean leaned over the table, keeping an eye out for the
return of their waitress. The last thing he wanted was
for the rumor mill to get started any sooner than it had
to. And while their waitress had been a mumbler, he
had no doubt her jaw would move a lot faster if she
had good gossip to relate. "As it pertains to Lisa? Not
a lot."

The intuitive professional across from him wasn't put
off. "And that which does not pertain to Lisa?"

He met her eye. "More than any sane person would
ever want to know."

She held his stare, unblinking, for a long moment, processing his words. Finally, Stacey glanced away, studying her own hand, which was wrapped around her drink.
Good thing the diner was the old-fashioned type and

used thick, heavy glasses. Were she clutching a foam cup, that tight grip would easily have crushed it.

"More videos?"

"Yes."

"You've watched them all?"

"Unfortunately."

She continued staring toward the table. "All the same?"

He could have downplayed it, but didn't. "Most are worse."

"My God." She lifted her eyes again. They were bright, moist, not necessarily with tears, but definitely with emotion.

They fell silent, hardly noticing the clink of tarnished silverware against chipped white plates and diner-issue coffee mugs. The chatter continued at tables all around them, waitresses greeting newcomers each time the door opened, someone calling out, "More coffee, please?" every few seconds. Meat loaf specials were consumed out of congealing platefuls of gravy, and every person at the lunch counter grumbled about the heat. The world continued to turn for everyone else in the place.

But not for her. Not for them.

"How can you stand it?" she finally whispered.

"I can stand it because I know that I'm going to catch the bastard who's doing it."

She crossed her arms, rubbing her hands up and down against them as if she was cold, despite the warmth of the day. That didn't surprise him. This was some cold shit they were dealing with.

What did surprise him was the way her movements emphasized the slenderness of her hands. She was so utterly strong and capable, but had beautiful, feminine hands with long, graceful fingers, as delicate and fragile as her neck and throat. He imagined she'd be as good at playing a piano as he suspected she was at firing a weapon.

He shook his head, tugging his thoughts away from where they'd quickly gone—to what else she might be really good at doing with her hands—because they were crazy. Insane. He was noticing way too much about the woman, from her hair to her hands, her voice, her slim-but-curvy body. Not to mention that quick brain and intuition.

"What the hell are you doing here?" he asked, unable to stop himself.

Her brow shot up. "What?"

"Sorry." He shook his head, cursing himself for opening his trap. "It's just . . . you seem to be really good at what you do. I'm surprised you stay here." What could this tiny town have to offer someone so bright, strong, and attractive?

"I like it here," she said, maybe insisting a little too hard. "It's my home."

"Sorry."

"As for what I do," she added, "it's family tradition. My father and my late grandfather held the job. It's expected that a Rhodes will be sheriff of Hope Valley." Her attention shifted to her mug, as if there were more to it, though she didn't elaborate.

He suddenly thought of her brother. Her angry, scarred brother, who hadn't followed family tradition. But he didn't bring that up. She'd wanted to pretend they hadn't overheard the ugly fight back at the station, and he wouldn't call her on it.

"Family expectations, yeah, I hear ya."

"Yours?" she asked.

"My dad's a steelworker; Mom's a hairdresser. From the time I was old enough to understand the spoken word, I knew they'd never forgive me if I didn't go to college and make something of myself."

She smiled, at least a little, that pretty smile that hadn't gotten much use since he'd arrived in town, as if she were grateful for the detour out of their dark conversation about the case. "They must be proud."

"I guess. Yours, too. Is your father aware of . . . ?"

She shook her head. "Not yet. But I might talk to him about it. He took care of this town for two decades. He might be able to help." She didn't say, *You have a problem with that?* The message came through in her cool, defensive tone.

"Smart," he replied, knowing he didn't have to warn her to be cautious. She was too good to be anything else. "Let me know if he has any thoughts."

A quick flash of appreciation appeared in her eyes, and she visibly relaxed again. "I won't give him the graphic details. I don't think my father or grandfather ever envisioned the job including something like this case," she murmured, her eyes gazing past him, looking at something in the distance. Perhaps the ghost of Lisa Zimmerman, which he suspected would live in her mind for a long time.

"Nobody envisions something like this coming into their life."

"What about you? I guess you see this kind of thing pretty often."

"Not this kind of thing. I was working Violent Criminal Apprehension until a month ago." He watched the waitress return with his tea, waited until she'd left, then added, "I thought I'd try cyber crimes to get away from some of the darkness."

Another of her small, rueful smiles appeared. "How's that working out so far?"

"Not exactly like I'd planned. I think I slept better tracking down average, everyday thugs." Unable to contain the sudden flare of anger that made his voice shake, he admitted, "But I won't rest until we've stopped this guy."

Her green eyes held understanding. Of course they

did; she wanted him stopped, too, even having known about the case for only a few hours. Anyone who witnessed what the monster was capable of would be chilled at the realization that he was still out there walking among them. She just hadn't figured out—not yet, anyway—that he might be walking a whole lot closer than she thought.

"I don't get the Cyber Division angle," she said. "This perp's not an embezzler or Internet fraud slimebag. I thought the ... what's it called, National Center for the Analysis of Violent Crime? I thought they handled this type of thing."

"NCAVC normally does. But we're a new type of Cyber Action Team. Every other one in the U.S. is on standby to respond to traditional cyber threats all over the world. Us? We respond only to Internet-related murder."

"Makes sense, I guess, in this day and age. With your background in ViCAP, a couple of IT specialists, you bring in a range of experience."

"Yeah, we're a mixed bag of specialties. Stokes, who you will meet tomorrow, is a forensics genius. And Wyatt's been trying to get a behavioral analyst to come over to join us, so far without much luck." Dean didn't always understand all that psychoanalytical mumbo jumbo those BAU guys spouted, but they usually got enough things right to make it worth including them in ongoing investigations. Especially investigations into serial murder. "In the meantime, he's found one who agreed to look at this case and come up with some kind of profile. But I don't know if they'll ever actually give us one full-time. That'd be making things too easy on us."

She appeared confused. Anybody who wasn't on the inside of the bureau probably would be. Because the machinations and competitiveness—and even spite—when it came to Wyatt didn't make a bit of sense.

Before he could even begin to explain, however, they were interrupted. "Hey, there, Stacey! How's my best girl? You been missin' me?"

Dean jerked back, shocked that he'd been so focused on his conversation with the woman sitting across from him that he hadn't even realized someone had stopped beside their booth. Glancing up, he noted a beefy, thick-chested guy, probably in his late thirties. He wore dusty jeans and a lightweight flannel shirt with the sleeves torn off to reveal strong arms, the right one paler than the left. His round face, made rounder by a receding hairline of puffy curls, was soft and jolly-looking.

But a longer glance revealed the stranger's deeply lined brow. And though he smiled down at Stacey, his eyes darted quickly about, nervous as an addict making a buy.

Or maybe Dean was imagining it. Because he didn't like anyone—least of all a guy who looked like the Webster's definition of a blowhard—talking to the capable, smart woman across from him as if she were a cute waitress without a brain in her head.

"Hey, Randy," Stacey said, obviously forcing a smile to her mouth. Dean had known her less than a day, but he recognized the effort she was making to appear normal. He saw it in her clasped fingers on the table, in the stiffness of her shoulders and the tiniest tremble of her jaw as the muscles in her cheeks tried to keep her lips curved up.

Strong fingers. Capable shoulders. Well-defined jaw. Nicely shaped lips.

He shifted in his seat.

"Been wondering how you're doing. Meaning to stop by and say hello to your dad, too. Just doing a lot of long-distance interstate runs this summer, delivering electronics to the big box stores. Heaven forbid folks don't have their new wide-screens and Blu-rays in time to catch the new fall shows next month."

"I'm sure Dad would love to see you," Stacey replied. She gestured toward Dean. "This is Dean Taggert. Dean, meet Randy Covey. My brother's partner in crime."

The stranger chuckled, obviously not hearing the steel in her voice.

Noting that she did not introduce him by title, Dean again appreciated the woman's common sense—a rarity among some of the local cops he'd worked with, or so it often seemed. But there had been no need to ask Stacey to keep his identity, and the reason for his presence in Hope Valley, a secret.

The burly man extended a thick hand, pumping Dean's with quickness and courtesy. "Nice to meet you. New in town? You stealing the prettiest little peace officer this side of the Mississippi?"

Mulrooney. That was who the newcomer reminded him of. Or he would have, if he were sarcastic and crude rather than aw-shucks friendly.

Give Dean sarcasm and crudeness over jovial friendliness any day. "Just visiting."

"Randy lives out by my dad's place. He's an old friend of the family."

"Old is right," the man said, sounding rueful. "Me 'n' Stacey's brother, Tim, kept this one from getting into too much trouble growing up." He suddenly glanced toward the door, where a young man hovered. "Son, say hello to the sheriff." Randy extended his arm toward the guy, who was probably around nineteen or twenty. Meaning Randy had probably gotten pretty lucky as a teenager.

The kid didn't much look like his brawny father. He was tall, lean, with white-blond hair and vivid red craters gouged into his cheeks from his losses in the acne wars. Despite the heat of the day, he wore long, oversize jeans that dragged the ground, which would probably reveal four inches of baggy boxer shorts if he weren't also wearing an oversize jersey that fell to his knees.

"Hi, Seth." Stacey smiled at the boy.

"Hey," he mumbled. He shoved his hands in his pockets and hunched his shoulders, his feet shuffling. Typical son, trying to remain invisible and pretend he wasn't related to Randy, who was, as all parents did, somehow embarrassing him.

God, he hoped Jared did not grow up to be like that. And that his ex didn't get her wish and make sure Dean wasn't around enough to help raise him the right way.

"Well, we better rock 'n' roll outta here," Randy said. "We're gonna be in hot water for being late for supper. If Mama finds out we stopped here for some onion rings first, there'll be hell to pay."

Not quite sure whether the man was referring to his wife, or really talking about his mother, Dean murmured good-bye, then watched the duo leave the diner. "Mama?" he asked once they were gone.

Stacey rolled her eyes. "Randy's wife walked out on him when Seth was little. Randy moved back in with his mother, who helped raise the boy. It's a shame, really. Last year Randy was dating a good friend of mine, Angie, who runs the new Internet café. But I don't think Mama liked that. She's a sour old thing."

"How about yours?" Dean asked, suddenly wanting to see that smile again. "Did she like that her sweet little girl took over as sheriff?"

Instead of a smile, he got a snort. "I was never a sweet little girl." She glanced down, stirring her iced tea with her straw. "Dad did his best, but he never managed to drill many feminine qualities into me."

He would argue that point. Noting the softness of her hair, the innate elegance of her movements, the huskiness of her voice that called to some deep part of him, he'd challenge anyone to call this woman anything but feminine. Strong, independent, yes. But still every inch a woman.

"My mother died when I was a baby, so it was just me, Dad, and my brother."

He opened his mouth, trying to come up with whatever kind of lame condolences people offered when they found out about the loss of someone else's parent. Not that he usually knew what to say to that sort of thing. Did anyone?

But before he could even find the right words, Stacey said, "About the case."

So much for personal stuff and sharing. Which, frankly, relieved him. He wasn't good at that. And the fact that she didn't appear to expect him to come up with something inane to say made his opinion of her go up even higher.

But it also made him wonder, did she ever allow herself to be vulnerable? How many rooms did she have in her subconscious to tuck away all the emotion she didn't allow herself to deal with?

"We're talking about a serial killer, aren't we?"

He could have thrown up defensive walls, given her the not-at-liberty-to-talk-about-it line. But something told him he didn't need to go that route, not with Sheriff Rhodes. She was tough. More important, he had the feeling they were going to need her. She'd proven her worth earlier by pointing them in the direction of the crime scene. And if this small town was like every other one he'd ever been in, she'd know every person here and could prove invaluable at narrowing down potential suspects.

"Yes, we are."

Her lips moved and her eyes drifted shut for a moment as she compartmentalized that information. Anyone in charge of the law in a town this size would react to having a nationally sought-after serial killer operating in her jurisdiction. For someone who knew the victim personally? Well, she was in for a rough time, no doubt about it.

"What do you have on him so far?"

"Not much. Most of what we know is from the videos."

"Can't even imagine them," she whispered.

"Believe me, you don't want to try."

Dean's jaw stiffened as a flood of images from the Reaper's sick home movies flooded his brain. There was so much darkness to this case that even he, an experienced professional, had found himself having a few nightmares in the past few nights. Nightmares involving those poor women, sometimes with the faces of his sister or mother replacing one of theirs. There had been even worse ones involving his son, though thank God none of the crimes had involved children.

She obviously read the viciousness of it in his silence. Because, for some reason, she reached over, extended her hand, and brushed it across the back of his. The touch was brief, devoid of anything more than simple human-to-human understanding. But it made his hand thrum for a full minute after she'd pulled hers away.

"How many victims altogether?" she eventually asked.

Flexing his hand, then fisting it on his lap, he got down to business. He ran down the pertinent details, giving her surface information that he'd share with any law enforcement official helping with the case, because that was what she was. Nothing more.

Something told him he'd need to remind himself of that throughout his stay here.

She listened in silence, her eyes occasionally closing, emitting a soft sigh of dismay here or there. He didn't get into details, especially not in-depth descriptions of the horrors playing out there in cyberspace to the twisted masses. But even the simplest explanation was enough to cause nightmares.

"So all the other bodies have been found. Lisa is the only one missing," she finally said when he'd finished.

"Correct."

"But no other victims were from around here. Lisa was our only missing person, and we haven't had a murder in this area since my grandfather was sheriff."

"Lucky you."

She nodded absently. "This guy was likely some stranger who wandered in off the interstate, saw Lisa getting drunk in Dick's Tavern, followed her as she stumbled out, and acted on the opportunity. Then he took off for his next town, next crime. Maybe he hid the body because it was his first murder, and he wanted to give himself time to make sure he could get away with it."

Dean said nothing. There were holes in Stacey's theory. He didn't point them out to her. She'd work it out in her own head, and reach the conclusion that would shock her even more. Her mind was quick and astute; she had spotted that unusual flash on the video and had known it meant something. She'd soon realize she'd seen something else equally as important.

"But a stranger couldn't have known what a perfect victim Lisa would be, that nobody would really take her disappearance seriously," she whispered, gazing into the air over Dean's shoulder, though, in truth, probably looking at nothing that existed here in this diner. She was visualizing *that* night. "Everybody at Dick's Tavern had been around at least a few times before. No newcomers. Dick confirmed that for me himself."

That made the thing she had missed even more important, though she couldn't realize that yet. Dean, however, immediately saw it was important, one more tidbit to confirm what he and the rest of the team already suspected. More than suspected: From the moment a bureau lipreading expert had told them what

Lisa Zimmerman had said to her killer before her death, they had known.

"And he had to be someone familiar with the area to know a place to take her where he could have a big enough clearing to move around, use spotlights, move his camera, all without being disturbed."

"Yes," he murmured.

The wheels in her brain clicked almost visibly. She'd grasped it. Her shocked gasp confirmed as much. "We're not talking about some stranger off the interstate."

Dean shook his head.

"The suspect was familiar with this area. He probably even spent some time around here beforehand."

"It goes further than that," he explained, knowing it was time to fill her in on what else they'd been able to learn from the video of Lisa's gruesome death.

"What?"

"At one point, she looks at him in shock and says, 'You?'"

Her jaw dropped. She understood. But he made it absolutely clear anyway.

"The Reaper personally knew his victim. And she most definitely knew him."

After he'd finished his twenty-minute-long phone call with the head of the Cyber Division, Wyatt considered joining Taggert and the very capable Sheriff Rhodes at the diner. Dean had texted him, not wanting to interrupt his calls, saying he'd run into the sheriff there and thought they could manage a somewhat decent meal.

Frankly, though, having heard everything his boss had to say about the endless machinations going on behind the scenes, and the grumbling about jurisdiction over this Reaper case, what he most wanted was a hot shower and a cold martini. He seldom drank, and never on the job. And even if it was technically after hours, being here in Hope Valley, Virginia, was being on the job. So a hot shower would have to do.

Ironic, really. His first supervisor, the man who'd given him the good advice against ever getting too comfortable with a martini glass while working for the bureau, was the same man Wyatt had helped bring down last year. His former friend had been right in the thick of evidence tampering, witness manipulation, coercion. The kind of corruption that went against everything Wyatt stood for and every reason he'd joined the bureau.

He lifted an imaginary glass and sadly murmured, "Thanks for the tip, old friend."

Shrugging out of his jacket and loosening his tie, he glanced at the room. Simply furnished, it held the most basic of hotel accommodations. He'd traveled enough to have predicted the number of drawers in the dresser and to visibly assess the comfort of the bed. He'd wager there was a Gideon Bible in the top drawer of the nightstand, and that somewhere within was a hand-drawn phallic symbol left there by a bored former occupant.

Fortunately, though, the whole place looked—and better yet, smelled—very clean. No greasy dust coated the slats of the air vent above the bed. No visible stains marred the worn carpet, and not a smudge of dirt or mildew darkened the bathroom tile. All in all, things could have been much worse.

Deciding to ask Dean to just bring him back a sandwich, he reached for his cell phone. But before he could even lift it and dial the number, it rang in his hand. "Blackstone," he answered.

The slightest hesitation and the quick, almost surprised inhalation told him even before she spoke that Lily Fletcher was calling. He smiled just a little. Lily, the newest member of the team, hadn't quite gotten used to him and never appeared to know how to act. Had he ever been so young and untried? So enthusiastic and eager to please?

Once. And look where it had gotten him.

"It's Fletcher, sir. Sorry to bother you; you're probably at dinner or something."

He sighed. "Please, Lily, call me Wyatt—especially on the phone and after hours."

"Sorry." A sudden hollow sound and subsequent knocking told him she'd dropped the phone and was fumbling to pick it back up.

His smile widened. He could almost see her at her desk, her petite form swallowed up in the oversize office chair they'd scrounged up for her from some old storage closet. Her blond hair would be mounded on top of her head, the small, wire-framed reading glasses perched on the end of her nose. Behind those glasses her eyes would be shining with intelligence or moist with heartfelt emotion—the latter not the best trait to have in this line of work, but no matter how often he warned her to remain detached, she was helplessly enslaved to her feelings.

Actually, those feelings had been one reason he'd brought her over to his team. She'd recently suffered a personal tragedy, the loss of her nephew and her sister. Almost desperate to get out of a closed-in office and into the field, if only to rebel against the impotence every crime victim felt, she'd asked for a shot, and he'd given it to her.

So far, he hadn't regretted it. Her personal history hadn't interfered with her job. Though he couldn't deny that whenever office conversation turned toward child abuse, like some of the sick goings-on at Satan's Playground, Lily Fletcher went whiter than any of the monuments gracing the city where they worked.

"Sorry, I dropped the phone," she mumbled a moment later.

Of course she had.

Before she'd dropped it, her desk phone would have been tucked in the crook of her neck so she could leave her hands free. The slim fingers would be flying across the keyboard as she coaxed miracles from the machine, just like Brandon Cole often did.

And that was the other reason he had hired her, despite her lack of field experience and her tendency to get too involved. The woman was as brilliant as Cole, but she played by the book. Brandon Cole did not. Frankly, Wyatt needed them both for exactly that reason. "It's all right."

"Listen, Brandon asked me to call you. Hold on; I'll put you on speaker."

He held, then heard, "Hey, boss! Hear you may have ID'd the first victim?"

"It appears so. You got the message that I want you and Lily here tomorrow?"

"Yeah, uh, about that."

"Yes?"

"Not sure we should leave. Something's happening, boss."

"What is it?'

"Hold up. I might have . . ."

Containing a sigh of irritation, he waited, hearing the clicking of keys in the background. As if realizing he was growing impatient, Lily explained, "He's trying to get back into the Playground."

"Bastards went underground again a couple of hours ago," Cole added.

Damn. In the week since Brandon had brought Satan's Playground to their attention, the group had changed servers twice. Brandon kept following them, like a child following a trail of bread crumbs, all over cyberspace. He wouldn't find anything as sweet as a gingerbread house at the end of his journey, and the evil waiting on the other side was darker than any children's tale could conjure up.

Finally, he heard a triumphant whoop. "Got you!"

"He's back in," Lily explained.

"I heard."

Brandon jumped into the conversation. "Okay, here's why I wanted to talk to you. It looks like the unsub is gearing up for a new auction."

"It's only been a month since his last one."

"I know. He's accelerating."

Never a good thing. "When will it take place?"

"I'm not sure," Brandon replied. "I haven't been able to break into the actual auctions yet; I don't even know whether they're real-time or silent. But I started seeing chatter about it right before the site went dark." More clicking. "I guess everybody gets excited when the Reaper gears up for his next kill."

Breaking into the auctions was on top of Brandon's priority list. If they could get inside and find a way to trace the money trail, they'd be able to nail somebody, either the auction winner or the Reaper himself. Right now, they wanted the killer very badly. But every member of his team also wanted to bring down the twisted clients who paid to have their evil fantasies carried out.

"How soon will you know?"

"I'll stay here all night if I have to."

Wyatt nodded, closing his eyes and rubbing at the corners of them. They hadn't expected this additional pressure, not so soon. The first auctions had been two or three months apart, the last few narrowed to about six or seven weeks. Now, barely a month. "What are the chances of disrupting the auction? Doing something to crash it?"

"Only if you want these sickos to know we're watching them," said Lily.

"Then they'll close up shop and dive into a hole so

deep it'll take months to find them again," Brandon added.

Damn. A cold rush of helplessness spread over him and Wyatt sank to the bed. All the other auctions had ended in someone's horrible death, which had been put on display at Satan's Playground within seventy-two hours. Meaning they had only days now, not weeks, in which to find the unsub and stop him.

Or else have front-row seats to another brutal, sadistic murder.

Chapter 5

They started the search early. With a lot of land to cover, and only seven people—Stacey, Taggert, three of her deputies, and two other FBI agents who'd arrived last night—to do it, the job was shaping up to be a major one. Better, in Stacey's opinion, to get started just after dawn and take advantage of whatever brief amount of coolness the day might provide. Despite their being shaded from the vicious sun by a thick canopy of pine, oak, and cedar, the woods hugging Warren Lee's fence had a closed-in, cavelike feeling that held the heat in and made even the simple act of breathing difficult.

Besides, it wasn't as though she'd slept for more than twenty minutes at a stretch all night, anyway. She'd lain awake, staring at the ceiling, trying to fathom what Dean Taggert had told her: that there might very well be a serial killer living right here in Hope Valley. It was so far beyond her comprehension, he might as well have told her aliens had landed.

That wasn't the only thing that had inhibited her rest. The mourning she'd done for poor, sad Lisa hadn't helped. And when she had fallen into minutes of fitful slumber, she'd found herself dreaming of Dean Taggert. Odd dreams she couldn't quite remember, but which had left her feeling tense and uncomfortable.

"You're sure your guys know what they're doing?"

She made an effort not to stiffen at Special Agent Taggert's bluntness as they paused, shoulder-to-shoulder, having cleared another section of their search area. He might have been Dean at the diner, but today he was again all hard-edged FBI agent. Which was fine with her. She'd spent enough time wondering why on earth she found a man who brought murder and horror into her safe, secure world so damned attractive.

She almost wished Taggert had been the one who'd left this morning, rather than his boss. Blackstone had stopped by only briefly before heading back to Washington, apparently because of a new lead in the case. Maybe that was just as well; she had a hard time picturing the supervisory special agent mucking around in the woods in his crisp black suit and highly shined shoes.

"They're not going to go tromping on any potential evidence, are they?"

"They're fine," she snapped. "Completely trustworthy."

Stacey had thought long and hard before deciding which of her deputies could be counted on to do this job right—not only the search, but keeping the reason for it quiet, at least for the time being. She'd have to tell Winnie Freed, and soon, but she'd be damned if she'd go to the woman without at least trying to find her daughter's remains first. News of a death was bad enough for anyone to deal with. Not having a body to bury meant Winnie would doubt—would question.

Would torture herself with false hope.

So Stacey had to put off telling the woman at least long enough for one good search for Lisa.

"We need to pick up the pace," Taggert said. "This is taking too long."

"Are you sure your guys know what they're doing?" she asked, not sure why she wanted to goad the man.

He frowned, his mouth pulling tight. Not a great sense of humor on this one.

"Pretty sure. Want to hear their qualifications?"

"I'm sorry. But we're not even sure what we're looking for, Agent Taggert," she said, her tone remaining cool. She was pretty impressed with how well her deputies had reacted today and didn't appreciate the implied criticism. She only wished her chief deputy hadn't put himself out of commission by falling off his damn roof.

"We're looking for anything," he said. "Absolutely anything we can use."

"Even if any blood could possibly survive in the elements, we know Lisa was standing on a tarp that would have caught most of it. I don't imagine we're going to stumble over an enormous red circle on the ground with a neon sign saying 'It happened here.' And I doubt this killer was stupid enough to leave his knife lying around for us to find."

He thrust a hand through his thick, dark hair, frustration oozing out of his every pore. "I know. But a complete visual pass is imperative. Then we'll move on to dogs, see if we can get something of Lisa's and try to get them to pick up a scent."

"That's a long shot."

"Tell me about it." His jaw flexed as he cast a slow look around the clearing in which they'd parked, and which he'd designated as base of operations. She sensed he was seeing the entire forest, not just the trees. "This whole thing is an incredible long shot, and God knows we don't have time to spare on a wild-goose chase."

Realizing he hadn't been criticizing, merely expressing his own anxiety, she unbent a little. Glancing at the sweat on his brow, the dampness of his unbuttoned dress shirt molding against his broad shoulders and thick arms, she murmured, "How are you holding up in this heat?"

"I'm fine."

"I sense you spend more time in an air-conditioned office than in the woods."

"You might be surprised. I've never been a desk-jockey type."

"Have you been a Boy Scout? Because any ten-year-old with half a brain would have known better than to dress like that today."

He jerked his head up, as if unused to women throwing snarky comments in his direction. A guy as tough and good-looking as this one probably got lots of compliments and come-ons instead.

A tiny smile that looked more menacing than friendly, as if it didn't get much use, appeared on his lips. His eyes narrowed, his dark gaze homing in on her, every ounce of his attention focused in her direction rather than on the search. The full onslaught of that heated concentration suddenly made her heart skip a beat in her chest. "I wasn't exactly the Boy Scout type. But something tells me you already knew that."

That frankly assessing look would have sent any self-respecting good girl running in the opposite direction. Stacey shivered despite herself. Because he was about as far from a Boy Scout as she was from a suburban housewife.

"Nobody's ever called me Mr. Nice Guy," he warned. And again, she had the suspicion he was talking about more than just this moment, this case. As if confirming that he might have spent some of last night thinking about her, too.

She wasn't scared off. Because nice guys? They were a dime a dozen in Hope Valley. And she was a good girl who'd been good so long she couldn't even remember why she kept getting her birth control pill prescriptions refilled.

She'd started having a suspicion, though, ever since he'd walked into her office yesterday afternoon.

"Maybe nice is overrated," she murmured.

Finally, as if realizing he was watching her a little too closely, building the already thick tension between them, he shook his head, hard. "You're right about the clothes. But I didn't exactly pack shorts and flip-flops."

She chuckled, unable to picture it, and glad he'd coasted back into safe territory. Away from that confusing awareness that seemed to wash over both of them at the most unusual times. Because if he wasn't as aware of her as a woman as she was of him as a man, then she had no business calling herself female. Every intuition she owned told her it was true. And the words he'd said when he'd joined her at the diner the previous evening—*If we're going to do this*—had repeated in her ears a whole bunch of times since.

He hadn't been talking about working together, having dinner or a drink together. Something had made him say those words in that way, and something in her had responded, even if she'd managed to keep her cool and pretend she'd misunderstood.

She hadn't misunderstood. She got the message loud and clear. She just didn't know what she was going to do about it.

Dean gestured toward her own pants and shirt. "You're not exactly up for a day at the beach yourself."

"At least mine are lightweight and light colored."

Unlike Taggert's dark trousers and long-sleeved shirt. She'd bet money he'd had a long mental argument with himself over whether or not to remove the suit jacket. If they'd been in public, where others could have seen the .40 Glock strapped in the holster at his hip, she doubted he would have, no matter what he'd had packed in his overnight bag for his trip to Hope Valley.

"Just make sure you drink plenty of water," she cautioned.

"I can handle myself," he retorted as he unbuttoned his sleeves and shoved them up his thick forearms. Every inch of tanned skin he revealed glistened, though they'd been out for only an hour. The muscles flexing in those arms confirmed his strength, the blunt power of him.

"I noticed," she muttered before she thought better of it. Oh, boy, had she noticed.

Fortunately, he either didn't hear the frank interest in her voice, or didn't correctly interpret it. "You look pretty capable of handling yourself, too."

"I guess," she admitted.

"You've been on the job somewhere else," he said, It wasn't a question.

"Virginia State Police down in Roanoke."

He studied her. Thought about it. "How long ago?"

"I quit in May of 'oh-seven."

She watched him make the connections. Saw the truth click in his brain.

"You responded to the attack at . . ."

"Yeah." She didn't want to talk about it. Didn't even want to remember what had happened that April day on that once-beautiful campus. The nightmares had finally ended. She'd do anything to make sure they didn't return, and she put up a big mental stop sign to keep the memories tucked away in the darkest recesses of her mind.

"That's rough."

She nodded, then quickly changed the subject. "And you were a street cop if I've ever seen one. Something tells me ViCAP wasn't your first stop in law enforcement."

"Baltimore Vice."

"Knew it."

"What gave me away?"

"Your boss screams fed. You don't."

"Was that a compliment?"

She stiffened, wondering how to answer. Because it had been. While she had noted his supervisor's handsome looks, Dean's outright ruggedness, the rough street edge, appealed to her more. A lot more.

Common sense said to keep that to herself. To maintain a professional wall, help this man get his job done, and push him out of Hope Valley as soon as possible. But Stacey suddenly wondered if common sense was just a little bit overrated.

The cop in her said it absolutely was not.

The woman who hadn't been touched intimately by a man in more than two years had other ideas.

Stacey honestly wasn't sure which of them was right. Their current situation demanded that she maintain a professional footing. Even so, she found herself unable to outright lie. "Yes, Special Agent Taggert. Unfortunately, I think it was."

Suddenly averting his eyes, he swiped the back of his forearm across his sweaty forehead. As if he'd bitten off a little more than he could chew, given their current location. She didn't know him well yet, but she suspected Dean wasn't used to this. He didn't know what the vibes between them were, what they meant, and where they were going. Hell, neither did she. But she wasn't about to pretend they didn't exist—there was that honesty thing again.

Having had enough of dancing around it, she cut to the chase. Stacey had learned as a kid that directness usually worked best with men. After all, she'd been raised in a house full of them, with no woman around. Maybe if she'd had a mother, she'd have learned the art of subtlety.

From her father, however, she'd learned bluntness. "Are you seeing anyone?"

His jaw unhinged.

"Look, we both know there's something here. What you said when you showed up at the diner last night proves it. Let's just get it out in the open so it doesn't get in the way of our work."

Silence. He simply studied her, as if shocked that she'd been so candid. But finally, he admitted, "My divorce was finalized ten months ago."

Oh. He'd been married. She had, of course, checked out his left hand to make sure she wasn't letting herself get interested in someone unavailable. She just hadn't figured him for the marrying type, which was probably pretty unfair, since most people saw her that way, too.

She'd get married someday. Probably. Maybe. If she found someone who understood her position on the whole kids issue. And if someone who could stand up to her—physically, mentally, emotionally—ever happened to wander into Hope Valley.

Her gaze lingered on him a moment too long. . . . *Not going there.* "Divorced, huh? Bet that was fun."

His gruff laugh acknowledged her sarcasm. "She remarried weeks later."

"Ouch." Knowing it was none of her business, she asked anyway. "I take it she . . . knew the guy before you two split?"

"Knew him? Oh, absolutely. In every way."

Bitch. Stacey had never laid eyes on the woman, but her intrinsic honor and basic values revolted at one who'd cheat. Who'd cheat on him. "That's rough."

He shrugged. "But maybe not so surprising. We got married right out of college. For some reason she thought being married to a cop would be exciting and impressive."

Snorting, Stacey replied, "Guess she doesn't read statistics very much." Divorce rates in law enforcement were staggering.

"She figured it out. Then she urged me to go for the FBI. I guess saying she was married to a special agent sounded more romantic at the watercooler than, 'My hubby busts dope dealers on Charles Street.'"

"ViCAP. Uh-huh. I've heard that's a regular hotbed of romance."

His shoulders started to shake as, unbelievably, he began to laugh. They were sweating and shooing away mosquitoes, looking for a crime scene in the middle of nowhere, talking about something two near-strangers almost never openly addressed, and able to laugh about it.

She liked this man. A lot.

"We're both better off. My son, however, is not."

Sucking in yet another surprised breath, Stacey absorbed that tidbit. A hard-ass FBI agent. A former street cop. The sexiest, toughest-looking man she'd ever seen.

And a father.

Tension churned in her stomach, but she quickly swallowed it away. She was contemplating a fling with the man. Not any kind of long-term relationship. So the fact that he had a child was completely irrelevant. "How old?"

"He's seven."

"Custody?"

"Not even standard. I get to take him to play at McDonald's every Wednesday night, and he sleeps on a futon at my apartment one weekend a month."

Wow. Less than standard, indeed. Thinking about it, she quickly realized a possible reason. "Is it because of the job?"

His eyes widened, the sun bringing a gleam to the brown depths, revealing a glint of emotion, either at the unfairness of his situation, or the fact that she'd figured it out so quickly. Or both. Then he moved again, into a pool of shadow cast by a towering overhead tree, and glanced away. "Yeah."

"I'm sorry."

"Me, too."

"Look, I know it probably doesn't help, but honestly, I'd much rather have had a part-time mom than none at all at that age. I know it isn't enough, but the time you spend with him is really important."

He fell silent and Stacey instantly regretted the words. She wasn't one of those people who always brought every conversation back to herself. In fact, she couldn't stand those types. Yet that was exactly what she'd done: taken his sadness over a recent divorce and how it affected his son and related it to her own childhood drama.

"I shouldn't have said that."

"No," he replied, watching her, quiet and contemplative. "Actually, you're right."

Stacey realized they'd taken a step forward. They were no longer near-strangers sharing an unexpected attraction. They'd first spoken less than forty-eight hours ago, yet they'd already reached a crossroads in their relationship, where secrets were revealed and hurts shown. And they'd passed it.

In the silence of the morning, where even the birds were too heat-exhausted to chirp, their stares locked. Words clamored to escape her throat—an invitation to dinner, to have a drink, to grab a beer later.

"Guess we should get back to it," he muttered before she could say anything.

"Sure."

He glanced at his watch. "Might be a good time to check in with the others first, though. See if they've found anything."

If they had, she probably would have heard the shouts of her own men from their search quadrant a quarter mile away. But she didn't point that out.

"I could use a water break, anyway," she said.

Taggert lifted his radio and got a brief report from Special Agent Stokes, leaving Stacey a moment to pull herself back together. And to remind herself of all the reasons she should not be letting herself grow more interested in this particular FBI agent.

He lived a dangerous life, worked a dark and bloody job. He was fresh off a divorce, a single father. He lived in a world she'd intentionally left behind when she'd moved back here from Roanoke.

But none of those things chased away the interest, the pure, electric attraction she felt for the man whenever she looked at him. Instead, she kept going over what she already knew about him, what she already liked about him.

He was strong and determined. Stubborn, even. Like her.

He was good at his job, wouldn't let anything stand in the way of doing it to the best of his abilities. Also like her.

He was smart. Intuitive. And deep down, beneath all the gruffness and the swagger, he had both a sense of humor and a genuine warmth. The latter appeared at the oddest of times, like when he'd tossed her that gum, when he'd tried to prevent her from watching the video of Lisa's death. Even now, when he'd genuinely appreciated the comment she'd made about his son.

Oh, yes, Dean Taggert had more depth than she'd first imagined.

And aside from all that, he was incredibly masculine, incredibly tough . . . incredibly big. *Incredibly sexy*.

That last one doomed her. Because despite resenting the darkness he'd brought into her safe, secure, nice world, she couldn't deny she wanted him. That was all, just plain wanted to go to bed with him.

It had been a long time since she'd been so aware of

a man. Longer since she'd been so aware of herself as a woman. That it should happen now, in the midst of this horrific case, confused her more. Not two minutes ago, in the middle of this nightmare, she'd had one of the most intimate conversations she'd had with a man in years.

No doubt about it, working with Taggert was messing with her head, putting strange ideas in it at the strangest of times. She'd found her stare tugged back to him time and again this morning, watching the way his white dress shirt grew damp with sweat and molded itself against his thick chest and muscular arms.

Unlike his boss, Taggert looked as though he knew how to get down and dirty. Despite the clothes she'd harassed him about, he seemed more than ready for some rugged action with that powerful body and that rock-hard determination in his jaw.

Get over *it already*.

She had to get over it. Because she needed to work with the man. Taggert was leading this investigation, and he was desperate to solve it. He hadn't told her the whole story, but she knew enough to know they were working against a clock here. This killer could be stalking his next victim right now. The thought that he could be someone she knew, someone she'd interacted with here in Hope Valley, made her stomach heave.

Anything she could do to help, she would. That included setting aside her response to the man and being one of seven people sifting through hundreds of acres of woods, looking for evidence that had probably been washed away months ago.

Utterly futile, perhaps. But she owed it to Winnie. And to Lisa.

By three p.m., Dean was beginning to regret not bringing the shorts he'd mentioned to Stacey. Heat radiated from each molecule of air, baking and assaulting the senses. His clothes clung to every inch of him, and his eyes had glazed over. His sunglasses didn't help; they merely steamed up, so he'd shoved them into his pocket early this morning and hadn't touched them since. If he had to inhale one more mouthful of hot, pine-scented air, dry and redolent with the must of decaying trees and ancient dead leaves, he was gonna gag.

The great outdoors. Give him the D.C. Metro during rush hour any day.

"Nothing," he muttered. "Absolutely nothing." The three teams scouring the perimeter of the fence hadn't turned up anything other than the remnants of an old, illegal campfire and a few crushed beer cans, there for a month at most.

"We've still got a lot to cover," Stacey reminded him. As if he needed reminding. With only seven of them working, this was shaping up to be a weeklong project. They'd expected to have more help with Brandon and Lily, but Wyatt had kept them in the city for today. Another auction could be taking place at any time, and the IT experts would be more valuable trying to track it than searching for the bloody needle in this forest-wide haystack.

"I know, but we've got to be thorough."

He'd seriously considered doing a trade-off when they'd all broken for a quick lunch: letting Stacey partner up with one of her men, leaving him with just about anybody else. Because despite the fact that he liked working with her, those moments this morning when things had gotten a little on the personal side had been a bonehead move.

He had no time to get personal. No interest in getting personal. No room in his life for anything resembling personal.

Right?

Keep telling yourself that and maybe you'll start to believe it.

Unfortunately, he wasn't able to hear himself say that when his head was filled with nothing but her words: *We both know there's something here*.

God, she was so direct, one more thing he really liked about her. That and the way her sarcastic sense of humor emerged every once in a while. The things he knew about the woman—the details she'd let slip—only made him want to know more. And despite the way she'd answered his question the previous night, he suspected he understood what she was doing here in small-town Hell Valley.

April 2007. Virginia Tech. Christ.

"I dunno. I somehow think I've seen this tree before," she mumbled as she leaned against a staggeringly tall pine. "Or maybe it was one of his nine thousand brothers."

He got the point.

"Can I be honest?" she asked. She didn't wait for him to answer. "I'm afraid this is a waste of time. The guy's smart. Would he really have left anything for us to find?"

"It's possible. You'd be surprised at the mistakes criminals make."

"But he's got to be a genius, right?"

"Not necessarily. Brilliant monsters are a Hannibal Lecter fallacy; most organized serial killers are of just slightly above-average intelligence. Disorganized types can have low IQs, but they're cunning. In fact, the less intelligent the perpetrator, the more persistent and brutal he can be. Like an animal going after a treat, he just doesn't give up. Doesn't relent. Doesn't see anything wrong with what he's doing."

"Doesn't have a conscience," she whispered.

"Exactly. No moral compass. Combine that with a bloody streak, a hint of cleverness, determination, and a good survival instinct and you've got yourself a John

Wayne Gacy, who was no rocket scientist, yet killed dozens before he was caught."

"He's savvy, though. Using the Internet the way he does . . ."

"Every sixth grader in America is savvy enough to utilize the Internet. You've got teenagers beating each other up and proudly sharing the video on YouTube. While it might be unbelievable, it's not that difficult. Any asshole with a digital camera and a DSL connection can get his fifteen megabytes of fame."

She fell silent. The reality of what they were facing was probably worse than what she'd been imagining. Because a brilliant criminal, while hard to catch, might trip himself up through his own arrogance and certainty of his intelligence. An average one often escaped notice, his sheer blandness allowing him to fly under the radar. For years.

"Okay. So maybe he left something." She shook her head, eyeing the hundreds of trees in all directions. "But seventeen months?"

There, he agreed with her. It was a long shot. And they were all exhausted. They needed more men, and they needed dogs.

About to call it a day and suggest he, Stokes, and Mulrooney start on their interviews of Lisa's family and friends, he paused when Stacey's staticky radio came to life on her hip.

"Sheriff? You better get over here," one of her deputies said.

Their eyes met and locked. "They found something?" he asked.

"What is it, Frank? Over."

"Sorry 'bout that, Stacey. I forgot about the 'over.' Uh, over?"

Dean's teeth clenched and his temples began to throb.

"It's okay. Tell me what's going on."

"We got company. Damn it now, Warren, you put that away unless you want to get yourself shot."

"Oh, hell." Stacey's slim body stiffened and she immediately began to move, her long legs pistoning as she blew past him. The radio at her mouth, she ran toward the next quadrant, where her three deputies had been working. Mulrooney and Stokes were south of them, too far to be of any use.

Dean took off after her, his feet tangling in mounds of overgrowth. Sharp branches and brush tore at his clothes, and he thrust them out of the way. Every instinct he had screamed at him to tell her to wait, and the sudden panic that she might be running into something dangerous made his feet fly over the ground. Still, he wasn't as nimble as Stacey at maneuvering through this crap, so she beat him to the others by a few yards and a few deep breaths.

His numbed brain started working again as soon as he skidded to a stop beside her, seeing that she was fine and totally in control.

Tense. But in control.

Stacey had unsnapped her holster, and the tips of her fingers hovered over the grip of her weapon. She didn't betray the effects of her hundred-yard dash by so much as a gasp, and neither her hands nor her chin trembled in the least. She was entirely focused, as she warily eyed the metal fence topped by that vicious razor wire.

On the other side of it sat a hulk of a man on an ATV.

With grizzled gray hair cut close to his skull, his dark green camouflage clothes, and combat boots, he could be nothing other than a vet. Something kick-ass and violent had shown this guy some action and had left his brains a little scrambled up about whether or not it was peacetime. The scowl—not to mention the shotgun lying across his lap—made that obvious.

His own hand went to his hip. But Stacey shot him a warning look, silently telling him to wait.

"Did he point that shotgun at you?" she asked one of her deputies, not turning her head, keeping her attention on the man glaring at them through the metal fence.

"No, Sheriff," one of them said. "Just waved it around a little."

She nodded but didn't lower her hand. "Warren, you want to fire up that four-wheeler and ride on back to your house right now. You hear me?"

Warren. The name sounded familiar. And suddenly Dean knew for sure who they were facing. This was Warren Lee, the man who owned the property on the other side of this fence. The violent one who Stacey seemed certain hadn't been the man in the tape.

Dean wasn't so sure. The shadowy figure who'd killed Lisa and the others had been covered from top to bottom, a black hood hiding his entire head, a shoulder-to-toes cape doing the rest of the job. But he'd been tall, and obviously strong, given the way he'd overpowered his victims. He'd also been disgustingly impressive with weapons.

The proximity and this man's violent personality meant they could be looking at the man who'd killed those women. Tensing, Dean slowly removed his side-arm from its holster, keeping it low, down by his side. He didn't want to inflame the situation, but damned if he'd be caught unawares if that mean-looking bastard started shooting.

Noting that none of the deputies had done the same, all following Stacey's lead, on alert, but not unholstering, he gave her the benefit of the doubt that she knew what she was doing. This was their territory; the man was one of their townies, whom they all knew.

"What's going on? What do you people think you're doing on my property?"

"This isn't your property," Stacey said, maintaining her cool so easily he wondered if she had a little ice in her DNA. "We're on federal land and we have every right to be here. Now, I mean it. Get on back to your house and put that shotgun away before you wave it at the wrong person and end up with a bullet in you." Despite the words, her tone was even, not exactly threatening but not one bit weak, either.

Damn, the woman was cool under pressure.

"This is my fence. . . ."

"And we're not touching it," she snapped.

"I got a right to protect my property and make sure you don't come on it."

"We're officers of the law performing a legal search, who have the right to respond if we find ourselves threatened. Do you understand what I'm saying, Mr. Lee?" Her hand wrapped around the butt of her nine-millimeter. She'd reached the end of her patience with the man. "I don't care if you're on your own property; if you point that gun at one of my men, or any other officer in these woods, they will be perfectly within their rights to take you down."

The man's eyes narrowed and he remained still for a moment, engaging in a staring contest with the female sheriff whose entire posture said she would not back off. Then, as if someone had whispered some sense into his ear, he pushed the shotgun, muzzle down, into a scabbard on his ATV. "Saw activity, had the right to arm myself to come out and see what was going on."

Dean wondered just how much this man actually knew about his rights. Because if he was stupid enough to shoot and kill anyone merely for stepping over his property line, the guy would be looking at manslaughter at the very least.

"We've talked about this, Warren. There's a big difference between protecting yourself if someone breaks into your house and you coming out here to look for trouble."

The tension drew out a moment longer, as the big, gruff-looking man continued to glare. Then, slowly, as if someone had poured a modicum of malicious pleasure into his brain, a creaky smile cracked his face. It looked more menacing than friendly, as though it didn't get a lot of use.

"Good luck on your search," he said with a sarcastic salute.

The smile widened, going from creaky to crafty.

All Dean's senses reacted to the change. He almost smelled the malevolent humor rolling off the man, as if he had a great, dark secret and knew the sheriff was wasting her time. He stepped forward, wanting to question Lee about whether he really knew something, as his expression and tone seemed to indicate. Before he could, though, Mr. Lee started the engine and revved it up.

"Stay on that side of the fence," Lee called before speeding away.

When he was gone, Stacey questioned her deputies. "Tell me everything he said and did."

Exactly what Dean wanted to know. Seeing her deep frown, he wondered if Stacey, too, had been struck by the unfriendly man's strange mood swing.

Her men, despite their rusty radio skills, proved pretty observant. They succinctly related the details of Mr. Lee's arrival, his belligerent attitude, and his comments. One thing was apparent: He did not immediately question what they were doing. He had been focused only on whether they were coming too close to his own property.

"He didn't ask what you were looking for?"

The deputy who'd been doing most of the talking, a

middle-aged guy with a bulbous red nose, answered, "Nope, he never did. Only . . ."

Stacey stiffened. "Only what?"

"Only, Carl mighta said something about us investigating a murder."

"Shit," Dean muttered.

The last thing they wanted was to tip off the Reaper that they were onto him. Getting out here and conducting a search as secretly as possible had been one reason for keeping the response team so small, despite the availability of some of Stacey's other officers. They did not want to scare the guy off and send him into hiding.

The revelation also made his impressions of Warren Lee tighten to a sharper point, a tension that pounded into his gut like every good instinct did. Because that man had *known* something. Dean would stake his career on it.

"God, I don't want to deal with this."

Stacey's heavy sigh reminded him that there was yet another reason they didn't want word to get out. When he saw her rub a weary hand over her eyes, and noted the slump of her shoulders, he knew what she was thinking.

"I'm going to have to go talk to Winnie Freed," she mumbled. "Lisa's mother."

Dean stepped closer, instinct making him drop a hand on her shoulder. "So soon?"

She nodded. "Warren's going to be screaming to anybody who'll listen that we're trampling on his rights while looking for a murder victim. There's only one missing person in this whole town. Word will get back to Winnie by nightfall." She finally appeared to notice Dean's hand. Staring at it, then casting a quick glance at her deputies, she stepped away, but not before offering him a small nod of appreciation. "I've never had to do that before. Personally notify the next of kin."

It was her job; she'd have to do it sooner or later, but he didn't envy her. He'd delivered that kind of news enough to know she was in for a rough scene. And her friendliness with the family was going to make it harder.

"Let me come with you," he offered. The idea made sense. He, Stokes, and Mulrooney would need to question the victim's family and friends. They'd intended to start after completing the entire search, but the potential exposure of the reason for their presence in Hope Valley had put them up against a ticking clock. Interviews were the better bet right now. Compiling a list of suspects, people who'd known Lisa, who'd been at the tavern that night, who frequently left town, who flashed new money around. There were lots of questions to ask, lots of people to talk to. The victim's soon-to-be-grieving mother was as good a place to start as any.

There was another clock clicking even louder in Dean's mind. The one at Satan's Playground. Another auction was going down soon; it could already have taken place. As much as he wanted to locate Lisa's body, he already feared that any evidence they found wouldn't give them enough to nail the bastard in time to stop him.

Or to save whomever he targeted next.

Amber Torrington's day had blown from the start.

First, her lame parents had refused to pay the deductible to repair her dented car. As if it was her fault dumbass drivers kept pulling out in front of her, or going too slow, causing her to hit them.

She'd broken a nail and couldn't get an appointment to have it fixed for two days. Time to find another nail salon, because they'd been rude on the phone when she'd demanded that they squeeze her in.

Then Justin had told her he hadn't been able to score tickets for tomorrow night's concert she'd been dying to go to. That fat cow Kelsey had acted all disappointed for her, rubbing it in that she had tickets. She'd even had the nerve to ask Amber to use her employee discount so she could get something new to wear to it.

This had to be her worst hair day ever. She felt a zit forming on her chin. And her psycho of a boss at the trendy shop where she worked had spent the last hour, after closing, grilling her about some missing clothes until they'd ended up in a screaming match.

Might be time to get another job. One where she could wear all her new clothes.

Thank God the day was almost over. There was only an hour for something else to go wrong in her life. God, what she wouldn't give to get into her convertible, head for 95, and drive south. Florida would be good. Anywhere but the boringest place on the planet, known as Rockville, MD.

Imagining riding with the top down along the coast— maybe with some Southern hottie who'd be way better than Justin—she didn't even notice that she was not alone until she almost ran into the black-cloaked figure in front of her.

"Watch where you're going, dickhead," she snapped when the guy stepped in her way as she walked through the darkened parking lot to her car. Too bad she hadn't parked it close to the mall exit. She always left her baby way out in nowhereland so no careless asshole would open his door and ding it up. But since it was already banged up from last weekend's fender-bender, she needn't have bothered.

"Can you help me?" asked the guy who'd almost bumped into her.

"No, I can't. Now get the hell out of the way."

"That's not very nice," he whispered. "Not very ladylike."

Finally really looking at him, she noticed his clothes.

He wore a long, dark coat, with the collar turned up to shield most of his face. On his head, covering his hair and tugged almost down over his eyes, was a plain black baseball cap. Not exactly normal dress for eleven o'clock on a hot summer night.

Suddenly uncomfortable, she stepped to the side, to go around him. He mirrored the movement, blocking her again.

"What's wrong with you? Are you some kind of a retard?"

He *tsk*ed, shaking his head. "You're a very mean girl. Nasty. Somebody should do something about that."

A hint of fear clutched at her spine and crawled up Amber's back like a tiny spider. "Leave me alone."

"I can't do that. Wouldn't be gentlemanly to leave you here all on your own."

Gentlemanly. Was this dude for real? "I can take care of myself."

She felt around in her purse, mentally kicking herself for not getting her keys out inside, like they always said you should. And for parking on the opposite side of the mall, far from where her boss usually parked. She was mad at the sour-faced witch, but right now, she would like nothing more than to see her come walking out that door, especially if she was accompanied by the security guard who'd stopped by the store fifteen minutes ago to see what all the yelling was about.

But she knew that wouldn't happen. The guy had gotten a radio call about an exterior break-in alarm going off at one of the big, high-end department stores. The last time she saw him he and the other guards had been racing there to check it out.

That store was all the way on the other side of the enormous mall.

"I mean it; get out of my way or I'm going to scream."

He laughed softly, as if knowing nobody was close enough to hear. "Go ahead."

Maybe he did know. *What if* he *set off that alarm*?

Even tenser now, she looked around frantically. Her car was a good twenty spaces down the aisle. The only other vehicle in sight was a covered pickup a few yards away. *His?* A thick stand of trees separated the mall from the closest road. Despite seeing the glimmer of color as yellow faded to red on the closest stoplight, she couldn't make out a single pair of headlights. Not one car. Not one person.

Nobody anywhere.

The blacktop suddenly seemed as big as a dark sea, the distance between her and her car enormous. Small puddles of gold fell here and there from the overhead lights but did nothing to spotlight the two of them. She suddenly realized why when she saw glass twinkling on the ground.

The closest one had been shot out. As had the one past that. And the next.

Growing frantic, she glanced toward the glass doors she'd just come through. There were video cameras posted above every entrance into the mall, and at least one guard was supposed to be watching them from the security office at all times. If she waved, maybe . . .

The camera was dangling by its own wires. *Oh, fuck.* She was in serious trouble.

"I heard what you said to that girl."

All the air left her lungs in a quick, shocked exhalation.

"The one who wanted to use your discount."

The guy had been watching her? Following her? And she'd never noticed?

"I heard you and your boss yelling at each other, too. Those were some bad words you were using, Amber. I could hear you all the way in the back of the stockroom."

He'd been in the stockroom.

Apparently seeing her shock and confusion, he explained, "Your boss probably should have locked the back door after that delivery."

The delivery. At six o'clock. God, he had been watching her for hours. He'd sneaked into the store through the rear employees-only entrance by the trash Dumpsters and they'd never even realized it?

Genuinely panicking now, she tried to dart around him, but he lunged after her, his fingers digging painfully into her upper arm. He spun her around, grabbing the other arm, keeping her in place.

She struggled violently. Her purse fell, its contents spilling onto the ground. Remembering a safety tip she'd once heard, she forced herself to let her legs collapse, leaving her entire body weight in his hands.

The move took him off guard, and he dropped her with a grunt. Amber landed on her knees, hard on the blacktop. She thought about the keys, but instead lunged for her phone. "I'm calling the cops!"

He stared down at her, not appearing the least bit concerned. Swinging his hand, he slapped the phone out of her fingers as easily as he would have shooed away a bug.

That was when she saw what was in his other hand. And fear turned to terror.

"They won't get here in time."

Chapter 6

Winnie Freed hadn't been home the previous evening.

Stacey had been prepared to break the news, as gently as possible, to Lisa's mother, but when she and Dean had arrived there, the small house had been empty. A neighbor had told them Winnie was working evenings through the weekend at the hotel. And Stan, who'd recently taken a second job to make ends meet, was pulling the night shift all the way over in Leesburg.

She hadn't known whether to be disappointed or relieved. Never having been the type to put off an unpleasant task, since the stressing over it was often worse than the doing, she was probably more the former.

Dean hadn't been happy, either. In fact, she'd sensed his frustration was even greater than her own. Learning why, when he'd told her this sick psycho killer was setting up his next crime, she understood.

She'd considered notifying Winnie at work. Since the woman had been away from town all day, however, she couldn't have heard any rumors yet. And she didn't expect Winnie to be able to help much with the case. Meeting with Lisa's mother would be more about comforting the woman in her grief than getting any real information that could help them, so she'd decided to wait until morning.

Spending the rest of the evening in her office with Dean and his two coworkers, Special Agents Stokes and Mulrooney, she'd given them everything she had on the case. She liked Jackie Stokes. They'd hit it off right away, possibly because they both knew what it was like to be a woman in a male-dominated field.

Kyle Mulrooney took a little getting used to. He was mouthy and he swaggered. But there was something about the twinkle in his eye and his genuine grin that enabled her to see past the blustery exterior. He might have been keeping up a series of running jokes in her office last night, when she'd briefed the three agents on everything she knew about the people in Lisa's life, but he also hadn't missed a single detail.

One of the most interesting things Mulrooney had pointed out was that Lisa was unlike the other victims in one way: They had been normal working women, students, all from good backgrounds, leading average lives. Lisa, however, had been one of society's throwaways. Nearly everyone had given her up as no good, destined only for a bad end, though most people had figured she was headed for jail rather than a cold, vicious death.

Stacey included, to her eternal regret

The realization had kept her awake for hours after she'd fallen into bed, exhausted but unable to shut her brain down. Her mind was awash with the case, the possibility that someone here in Hope Valley might have murdered eight people.

When she'd finally thrust those thoughts away, late in the night, Dean Taggert had taken up residence in her head and done his little number on her, too.

"Not gonna go there today," she reminded herself as she got into her car at seven a.m. Saturday. She had made a mental deal with herself before finally succumbing to sheer fatigue the night before. She'd remain all business with Taggert until he made it clear he was interested in more than that.

Stacey was no old-fashioned, the-guy-has-to-make-the-first-move kind of woman, but the stakes were too high for her to do anything else. She was out of her depth, unsure how to proceed. If exploring the unexpected attraction between them was okay on his part despite his job, this case, and his obviously screwed-up personal life, it'd be okay with her. But she couldn't make that decision for him.

"So for once, let a man take the lead," she muttered as she backed out of her driveway. Even though she already hated the very thought of it. She'd called the shots in every relationship she'd ever had. *And maybe that's why you haven't had very many.*

Ignoring the little voice in her head, she took off, heading not downtown, but toward the road leading out of Hope Valley. Though she had plans to meet the FBI agents at her office at eight thirty, she had a stop to make first. There weren't many people she could talk to about this case; not many who'd even be able to comprehend it, much less treat it with the absolute secrecy that it demanded.

She could, however, think of one.

"Hi, Dad," she said when he answered his front door about ten minutes later. Normally, since she had a key, she would have let herself in. Peeking into the window of the closed garage, however, and seeing Connie's car parked inside, she hadn't done it.

Let them think they were fooling the town. They both deserved a little happiness in their not-so-secret affair.

The look on his face—concern instead of embarrassment at potentially being caught with an overnight girlfriend—confirmed that he already knew what was going on. "Figured you'd be showing up soon."

An early riser all his life, Ed Rhodes had never gotten used to the habit of being a layabed, as he called it. He was already dressed, in long khaki shorts and a tropical shirt. Stacey hid a smile; Connie had obviously picked out this ensemble.

"Come here and give your old man a hug." Reaching out, he enfolded her in his arms and drew her against his solid chest. Stacey closed her eyes, hugged him, and let herself be his daughter for a moment.

But as soon as he released her, she went back to being his successor as sheriff. "Got some time to talk?"

"Coffee's on. I'll grab us some and meet you back here."

Nodding, she walked across the porch, hearing the familiar creaks of the old wooden planks, once a bright white, now faded to gray, with chips of paint peeling up at the corners. Tim had lived here for the first year after he'd come back from overseas, and had promised to do all kinds of needed repairs. As was so often his habit lately, her brother had done nothing but stay to himself, vacillating between bouts of anger and sorrow, lashing out at anyone who even tried to help him.

Now Tim had his own small place, and their father was once again alone, but he'd never leave. Her family had lived here for fifty years, starting with her grandparents. And though she sometimes worried about Dad being outside of town, two miles from the closest neighbor, she couldn't imagine him ever living anywhere else.

Dropping her elbows onto the railing, she stared at the thick woods, the lake, and the old red barn in the distance. Then, hearing the scratch of nails on the steps, she realized she had company. "Hey, girl," she murmured with a smile. "Out getting into trouble?"

She bent to scratch the tired old mutt who had shown up on her father's porch a few winters ago and never quite left. Her dad had originally called his unexpected pet Tramp, because of the dog's wandering tendencies. Then he'd realized she was a Lady. But she still wandered.

"Don't be mad at Connie for telling me," her father said as he joined her at the railing. She hadn't even heard him come back out.

"I figured she would."

"She's not a blabber; it didn't go anywhere beyond me."

"I know." Accepting the cup he offered her, she sat in one of the wicker rockers by the door, waiting for him to sit beside her. The dog curled up at her father's feet, resting her head right on top of his leather loafers.

"So what did she tell you?" Honestly, Stacey wasn't sure what Connie knew, whether she'd been listening through keyholes or just making a lot of assumptions.

"That the FBI is here looking for Lisa Zimmerman's body." Her father's big, competent hands, gnarled with the rheumatoid arthritis that had forced him to retire before he was ready, tightened on the armrests of his chair. "That there's some kind of movie of her being killed, and you had to watch it."

Listening at keyholes. Thank God the video had been a silent one.

She sipped her coffee, trying to decide how much she could share. Her father was no random bystander; he'd been sheriff of this town for more than twenty years and had lived in it for more than sixty. She trusted him like she trusted no other person on earth.

Most important, he knew every person in the county. And while he'd probably have as much trouble as she did imagining that one of them could be a serial killer, having another set of eyes evaluating possible suspects could be very helpful.

"This is going to be hard to hear," she warned. "I know you were friendly with Lisa Zimmerman's father."

He nodded once, indicating he was prepared for what she had to say.

So she told him. How Lisa had died, where, and when. Everything the FBI had on that case. Respecting Dean and his team, she made a point to avoid discussing specifics on other murders, expanding only on the facts that affected Hope Valley.

That was enough for any normal person to digest, anyway. She saw no need to describe how those seven other women had suffered. Hearing the details last night had been enough to make her physically ill again.

By the time she was finished, her big, blustery father had grown pale and glassy-eyed. "Lord almighty."

"Yeah."

"That poor little thing. This will crush her mother."

"I know."

He fell silent, thinking about it, slowly stretching and massaging his pained knuckles by long force of habit. Finally, his gaze focused somewhere on the woods beyond the house, he murmured, "Do you think they're right? That somebody from around here killed her and those other women?"

She did. Mentally, she had accepted that as a likelihood. But damn, did it hurt to admit it out loud, especially to someone who loved this town so very much. She couldn't lie to him, though; never had been able to. So she nodded. "I do."

He closed his eyes, a low, small shudder rolling through him. The cup shook in his hand, and Stacey reached for it, worried his poor, tortured fingers would lose their grip on it and spill hot coffee all over his lap.

But he waved her away, lowering the cup to a small table himself. "I'm all right. Just . . . not something I ever thought I'd hear about Hope Valley."

"Me, either."

"I investigated a murder once, you know. More'n

twenty years ago. And damned if it didn't involve two good old boys who'd had a fight out at Dick's one Saturday night." He shook his head ruefully. "I can't help thinking lightning shoulda struck and burned that place clear to the ground by now, with all the trouble it's been."

She hadn't known that, but wasn't surprised at her father's sentiments regarding the rowdy tavern. It had been the bane of many of her weekends since taking office, and many of his before her.

"Have you got anybody in mind? One of Lisa's no-good boyfriends? I heard she was dating some ex-con biker."

"He'd been in a Georgia jail for a few months when she disappeared," she said, already having looked at that angle as soon as Winnie had reported Lisa missing.

"I suppose, if there are other cases you're not telling me about, that it's got to be somebody who can go out of town without much notice."

"Possibly, though I think all the other murders were within a few hours' drive of here." The Reaper had been able to do his dirty work in a single night, in most cases.

"Still, that many overnights, wouldn't be easy for a family man to be gone nights, unless he had a reason to be. Night job, or one that required travel."

"True."

"I think there are a lot of marriages around here that had some ups and downs because of that girl, so it could be a married man. But I bet you're looking for a single fella. Somebody who hasn't had much luck with women."

Stacey's brow rose. "Maybe you should go to work for the FBI as a profiler."

He shrugged. "Common sense. If he's as vicious as you say he is toward women, he obviously hates them." Frowning darkly, he mumbled, "That Warren Lee, somebody sure dropped him in a whole barrel full of crazy somewhere along the line."

"But he hates everybody, not just women. When he goes . . ."

"He'll go postal," he said, finishing her sentence.

"He did act strangely yesterday, though," she mused, more to herself than to him.

"Stranger than usual?"

"Good point."

Her father fell silent for a few moments, gazing toward the lawn. Then, in a low voice, he said, "That stepfather of hers is a mean son of a bitch."

Stacey concurred, but she'd rarely heard her dad use foul language and always made a point of cleaning up her own around him. "Did you ever think, ever wonder . . ."

"If he abused her? Hell, yes, I wondered. Something made that girl change right after he moved into her mama's house."

"I sometimes see bruises on Winnie's arms," Stacey admitted. "Whenever I ask her about them she says they're from work."

He sneered. "Yeah, those laundry carts have big fists on 'em, don't they?"

Deep in thought, she whispered, "I never saw bruises on Lisa. But maybe the abuse was different."

Dad's hands clenched into fists, though it must have pained him terribly. "I asked her once when she was a teenager."

Stunned, Stacey felt her mouth fall open. "You're kidding."

"Nope. You were with the VSP when the worst of it happened. She went so wild, and I had to haul her in for dealing. When she begged me to let her off, saying she was pregnant and desperate, I flat out asked her if Stan was the father."

"Oh, my God," Stacey mumbled, never having heard this part of the story.

"She denied it. Told me if I went to Winnie about it, she'd run away forever."

Which just made it more likely.

"I knew by the look in her eyes that she wasn't lying about the pregnancy, but I guess she miscarried, or went out of town and took care of it. Never saw her have any baby. She was probably, oh, fifteen at the time."

The story stunned her and broke her heart all over again for Lisa. By the time Stacey had come back to Hope Valley, she'd simply accepted the girl as the town tramp and druggie, not even recognizing her. If she hadn't left, if she'd moved back after college, might she have been able to do something? Lisa had looked up to her once, had treated her like a big sister. If she'd been around, could she have helped her escape the nightmare her life had become?

A nightmare that might have included sexual molestation by her stepfather?

She couldn't even bear to think about it, that poor little girl slowly turning into the helpless, desperate young woman she'd become, so hungry for escape and for love that she sought them both from any man who'd show her a little attention.

The dark thoughts churned in her mind; her stomach clenched and heaved. And in the darkest corner of her brain the images anchored and took root. Bloody images.

"Could he have wanted to shut her up?" she whispered. "Or maybe she was older, strong enough to turn him down, and he snapped?" Had that sent the man on the path of savagery the Reaper had let loose upon the world?

Her father said nothing, continuing to rock, slowly,

absorbing the possibility just as Stacey was. Finally, though, he mumbled, "It's a damn tragedy. I can't imagine how different things might have turned out if her daddy hadn't died in that accident."

Stacey didn't even want to think about how Lisa's world had blown to bits with her father's death and her mother's remarriage to a complete bastard, one in a long line of mean men, if the stories about the Freeds were true. Lisa's life might have been very different, indeed.

"I know." Reaching over, she took her dad's hand as gently as possible, thinking not for the first time how lucky she and her brother were. Her life might have gotten just as screwed up as poor Lisa's had he made some different choices. Lord, when she thought about how Tim and Randy used to scheme to get their widowed father together with Randy's widowed mother . . . She shuddered at the very thought of having grown up with that wicked witch of a stepmother. But her father obviously had much better taste. He'd steered well clear of Alice Covey, and all the other divorcees and widows who'd set their eyes on the handsome widower, devoting himself just to her and to Tim.

Which was one reason she was so happy he'd finally reached out and grabbed some personal happiness with Connie.

Thinking about her brother, she said, "Tim came to see me the other day."

His mouth turned down at the corners. "I heard."

Oh, she'd just bet. She doubted the news had come from Connie, who tried to avoid upsetting Dad as much as possible. Her brother had most likely come out here screaming at the injustice that his bitch of a sister wouldn't help him out in his time of need. As if she and everyone else hadn't been doing exactly that since the day he'd come home two years ago, injured and so messed up in the head that she barely recognized him.

"Dad, he'll never help himself if we keep bailing him out. He doesn't need his family to keep rescuing him, or his buddy to keep dragging him into trouble."

"Randy's been there for him."

"I know. But a friend who encourages him in his anger and resentment, who takes him illegally out-of-season hunting, or drinking seven nights a week, is not what he needs right now. He needs to get back over to the vet hospital and talk to that shrink. He shouldn't have stopped going after only a couple of months."

He met her stare evenly. "I know you're right. Logically, I know that." His free hand dropped over hers, covering it. "But he's my boy. I look at him and I see those scars and I think about what he's been through and . . ." He didn't ask her. Didn't make the request out loud. But he made it just the same, with his pained eyes.

Shaking her head, knowing tough love would be the first thing her father would suggest for anybody else's kid, she pulled her hand away. "I'll see what I can do."

"Thanks, sweetheart."

She wondered if he'd be thanking her if Tim never got his shit together, never emerged from the dark cloud of anger that had swallowed him up and eradicated any sign of the guy who used to play football and bass guitar. The one who used to smile.

He sure wouldn't if he kept hanging around with Randy, the two of them getting drunk and raising hell like a pair of teenagers. Randy had gotten Tim into enough trouble when they were growing up, for stealing and fighting. She truly wished her brother hadn't renewed the friendship when he got home.

"I should run. You'll think about the case, won't you? And let me know if you can come up with anything you think could help?"

"I will." Rising, he put his hands on her shoulders and, staring at her with worry in his eyes, he said, "You be careful. Let those FBI guys take the lead on this. The last thing I want to even think about is you going head-to-head with someone so evil."

Evil. Yes. That described the person they were after. Could Stan Freed, while a mean and possibly degenerate brute, be that evil?

"I know this isn't what you bargained for when you came back here to take over for your old man," he murmured, staring into her face as if looking for signs that she might break. As if he feared the violence that had followed her here to her small hometown had assaulted her personally and she'd be unable to bear the strain.

It hadn't. And she'd bear it. Period.

"I'll be fine." She kissed her father on the cheek, acknowledging his right to fear for his daughter, rather than support the sheriff. Then, turning to walk down the steps, she glanced over her shoulder, smiled, and said, "Tell Connie I said good morning."

His surprised chuckle made leaving him alone on the porch a little easier. And gave her what she knew would be one of her few bright moments of the day.

With Stacey's office as the base of operations, Dean, Stokes, and Mulrooney headed there first thing in the morning after making a quick pit stop at the little coffee bar, where they'd all filled up on liquid fuel. Grabbing an extra cup for Stacey, he realized he didn't know how she took her coffee. Or even if she drank it. Didn't know a lot about her at all, as a matter of fact.

He just knew that as he entered the sheriff's office promptly at eight thirty, his pulse picked up its pace a little in his veins. Because he wanted to see her.

She met them right at the front door. "Good morning."

Unlike yesterday, when they'd been tromping in the woods, Stacey again wore her crisp, starched uniform. Probably because of where she and Dean were headed in a few minutes. She'd need that self-protective armor when she made the notification to Lisa's mother.

She eyed the foam cups of coffee in his hands. "Thirsty?"

He extended one. "Wasn't sure how you take it."

"In this weather, usually iced. But considering how little sleep I've gotten the past few nights, I'll take anything I can get." She reached for the cup, her fingers brushing against his. "Thanks." She sipped, then glanced at Stokes and Mulrooney. "You guys doing okay at the inn?"

"It's not as bad as it looks," Jackie replied.

Mulrooney stretched, arching his back, sticking his belly out. "I slept like a baby. A baby having nightmares about a black-cape-wearing bogeyman, but a baby."

Dean merely grunted, as usual not quite sure how to take Mulrooney's odd sense of humor. But he had to concede that when the older man was on his game, he was pretty intuitive. And pretty brave, given the stories Dean had heard.

"Let's go into my office," Stacey said.

They followed her, sat around her desk; then Dean filled her in on the morning's developments. "We got a call from Wyatt. Turns out the PD in the Maryland case had a tire print at the dump site that they just now let us know about. It's a 7.50R16LT. Pretty standard-issue on late-model American-made light-to-medium-duty pickups and SUVs."

She frowned. "Which describes vehicles driven by half the men in this county."

"It's something."

"Didn't you say one of the victims was . . ." Her voice the tiniest bit shaky, she quickly rephrased her question. "There was a semi truck involved somewhere, right?"

Dean shook his head. "The MO was out of an old movie that involved a semi, but the unsub didn't use one. It's clear on the video that he was driving a monster SUV, which he'd stolen." He didn't want to think about whether the less powerful vehicle had made the victim's death any worse, but he suspected it had taken longer. "It was found a few days later, in another town, and treated as a standard auto theft. The locals didn't know it was involved in a murder until we brought the case to them last week."

"No prints?"

"Not a damn thing. If they even dusted for them."

In a standard auto theft case, with a vehicle recovered within a few days, he'd bet they hadn't bothered. He assumed the perp had cleaned off the back of the SUV, or even small-town, inexperienced guys would have recognized blood on the bumper and done at least something to investigate.

"After it was recovered, the SUV was traded in. We tracked it down to its new owner in Ohio, and had it picked up. There could be blood on the undercarriage even after all these months."

She didn't look particularly hopeful about that possibility. Considering Dean felt the same, he didn't blame her.

"Too bad about the semi," she said. "That would have narrowed things down, since they're not something just anybody can jump into and drive."

"Tell me about it. If the unsub was a licensed trucker, he'd be easier to track."

Mulrooney cleared his throat. The quick, curious glance he cast between Dean and Stacey made Dean stiffen in his chair. They'd been talking as though the other two agents weren't in the room, and while it had been strictly business, something made him wonder if the personal connection he shared with the sheriff had been noticed by others.

"So your guys are out stomping through the woods on

their own today, right?" Mulrooney asked. "Better them than me. It's going to be even hotter than yesterday."

Stacey nodded, busying her hands with some blank sheets of paper on her desk. As if she, too, had realized they'd been ignoring the other agents. "Yes, the same three deputies. They know that if they find anything, they are to call immediately and not touch a thing."

"Hope that crazy-as-a-jackrabbit guy on the ATV doesn't show up," Mulrooney said. "You sure we shouldn't be searching on the inside of that fence?"

Stacey frowned. "I'll handle Warren. But my opinion hasn't changed, based on a lot of things, including the way the man in the video moved and acted."

"I think there's something there," Dean said, flatly convinced of it. "I didn't like that smile when he took off yesterday."

Nodding, Stacey admitted, "I noticed it, too. Maybe he is hiding something. But I have a hard time picturing him as deliberate and patient as the Reaper." Swallowing, she added, "If you want me to watch the other video files to see if that changes things . . ."

"Forget it," Dean snapped, not even willing to consider letting her put herself through it. "Let's do our interviews, see if Mr. Lee was anywhere near the tavern the night the victim disappeared. Look for any possible connection there. Then we'll decide if we need to go have a talk with him."

Jackie, who'd been jotting some notes on a small pad, rose. "Okay, guess that's our cue to get moving. Kyle and I are headed to talk to"—she consulted the pad—"Mrs. Baker, who runs the drugstore where Lisa was last employed."

Stacey grunted. "Good luck with that one. She fired Lisa for stealing from the register. I imagine she'll have a lot to say about her, but none of it will be nice."

Mulrooney shook his head. "There's that bad-girl

angle again. All the others were described as—how'd you put it?" he asked Stokes.

"Determined, headstrong," she replied with a quirk of her mouth. "Which I took to mean they weren't very well liked, but nobody wanted to speak ill of a murder victim."

"But all successful, workers or students," Mulrooney said. "No other druggies, ex-cons. She stands out."

He'd noted the same thing the previous night, but obviously, judging by the thoughtful look on his face, Mulrooney considered the idea worth repeating. And Dean thought he was right. Every detail about Lisa's case that made her unique from the others shored up their theories about her murder.

"Somebody who wouldn't be missed," Dean muttered, "somebody he could experiment on without too much fear of causing a big search and rescue."

Stacey, who had just risen from her chair, stiffened and her jaw tensed. Dean saw a flash of emotion in her eyes, a hint of guilt in her tight mouth, and realized he'd just added to the weight of responsibility she'd already piled onto her own shoulders.

Stupid. He glanced at the others, wanting to reassure her, but not wanting to embarrass her in front of their colleagues. Knowing he would be alone with her in a car in a few minutes, he figured he'd have time to talk to her then. He'd let her know she had done absolutely nothing wrong and had reacted as anybody in law enforcement would have.

Before he could rise to leave, the door to Stacey's office burst open. A wide-eyed young man, probably in his late twenties, erupted into the room, swinging an arm that was encased in a cast from the wrist to just above the elbow. "Is it true? Was Lisa murdered?" he bellowed, not even appearing to notice that three FBI agents and one annoyed-looking sheriff had all leaped to their feet and gone on alert at the unexpected interruption.

Stacey put a hand on the younger man's arm. "Mitch, calm down."

"I heard you were out in the woods looking for her body." He thrust his good hand through his sandy blond hair, then noticed the others in the room. His face reddened, but he didn't back out with an apology. Instead, his chin thrust forward, his expression going a shade grimmer. "It's true. They're FBI, aren't they."

"Yes, they're FBI." She released the man's arm, watching him closely.

She probably wasn't watching him as closely as Dean, Stokes, and Mulrooney were; however, it wouldn't be the first time a perp had insinuated himself into a police investigation. Many serial killers had been well-known to the police before they'd been caught. And this guy had obviously known the victim very well, judging by his obvious dismay.

"And yes," Stacey added, "we're looking for Lisa's remains."

The truth of it seemed to deflate the young man, because he staggered back, his shoulders hitting the closed office door. He bent over at the waist, clutching his middle. "Oh, my God. She's really dead."

"Who is this?" Dean finally asked.

Stacey kept her eyes on the newcomer, giving him a frown of warning. "This is my chief deputy, Mitch Flanagan."

Now it was Dean's turn to be surprised. Her chief deputy? A guy in a cast with no sense of professionalism, since he'd burst in on a closed meeting? A guy who, judging by his behavior, had been involved with their victim? He and Jackie exchanged a quick glance, and he knew he wasn't the only one in the room who wanted to know more.

Stacey returned her attention solely to Flanagan. "Were you friendly with Lisa?"

His mouth opened, no sounds coming out. Then he nodded. "We were close."

Damn. Lovers. Stacey looked shocked. "How long had that been going on?"

"Nothing was going on. Not in that way."

Doubtful. Or at least, not for lack of trying on this guy's part.

"But we were friends. She could talk to me, and I was trying to help her." He rubbed a hand over what Dean suspected were tearstained eyes.

Or maybe Flanagan just wanted them to look that way.

God help him for a cynical bastard. He just didn't trust anybody, especially not immediately after meeting them. Which, he supposed, made his instinctive reaction to Sheriff Stacey Rhodes that much more surprising.

"I want to help with the search."

"Absolutely not."

"Stacey, come on, you need my help."

"You're on medical leave and I want you home." Her eyes narrowing, she added, "I mean it, Mitch. Stay out of this. If you were personally involved with Lisa in any way, the last place you can be is in the middle of this investigation."

"Who *wasn't* personally involved with her in this town?" the guy said, suddenly sounding angry. Angry enough to incite Dean to take a step forward, sending a hard look in the younger man's direction.

"Fine. Whatever." Swinging around, Flanagan grabbed the doorknob. But before he twisted it and stepped out, he muttered, "Just tell me when you find her." Looking back over his shoulder, he offered one more pleading glance at his boss. "Please."

She nodded, saying nothing as her deputy stormed out as quickly as he'd burst in.

"Well, that was exciting," Mulrooney said with a lazy smile, sounding anything but excited. It took a lot to get the big man's juices flowing, and Dean suspected he wasn't even fully conscious until he'd had at least three cups of coffee. Nice to know some things were still normal in this very un-normal place and situation.

"You'll need to find out just how close those two were," he told Stacey.

She frowned, not liking it one bit. "I know."

Her shock hadn't been feigned; she apparently hadn't had any idea her chief deputy had been involved with the missing woman. It had visibly shaken her. He understood why. Stacey was pretty damn confident in her own abilities, and not knowing something she must now see as obvious had to burn.

"Okay, enough for now. Can we get out of here?" Dean asked. But before he could take one step toward the door, his cell phone rang. "Damn it." Then, recognizing the number on the caller ID, he put a hand up to tell the others to wait. "Taggert."

"It's Wyatt. I'm sending you a file and you need to look at it."

"Good Lord, not another one," he muttered. Glancing at Stacey, he pointed to her desktop computer, and she nodded her permission.

"It's another kind of file; not a video."

Thank heaven for small favors. But hearing the obvious tension in his boss's voice, he knew whatever Wyatt was sending was bad. Dean sat in Stacey's chair and faced the desktop, accessing his e-mail. "What is it?"

"Brandon found the auction. It's already over."

Damn. They'd thought they had a few days, at least, before the next seventy-two-hour countdown started.

His pulse throbbed in his temple and his fingers curled tightly on top of the keyboard as he kept refreshing the screen, wanting the thing to hurry up. Yet somehow, not ever wanting to have to see it at all. "When?"

"Looks like it went down yesterday around noon."

The words stunned him, every muscle in his body clenching reflexively. "The unsub's already got almost twenty-four hours on us? How could this have happened?"

He saw the others react to the news. With his few words and his visible frustration, they already knew as much as he did. Stokes and Mulrooney both sat back down across from him, leaning over Stacey's desk, tense and completely at attention.

Wyatt continued. "Brandon thinks the site owners are paranoid about being compromised, especially as more and ever more illegal activity is turning up there, child pornography and the like. So the security has gotten more intense. There was some Reaper chatter; then the site went black with a 'Be Back Soon' message scrolling across, followed by a line of gibberish."

"Code for the members to find their way back in?"

"Perhaps. Or information on how to get into the invitation-only auction. It's open only to the members who like that sort of thing and who can afford to pay for it."

Dean would love to think that was a small group. But his gut told him it wasn't. With a whole world full of deviants the possibilities boggled the mind.

"When Brandon got back in this morning and saw more chatter that it was over, he went deep and finally found a transcript. Have you got it yet?"

Refreshing the screen, he saw the e-mail. "I've got it. It's opening."

Wyatt waited, saying nothing.

When the screencap appeared, Dean resisted the urge to dive to the bottom of it to find out what they were up against and started at the beginning. He read quickly, feeling his stomach heave at the excited chatter between Satan's Playgrounders with handles like Twistedsister, Thebutcher, and Marquisdesade. One persistent bidder whose name hinted at his true proclivities, Lovesprettyboys, tried to persuade the Reaper to let him choose the victim, but had been shot down. The others seemed content to merely toss out suggested means of death. Things so sick Dean wondered just how far the depths of the human mind could reach.

"I think I'm gonna puke," Mulrooney said.

Dean didn't turn around; he merely pointed to a trash can and kept reading. All the way to the bottom, to the winner's final bid. And his choice.

"Good God," he whispered.

"Taggert?" Wyatt's voice asked from the phone. "Do you see?"

"I see."

"We've got to stop him."

"I know."

"You gotta be kidding me," Stokes snapped, as she, too, read the final few lines.

Mulrooney was more blunt. "Fucking medieval."

Good description. Barbaric, horrific. Though, considering the viral popularity of some online videos, like the ones of the overseas assassinations of Americans by terrorists, not necessarily something nobody had ever heard of.

Stacey, who was seated on the corner of her desk, out of eyesight of the screen, asked, "What is it?"

Dean didn't answer. He merely turned the monitor so she could read the words for herself. She did so, then paled, closing her eyes and turning away.

"Lily's trying to track the payment," Wyatt said, meaning all three of them were in the office this early on a Saturday morning. Good to know the whole team was so anxious to catch this guy.

"You can see the winning bid was thirty-five thousand," Wyatt added. "He can't move that much money around the Internet without somebody noticing him. This is the closest to real time we've ever gotten, and she's making the most of it, focusing first on trying to find accounts that lead to anywhere in Virginia."

Another voice suddenly came through the phone. "There he is! I see the bastard."

Recognizing Brandon's voice, Dean asked, "What's he got?"

"Hold on," Wyatt replied. A low rumble of conversation followed, until Blackstone came back on the line. "He's in the Playground right now."

"The Reaper?"

"Yes."

"I see you," came Brandon's voice from the background. "Why don't you come out from under that cape, you little prick."

Unreal. They were watching a cartoon version of the sadistic killer freely strolling through his cyber world and couldn't lay a finger on him. "Can he trace him?"

Wyatt seemed distracted. "Why is it going in and out? Are you losing him?"

"Shit! Oh, no, you don't!" Brandon shouted, frustration making his voice throb.

Wyatt snapped into the phone, "I've got to go. We're doing what we can; I think we're going to lose him again. One thing we know at this point: The Reaper is online, playing in the Playground, right this minute. If you're going to conduct interviews this morning, you might keep that in mind."

"Got it," Dean said, ending the call. He tucked the phone away and related the information to the others.

"So let's go knock on good old Mr. Lee's door, tell him

we'd just like to chat, and see if he's online," Mulrooney said. "I bet he's got some high-powered security equipment out there, run by a state-of-the-art computer."

The idea had merit, but he saw by the look on Stacey's face that she genuinely believed they'd be wasting their time. And frankly, they didn't have time to waste.

He trusted her. He hadn't known her long, but he already had faith in her instincts, and if she thought they'd be barking up the wrong tree, he intended to take her at her word. "Let's stick with the original plan," Dean said.

He glanced at the computer screen again, unable to keep his eyes off the final words, the sick desires of the winner. And the Reaper's agreement.

God, he hoped they found this guy before he grabbed his next victim.

He enters the Playground through the south gate.

The palette of odd colors is familiar, welcoming. The eerie, gray-streaked blue sky casts a perennial storm cloud over the preternaturally cheerful Playground. The grass is too green. The sun too yellow. The images too surreal, at odd angles, with unnatural curves and sharp edges.

It's Dalí's version of Sesame Street.

Only if you look closely can you see the writhing forms of anguished souls carved into the base of the tree holding the tire swing. At first glance, the yawning opening beneath the sliding board, which falls away into a pit of flame and torture, appears to be only a shadow. The metal rings hanging from a jungle gym seem simple gymnastic playthings—until you notice the screaming man hanging from them, begging for mercy as a fire is lit beneath his feet.

As always when he comes to the Playground, peace washes over him. Happiness fills him from his core to the tips of his fingers and the very ends of each strand of hair on his body.

Ahead of him, the morning crowd is thick and buoyant as the weekend begins and earthly workweek identities fall away. Possibilities abound; excitement ignites the air. Convention and morality and mundane laws simply do not exist in this world. Nothing is taboo, nothing sacred.

No one ever says no. No desire is too dark to fulfill.

Here is a woman being beaten by a long, spiked whip. There a man is led around on a leash like a dog. A crowd encircles a duo taking turns raping the brunette they have pinned to the ground.

And a tall, skeletally thin man draped in expensive clothes takes yet another child by the hand and leads him through an elaborate gate marked PRIVATE.

Then, at last, they notice his arrival. All fall silent. Watching him. Waiting for him. They part like the sea spreading for some biblical being.

As they should. This is his kingdom and he stalks it like an all-powerful, all-seeing deity. Death ravaging the earth with every step he takes.

His black cape ruffles in the breeze, casting a long shadow of dread across the landscape. His scythe, sharp and vicious, swings side to side as he cuts a path toward his destination, everyone backing out of his way, bowing to him, whispering words of love and praise and adoration.

He doesn't love back. In this world. In any world.

But he is fond of them, as a god is fond of his worshipers. He bestows benevolence upon them, emerging from his dark fortress every so often so they may bow at his feet. He occasionally allows them the privilege of touching his robe, of getting close enough to death that they will experience endless nightmares.

The power invigorates him. He needs no sleep. No sustenance. Just this.

He reaches the marquee for the theater. Swiping his

*gloved hand across it, he erases the mundane titles prom-
ising sexual delights for those who enter.*

    He replaces it with words of his own:

COMING SOON . . .

BEHEADED.

And the crowd erupts.

Chapter 7

In the car on the way to Lisa Zimmerman's mother's house, Dean forced himself to focus on the unpleasant task ahead. Notifying next of kin was never easy. With a murder case, it was a hundred times harder.

He wanted to focus only on the unsub, on what he might be doing this minute to another innocent victim, but he couldn't allow himself to. Being distracted by that would make him less effective in his job, and he needed every brain cell in his head focused and in control. And every emotion he had shoved away to be dealt with later.

He needed Stacey to be the same way. Remembering what had happened before Wyatt's call, when he'd realized just how much she blamed herself for what had happened to Lisa, he wanted to get that out of her head. Though he wasn't the king of comforting women, and he knew she wasn't the type who would be interested in being comforted, he couldn't help saying, "It wasn't your fault."

Her hands clenched on the steering wheel.

"Stacey, you know as well as I do that she was dead by the time she was reported missing. There was nothing you could have done to save her, even if she'd been the mayor's wife and the whole town had been in an uproar over her disappearance."

"Tell her mother that," was the flat reply. "Explain to Winnie that the past year and a half of crying and waiting and hoping and praying wasn't my fault for not really believing something bad had happened to her daughter."

He knew he shouldn't, but something made him reach over and touch her shoulder. She flinched, taking her eyes off the road for one moment to glance at him.

"Anybody would have thought the same thing," he insisted, focusing only on getting Stacey's head back where it needed to be, in the now, rather than in the recriminations of the past. He squeezed lightly. "I would have. Wyatt would have. With someone like Lisa, who you admitted had disappeared before—"

"I know," she acknowledged, shaking her head. "But that doesn't make it right."

He pulled his hand away, knowing Stacey wouldn't be forgiving herself anytime soon. Sometime in the future, when they'd nailed this bastard to the wall, maybe she'd give herself a break. But not before then, if he was any judge of character.

Maybe that was one more reason he liked her. The incidents in her past that had forged her into the powerful woman she was today had also instilled a strong moral boundary within her. And the need to make a difference. He found the combination of sexy, sometimes playful, woman over that solid, implacable center incredibly appealing.

It could have been that the steel core inside her had been forged by fire in the heat of brutality she'd witnessed as a state cop. God knew, he'd never experienced anything like she must have at Virginia Tech. And part of him—a big part—wanted to pull her into his arms and comfort her for the awful memories that he suspected haunted her.

He couldn't, of course. She'd never accept that kind of gesture without reaching out for it first.

He only wondered what it would take to make her reach out.

Considering he'd never been able to acknowledge his own emotions about anything in his personal life until that life had been completely disrupted by his ex-wife's choices, he couldn't even venture a guess. He just hoped that whenever the moment did come, someone who really understood her would be there to respond.

"Do me a favor, okay?"

"Of course," he said.

"When I tell Winnie, keep a close eye on her husband, would you? He's not the nicest man in the world."

His eyes narrowing, he tried to read between her simple words, wondering if Stacey suspected Lisa's own stepfather of killing her. That seemed like a long shot, the Reaper being reckless enough to kill someone so close to him. But he'd certainly seen criminals do reckless things. "Of course."

When they reached the same small, dingy, shuttered house they'd visited the previous evening, Dean noted the beat-up old hatchback in the driveway, as well as a dusty sedan with a smiling laptop logo on the side, and heard Stacey's slow exhalation. "They're both here."

"It's a rotten part of the job, but you'll do fine," he murmured.

When he saw the thin, wasted-looking woman appear in the doorway before they'd even exited the car, however, he had to rethink that. She didn't look strong enough to carry a gallon of milk, much less hear news of her only child's murder.

The victim's mother had obviously heard from her neighbor that the sheriff had come looking for her the previous night. She walked down the steps toward them, looking both hopeful and terrified. "Sheriff?" she called. "You got some news?"

Stacey reached for her hat, which she'd set between the front seats, and put it on her head as she stepped out of the car. It was the first time he'd seen her in it, and somehow it completed the whole image of a strong, in-control professional.

The slight tremble of her lips, however, said a thousand times more about the woman wrapped up in all that professionalism.

His heart twisted in his chest, an unfamiliar sensation that he'd only ever experienced with Jared, when his little boy had been hurt or was afraid. He wanted to soothe her, to protect her, to take this burden from her. But Dean knew he could only cover her back. And be there for the inevitable recriminations and emotional overload once she had done her job and gotten far away from here.

"Can we speak in private?" she asked.

The woman paled, her eyes darting frantically, as if she half expected to see her daughter appear, safe and sound, maybe in handcuffs but okay. Alive. Accounted for.

"Please, Winnie. Let's go in out of the heat."

The older woman nodded, twisting her hands in the front of her drab, shapeless housecoat. "All right."

The house, with its dingy and weather-beaten exterior, was equally as morose on the inside. From the cluttered foyer, he noted that every curtain was drawn, each visible room cast in shadows that defied the bright morning sunshine. As if it weren't welcome here, as if the whole place were already in mourning.

He supposed it had been, for seventeen months. But for Lisa's mother, the true mourning was about to begin.

"Winnie, this is Special Agent Dean Taggert, from the FBI."

He extended his hand. She merely stared at it, as if it were a snake ready to bite. Maybe she thought not acknowledging his presence would forestall the dark news she already sensed was coming.

"Is Stan here?" Stacey asked.

"He's sleeping. He works nights a lot now."

"Maybe you should get him."

"He'll be mad," the woman whispered. "Tell me about Lisa."

Stacey took her hat off, holding it at her side. "We should wait for Stan."

The two women stared at each other, Stacey resolute, Mrs. Freed visibly afraid. Finally the older woman looked away, knowing in her heart what was coming, wanting to forestall the inevitable moment when reality could no longer be evaded. "I'll go get him. Have a seat in there," the woman said, gesturing toward a shadow-filled living room.

They watched her trudge down a hallway, open a door, and descend into what must be a finished basement. Separate bedrooms in the Freed marriage, perhaps?

When she was gone, her slow, aged footsteps growing lighter until they disappeared altogether into the bowels of the house, Dean stepped into the cavelike living room. Cluttered with a mishmash of furniture, it was as hot as an oven despite the closed curtains blocking out the sun. A sad assortment of ceramic figurines covered the surface of the coffee table, shepherds, milkmaids, and farm animals, gathering dust and ignored. The room had an abandoned feel, and he suspected that when Mrs. Freed was in this house, her existence consisted of sleeping, bathing, and eating. Not really living.

Catching sight of a number of framed photographs on the wall above the well-worn couch, he leaned closer.

"Lisa?" he murmured, eyeing the sweet-faced little blond-haired girl in school pictures like the ones he had of Jared back at his place.

Stacey joined him, though she looked as though she'd rather be anywhere else. "Yes."

"I wouldn't have recognized her. She was so pretty, so innocent," he said, having to swallow hard as suddenly something clicked in his brain. He recognized it as the moment that came in almost every case, when the victim became a person. Someone's loved one, someone's daughter. "Sad."

"She was a doll," Stacey admitted through a throat that sounded tight. "I used to babysit her. Can't tell you how many puzzles we did together right on that table."

He jerked his attention from the half dozen photographs of the ponytailed child, and stared at the woman standing so stiffly beside him. Stacey had admitted she knew Lisa, just not how well she'd known her. Realizing how much this had to be personally affecting her, he again felt the urge to put his hands on her shoulders and tug her close to enfold her in his arms. He sensed she didn't lean on anybody very often.

"I'm sorry," he mumbled, knowing he couldn't reach for her, couldn't make this personal. Not here, not now.

Not until she made it personal.

"I've got to catch whoever did this, Dean." Her voice shook with angry emotion, her slim body suddenly seeming too fragile to handle the weight that had been dumped on it. "I can't live the rest of my life without catching him."

Hearing the depth of her frustration, he couldn't resist putting one hand out, touching the tips of his fingers lightly to her arm. He wanted her to feel the unvoiced support he was offering her. "We'll catch him. I promise you."

She glanced at his hand, but didn't pull away. Instead,

she lifted her own and covered his fingers with her soft, capable ones. And in that moment, the touch, intended to be comforting and impersonal, simply became more. It secured an invisible connection between them, reinforcing his promise that he was here and wouldn't let this case go unsolved. And underscoring her belief in that promise.

It also acknowledged that they both knew there was some personal force at work between them that went beyond the job, beyond the case. Beyond this room in this house.

"Thanks," she murmured. Nodding and clearing her throat, she ducked away and turned her back on the photographs, as if unable to stand the innocent eyes that he knew she saw as accusing. Glancing at the floor for a moment, then at the figurines on the table, she suddenly stalked back out of the room to wait in the foyer.

He followed, knowing she couldn't stand being in that room with those memories.

A moment later, Mrs. Freed returned from the basement of the house, still wearing her faded housecoat, but having pulled her hair back off her thin, bony face. The style emphasized the dark circles under her eyes and the haggard folds of skin hanging on her neck. "He's comin'." As if realizing they might be curious about why her spouse was sleeping in the basement, she grudgingly added, "Air's not very good up here. It's cooler down there, so he sometimes sleeps on the sofa in his office."

"Understandable," Stacey said, shifting on her feet. She obviously hated the delay and wanted to get this over with.

Mrs. Freed glanced toward the room they'd just exited, then at Stacey. "Want to go into the kitchen for a cup of coffee?"

Nodding once, her back stiff, Stacey followed the woman, Dean taking up the rear. Though small, the kitchen appeared immaculately clean. With no shades or curtains to darken it to a tomb, it was better, less cloying than the rest of the place.

Gesturing for them to sit at the round table, Mrs. Freed prepared two cups of coffee and brought them over. She pointed at the sugar bowl, plopped a small carton of milk beside it, and mumbled, "I'll go see what's keeping him."

The woman had been morose and frightened when they'd arrived. Now her tension had shifted, worry changing to jittery nervousness, and he wondered just what her husband had had to say to her when she'd awakened him. Was it even possible that her motherly concern had been diluted by the annoyance of an angry husband? Given the few comments Stacey had made about the victim's stepfather, he imagined so. Winnie Freed looked cowed by life, by tragedy, and also, perhaps, by the man she'd married.

When that man entered the room a moment later, Dean felt sure of it.

"What's this all about?" the man asked, his tone nothing less than surly.

Stan Freed was a head taller and about a hundred pounds heavier than his waif of a wife. With heavy, bloodshot eyes, a deep frown on his brow, and a belligerent jut to his chin, he obviously didn't appreciate being awakened.

Stacey immediately rose to face him. "You and Winnie might want to sit down."

"Don't tell me what to do in my own house, young woman."

Dean stiffened, already disliking the man intensely.

Ignoring him, Stacey turned to Lisa's mother, putting a hand on her shoulder and taking her arm. She gently pulled her forward and helped her down into a chair, then sat directly in front of her. Bent at the waist, with her elbows on her knees, she took Mrs. Freed's hands in her own. "It's about Lisa."

The other woman sniffed, staring at her own lap. Before Stacey said another word, a drop of moisture dripped out of the woman's eye, slid down her cheek, and landed on the women's joined hands.

"I'm very sorry to tell you this, Winnie, but we have evidence that Lisa is dead."

The older woman's shoulders shook, and the single teardrop was joined by another. And another. But her grief remained silent, pent-up.

"We believe she died a long time ago, probably the same night she disappeared."

"Well, that's a fine job you've done as sheriff, then, isn't it?" Stan Freed muttered. He remained stiff and scowling, his arms crossed over his chest, watching the scene as if it didn't affect him. As if he hadn't just learned that his stepdaughter, his wife's only child, was dead.

Dean felt heat rise from low in his body up into his head until his pulse throbbed in his temple. He struggled to keep a lid on it, to not let anger drive him, to avoid giving his temper free rein by saying what he really wanted to say to the man.

Stacey remained remarkably calm, ignoring the husband, focused only on the wife. "I wish this had turned out differently. I can't tell you how sorry I am."

A long shudder racked the woman's body; her chin jerked; her thin shoulders banged into the back of her chair. She managed to bite out one strangled word: "How?"

Stacey glanced up for a brief moment, meeting Dean's eye. He offered her what silent assistance he could, knowing she'd be careful in what she revealed.

"It appears she was murdered, Winnie."

The woman moaned, then tilted her head back, looking at the ceiling. A low, keening wail began to fill the room.

"Knew that girl would get herself killed one day," Stan muttered under his breath.

Stacey finally put her attention squarely back on the man, leveling him with a glare so heated it was a wonder he didn't singe.

As if just realizing the hateful words had actually left his mouth, he flushed a little. Then the mean-spirited husband reacted in a somewhat normal way, finally stepping over and putting a hand on his wife's shoulder and squeezing it. Hard.

Dean frowned. Freed's hand went white as he squeezed. *Temper. He doesn't like to be challenged.*

"Mr. Freed?" he said, no longer able to remain out of this strange situation, not when he suddenly realized just how cold and detached Lisa's stepfather appeared about her murder. As if he wasn't surprised. As if he didn't give a damn. And that harsh hand on his wife's shoulder seemed more threatening than comforting. "Why don't you and I go talk in the other room?"

Mrs. Freed's hand came up and she covered her husband's, clawing at it frantically, not letting him go, even though his grip appeared punishing. "Please . . ."

"I'm not leavin'," he said to both of them.

Dean nodded in concession, but also held the man's eye, making sure he knew they would be having a conversation sooner or later. Because Dean was suddenly very curious about Lisa Zimmerman's stepfather. How they got along. Whether the man had a history of violence. If he'd ever been arrested. Whether he was really going to work at night, as his wife had said he was.

And suddenly, remembering what Wyatt had told him earlier, he found himself wondering if Stan Freed really had been asleep downstairs in his office.

Or if he'd been online.

Mrs. Freed swiped her arm across her eyes. "Who did it?"

"We don't know yet," Stacey said. "But we'll find him. I promise you. We're working on it; the FBI is working on it; he won't get away with it."

The woman shook her head, hard, as if to wake herself from a dream. The low wailing continued, whimpers bubbling up in her throat and falling out of her mouth like helpless coughs. "When can I see her?"

Stacey glanced at Dean again, wariness visible in the tense lines of her face. She'd worried about this moment; she'd admitted that last night. Knowing from experience that some people simply would not accept a loved one's death without seeing the visible proof, Dean understood completely. Though, in his mind, it was unfathomable to think of a parent witnessing the remains of a child who had been dead for a year and a half.

In this instance, it was almost a blessing that Lisa had not yet been found.

"Mrs. Freed," he murmured, taking the situation out of Stacey's hands, "while we are sure that Lisa was killed, we have not yet located her remains."

The woman's head jerked as if she'd been slapped. So did her husband's. They both gawked at him. "Well, how do you know she's dead?"

"Ma'am, we have irrefutable proof."

"Maybe it's not her; maybe she's not—"

Stacey cut her off. "I saw the proof, Winnie. It's her."

"I want to see this proof."

"No," Stacey said. "I identified her myself; there's absolutely no doubt in my mind, and I've known her since she was a baby."

The woman stared, saying nothing.

Leaning close, still holding those tired, trembling hands, Stacey lowered her voice, sounding like a parent comforting a child. "Please do yourself a kindness. Remember your daughter by those photographs in the living room, and mourn the child you raised. I know you have lots of wonderful memories. She was a happy little girl and she loved you very much. Let that be enough. I'm begging you."

Stan cleared his throat, obviously reading between the lines how graphic their proof must be. For the first moment since they'd arrived, Dean saw a hint of humanity in the man's hard-eyed stare. His shoulders slumped, and he cleared his throat and mustered a concerned tone. "Sheriff's right, Win. You shouldn't be cuttin' yourself up like that."

Human tenderness? Or guilt?

Whimpering, Mrs. Freed gave it one more effort. "But what if they're wrong?"

Dean met Stan's eye, shook his head once, expressing every bit of confidence that they weren't.

"They're not wrong. And you're not looking at that proof, Winifred, so get it outta your head." Stan slid his hand across his wife's shoulders, tugging her hard against his side to underscore his command. She flinched, then allowed it.

That flinch said more than a million words Winnie Freed might have uttered.

If this scumbag hadn't beaten his wife at least once a week since he'd married her, Dean would give up his badge. Nearly choking on the disgust of it, he had to turn away and stare out the window, noting the decrepit, rusting swing set rising like an ancient ruin from the scraggly, knee-high grass.

Poor Lisa. No safe, happy playgrounds for her. Not for a very long time.

"I promise you, we'll catch whoever did this," Stacey added. "And God willing, we'll find her remains soon so you can bury her."

The victim's mother must have heard the resolved certainty in Stacey's tone. That word *bury* seemed to sink in like nothing else had. The finality of it. The harshness of it. Because she stopped moaning, stopped shaking, stopped hoping.

As he entered Brandon and Lily's joint office Saturday afternoon, Wyatt felt the frustration thick in the air. It was evident in their frowns, the tension of their bodies, the angry jabs of their fingertips on two computer keyboards.

His two IT specialists had been working since just after dawn, trying to keep up with the sick inhabitants of Satan's Playground. Especially one sick inhabitant. But the site kept throwing up barricades, stumbling blocks that its "legitimate" users obviously knew how to get around. Unwelcome visitors, however, didn't find it as easy. Even visitors as brilliant as Brandon Cole.

"Have you found anything else?" he asked. He hadn't checked in since noon, not wanting to pressure the two, who'd put in hours just as long as his own since this Reaper case had started.

"He's gone. He put up that sign, let the crowd worship him, then disappeared." Brandon sprawled back in his chair and shook his head. The young man scowled at the monitor in disgust, watching the sick acts taking place all over it. "He crawled back into his hole and hasn't come out again, though I can tell by the users list that he's online, watching. Just not participating."

Or maybe not sitting in front of his computer. But always there, hovering, like some damned malevolent presence.

"Keep trying," he said.

Lily, he noted, kept her head down, focused only on the long strings of numbers rolling across her computer screen. Her chair was turned, slightly, as if to absolutely ensure she didn't get a random glance at anything happening on Brandon's monitor. Something had hit her hard this morning; he had the feeling it was witnessing the actions of one cartoonishly frightening predator in the Playground, who'd made a great show of taking young children into his gated mansion.

He knew enough about her to know that she wouldn't let herself be distracted from the job. He also knew that if she had the chance, she'd do whatever she could to bring down the pedophile.

Now, though, her thoughts went in only one direction: toward the Reaper. But the frown of concentration and the curl of disappointment on her mouth said she wasn't having any better luck with the financial tangle than Cole was with the site itself.

"I've been making calls, keeping an eye on all missing persons cases," Wyatt said. "Nothing new has come in, not yet, anyway."

"Meaning he hasn't grabbed his victim?" Lily asked, appearing, for the moment, hopeful. "He usually gives himself seventy-two hours, right?"

True. But Wyatt wasn't sure he agreed with her. They'd already lost a full day. And they knew their unsub was very careful. He'd allow himself plenty of time to commit his crime, record it, then go over every millisecond of that recording to ensure he didn't leave anything that might hint at his identity.

He didn't want to admit it, but Wyatt suspected there was a better than fifty percent chance they were already too late. Just because no young woman had been reported missing in any nearby state didn't mean one hadn't already been removed from her life with surgical precision. There could be any number of reasons for a delay in a report—a victim living alone, one who was known to travel. All kinds of possibilities.

"I mean, he'd have to find someone first, right?" Lily said, her usual optimism not allowing her to give up on the idea. "The conditions would have to be just right; he can't simply snatch a woman the moment the auction is over."

"Unless he's had one under surveillance and knows exactly who he's going to grab each time," Brandon said. No optimism there. He was thinking along the same lines as Wyatt. "He might have a whole list of possibilities that he keeps tabs on, knowing how and when to make his move, given the location and time of day."

Wyatt revealed something he'd just discovered when scouring through every word of the case files. "One of the victims told a friend she'd seen a strange-looking guy in a long black coat watching her a few weeks before she was snatched. The friend didn't think too much of it, until after the victim's body had been found."

"Oh, God," Lily murmured, a stricken look appearing on her face.

"He wouldn't leave anything to chance," Wyatt explained, gentling his tone. "In every previous case, he's known exactly where and when to strike to minimize the possibility of witnesses. In one case, he shot out surveillance cameras. He doesn't leave anything—like waiting to choose his prey—until the last minute. I don't think the unsub would have scheduled the auction if he didn't have his eye on his next victim."

The two computer experts remained momentarily silent, acknowledging what he was saying. Then both, as if sharing the same mind, spun in their chairs and went back to work, more determined than ever to find something they could use to stop the nightmare.

Stacey and Dean spent much of the morning in the stifling little house on State Street. They told Lisa's mother what they could, offering few details, but a lot of comfort and promises of justice.

And they asked questions.

These people knew Lisa the best. If there was a personal connection between her and her killer, here was the best place to start trying to find it. They needed to learn everything they could about the men she'd dated, those she'd fought with, anything that might have been a motive for murder.

So far, they'd learned nothing Stacey hadn't already known about the young woman.

"I don't know who her boyfriends were," Winnie said, probably for the tenth time. "She was a popular girl; she was so pretty. Nobody would want to hurt her."

Stacey didn't quite accept prettiness as the reason for Lisa's popularity. And she knew plenty of people who had reason to dislike the young woman. But she let it go.

Across the kitchen, Stan mumbled something, apparently in response to his wife's statement. It wasn't the first time he'd had an under-the-breath comment. So far, nearly all his answers had held a note of belligerence, and more than once he'd made a disparaging remark about his stepdaughter. *Prick*.

Seeing the way the cowed woman's eyes constantly shifted toward her husband before she answered anything, Stacey finally had enough. "Winnie, why don't you and I go into Lisa's room to talk, while Special Agent Taggert gets a few details from Stan."

Her husband immediately began to object. Winnie, though, leaped from her chair. "Yes, yes. Her room. It's exactly the way she left it."

"Win ..." Stan said, his voice holding a note of warning.

"Mr. Freed, if you wouldn't mind," Dean said, smoothly distracting the man by stepping between him and his wife. "I really would like to talk to you."

The older man frowned. "I need to go shower and get ready for work."

Work. Hours after being informed of his stepdaughter's murder. That really ought to go on his husband-of-the-year application.

"I'm sure they'll understand if you're late, given the circumstances," Dean said, somehow managing to disguise the disgust she suspected he felt. His quick, unguarded glance in her direction confirmed it.

"I'd appreciate more information about how your stepdaughter got the keys to your car. You said she borrowed it without permission?"

Mr. Freed was well and truly distracted. "More like stole it," he spat. "And that's a company car; I don't own it, and if she had gone out and wrecked it, I could have been fired. After all I did for her, she didn't even care that we could end up on the streets."

To Stacey's knowledge, the house belonged to Winnie. She'd certainly lived here before her first husband had died, and had come into some kind of insurance settlement after that drunk driver had killed him. Where that money might have gone was anyone's guess.

"All right, then," Dean said, "let's go discuss it."

"Fine. Do you want to go outside and look at the car?"

"That's an excellent idea."

Stacey blessed the distraction. Stan had seemed reluctant to get out of earshot from his wife, almost as if he feared what she might say. Now, he seemed focused only on sharing his grievances about his stupid car.

She suddenly wondered if Stan's employer provided other vehicles for their tech guys. Like pickup trucks ... It was worth checking out.

"Come on," Winnie said, only a small furrow of her brow revealing what she thought of her husband's actions. Stacey suspected she'd gotten quite adept at hiding her feelings. And her pain.

Following Winnie down the back hallway, Stacey steeled herself for whatever they might find in Lisa's bedroom. She had no doubt Lisa had been doing drugs and hated the idea of finding paraphernalia in front of her heartsick mother. But when Winnie pushed the door open with a creak, and she stepped inside the immaculately clean room, she sucked in a shocked breath.

Because it wasn't just in the same condition it had been in on the day Lisa had disappeared. It was the same as it had been when she was a child.

The twin-size bed was made with a frilly pink cover and a profusion of lacy pillows. Wide-eyed, pink-lipped dolls sat on a white wicker rocking chair in the corner. A bookshelf laden with childhood titles stood beside a small dresser sized for a young child's hands to open. Framed prints of butterflies and puppies hung on every wall.

Stacey's breath caught in her throat; she could neither inhale nor exhale. She could only stare as the awfulness of it washed over her.

It was as if Lisa had stopped growing—stopped aging—at around the age of twelve.

The only concessions that an adult woman had lived here were the closet, which contained jeans and sheer blouses, spike-heeled boots, and carelessly tossed lingerie. And the faint, lingering scent of cloying perfume emanating from the bottles on the dresser.

"Neat as a pin, my Lisa was," Winnie mumbled. She stood in the middle of the room, unwrapping her arms from around her body only long enough to gently smooth the soft, fluffy bedspread. A half laugh, half sob burst from her throat. "Except for her closet. Never could get her to keep that closet clean. I think she liked it cluttered and dark because she'd go in there and play cave explorer. I'd find her in there all the time when I'd get home from work, even when she was a teenager."

Hiding in the closet. God in heaven, was it really possible this woman had had no idea what was happening in her own house, to her own daughter?

Stacey found it hard to speak, but somehow managed to ask, "Did Lisa say anything to you, before she died, about anyone who might have threatened her? Or frightened her?"

And would you have heard her if she did?

"Everybody loved my little Lisa."

"She was a sweet child." Knowing she needed to tread a fine line, she still said, "But we both know Lisa had her troubles when she grew up. Those died with her, but they could still mean something. I need you to be honest now, and think about the way things really were right before she disappeared."

The older woman's mouth tightened into a tiny, dime-size circle. If Stacey pushed her into thinking about the way her daughter had really been, she might not cooperate at all. So she proceeded very carefully. "Had Lisa been feeling all right?"

"Of course."

"No illnesses?" She thought of the teenage pregnancy scare, wondering if Lisa's mother had ever even known about it. "No signs that anyone had hurt her in any way?"

"Hurt her?"

"Yes. She didn't appear injured—bruised, did she?"

Winnie's right hand instinctively moved up, rubbing her left arm below the shoulder before flinching in obvious discomfort. If that housecoat was sleeveless, Stacey would lay money a large bruise would be visible on the woman's parchment-thin skin.

Stacey shoved her hands into the pockets of her khaki trousers to keep from fisting them in visible anger.

"No, no, nothing like that."

"You're sure?"

"Yes," Winnie snapped. "She was just fine." Lowering her voice, she mumbled, "I took her to the doctor all the time when she was growing up. To make sure . . ."

"To make sure of what?"

The woman's head rose defiantly. "To make sure she was absolutely healthy and nothing was wrong with her."

So Winnie Freed had suspected.

"You can talk to the health clinic downtown; I'll give permission if you need it. Lisa was troubled; I'll admit that. But she was not being hurt in any way. By anyone."

I wouldn't bet on that.

"Okay, then. I'll try to stop by and see if they can tell me anything Lisa might not have felt comfortable talking to you about."

Winnie's pale face lost what little was left of its color, as if she were more frightened of that mild threat than she'd been of anything else. But the good mother still existing somewhere deep inside of her must have wanted to know the truth, too. No matter how painful. "All right. You do that."

Stacey knew she wasn't going to get much more from the woman, but she couldn't walk out of this house without making an effort. So she asked a few more questions, steering clear of the triggers that might make Winnie shut down—including anything suggesting that her daughter had been abused, perhaps right here in this house.

Finally, though, knowing she'd gotten as much information as she could, she had to push one more time. "So that night that Lisa disappeared," she said, casually flipping pages of her notebook instead of looking at Lisa's mother, "you and Stan were where?"

"Right here." Winnie's coldness could not disguise her sudden nervousness as she twisted her hands together.

"All night?"

The woman thought about it, biting so hard into her bottom lip Stacey thought she would break the skin. "Oh, I remember now," she said, her face flushing with color. "I had a little accident, fell down the porch steps going outside to watch for Lisa. Stan had to run me up to the emergency room in Front Royal."

That bastard. Stacey could almost see how it had played out: Stan furious that Lisa had taken his car, punishing Winnie for it, hurting her enough to put her in the hospital. The scenario didn't surprise her, but it did make her very anxious to talk to the hospital about the time Winnie had been brought in. And whether her husband had remained with her the entire night, or had possibly taken a trip back down here to Hope Valley in search of his hated stepdaughter.

"Okay, then," Stacey mumbled, putting the notebook away. She already knew it would do no good, but her job, and her sense of humanity, demanded that she try to help the defeated woman. "What about you?" she murmured, intentionally looking away, as if fascinated by Lisa's doll collection. "Have you been seeing the doctor?"

"For what?"

Stacey brushed the tips of her fingers across one plump, blond curl on the head of what she remembered was Lisa's favorite. "You haven't been looking well, Winnie." Finally turning her head to meet the woman's stare, she added, "I've been worried. So has Dad. Is there anything we can do to help you?"

Winnie's mouth opened and closed twice. Her lips quivered, her jaw, too. She blinked rapidly, the thin lashes doing little to get rid of gathering tears. As if the idea that she might have friends, people who cared about her, who might help her, were almost too much to grasp. Finally, though, she cleared her throat and jerked her head up and down once. "Yes. There is."

Stacey waited.

"Find my daughter so I can bury her. And catch her killer."

                    *   *   *

Stan Freed stood on the sagging front porch of the crummy little house he hated and watched that bitch of a sheriff and the nosy FBI agent get into her squad car. His hands gripping the railing, he forced himself to remain there, nodding his thanks as they backed out of the driveway. That was the normal thing to do.

Above all, Stan liked things to appear normal.

It was only once they were well down the block that he let go and saw the impression the wooden railing had made on the insides of his big hands. Splinters protruded from the puffy flesh of his palms and his fingertips. He hadn't even noticed, hadn't felt any pain. He'd been too focused on grabbing something, needing to remain in control. Keep cool. Stay normal.

Everything would be fine if he didn't lose his head, kept things going the way they had been. The cops couldn't prove a thing. Winnie knew better than to shoot off her yap, even if she did know something, which she didn't. And the only other person who knew a damn thing was dead and rotting. So there was no reason to panic. No way could that little bitch reach out from the grave and ruin his life now, after all this time.

Lisa. How he'd loved her. How he'd hated her. She'd been so beautiful, so perfect, an angel.

Then she'd grown up to be so hard, so ruthless, a whore.

He'd wanted to give her the world once, and she would have taken it. She might have pretended otherwise, but she had loved him, too. And she'd wanted him. It was her nature; she'd liked what they did in this house when her mother was at work or asleep.

Until she got older and began whoring herself out to other men. She'd started resisting, calling him names, acting like she hadn't been into it all along. And had laughed in his face just a few days before she'd disappeared. *Good riddance.*

"Stanley?"

He stiffened at the grating sound of his wife's whiny voice. God, how he hated it. Hated her. Hated everything about this place, where he'd been trapped for eleven years. If only he'd found out exactly how much—or how little—insurance money she'd gotten after her first husband's death before he'd married her, rather than listening to rumors. His life could have been so different.

"Stanley, please . . ."

"Quit whining, woman," he snapped as he spun around and entered the house. He slammed the door shut behind him with enough force to shake the frame. "Just quit your goddamned whimpering and let me think."

She'd been standing in the front hall, still wearing that ugly rag, her face red and splotchy from the tears she'd shed over her no-good daughter. And suddenly, he couldn't even stand to look at her.

"I'm going to work," he growled, heading toward his room.

She reached for his arm. "No, please."

He threw off the touch, backhanding her across the cheek for good measure. And she shut up. Like usual. "Have my lunch ready in a half hour."

He didn't bother turning around to see whether she'd hop to it and obey him.

Because she knew what would happen to her if she didn't.

Chapter 8

IT specialist Lily Fletcher was sickened to her very soul by the things the Reaper had done to his victims. Naturally empathic—one reason she'd been warned she'd never make it in the bureau—she'd had a hard time getting their faces out of her mind since the day Brandon had discovered that first video. She'd said prayers for them in private moments, promised them justice, and grieved for their loved ones dealing with such tragedy and pain.

She understood tragedy and pain. She understood them much too well.

Maybe that was why, as she dug deeper into Satan's Playground trying to find any cyber string that might lead to their unknown subject, she found herself unable to tear her attention away from that menacing, skeletal figure who called himself Lovesprettyboys. The small, cartoonish avatar cast off such malevolence, it was as if he'd been dipped in evil and formed out of hatred and vice.

He had invaded her thoughts and sabotaged her peace of mind, becoming the focus of all the anger and anguish that had been building in her for so long. The Reaper terrified her. Lovesprettyboys revolted her. And she wanted them both gone, out of the world, far away so they could never hurt another woman or another child. No one would ever convince her that tall, thin monster hadn't abused children in real life, the way he did in the Playground.

Which was, perhaps, why he'd become her side project. Stopping him would never change what had happened to her own family. But she had to do it anyway.

"Sir?" she asked as she knocked on Wyatt Blackstone's door late Saturday afternoon. "Can I speak with you for a minute?"

He beckoned her in, not looking up from the papers, saying, "Wyatt, please."

She had a hard time with that, calling him by his first name. Not just because she wasn't used to supervisors who were so much a part of a team, but also because the man intimidated her like crazy. The supervisory special agent was everything an FBI agent should be, from the top of his handsome head to the bottom of his shined shoes. Intelligent enough to keep up with even Brandon, street-smart enough to hold his own with Dean Taggert. Wyatt was out of her league in every way. She was often left tongue-tied around him.

"Anything new?" he asked when she took the seat on the other side of his desk.

"I've found a few accounts that look promising. I've contacted someone at Treasury to get information about some transfers, but I won't hear back until Monday."

"I am afraid our unsub probably works weekends," he mused.

She had no doubt he was right.

"Good work."

"Thank you, sir." She fell silent, looking at her own clenched hands in her lap, wondering how to broach the subject that had driven her to seek him out.

"Is there something else?"

Taking a deep breath, she hoped her voice remained steady and didn't betray how personally involved she was. "I was wondering . . . I know the Reaper is our primary target here, but some of the other things going on in that site are keeping me up nights."

"The pedophiles."

"One in particular," she admitted, not surprised that he had immediately known where she was headed. Blackstone had been very kind during her interview, when he'd asked how she was coping with what had happened to her family a short eighteen months ago. She'd been incapable of lying about the rage she still felt toward the man who'd brutalized her nephew and the anguish over her sister's resulting suicide. So yes, of course he understood her personal demons.

"The Cyber Division has a unit devoted to catching those monsters, Lily."

"They don't know about him," she snapped back. There was such a mine-is-bigger-than-yours attitude pervading this building that she had no doubt Blackstone was keeping this case close to his chest.

But he immediately proved her wrong. "Yes, they do."

Her jaw falling, she realized she'd completely misjudged him. "You mean you—"

"Of course. You can't possibly think I would keep Satan's Playground a secret from the rest of the division in some kind of we-found-it-first foolishness."

That was exactly what she'd thought. Now who was the fool?

"There are people working on it, I assure you. Another CAT, for one, and top agents who work crimes against children."

Relieved by that, she still couldn't contain the need to do something—which had driven her here to begin with. "I want to help."

One fine brow arched over a dark blue eye. "We're not keeping you busy enough?"

Flushing, she shook her head. "I would never let my personal history distract me from my job." Meeting his stare, she added, "I promised you that when I asked you to take me on."

He nodded once, conceding the point.

"But if I were to offer some assistance in my spare time . . ."

"You don't have any spare time," was the flat reply. "The unsub has to be stopped. If you have time to work on anything, it's got to be on him."

"I meant afterward, once we've got him. I certainly would not deviate from the first priority, to stop the murders."

She meant it. Despite wanting to go after the sickos playing out their child-rape fantasies in the online Playground, she knew her job. She had no proof Lovesprettyboys had ever actually acted on his proclivities, just suspicions. The Reaper, however, had shown in full, blazing color what evil atrocities he was capable of in real life.

"I'd like to volunteer to assist in the other investigation after ours has been successfully concluded. My experience working on the Satan's Playground site in this case might prove beneficial in that one."

His frown said he didn't like the idea, but his words were careful. "I thought the change of jobs was about you moving beyond the past. Trying to get on with your life." His words were cautionary, his tone sympathetic.

"Getting on with my life does not mean I can't try to stop the kinds of criminals who affected me and my family," she replied, resolute. "The man who killed my nephew is in prison and he'll remain there for the rest of his life. I'm not confusing the deviants on this Internet site with him."

Blackstone was quiet for a moment, rubbing the tips of his fingers on his temple, as if battling a headache. She imagined he had a lot of them in this job. Finally, he murmured, "You know he's filed an appeal?"

Lily closed her eyes briefly, not wanting her boss to see the rage and frustration in them. The knowledge that Jesse Tyrone Boyd was trying to overturn his conviction for the rape and murder of the little boy she'd loved with her entire soul infested her brain and tormented her every minute of every day.

"He was rightfully convicted. He won't get off." She bit the words out from between clenched teeth.

"But while that's going on, do you really want to immerse yourself in something so similar?"

"We don't know that it's similar," she insisted. "Or that this Internet guy has ever committed a real crime against a child." That was a lie. She knew. Something deep inside of her was certain that the monster lurking in the cyber playground had done his share of lurking in real ones. But she had to play this cool, by the book, remain completely detached and professional. "I simply want to do whatever I can to help stop him."

Blackstone studied her intently for a long moment. She managed to keep herself calm and collected through sheer force of will.

"All right," he finally murmured.

Lily suppressed a sigh of relief, thanking him as she got up to leave. And as she walked out of his office, she mentally told herself that he was correct.

Not personal. Not personal. Not personal.

Maybe if she kept thinking that, she might actually start to believe it.

Dick's Tavern had been built in the sixties, and from day one it had attracted a certain kind of crowd. Back then, it was a haven for roughnecks wanting to avoid hippie freaks. In the eighties it had been a haven for roughnecks wanting to avoid yuppie scum.

Now it was a haven for roughnecks wanting to avoid anything resembling law and order. Or politeness, decency, courtesy, or class.

Stacey hated the place almost as much as her father did. But there wasn't a whole lot she could do about it, aside from responding to the inevitable brawls that sometimes spilled out into the road. The proprietor, Dick Wood—wasn't that a porn star name if there had ever been one, and didn't he just act like he'd earned it?—kept his nose clean in the two areas that could destroy him: He didn't allow dope deals anywhere on the premises and he had never been caught serving minors.

If he had been, she'd have had him up on charges so fast the man wouldn't have had time to lock the door before she'd slapped a CLOSED sign on it.

"Classy place," Dean said as they pulled into the parking lot, already crowded with mud-encrusted off-roaders, rusty pickups, and crotch rockets that had seen much better days. "I don't suppose they have a lunch menu? That might explain the crowds at three o'clock in the afternoon."

"Only if by lunch you mean peanuts, whose shells are about an inch thick on the floor in some places. This is why I figured we'd be safe coming out here this afternoon rather than waiting until tonight, when they got really busy. The regulars are already parked on their usual stools; I guarantee it."

Dick's was always busy on weekends, from the time the doors opened at ten a.m. until they closed, often with a last drive-by warning patrol by Stacey or one of her deputies at two. At any hour in between, beer was being poured or vomited back out on the sticky floor. Darts were being flung. Fights were breaking out. Sex was being had in the dirty, dingy back hallway or up against the side of the building.

"How often do you have to come out here?"

Swinging the patrol car into the lone vacant spot out back, she left the engine running to combat the heat. Stacey pushed her dark sunglasses onto the top of her head and glanced at her passenger. "Once or twice a week. More on weekends and holidays, when we set up sobriety checkpoints."

"Like shooting fish in a barrel, huh?"

"Absolutely."

"Is Stan Freed a regular?" His simple question didn't disguise the genuine dislike he obviously held for the man.

"Not that I know of."

"That guy's total scum; you know that, right?"

Hell, yes, she knew it. "Yeah, he is." She quickly told him what Winnie had said about their visit to the hospital the night Lisa had disappeared.

"Easy to check her. Not so easy to find out if he sat in the waiting room all night, or left."

Something else she'd already considered.

He looked at the tavern again and sighed audibly. "Too bad the place is such a pit. I have a feeling I'm going to wish for a beer after today."

"You definitely don't want to drink here." Something sent a few more crazy words across her lips before she could think better of them. "Stop by my place tonight. I have a six-pack in the fridge. I suspect we could both use a cold one."

So much for letting the guy make the first move. That resolution had lasted all of, what, eight hours?

A small smile tugged at his mouth and an amused gleam appeared in his dark eyes. The hard-ass FBI agent had been replaced by the sexy hottie she'd met once or twice since Special Agent Dean Taggert had come to town. The one who made her forget the uniform and remember the woman wearing it. "You asking me on a date, Sheriff?"

She snorted, sensing that teasing didn't come easily to this man, especially while he was on the job. Maybe he needed a break from the tension as much as she did.

"Could be."

"Your timing is interesting."

"Yours sucks."

One brow shot up.

"I mean, you've been here a couple of days already and you still haven't worked your way up to making the first move."

He laughed out loud, a low, masculine sound. "We're just going to skip the part where we gradually get to know each other and feel our way around to determining if we're interested in more, right?"

"Uh-huh."

"Blunt."

"I never learned to be any other way." In for a penny, as they said. "Besides, like I said yesterday, we both know we're interested. I was going to be all female and let you take it from there." Her good humor fading a bit, she admitted, "But to tell you the truth, this case has me a little rattled. I'm finding it hard to stay completely aloof. And, honestly, I could use some company after hours."

She didn't up the ante, didn't say she could use some company in the long, empty nights when the bad dreams and her own need for physical connection kept her from any real rest. She wasn't trying to fool herself. Stacey had no doubt she wanted to go to bed with the man sitting beside her. But there was only so much even the bluntest of women could say to a guy she had known for only a few days.

"I've been wondering if you were going to make this personal." He reached over and touched the tips of his fingers to a strand of her hair, which had loosened from its bun and fallen to her cheek. Rubbing it between his thumb and index finger, he murmured, "I know better, but still, part of me wanted you to."

"You know better?"

"I am in no shape to get involved with anybody."

"You're preaching to the choir here, Special Agent Taggert. I'm not looking for any kind of long-term involvement." Especially involvement with somebody like him, who would leave here soon and continue making his way through the bloody world he inhabited. The one that had briefly invaded her little corner of the universe, and which she wanted gone just as soon as they nailed the bastard they were after.

"I'm so far out of practice with this game, I don't remember the rules."

"Rules aren't laws. They're sometimes made to be broken," she said, a tiny shiver coursing through her. It had nothing to do with the chilled air pouring from the vents in the dashboard and everything to do with the way his fingertips oh-so-gently brushed her cheek before he slowly pulled them away. "Besides, I don't feel like playing games."

"Me, either." He blew out a frustrated breath. "That doesn't change the fact that I'm bad at this, Stacey. I never even noticed my wife falling out of love with me."

"Jeez, I didn't ask you to marry me; I asked you to come over for a beer," she said with a forced chuckle. This needed to stay light and easy, for both their sakes. He was one year off a divorce. She was two years out of the worst period of her life. He was saturated in death and violence. She'd moved back here specifically to escape that darkness. No way did they have anything that could resemble long term.

Simple. No strings. That was all either of them could afford.

She knew all that. But she still opened her dumb mouth. "Have you fallen out of love with her?"

He thought about it, staring out the windshield. "Yeah. I guess I had long before we split up. I just didn't realize it until she forced the issue. The divorce didn't bother me much. The custody, though, that's pure hell."

"I'm sure."

As if wanting to scare her off, to make one more effort to put up barriers for *her* protection, he admitted, "It's been a long time since I've been with anyone else."

Been with—as in, had sex with. The tension in the close confines of the car shot up a notch. Or a hundred notches. She felt the warmth of his strong body, heard the slow breaths that seemed as deliberately cautious as her own. Smelled the clean scent of soap and an earthier one of pure masculinity that encompassed him from head to toe.

And every female particle inside her reacted. "You're not alone," she finally said, the words shaking as she tried to keep them light. "I'm not exactly a man magnet myself."

Man repellent would be more like it. The last guy she'd been with had been an attorney down in Roanoke, who'd been able to separate his job from his emotions. He couldn't understand why she couldn't get over what had happened. Of course, he hadn't been an early responder to one of the worst mass killings in U.S. history.

"I find that hard to believe. You have a whole townful of people who like and respect you." That sexy, amused glint returned to his eye. "You have at least one admirer."

Thinking of the scene with Rob Monroe in the diner, and in the doughnut shop the other morning, she visibly shuddered in distaste. "Not a chance in hell."

"Is he the only available guy around?"

"No. But knowing everyone here is a double-edged

sword. Since nearly every man in this county is either scared of me or hates my guts, the social opportunities aren't exactly limitless. Believe me, I don't have much of a personal life." Shrugging, tired of dancing around it, she could only meet his direct stare and be entirely honest. "I'm attracted to you, Dean, for any number of reasons. And I think we're both in the right place right now to do something about it."

He didn't argue; they were past that. "Attracted physically."

And mentally. And possibly even emotionally. But that was miles ahead of where she would consider walking, even in her own head. "Yes."

He hesitated, then merely murmured, "Well, okay, then."

"Okay, then?" Whatever that meant. A beer? Dinner? More?

"Okay," he explained, "I'd love to come over for a beer."

And maybe more. She'd just have to wait and see what.

Smiling in self-satisfaction, as she acknowledged that waiting for a guy to take the lead had never gotten her anywhere, Stacey cut the engine. "Guess we'd better get on with it. The crowd's not getting any more sober in there."

Stepping out of the car, she spotted one very familiar, dented four-by-four, and couldn't contain a frown. *Damn it, Tim.* Her brother had sworn he wasn't getting in over his head with his drinking or with Randy and his rough-edged new friends. Who, she suspected, appealed to him, since many of them carried scars of their own, physical and emotional.

She also suspected the shrink Tim refused to go back to would say he was trying to escape from his former world into a new one where he didn't have to give a damn about anyone. Even himself. One where he could escape the memories of whatever had been done to him—and whatever he'd done—in the Middle East, before a roadside bomb had shattered not only his face, but his spirit as well.

"Let's get this over with." Pushing her sunglasses back over her eyes and donning her broad-brimmed hat, she took a deep breath, determined to remain the sheriff no matter what happened inside. If her hardhead of a brother started anything, he'd be talking to her back at the station.

With Dean at her side, she strode around the side of the building, her gaze scanning the parking lot. As she walked, she also checked for expired tags, unsafe vehicles, and, mindful of the case, any late-model American-made pickups. That there were a good dozen of them right here in this one parking lot said a lot about how that lead was going to pan out.

Just inside the doorway, Stacey paused, but didn't remove her sunglasses. She knew from experience that the dark lenses, and the inability to gauge her expression, was intimidating to people. Especially people she was questioning.

She allowed her eyes to adjust to the dim lighting, a sharp contrast from the bright sunshine, then scanned the place. She instinctively counted the bleary-eyed men sidled up to the sticky bar. Two slow-moving couples rubbed against one another on the dance floor, their feet scuffing the oak planks rubbed smooth and chalky gray by a thousand couples before them.

Patrons sat at every wobbly table in the room. Loud, twangy music emerged from the ancient jukebox. The yeasty scent of newly tapped beer was overpowered by the stench of unwashed bodies and puke from the Friday-night crowd who'd left here a little more than twelve hours ago.

She'd sooner spend a day in lockup than in this place.

Stacey's pulse skipped as she spotted her brother. Tim was playing darts with Randy Covey in the far corner. A half-full pitcher of beer, and an empty one, sat on the closest table, and they each had mugs in their free hands. Neither had noticed her arrival.

That was fine. She'd make her presence known to them in very short order. She had a few things to say to Randy for backing up Tim's idiocy and drinking hard with him on a Saturday afternoon.

"Back exit," Dean murmured.

Stacey glanced in that direction. A heavyset, bearded biker type watched them closely, edging step by step toward the door. She'd wager there was a warrant out on him somewhere. "This is your lucky day, pal," she whispered.

Finding Dick behind the bar, she stepped over and rapped her knuckles on the worn surface. She knew damn well the man had looked up and seen her enter, but he'd made a show of continuing to draw beer and pour shots, ignoring her presence.

"Oh, hey, there, Sheriff. Surprised to see you here in the middle of the day. Stop in for a cold one?"

Shaking her head, Stacey saw the way his hand shook and knew he was nervous. The sixtyish, skinny, balding little man knew how thoroughly Stacey disliked the place. She could never hide her disdain when she came in. Just because she'd never caught him doing anything illegal didn't mean she believed he wasn't. "You know better than that."

The bar quieted as others noticed her arrival. Her appearance—uniform and hat, stiff form, jutting jaw, the dark glasses—screamed rigid law enforcement, and since most of the clientele were ex-cons, drunks, or druggies, everyone went a little on edge. That was one reason she always unsnapped her holster when she entered the place, though she'd never actually had to pull her weapon from it.

The club, yes. She'd broken up a few fights with it. One had involved one of her own deputies, who'd been attacked by a huge, drunk redneck whose thick skull hadn't even registered the first blow.

"This is Special Agent Dean Taggert," she said. "We're here to talk to you about the night Lisa Zimmerman disappeared."

Dick made a great show of sympathy. "I heard the rumors. Is it true? She's dead?"

"We need a list of everyone in the bar that night."

"That was a long time ago, Sheriff. I can't be remembering everybody in my place." He glanced around nervously, as if worried his customers, who valued discretion, would realize he was a rat who'd turn anybody in to save his own narrow ass.

Stacey pulled a small notebook out of her back pocket, reading off the notes she'd jotted when she'd originally investigated. "You said there were no strangers, only regulars. About thirty of them, and you named several." She scanned the list, as she had a number of times in the past few days. Her eyes zoned in on a few names, men she knew drove American-made pickups. Warren Lee being one of them. "All I'm looking for is anyone else you remember. And any details that made that night stand out."

Her voice was loud enough to be heard by those close by, and Dick's eyes narrowed in annoyance. His gaze darted around the room, then lit upon the dartboard in the corner. "Why don't you go ask your brother and his good friend Covey over there?"

Her jaw clenched. "What?"

"They were both here. Or didn't you write that part down in your little book?" The man laughed, though his amusement was overshadowed by pure malice. "Matter of fact, I seem to recall Lisa bein' a mite short with Tim." Leaning forward in a pretense that he intended to whisper, but doing no such thing, he added, "I think he got his feelings hurt that she didn't like his scars and wouldn't dance with him."

Her eyes instinctively shifted. Tim, across the room, had just sent a steel-tipped dart toward the board. It landed in the center ring. Bull's-eye. But he didn't react by so much as a laugh or a high five with Randy.

Because he was listening. The tension in his ramrod-straight back made that clear.

Angry and protective of her brother, despite being here in an official capacity, she sneered at Dick. "Oh, don't you worry; I'll be tracking down a whole bunch of your regulars and talking to them. After I do a little background checking on them, of course."

The man visibly paled, realizing his jab had done nothing more than dig him in deeper. He wiped his hands with a dirty cloth and mumbled, "Honestly, Sheriff, I don't remember that far back. I can make some guesses, though."

Dean, who'd been silently watching the exchange, covering her back, interjected: "What about credit card receipts from that night?"

The tavern owner snorted. "I don't think a soul in this place could get one."

"But you can still check," the special agent insisted, his voice low and steady, the very confidence of it enough to scare the hell out of any man who had something to hide.

Or to arouse the feminine instincts of any woman with a hint of estrogen.

"All right," the man muttered. "Not that it'll do any good."

"Thanks for your cooperation," Stacey said, knowing she sounded steely and anything but grateful.

"Not a problem. Surprised you don't already know who was here that night. Didn't you have deputies watching the place around then?" Dick attempted a weak smile. "I know you were trying to sting me, sending underage kids in here, but I don't serve nobody without ID."

Stacey frowned. Though the idea wasn't half-bad, she wasn't naive enough to think Dick would fall for it; he was far too crafty for that. Besides, he knew the names and ages of just about every teenager in the county. "I don't know what you mean."

"Well, last spring, a couple times kids came in here thinkin' they were gonna be able to score beer." He scratched his grizzled chin. "Now that I think about it, there was a ruckus the night the Zimmerman girl went missing. Had to have that Flanagan kid hauled outta here."

Flanagan. Mike Flanagan. Why was she not surprised?

But even as she discounted the idea that teens trying to buy beer might have anything to do with Lisa's murder, she realized she needed to talk to Mike. Because if he'd been tossed out, he might very well have lurked around outside. Kids like that wanted to get even. She wouldn't put it past him to flatten a tire, break a window, do something to throw a young man's fit at not getting what he wanted.

And if he'd been hanging around, maybe he'd seen something.

"Only other thing I recall is that Lisa's stepdaddy called here lookin' for her around midnight, mad as hell about his missing car."

That was something she hadn't known. "Stan Freed? Did you tell him she was here?"

The man's scrawny chest puffed out and his voice increased in volume. "Nah. I don't go tellin' tales. Didn't let on she was here."

Had Stan gone out looking for her, by chance?

"Oh," Dick added, as if suddenly remembering something. "And Warren was on a rant about the gov'm'nt conspiring to keep gas prices up, part of their 'master plan' for the rich to take over the country."

More unsurprise. Her list of interviewees was getting longer by the minute.

That should have been a good thing. More leads meant more chances to solve this case and stop the brutal crimes.

If only one name hadn't been on the list. Because questioning her own belligerent brother was going to be anything but pleasant. And frankly, it would be worse if she tried to talk to him here. He would swagger and puff up, not wanting anyone in the place to think he was at all intimidated by his cop sister.

She'd talk to Tim herself, but she might ask Dean or his fellow agents to deal with Randy. The man made her teeth hurt. He seemed to bring out the worst in her brother in terms of recklessness and overblown testosterone. They had done some stupid stuff as teens, Randy even getting arrested for theft before he had gotten his girlfriend pregnant and Tim had left for the military.

What a nice contrast to be with a man like Dean, who oozed masculinity, yet had no problem with the fact that Stacey had been the bold one in the car. He had to have self-confidence by the boatload to go with that intelligence and strength. It was an incredibly intoxicating combination.

A lack of self-confidence was one trait her brother shared with his best friend. Tim because of his injuries and scars. Randy because, well, probably because of his whole disappointing life.

"Want to split up?" Dean asked. "Work our way through the room faster?"

Stacey shook her head. "I don't think so. I know these

guys. Some of them will do better with you—I'll let you know which—but some won't give you the time of day." Not that they'd do much more for her. But at least she knew their weaknesses.

Spying a couple of the men Dick had named during her original investigation, a pair of roughnecks who lived downstate but came here to do their drinking and raise their hell, she strode to their table, pulled out a chair, and sat down. "Afternoon, gentlemen."

They both eyed her sullenly. The smaller of the two, a weasely sidekick by the name of Lester, tried to act tough. If his big buddy weren't sitting beside him, he would already be spilling his guts. "You looking for some company, pretty lady? You need a couple of men to remind you what you got between your legs—and what you ain't?"

Feeling an almost tangible burst of heated fury from Dean, who stood beside her chair, Stacey shook her head once. Eyes narrowed, she dropped her elbows onto the table and stared, hard, into Lester's bloodshot eyes. "You don't want to compare balls with me, boy. Remember, I busted your naked ass for public indecency last year. So I know how *small* the chances are that you've got anything I'd be interested in."

His companion, a big, hard-looking dude who rode one of the choppers outside, snorted at the put-down. "You better shut up while you can," he told his friend. Lifting his mug of beer to his lips, he drained it. Streams of amber liquid and foam slid down either side of his mouth to soak his thickly bearded chin. When the mug was empty, he slammed it down, the table shaking beneath the force of the blow. As if both fortified and confident of the manly display he'd made of his supermacho ability to chug a beer, he nodded at Stacey. "Go ahead," he said. "Ask whatever you want."

"But—" Lester interrupted.

"If you ain't smart enough to remember what she can do with that club on her hip, I am." The man rubbed his head, obviously remembering when Stacey had stopped him from breaking any more furniture right here in this room during a bender last fall. The big man's fierce frown faded. "Besides, I know what you want to hear about. That little Zimmerman girl was messed up, but she was a sweet young thing once upon a time. And if somebody really murdered her, chopped her up, and fed her to some wild pigs, I hope you fry the bastard."

Hearing Dean's disgusted sigh, she contemplated correcting the crazy story. But it was already too late. The rumor mill was hard at work, and no matter what she said, the stories would persist, growing wilder, until Lisa's remains were found and the cause of death made public. And even then the conspiracy theorists would continue to embellish.

"I might not be on your side most of the time," the burly guy added, "and I might hate your guts. But I'll help if I can. For that little gal's sake."

"Fair enough," she said.

She flipped open her notebook, not entirely surprised at the man's reaction, because even tough guys had a code. His line between right and wrong might be wider than Stacey's, but he knew enough to recognize when it had been crossed.

Cooperation from one of the most badass regulars at the skankiest establishment in the county, that was a good start. But she knew it wouldn't last. If she got cooperation from everyone else in the place, she'd trade in her badge for a case of Mary Kay cosmetics and her squad car for a pink Cadillac. Because things were just never that easy.

They were looking for Lisa Zimmerman's body.

When he'd first heard the FBI was in Hope Valley, he

hadn't worried. What could that possibly have to do with him? He'd done nothing close to home in ages, nothing to draw attention to himself. His fun in the Playground couldn't lead back here to his real door. He'd been far too careful for that.

Then he'd heard about them digging near Warren Lee's place. That was a bit troubling, but still nothing to panic about.

Eventually, like always, the gossipers got everything jumbled up. The stories about Lisa's disappearance and a potential murder victim being sought by the FBI had gotten twisted together into one big, very plausible rumor.

Then came the confirmation: It really was Lisa they were looking for.

As he sat alone in his most secret place Saturday evening—a room to which he alone had access, concealed from any prying eyes—he had to concede a certain sense of alarm. Not fear. He never experienced fear, just as he never experienced pain. He'd done far too much, inflicted agony and visited death on far too many, to worry about it coming for him. He was death, after all.

No, his concern was the inconvenience of it all. The descent of a bunch of FBI agents chasing bodies they would never find might interfere with his plans and restrict his movements.

It also might bring exposure of other things. Things he wasn't responsible for. Someone else was.

"You asshole," he hissed, suddenly enraged. Because if those other activities were uncovered, the interest in those crimes might spill over onto him. People might come around, ask questions, do a search.

"Don't panic," he reminded himself, focusing on the main issue. Lisa.

How did they know she was dead? For the past year

and a half everyone had accepted the fact that the little slut had run off somewhere on her own. Why had that changed? What evidence could they have?

"They're bluffing," he told himself. "They must be."

Wanting a distraction from the worry, he busied himself tidying his special room. He kept it clean and normal-looking, on the off chance that anybody came in here. The idea of somebody invading his privacy, learning about his other life, was enough to make him sick. Nobody could interfere with that life. He wouldn't allow it.

What if they know about the Playground?

Impossible. The security was rigid, the existence of it shared in cyber whispers. He doubted there was another person within two states of here who was a member.

Or perhaps his closest neighbor was.

That was one thing that made Satan's Playground so wonderful.

But there had been a lot of extra security in recent weeks. *Maybe someone hacked in. . . .*

Maybe he should quit.

Bile rose in his throat at the very thought of it. Quit? Leave the only place he'd ever belonged? No. He'd never do that.

In fact, he'd do whatever it took to keep that world safe and intact. Including removing anyone who threatened its existence. FBI agents. The sheriff. Anyone.

He could. So easily. They would never even realize he was the enemy until he took their heads off their bodies. Just as he had with that girl from the mall. The loud one. The mean one. The one who had screamed awful language and was no lady, just another whore. She hadn't used those words on him for long.

Almost smiling as he realized just how little anyone in this drab, colorless place knew him, he was startled by a sudden ding from his computer speakers. He had mail.

Not in the playground, but an e-mail to the identity he wore in the dirt world.

Not recognizing the generic address, he almost ditched it as spam. But the subject message—*You'll Want to Read This*—intrigued him. It seemed different, though it was probably someone offering to make him wealthy, or teach him the secret to better sex.

Ha. There was no secret. Because sex could never be as good as draining the blood out of a woman until the light left her eyes and the spite left her lips.

Nothing could.

Bent over his chair, he leaned down and clicked on the message to open it, ready to delete it at once.

Then he read the words on the screen. His heart pounded.

He saw the image below the words. His pulse surged.

He read the final demand. And he slowly lowered himself to the chair.

The message was simple: *I know what you did.* Below it was a fuzzy, black-and-white photograph, apparently taken from a surveillance camera. It wasn't very good quality. But it didn't need to be. The image clearly showed the two most important things: his draped form putting a large, body-size wrapped object into the back of a truck. More disturbing—an easily recognizable license plate.

"No," he began to whisper, the word rising in volume as fury crawled up his throat and began to choke him. "No! You can't do this!"

But the message writer apparently thought he could.

The anonymous e-mailer wanted money. A lot of it, which he didn't have. And he wanted it within seven days.

Or the picture would go to the FBI.

Chapter 9

Though he'd seldom played standard investigator games throughout his career, in the few times he'd done so, Dean had always found himself in the role of bad cop. His naturally stern, unsmiling demeanor and size made him the tough guy, the ball-breaker. He was the one ready to throw the book at a suspect, the angry official who'd convince the perp he'd spend the rest of his miserable excuse of a life in a ten-by-ten cell if he didn't cooperate.

Today Stacey was bad cop.

And it was just about the sexiest thing he had ever seen.

"Don't shoot me for saying this, okay?" he said as they entered her private office a few hours later, after having interviewed most of the people at the tavern. Except her brother and his friend, whom Stacey wanted to deal with on neutral turf.

She pushed the door shut behind them. "What?"

"When you grabbed that guy playing pool by the front of his shirt, and told him you were going to dig into his past until you found out if he'd stolen a piece of bubble gum as a kid, I almost got a hard-on."

Surprised laughter erupted from her mouth. She probably wasn't as surprised as Dean. That kind of frankness hadn't been part of his vocabulary in a couple of decades. His ex hadn't exactly been the sexy-innuendo type. She'd been a combination of Martha Stewart and Fran Drescher. Domestic wannabe with an annoying voice. And no interest in snappy verbal foreplay.

But with Stacey, he didn't feel as though he had to watch his mouth. In fact, he felt capable of saying absolutely anything. It was, after all, only the truth.

She hung her hat on a peg and slipped out of her uniform jacket, revealing a few more of the curves she usually kept buttoned up tight. "I guess most women wouldn't know how to react to that. But since I've been pretty damn hot to see you handle the Glock on your hip, I think I get it."

"Does that make us a couple of violence-loving wackos?"

Shaking her head, Stacey stepped closer. Closer. Until the tips of her boot-clad feet touched his shoes and their clothes brushed. The place was wrong; the timing was even more wrong. But everything else about the moment felt utterly right. So no way in hell was he going to put an end to it.

"No. I think it just proves what we were talking about earlier in the car. That we're attracted."

Then she proved the attraction. This time, his was the shirt bunched in those slim, capable hands. He was pushed until his back hit the door.

And he was being kissed.

Her mouth connected with his, hot and hungry. She parted her lips, deepened the kiss, all warm, spicy woman. Stacey tasted so damn good to him after the long drought of personal connection; she quenched his thirst, emptied and refilled him at the same time. That slender body, pressed against the length of his, emphasized her femininity, despite her undeniable strength. The combination intoxicated him until he was almost out of his mind with the need to touch every inch of her.

He let her have control for a few seconds, then took it back, turning her until she was the one backed into the corner. Their mouths continued to meet; they exchanged kiss after kiss. Each sweet, wet thrust of her tongue sent another surge of lust coursing through him and refilled the dry, empty well of physical need that had tormented him for so long.

Groaning low in her throat, Stacey pressed herself harder against him. "God, I've wanted this," she mumbled against his mouth. Tangling her fingers in his hair, she kept kissing him, as if once she'd started she couldn't possibly stop.

Not that he wanted to. Huh-uh.

Dean dropped his hands to her hips, sliding his palms across the generous curves to tug her even harder against his aroused body. When she felt the rigid proof of that arousal, Stacey sagged a little in his arms, as though her legs had suddenly lost all their strength. His hands and the office wall kept her upright, pressed against him, exactly where he wanted her.

Finally, though, voices from the vestibule pierced the hazy cloud of sensuality filling his head. With utter regret, he let go of her, ended the kiss, and stepped back. They stood staring at each other for a good thirty seconds, both sucking in ragged breaths, both asking a million silent questions, and answering them with only their eyes.

"You are going to come over for that beer, right?" she asked once they both seemed to have gotten it under control.

He nodded, then had to at least pretend to play the gentleman. "I don't expect—I mean, just a beer is fine."

"Yeah, uh, I don't think so."

Wondering how this woman could so easily work him straight from pulsing desire into pure amusement, he had to laugh. "I bet you were hell on wheels growing up."

"I didn't play with dolls, if that's what you're asking." Her lashes half lowered, her mouth suddenly twisting down. "Except when I babysat Lisa."

She'd been a passionate, wild woman in his arms a moment before. Now the regret almost visibly washed over her. She'd allowed herself to forget for a moment. But he knew those snatched bits of happiness wouldn't drive away the guilt until this case was solved.

Still, she made a concerted effort. "Enough. My brain is ready to explode from the defensive ramblings of a dozen drunks. And I am sure I reek from having been inside that place for so long." She glanced at her watch, then bent over her desk and scrawled an address and directions on a small sheet of paper. "Let me go home and shower. Then you can meet me at my place in forty-five minutes or so."

"Sounds good."

"Wait." She straightened, not yet handing him the paper. "Do you have a way out? Didn't your boss take your car back to D.C.?"

"Yeah, but Jackie and Kyle drove out in two cars so we'd have an extra vehicle."

"Oh, good. That means I can get home and take out a couple of steaks for us to throw on the grill, and still have time to wash the tavern smell out of my hair."

Her hair. He was very much looking forward to seeing it down around her face, knowing it would softly frame her fine features. "Leave it down," he murmured.

She lifted a questioning brow.

"Please." After their sensual encounter, he shouldn't have felt strange making the request. But he did. Because it seemed intimate. Something a lover would ask.

She swallowed hard, her throat quivering, as if she

knew how often he'd pictured wrapping those straw-berry blond strands around his fingers, then whispered, "All right."

He left the office without another word, without a touch. Because if he reached for her, or she reached for him, one of them would be backed against the wall get-ting their lips kissed off.

"You're taking a cold shower," he told himself as he left the sheriff's office and walked toward the inn.

It was only after he'd reached the corner that he began to wonder what, exactly, he was going to say to Stokes and Mulrooney about why he wasn't joining them for dinner. But, hell, the truth was as good as anything. Because if they hadn't noticed the tension between him and the sexy sheriff, then neither of them deserved to carry a badge.

Fortunately, though, when he got back to the flea trap a few minutes later, he saw a note taped to his door. The two of them had gone to check out the steak place just outside of town. So he didn't have to explain a thing.

Or maybe he was right: They were good enough agents that they'd definitely noticed and were giving him a night alone without requiring excuses or explanations.

Dean's cold shower lasted a long time. He felt every bit as grungy after their day as Stacey did, and he had extra incentive. Not having had sex in more than a year, he needed to bring his body temperature back within normal range; otherwise he was likely to go up in flames if she touched him at her front door.

This wasn't how he was supposed to get back in the saddle. Stacey wasn't a mindless bar hookup. But he just couldn't bring himself to care.

He wanted her. He liked her. He admired her. He re-spected her.

Why on earth would he even think about being with anyone else?

It would be just sex, no question about that. Neither

one of them was up for anything else, and they both damn well knew it. But sex between two people who liked and respected each other . . . what was wrong with that?

After dressing and calling his son to say good night, he shoved the address and directions Stacey had given him in the pocket of his jeans. A quick stop at the liquor store on the corner—if she was supplying the steaks, he could show up with an extra six-pack—and he headed out of the main section of town.

Unable to keep the smile from his face as he drove, he had to acknowledge that for the first time in months, he felt genuinely good about something that did not involve Jared. He hadn't felt that way about anything else in his personal life since he'd realized just how far he and his wife had drifted apart. That had been about a month before he'd found out she was cheating.

All that, however, was in the past. And, when he thought about it, he had to acknowledge a certain relief that she'd handed him an easy out of their cold marriage.

Surprised by that self-realization, Dean almost drove right by Stacey's house as he turned into her neighborhood. Spying the number on the mailbox, he swung into the driveway, parking right behind her dusty cruiser.

He sat there for a moment, wondering whether he was losing it. Because coming to that kind of conclusion about his breakup after more than a year of feeling like the wounded party was both shocking and a little freeing. And it made him wonder if he would have arrived at it now if he hadn't met a woman who'd driven him crazy with lust since the first time he'd shaken her hand.

Maybe. Maybe not. Either way, he was looking forward to seeing just what else he figured out about himself and about Sheriff Stacey Rhodes. Starting tonight.

Smiling in anticipation, he grabbed the beer and

walked toward the house, up the curving sidewalk lined by tall, ragged hedges. He came around the corner, intent on avoiding the sharp thorns on the ivy bushes. So intent he didn't at first notice what was happening just a few feet in front of him.

Then he saw it: the front porch stained red. The woman kneeling on it.

The woman covered in blood.

And he stopped smiling.

Wyatt didn't generally watch television. He had one, of course, and occasionally flipped on the news when he was making dinner or waiting for his coffee in the morning. But as for regular programming, he'd rather read a book. If, that was, he had time to read anything other than case files and reports.

Considering the last work of fiction he'd read had been that da Vinci book everyone had been raving about, he supposed some would say he was bringing a little too much of his work home with him. Including tonight.

For some reason, though, as he warmed up the meal his housekeeper had left for him, he flipped on the television, barely listening to it. Having it on, hearing the low murmur of other voices in the background, helped remind him that a normal world existed out there. Everyday people lived and laughed, completely unaware of just how cruel and capricious life could be. While he buried himself in these quiet, still places, drenched in horror as he tried to make sense of the crimes committed by the Reaper, the earth continued to spin.

The antique dining room table he'd inherited along with this house in Alexandria was covered with files and photographs. Autopsy reports, interviews, and investigator's notes competed for space. Additional boxes full of files sat on the chairs. Every piece of information currently available on each Reaper case was scattered across his elegant home, which had once belonged to his grandparents. With it came a wealth of darkness, entirely at odds with the serenity and calmness that had defined the lives of that kindly couple.

"I'm glad you never saw anything like this," he murmured as he spread out the brutal crime scene photos from the third murder and examined them yet again. Because there had to be something in them that would help them break this case. Like rereading a book, though, the more he studied them, the more his mind filled in what his eyes tried to skim over as too familiar. So he took out a small magnifying glass, going over each inch.

Nothing.

Hearing the beeping of the timer, he put the photograph down, wondering how normal people would react to consuming a nice pasta marinara on a table covered with proof of human suffering and cruelty. The job had hardened him to it, but it hadn't immunized him. So he took the plate to the couch, sat down, and put his feet on the coffee table, leaving the photographs in the dining room.

He'd taken two bites when a news story came on that captured his attention. A photograph filled the screen, the headline scrolling across the bottom. Reaching for the remote control, Wyatt punched up the volume.

He barely even noticed a moment later when his plate of pasta marinara slid off his lap onto the floor.

At first, when she'd arrived at her house and seen the horror on her front porch and door, Stacey thought a teenager she'd busted had gone crazy with a can of spray paint. But she'd quickly realized the awful truth: The saucer-size circles and long, thin smears had not been made from paint.

It had been blood.

Thick blood, congealing into brownish pools and

drawing flies in the hot summer evening. The coppery scent filled every breath she took. Overwhelmed by the smell—and by those awful, vivid memories that scent and the feel of the slick fluid inspired—she had just stood there, gasping for untainted air.

And then she'd spotted the body, recognizing her immediately. The sad, lean corpse was mangled and broken, the once soft fur matted and sticky. But there had been no mistaking those gentle brown eyes, now blank and glazed with sudden, shocking death.

Dad would be heartbroken, utterly devastated, and Stacey already dreaded telling him. For there had been no doubt the poor, pathetic creature was Lady, the free-wheeling stray who'd adopted her father and made him her own.

"He loved you, girl," she whispered, her voice breaking. "You did have a home and a family, whether you wanted them or not."

Those were the first words she'd been able to manage in the half hour since she'd arrived home. Before that, she had been too shocked to speak. She'd felt as thoroughly assaulted as if someone had beaten her. Just as whoever had left this vicious surprise here had intended.

Someone really had killed a sweet, lovable old dog whose only fault was occasionally sleeping on a porch step and allowing herself to be tripped over.

Stacey had paused for a second to pray that Lady had been killed by accident. She'd seen animals struck by cars plenty of times; those kinds of emergencies usually generated a 911 call here in Hope Valley. Especially on the winding country road where her father lived. She and Tim had lost more than one pet to that road during their childhood, each of them looking in death much like Lady did now.

But she couldn't comfort herself for long. Because

Lady hadn't limped several miles here to Stacey's house. She hadn't smeared her own blood all over the porch and door.

And she absolutely hadn't scrawled the word *bitch* in spiky letters across the cheery WELCOME HOME mat lying in front of the door.

Jesus. Sweet Jesus.

If Lady's death had been accidental, her disposal most certainly had not been.

Stacey had spent ten minutes on her knees, with the dog's head cradled in her lap. Those dark, betrayed eyes had stared up at her as if to ask how such a thing could happen. Finally, thinking of one of the neighborhood kids riding past on a bike and catching sight of the horror, she had gotten some supplies and gone to work cleaning things up.

"I'm sorry. I'm so sorry," she murmured as she worked around the body, rinsing the pink-tinged rag in the pink-tinged water bucket. She'd already changed the water once.

She didn't really cry, though dry sobs had filled her throat at first. Tears had formed in her eyes, and two had even erupted from them, sliding down her cheeks in twin salty streaks that had disappeared on her lips. But the rest remained locked inside her. As if deep in her subconscious, she knew that if she gave release to all the emotions surrounding the sorrow and tragedy she'd been dealing with in recent days, there would be absolutely no holding them back.

"You poor, sweet old girl," she whispered, knowing that whatever anguish she felt would be multiplied a hundred times by her father's. "You deserved so much better than this, and I'm sorry I wasn't here to protect you."

"Jesus," a voice said.

Dean.

He fell to his knees beside her, right into the congealing pool of blood, grabbing her upper arms. "What happened? Stacey, are you all right? All this blood . . ."

"Someone killed her." She finally raised her eyes to meet Dean's, and she shook her head, though with sorrow or unreleased fury, she honestly couldn't say. "Who would do such a thing?"

He wrapped his arms around her shoulders, tugging her close, ignoring her bloody hands and clothes, Lady's body right beside them. Sliding his hands into Stacey's hair, he cupped her head, holding her tenderly, making soothing sounds of comfort and tenderness. "Shh. It's okay, honey."

Part of her wanted to cry like she hadn't cried for a long time. The few teardrops she'd allowed herself in recent years hadn't been nearly enough—not for the kind of horror she'd seen. Not for the nightmare of Virginia Tech. Not for poor Lisa.

An ocean of unreleased grief had backlogged behind her eyes. It was being held there by the tiniest remnants of her strength. And this poor, brutalized dog was on the verge of becoming that one final drop that forced all that restrained emotion out of her. This single event might just pull the plug on her sadness, sending the tears spilling out of her like a flood over a causeway for all the tragedy and horror to which she'd borne witness in her life.

"Why would someone do this?" she muttered through ragged breaths. The air kept catching in her throat until she almost choked on it, the words emerging in spurts. Each was underscored by an anger she hadn't yet allowed to overwhelm her, knowing that when it did she would be completely lost in the fury of it.

He pulled away, but kept an arm around her shoulders. "Is she yours?"

She shook her head. "Just a sweet old stray my dad unofficially adopted and took care of."

With infinite tenderness, he stroked her jaw with the back of his thumb, a simple, quiet reminder that she was no longer alone. "I'm sorry. There are some really sick people in the world. Somebody wanted to hurt you, or to scare you."

"By slaughtering a poor, defenseless animal." She shook her head, not knowing why she was surprised. Considering the things she'd witnessed, she knew man was capable of incredible cruelty. She just hadn't expected to literally stumble across it right on her own doorstep.

He continued to stroke her hair, kind and calm. She suspected he wouldn't be if she hadn't tossed the obscenity-smeared doormat into the trash before his arrival.

"Come on, Stace; go inside. Get cleaned up. I'll finish this."

She tried to resist, but Dean wouldn't take no for an answer. With a soft sigh of sadness, he took the rag out of her hands. His expression revealed so much about the man. There was no revulsion, no concern about his clothes, not a wince of distaste. Just tenderness, goodness.

It told her more than she'd known about him to this point. That simple act revealed a man she suspected was a wonderful father to his little boy, a good friend, a loving son and brother. A man with depth.

A man she could care about.

"I'll take care of her." He brushed his lips across her temple. "Let somebody help you for a change, okay? You don't have to do it on your own."

And suddenly she knew he was right. She didn't have to do this by herself. Not today.

"Go on inside. I'll take care of everything."

God, when was the last time she'd let anyone take care of everything? Or anything at all? She honestly couldn't remember. She only knew that she trusted Dean, and that it felt good to have someone else to share the burden with, if only for a while.

He helped her to her feet. "Do you want to bury her?"

She nodded once. "At my dad's." Glancing at the body, she added, "But I can't tell him everything. Not yet, maybe someday. But for now . . ."

"We'll tell him she was hit by a car."

It was as if he'd read her mind.

"Bring me a box, and some more rags and bleach, too, okay?"

"No, you don't have to."

"I know that. But I want to." He pushed her toward the door. "Just get the stuff; then you go take a shower and try to wash this whole thing off."

Wash off the ugliness like she'd wash off a day's worth of dust and sweat? She didn't think the slick, sticky feel of the blood on her hands would ever wash off. But Stacey couldn't deny how much she desperately wanted to take him up on his offer.

Unlocking the door with shaking hands, she stepped inside. Her booted feet immediately skidded on the tile floor, leaving twin streaks of red. Emotion welled even higher at the sight, but she swallowed it down. She unlaced and kicked the boots off, then went to the kitchen and got more cleaning supplies and a large box from the garage.

Dean didn't even let her step outside when she returned with them. "Okay. Now you take a shower."

Somehow managing to control the disgust, rage, and sorrow, she staggered through the house. With each step, she tore off her clothes and dropped them onto the floor a piece at a time, wanting nothing against her skin. By the time she entered her bedroom, she wore only her underclothes. They were off before she'd gotten to the bathroom door.

The evening remained brutally hot. Most nights she took a cool shower to comfort her overheated body. Now, however, she needed steam and heat in order to feel clean. So she turned the controls as hot as she could stand and stepped inside, closing her eyes and turning her face up to the showerhead like a penitent seeking absolution.

She kept them closed for a long time. Piercing streams of hot water gushed through her hair and down her body. And it wasn't until she felt sure the soap wouldn't turn the color of blood that she reached for it and began to wash.

She didn't know how long she stood there scalding herself, but eventually she reached for the controls and eased the water to a cooler temperature. But the unshed tears behind her eyes continued to burn. She didn't expect that to stop anytime soon.

She'd just finished rinsing the conditioner from her hair when she heard Dean calling from the next room.

"Hey, you okay in there?"

"I'm fine." She clenched the shower curtain in her fists, leaning toward the opening in the front. "Are you finished?"

"Everything's taken care of."

"Thank you," she whispered, knowing he wouldn't hear.

"Listen, maybe I should just go back to the hotel. I need to clean up."

No. God, no. The very last thing she wanted was to step out of this shower and find herself alone. Alone to pick up her red-stained clothes. Alone to wash the floor. Alone to think about the fact that someone hated her so much he wanted to punish her by killing an innocent animal and spattering its blood across her front door.

Alone to fall into bed and add one more layer to her dark dreams.

"Don't go," she said. Realizing she'd whispered again, she cleared her throat. "Dean, please don't leave."

Silence. Then, "I'll wash up in the other bathroom."

"No." Leaning her face against the warm tiled wall, she added, "Come in and use this one."

He didn't reply at first, and she waited, wondering if she'd just lost her mind. Yes, she'd invited him here tonight fully intending that they'd end the evening in her bed. That was supposed to happen after a beer, some good conversation, more flirting. After at least she'd fixed her hair and maybe scraped a little bit of shadow across her lids. They'd act on the attraction, keep it light and simple, and then proceed.

But now everything was different.

Not only could she barely keep herself upright, but she didn't look like a woman about to take a lover. She was, in fact, a complete nightmare. Her lips were twisted in grief, her body flushed and reddened from the heat of the water. Her eyes were so damned heavy and sore from unshed tears. Yet she'd asked him to come in.

And that was what he did.

"You holding up?" He stood just inside the doorway, big and powerful, a look of utter tenderness on his face. "Can I do anything?"

That someone so strong and serious could be capable of such compassion and sweetness nearly took her breath away, and she felt on the verge of shattering into a thousand pieces. She hadn't broken down in ... well, ever, really. Yet all the years' worth of just dealing with things as they came had apparently taken their toll. Because right now, after one small, hateful act, she wasn't sure she was going to be able to make it one more day.

But with Dean, maybe she could.

There was such a depth of humanity in him. A wealth of goodness and understanding, which was contrary to all the things he had to have seen and investigated in his career.

She envied it. More, she wanted it.

Still mostly blocked by the shower curtain, she managed a single word. "Please."

His eyes met hers. Sealed the connection. Then, without a word, he reached for the top button of his shirt and slipped it open. Though his gaze remained locked with hers, the strong hands moved down, slowly unbuttoning, until he shrugged the shirt off, tossing it to the floor.

Stacey's heart thudded as she noted the breadth of his shoulders, his massive chest rippled with muscle, and his flat stomach. Clothed, he'd been powerful and hard. Beneath those clothes was a man built to make even a tall, strong woman like herself feel utterly feminine and delicate. Her body, weak, drained, almost physically battered just moments ago, began to thrum again. Heat skittered through her veins, sending blood pulsing back into places where she'd felt empty for a very long time.

This was what she needed. Maybe not for the long term, maybe not even for tomorrow, but for right now, she needed physical connection. With him.

Entirely sure of what she was doing for the first time in forever, she returned her attention to his face. That handsome, concerned expression said he was ready to stop, to leave if she so much as quirked a finger toward the door.

Instead, she drew back the shower curtain.

Dean swallowed visibly, his neck and throat flexing as he studied her. Desire tightened the muscles in his jaw, and his eyes narrowed. He hadn't touched her with more than a heated stare, yet as he unfastened his jeans and let them fall off his lean hips, she could see the way he swelled in reaction to her nudity.

"You're sure?" he murmured, the words sounding

drawn from the very last wellspring of resistance he owned.

"I need to be with you."

He didn't question it. Didn't focus on the way she'd worded her desire for him. Maybe she was being selfish, but he didn't call her on it. Instead, he removed the rest of his clothes and stepped to the tub.

"So be with me," he said as he joined her.

The water had cooled a bit, but she suddenly felt hot again. In silence, he took the soap and washed his hands and arms. When they were scrubbed clean he reached out to touch her. It was the simplest, most tender scrape of his index finger against her jawline.

She felt the connection down to the soles of her feet.

Without a word, she slid her wet hands onto his shoulders and moved closer, until their bodies brushed ever so lightly, hers wet and pliant, his hard and slick. Her pebbled nipples scraped against the dark hair of his chest, sending delicious sensations racing through her.

Dean groaned low in his throat, as if he hadn't been entirely sure what to expect. Had he thought she merely wanted comforting? A pair of strong shoulders to cry on and a hard body to lean against?

He'd soon know better.

She wanted to grab hold of those strong shoulders, to touch every inch of his hard body. To lightly bite him, and to scratch his powerful back. She wanted her thighs wrapped around his hips, wanted him driving into her with heat and lust until there was no room for thought.

And as she felt him swell and harden to a dizzying size against her hip, she knew she wanted it all twice.

"I want you so much," she whispered, eliminating all subtlety. "Please don't make me wait any more."

Twining her hands behind his neck, she ran the tip of her tongue along his collarbone, needing to taste him. He was salty and warm and masculine; she breathed in his scent and sucked up the delicious heat his body provided.

"Looking at you pulls the breath right out of my lungs," he admitted, his tone thick and husky with need.

With patience she didn't know the man could possess, he skimmed his palms over her shoulders, brushing the long, wet strands of hair behind them. It seemed to take forever for his mouth to move toward her temple, then, still with that maddening slowness, down her cheekbone toward her lips.

"Kiss me, Dean."

He did, giving her not the deep, hungry kiss she'd taken from him in her office, but a lovely, tender one. Softly, gently, he touched his mouth to hers. The water from the shower streamed down their faces, blending on their joined lips and sliding between.

Focused solely on the delicious taste of him, Stacey didn't have time to prepare herself for the deliberate, steady assault on all the rest of her senses. The pulsing jets of water were not loud enough to drown out the thudding of her heart. The intoxicating scents of warm man and soap and sweat and sex filled the steamy air, drugging her with each inhalation. His hands moved down her sides, tender and deliberate, each stroke both inciting desire and offering incredible pleasure. And when she looked down at him, saw the glory of that masculine body and the powerful erection she would soon take into herself, she quivered with hunger.

"I've wanted this since the minute you walked into my office," she admitted.

"I've wanted it since you told your brother to get the hell *out* of your office."

Unbelievably, she found a laugh deep inside herself and let it spill softly from her lips.

He cupped her breasts in his hands, gently toying with her sensitive nipples. Gasping, she sagged against him, knowing he wouldn't let her fall. One strong hand slid down her side to her hip, where he grasped her possessively; then he pushed her back to lean against the wall. Kissing his way down her neck and nuzzling into the hollow of her throat, he murmured tender, sexy promises, the hunger in his voice making her throb with the need for him to follow through on them.

When he covered her nipple with his mouth and sucked deeply, she cried out, tangling her fingers in his thick, wet hair. The water grew cooler, now just tepid against their hot skin, but neither of them suggested getting out.

"Mmm, yes," she groaned as he moved his other hand down, stroking her belly before tangling his fingers in the curls between her thighs.

Her groan was echoed when he slid his fingers lower and stroked her to insanity. She shook and quaked with the intensity of it as he brought her higher and higher, kissing her again when she cried out her climax.

She hadn't even had time to come down from it when he deepened his caresses, toying with her and testing her wetness. She was drenched and ready, and while there were a million things she wanted to do with this man, the most important one, right now, was to connect with him completely.

She lifted one leg and wrapped it around his, tilting herself up in both invitation and demand. Dean cupped her face in his hand, staring at her with one final question.

"I'm on the pill," she told him. "And I want this more than I've wanted anything."

A slow, sexy smile preceded his response. "You won't regret it."

Hell, no, she wouldn't regret it. She already didn't regret it. She especially didn't regret it when he lifted her leg higher, making room for himself and moving between her thighs. When that thick, hot shaft began to ease into her, she almost cried out her not-regret.

He went slowly—so slowly—gliding into her an inch at a time, kissing her face, her neck, her mouth. Stacey wanted more. She thrust greedily, demanding more. Until, with a helpless groan, he gave it to her and plunged deep.

Yes.

They didn't move for a second, just gasping as sensation exploded and pleasure erupted. Helpless to the demands of both their bodies, they began a slow, sultry tango. He filled her; he pleasured her; he offered her tenderness and delight and strength. Dean made her feel, for the first time in ages, that she wasn't alone, and that there was still goodness and light and beauty to be found if she just opened herself to them.

They loved until the water grew completely cold and they both cried out their ultimate release. But it was only afterward, when he gently lifted her from the shower and carried her to her bed, that she realized the dam had burst. The tears had been released.

And she sobbed quietly in his arms until she fell asleep.

Chapter 10

Dean hadn't held a sleeping woman in a long time, and he liked it.

As Stacey's ragged breathing smoothed and evened, and the tears dried in her eyes, he watched her succumb to exhaustion. Her long lashes rested on her pink cheeks, her lips parted slightly as she breathed over them. Her hair was still wet, spread across the pillow and his chest.

He just kept watching her. Wondering what he'd gotten himself into here, and why he didn't regret it.

By the end of his marriage, he'd been sleeping in the spare room. Dean had been working crazy hours back then, traveling a lot, getting home late in the night. His wife hadn't wanted to be awakened, since she had to get up early in the mornings to get Jared off to school. He'd understood. More, though, he'd been relieved.

That should have been a big tip-off about the state of his marriage. He hadn't given a damn. He'd had no physical interest in the woman he'd married. Between his absorption with his job and focusing every spare thought on his son, he'd been entirely oblivious that she was walking out of their marriage.

He really had been a lousy husband.

With all these realizations that had been hitting him in recent days, he was seeing the whole sorry mess clearly for the first time since he'd been so blindsided by her request for a divorce and her confession about the affair.

He'd been furious. Humiliated. Ashamed.

But not heartbroken.

It had taken him more than a year to realize that truth. She hadn't broken his heart. Because it hadn't been hers to break anymore.

Stacey sighed in her sleep, her bottom lip quivering. Drawing the sheet up, he covered her naked body—so feminine and curvy for a woman so tough and capable.

"Maybe too tough," he murmured, swiping the tip of his finger down her cheek.

In another time and place, the idea of a woman bursting into tears and sobbing her heart out right after they'd both had orgasms that nearly blew the tops of their heads off might have been a little disconcerting. Even worrisome.

But he knew why she'd cried. She had at last been releasing those closed-up boxes of dark emotion that he suspected had been building in her head for a very long time. She'd needed to let them go. That the catalyst for the final emotional meltdown had been a poor pup someone had left on her front porch meant only that she'd been ready to break anyway. He was just glad he had been here when she did.

"Dean?" she murmured, not even opening her eyes.

"Hmm?"

"I'm sorry."

He tightened his arm around her waist. "I'm not."

"I mean, sorry that I broke down."

"Repeat: I'm not."

She nestled closer, her face against his neck. "I don't usually do things like that."

Unable to help it and wanting to lighten her mood, he replied, "Really? You're incredibly good at it."

She chuckled a little against his throat, but didn't reply. And within moments, her breathing returned to its deep, steady pace as she drifted off again, obviously feeling completely safe right here with him.

Well, wasn't she? Because he'd do anything to make sure she didn't get hurt. Except he somehow had the feeling he'd already hurt her, at least a little. By showing up in her town and invading the nice, safe world she'd invented for herself after she'd escaped from the horror she'd seen in her previous job, he suspected he had hurt her badly. She either hadn't realized it yet, or just didn't want to acknowledge it.

"I'm the one who's sorry," he whispered into her hair.

From the bathroom a few feet away came the ringing of his cell phone. Dean normally would have ignored it, but not now, not while he was on a case—especially this case. Carefully disentangling himself from her, he padded naked across the room and grabbed his jeans off the bathroom floor. Tugging the phone from his pocket and seeing the familiar number, he couldn't keep a smile from his mouth.

Not the case. Not the job. Something much more important.

"Hey, big guy," he said, keeping his voice low. "Isn't it past your bedtime?"

"Hi, Daddy. We gotta talk."

Smothering a chuckle at Jared's serious tone, he knew before the words left the boy's mouth what the problem was.

"They're back."

"No way."

"Yes way. They're under there. I hear 'em."

"Impossible, dude. You know your mom wouldn't

stand for any dust bunnies under your bed, so there can't be any dust-bunny-eating monsters."

From across the room, he thought he heard a sound. A quick glance, however, revealed that Stacey was still sleeping soundly.

"I think they eat candy wrappers now."

"Well, that's a different story, then. Have you been tossing candy wrappers under the bed?" Candy. He almost snorted. His ex and her dentist husband would have a fit.

"Maybe one or two."

Or maybe his son just wanted to say good night once more. It wouldn't be the first time they'd shared a second good night phone call since he'd given Jared the cell phone. His ex hadn't liked it, but too bad. Dean wanted Jared to be able to reach him whenever and wherever he wanted.

"You're gonna get those wrappers out of there in the morning, right?"

"Yep. But until then . . ."

"Okay."

Cupping his hand around the mouthpiece of the phone, he began to recite the rhyme he'd made up when Jared was five and had first started hearing monsters under the bed. They banished them with invisible laser beams. Luke Skywalker and Darth Vader—who'd somehow become a hero between Dean's generation and his son's—helped. So did Jared's favorite stuffed bear, which he still slept with but hid from his buddies by day.

"Jared's not coming down there; you can wait all night. So just get going or we'll have another fight," he concluded, hearing his son sigh in sleepy happiness at the end. The boy barely even murmured good-bye, already half-asleep.

Dean was smiling as he stuck the phone back into his pocket and carried his jeans into the bedroom. At least until he saw that Stacey was now awake, climbing out of the bed, not meeting his eye. And definitely not smiling.

"Where are you going?"

"Are you hungry? I'm hungry. I forgot about that steak. Let's go eat."

"Better idea. Let's go back to bed."

She did that weird take-the-sheet-off-the-bed-and-wrap-it-around-yourself thing that he had only ever seen in movies. As if he hadn't explored just about every inch of her body in the shower less than an hour ago.

It didn't take a rocket scientist to figure out why. "Stacey, look, if anybody was due for a meltdown, it was you. Don't wig out because you happened to let some of the pent-up emotion in your head come out through your eyes."

She stared at him, snagging that full bottom lip between her teeth. Sniffing, she murmured, "Thank you for that. I guess I needed to let it go."

Exactly. But that damned sheet stayed in place. And she actually headed toward her dresser and began pulling out clothes. Sensible, nonseductive Stacey clothes, including a simple white bra and boy briefs that he knew would look sexy as hell on her.

He didn't, however, want anything on the woman. Except himself.

"What's going on?"

She pulled on the underclothes, dropping the sheet. *Yeah. Supersexy.*

Grabbing a brush, she yanked it mercilessly through her long hair. He knew she was putting up barriers, but damned if he was going to watch the woman rip those long strands out by the roots. Stepping into the bathroom again, he grabbed his briefs, tugged them on over his naked body, and walked up behind her. Dean took the brush out of her hands and began working it through the tangled, damp mass of hair, which had begun to curl softly against her skin as it dried. Such beautiful hair, kept so tightly restrained. Like the rest of her.

"You don't have to do that."

He met her stare in the mirror over her dresser, unsmiling. "I know. It's not a problem."

They remained silent while he worked out the knots, sliding his fingers through the strands as each one was freed. With each stroke of the brush and his fingers, he silently gave her time to figure out what she wanted to say to him. Because he knew her well enough to keep his own mouth shut, not asking her what was wrong. Something was; that was clear. She'd let him know when she'd figured out how to tell him.

Finally, when he'd finished and placed the brush on the dresser, he put his hands on her shoulders and stared at her in the mirror. "Okay?"

Her eyes were moist and red from her crying jag. But they also swam with fresh emotional uncertainty.

"You're wonderful," she whispered.

He rolled his eyes.

"It's true. You're all hard-ass and tough, but you're also utterly wonderful."

"You're nuts. I told you before, I'm no nice guy." He had an ex and a bunch of other people, like those he'd busted and some he'd worked with, who'd confirm it.

She turned around in his arms, her body pressed against his as she looked up into his eyes. "Yes, you are. That's what's killing me here."

"I so don't get you."

"I heard you on the phone with your little boy."

He shrugged. "He's afraid of monsters under the bed."

"You love him. You're a wonderful father. You gave me exactly what I needed just now. And I can't have that."

Her seriousness told him they'd finally reached the point. "Care to explain?"

"This is a fling, damn it. Just sex, just while you're in town, just because I'm lonely and you're newly single."

Ahh.

"No strings, no emotions. No wonderfulness. No hearing you on the phone with the kid you adore, when I don't even want kids."

Taking the same tack she'd used earlier in the car, he forced a dry laugh. "Hey, I came over to have a beer, not knock you up."

She saw right through him. Putting one hand on his chest, she pushed him back and ducked away. "I could fall for you."

"Don't," he warned her, knowing that she was right. This was just a fling. A get-back-in-the-saddle interlude for them both to gain a little release. The fact that she was someone he already cared about was something he'd fully intended to ignore when he'd shown up tonight.

And the idea that she could care about him? Inconceivable. He didn't have to hear her say it to know that her coming back here to Hope Valley had been all about getting away from men like him, in jobs like his. And he had already proved once that he totally sucked at the whole relationship thing.

"Stacey, I get the picture," he insisted. "I agree. It's sex, great sex, no strings. That doesn't mean we can't like each other. In fact, liking you makes it better, in my book. Less . . ."

"Impersonal?"

He nodded, liking how quickly she got him. "God knows the situation couldn't be much worse, but the timing, at least, is right. We both need exactly what we're getting. No more, no less. Not a one-night stand with a stranger, and not a lifelong relationship. Something in between that works for both of us."

She eyed him warily. "Really?"

"Really. You're not falling for me; you are attracted to me and you like me. And there's not a damn thing wrong with that. We're friendly lovers."

"Not *loving* lovers."

Yeah. Right. Exactly. At least for now.

If his expression changed with that crazy thought, she didn't appear to notice. Instead, she seemed almost relieved, mumbling, "Okay." She glanced at the bed, then down at his body. "Still want that steak?"

He reached for her, sliding a hand around her waist and tugging her against him. "The steak can wait." Then he covered her mouth and kissed her deeply, with slow deliberation. He'd had her up against a shower wall before. Now he wanted her in bed. For hours.

Before he could take her back there, though, his damn cell phone rang again. "I'm sorry; I can't turn it off."

"I wouldn't expect you to."

Not allowing himself to get frustrated, since he knew Jared's calls were more about staying connected to his dad rather than any real fear of monsters, he got his phone. But the caller ID said it wasn't Jared.

"Hey, Wyatt," he answered. He immediately pulled his head back in the game, shaking off his sensual lethargy. And willing down his hard-on.

He listened to what his boss had to say, the information doing a lot to remove from his brain any thoughts of sultry sex with a sultry sheriff. In fact, by the time Wyatt was finished, Dean's mind was filled with nothing but red rage.

Because it appeared they were too late.

"What is it?" Stacey asked after he'd disconnected the call.

He'd already begun pulling on his jeans, hoping the

shadowy room, and the fabric, were dark enough that she wouldn't notice the bloodstains on them. He'd change the minute he got back to the hotel.

"Dean?"

"They think they've identified the latest victim."

"Oh, my God," she whispered, drawing a hand to her mouth.

"She's a teenage girl who disappeared from a mall in Bethesda, Maryland, Friday night. She'd fought with her parents that day, and then with her boss, and the local guys figured her for a runaway. But when they found her wallet and her car in the mall parking lot, and all the security cameras in the area shot out, they changed that theory."

"Cameras shot out?" she whispered.

"It isn't the first time. Our guy's damn good with a twenty-two rifle. He shot out the cameras at another location when grabbing the third victim."

"So there's no doubt he's got her?"

"Very little."

She covered her eyes, as if wanting to block out a horrible sight.

He knew exactly what she was trying to block out. Because the same vision had filled his mind from the moment he'd read the transcript of that last sick online auction.

Beheaded.

"Twenty-four hours," she finally whispered. "Is there any chance she's still . . ."

"No," he snapped, crushing his own tiny bit of hope that the girl, Amber something, was still alive. "I don't think so." He finished yanking on his clothes, then kissed her roughly. "I've got to go to Maryland. I'm going back to the hotel to meet up with Stokes and Mulrooney so we can all go."

She nodded. No tears, no regrets, no sighs that he was

walking out on her right in the middle of their first night together.

Damn, he liked her.

"Call me when you have more news."

"I will." He kissed her again, more gently this time. Stroking her soft, almost-dry hair, he murmured, "Be careful. Keep your head down and leave this alone until you hear from me, okay? I don't want you doing anything to attract this bastard's attention."

"I wouldn't do anything to hurt the case."

"I don't mean the case, Stacey." He cupped her chin, forcing her to look at him. "I mean you. Just because we're friendly lovers doesn't mean I can't worry about you. I want to know who the hell left that hateful message for you on the porch." Frowning because he wouldn't be around to help her deal with that situation, he quietly added, "The box is in the trunk of your squad car."

"Thank you. And don't worry about me," she said. "I'm sure that isn't connected to the Reaper case."

"I know. It's not his style." He offered her a grim smile. "Believe me, if I thought it was that bastard, I wouldn't be leaving you here alone."

She nodded, completely understanding, not arguing. She saw the sense in what he was saying without his having to explain a thing or justify himself. What a rarity.

Damn, he could love her.

Which was the last thing he could afford to think about as he said his good-byes and left to go try to find the Reaper's latest victim.

For the first several hours after receiving that anonymous e-mail message, the Reaper lost himself in the Playground. He disappeared from the dirt world, the one some people called real, but which he considered only dark, drab, ugly, and colorless. No life at all, just existence.

In that world, someone was trying to do him harm. Someone actually believed he could be blackmailed. Unacceptable.

He needed to escape in order to think about it and decide on a course of action. He couldn't panic, couldn't allow rage to make him do something stupid. Only one location calmed him now; only one provided any real escape. In the sunlit, warm, beautifully colorful world that was the Playground, no one could ever touch him. He'd never be betrayed. Never criticized. Never hurt.

He did all the hurting, of both the game-generated 'bots who inhabited Satan's Playground, as well as personalized avatars created by those who wanted to see what it would feel like to be murdered.

And now it was even easier to do. He had lots of new toys to try out. He'd just bought some new custom-made weapons and implements to enhance the torture chamber that existed in the dungeon of his cyber castle: vises and blades, whips and chains, a stretching rack, gallows, and a spike-lined box. All perfect.

He'd filled a pit of snakes and rejoiced as a dumb bitch had broken her ankles and been devoured after he'd tossed her in. He'd finally experienced the excitement of seeing someone drawn and quartered. How wonderful a death; and how weak and pathetic people were to have stopped using it so long ago.

He loved his new toys. Worshiped them. He couldn't stop touching them, testing each one several times as he acknowledged just how perfectly equipped he was to do his job now.

And he did it. Throughout most of the night, he gave free rein to his violent fantasies. Walking among the others, he plucked victims randomly, bringing them back to his lair and spending hours doing things to them.

If life were fair, he could have such a chamber in this cold, ugly world. Hearing the real cries, smelling the blood, tasting the fear that dripped from every pore of his victims, that would be heaven on earth. Acting furtively in the night no longer gave him enough satisfaction. He longed to take his time and enjoy it, to play and play, as he could in the Playground.

And now, even that could be lost.

Which was why he finally said his farewells with a few more swipes of his scythe and emerged from the light back into the darkness. Damp air assaulted his nostrils, and from within the walls he heard mice skittering around. Whenever he'd gone on a long visit away, his senses were always heightened upon his return. Even his eyes saw clearly into the darkness of his basement hideaway, and he couldn't help picturing it laid out as a second dungeon.

There would be no room for the gallows, or for the pit. But a table with chains at the head and foot, a spike-covered board, those would be just fine.

"I will," he whispered. If he got through this new threat to his safety and security, he'd do it. Somehow, he'd bring prey here and enjoy them for hours. Even if it meant removing others who might stand in his way.

Starting with the blackmailer.

Because in the long night of violent pleasure, when his mind had been washed clean with blood, the truth had come to him. He'd seen with utter clarity what he should have realized right away.

He knew who'd sent the message. There was only one person it could have been.

Warren Lee.

Everyone knew the crazy man had cameras protecting his house. That he'd have them along the perimeter of his property, seeing into the adjacent woods, should have come as no surprise. He should, in fact, have expected it and done something about it before Lisa. But he gave himself a break. After all, it had been his virgin experience.

The black-and-white photo was fuzzy, and shot from above, probably the top of the whacked vet's fence. Lee must not have realized the significance of what he had. But he'd held on to it, knowing it meant something.

Then the FBI had started poking around, looking for Lisa's body. And Lee had put two and two together and come up with murder.

"He won't be easy to get to," he muttered, his own voice stark against the silence. "Not easy at all." The man lived in a fortress of his own. And he would defend it. Violently, if necessary.

"Damn him." Why did that old bastard have to go putting his nose into it? What did Warren Lee need with money, anyway?

Someone should teach him a lesson about minding his own business. In fact, a few other people in this town might be due for lessons, too.

It could be done, taking Lee down. But he might not be able to do it soon enough to meet the deadline. Which meant he had to have a plan B.

Coming up with the money and using it to pay off Warren Lee long enough to get him alone and take him down. That was plan B.

He knew of only one way. That way both thrilled him and terrified him.

He'd have to hold a very *special* auction, where the potential gains could be huge.

But where all restrictions were off.

Stacey probably should have gone into work on Sunday, but after the week she'd had, and mindful of her promise to Dean to keep her head down until she heard from him, she didn't. Instead, she drove out to her dad's, gave him a carefully edited version of the news, and helped him bury Lady's body. God, how it hurt to see the sadness in his eyes.

Stacey hadn't kept a secret from her father in years, and she hated to start now. But causing him pain, and making him fear for her, would be much worse.

Afterward, she drove back to town, focusing her thoughts on the one case she could investigate. She'd promised Dean she wouldn't do anything involving the Reaper case. But she hadn't promised not to try to find out what had happened to Lady.

She desperately wanted to know which sick bastard had slaughtered that poor, sweet dog.

It occurred to her for only a moment that the cases were connected. Psychos like the Reaper didn't waste time scaring off small-town sheriffs with sick pranks. Even Dean had realized that right away. Whoever had done it probably hadn't even intended to scare her. He'd just wanted to hurt her. To pay her back for something. To call her a bitch and to underscore the point as graphically as possible.

The list of people in this town who had a grudge against her wasn't exactly as long as her arm, but it probably reached her elbow. Once she'd mentally drawn up that list, including some of the men she'd undoubtedly pissed off at the tavern the previous afternoon, she canvassed the area, trying to narrow it down. Her closest neighbors—the ones she trusted to keep this under wraps—had been devastated to hear about what had happened, and any one of them would have helped if they could, but they hadn't been able to give her any leads that might help her investigation.

The mailman, who lived up the street, said everything had been just fine at noon, when he'd dropped her mail in the slot. Meaning the creep had to have done his nasty work between then and when she'd gotten home.

Broad daylight on a sunny Saturday, and nobody had seen or heard a thing.

It wasn't hard to figure that he had parked on the quiet lane running behind the neighborhood, and approached her house through the thick woods running behind it. Easy enough for him to climb over the low fence, shielded from view by the huge evergreens that had attracted her to the area in the first place. A quick dash down the side of the house, hugging the late-afternoon shadows, and he'd be at her door. The porch was hidden from the street by the out-of-control hedges she never had a chance to cut back. He could have taken his time then.

Bastard.

After striking out with the neighbors, she'd worked out her frustration by cutting back those stupid hedges. Brutally. Until her arms and neck were scratched deeply enough to draw blood. And until some of the rage began to leave her.

Last night, in Dean's arms, she'd been crushed. Now she was just damn furious.

By late in the afternoon, knowing she was going to have to go talk to some of the people who might have it in for her, she got into her squad car and headed downtown. But instead of going to the station, she detoured to Tanner Road, long considered the "wrong side of the tracks" in Hope Valley.

The Flanagan house had probably been beautiful when it was new. An old Victorian, it still exhibited graceful lines and genteel porches. But those lines were blurred by thirty years of dried, peeling paint, and the porches were falling off the sides.

Mitch and Mike's father had lots of recriminations and a ton of blame for others when it came to his sorry lot in life.

Parking in the driveway and approaching the door, she saw the man eyeing her warily from the open garage. He'd been poking under the open hood of a rust bucket disguised as a pickup, complete with gun rack and Confederate flag on the back. Classy.

"What do you want?"

"I'd like to talk to Mike."

He immediately hunched, his fists clenching at his sides. Damn, she didn't want to bring the man's wrath on the kid if Mike was innocent. But she needed to question him, because leaving a dead dog on her porch seemed like exactly the atrocity an angry, violent teenage boy would commit.

Still, there was a chance he hadn't done it. "He's not in any trouble," she muttered, wondering how Mr. Flanagan didn't hear the insincerity in her voice. "He just might have seen something that could help with a case I'm investigating."

She'd promised Dean she wouldn't investigate. But Dean didn't know Mr. Flanagan. Or his beefy fists. And if she had to use the other case to get Mike alone for questioning, without setting him up for a beating from his father as soon as she left, she'd do it.

"You sure he didn't do nothin'?"

No. She wasn't. Nor, however, was she sure he had. "I just need to talk to him."

"About that trashy Zimmerman girl?"

She wasn't wearing her uniform. But she could still convey her office with a look. The disdainful one she gave him obviously came through loud and clear. He mumbled something, then hauled himself up the steps. Opening the door, he yelled for his son.

When Mike stepped outside, she watched for any sign of guilt on his face. She saw bloodshot eyes, a haggard frown, and a hint of a bruise on his cheek. She also saw a glimmer of fear. But it was not fear of her.

"What'd you do, boy?"

"As I told your dad," she said, stepping forward, "you're not in any trouble." *Yet.* "I wanted to ask you if you saw anything that might help with a case I'm investigating."

He nodded quickly, his head jerking up and down, all evidence of that cocky little prick at the doughnut shop gone. Which just made her despise his father even more. Thank heaven Mitch had escaped this nightmare. He'd done what he could to help his kid brother, though not going so far as pressing charges against his father.

A deep kernel of pity for the boy made Stacey hope Mike someday got out, too. But her pity extended only so far, and was conditioned on whether he'd left that horrid surprise for her on her porch.

"Will you excuse us?" she said to the father.

"Maybe I don't want to."

Eyeing Mike, she turned her head enough so his father couldn't see and mouthed, *Get rid of him.*

Paling, the kid shoved his hands in his pockets. "It's okay, Dad. It's all good." She could see the wheels churning in his head. "Coach says scouts like it when you get involved with the community. And I want to help if I can."

Yeah, uh, bullshit.

But given that the only thing Mr. Flanagan had any pride in was his son's ability on the football field, the line worked. He returned to the garage, leaving them alone.

"You're not here about the other day?" Mike immediately asked.

Stacey shook her head once. "I really do want to talk to you about a case I'm working. But first I need to ask you something. Where were you yesterday?"

The kid showed no sign of guilt. "Practice. Coach was pissed about how we did last week and made good on his threat to make us come in on weekends."

"What time?"

"Around ten. He worked us for hours. It was dark by the time we left."

No wonder the kid looked bleary-eyed and bruised.

"He wants the state championship this year." Sneering toward the garage, Mike muttered, "It's my ticket outta this hellhole."

"The coach will confirm that?"

"Sure. We never left the field. We got five-minute piss breaks and ten for lunch. That was it."

The school was a good distance from her house. So if the coach and other players backed up his story, it eliminated Mike as the one who'd killed the dog. She wasn't stupid enough to take his word for it, but the alibi was easily checked, so she had to assume he was telling the truth. A weight lifted off her shoulders that she hadn't said anything to his dad about the real reason for her visit. "Okay."

"Are we done?" He looked up and down the street, as if worried some of his thug buddies would see him cooperating with the cops.

"No." Letting him know she was aware he'd tried to buy beer at Dick's that March night when Lisa had disappeared, she asked, "Do you remember that night?"

He put his hands up, palms out. "Hey, he didn't sell me any. And I wasn't the only one trying it, not by a long shot."

"I'm not accusing you of anything, and I'm not busting your chops about trying to buy beer. I just want to know if you saw anything. Did you hang around outside, or come back after you got thrown out? See anyone suspicious in the parking lot who might have been paying particular attention to Lisa?"

Mike, finally realizing she truly was here for another reason, crossed his arms. "Mitch hauled my ass home and dumped me in the driveway at around midnight."

Mitch had been at the tavern? The bar owner had said he'd had the teen thrown out; he just hadn't mentioned who had done the throwing.

Why hadn't her trusted deputy mentioned it? Maybe at first, when everybody had thought Lisa had skipped town, he hadn't thought it relevant. But now, knowing she was murdered, he should absolutely have said something.

"What did you do afterward?" she asked, not wanting Mike to realize how stunned she was by the tidbit he'd inadvertently provided.

"Nothin'. Stayed home. Isn't that what all nice, wholesome teenagers are supposed to do?"

He wouldn't know a wholesome teenager if he landed on one.

She wasn't sure she believed him. Mike's cocky attitude was back again, now that his father was out of earshot and he'd realized Stacey wasn't going to rat him out for the crap he'd pulled at the doughnut shop. Frankly, she wondered why he'd been worried. From what she knew about Mr. Flanagan, he'd probably have some kind of that's-my-boy macho reaction to the news that his kid had been leading a gang of boys in frightening a teenage girl. Mr. Flanagan was the type who'd laugh if his sons beat up other kids, who'd had them out hunting out of season by the age of four, who'd been horrified when Mitch had decided to be a cop. Father of the year.

Mike suddenly smiled. A nasty, knowing smile. "You want to know what was up with Lisa? Man, that girl was drunk as shit, dancing with every guy like she'd give it up right there on one of the pool tables. My dick of a brother tried to get her to leave with us, but she laughed in his face. He sure was pissed."

She kept her face blank. Mitch hadn't just been there; he hadn't merely seen Lisa in passing. He'd interacted with her. And nobody at the tavern had thought to mention that.

Could be they figured she already knew, since Mitch worked for her. Or could be they were scared to mention it, knowing how highly Stacey thought of her chief deputy.

Whatever the reason, she needed to find out exactly what had happened between Mitch and Lisa—both that night, and before it.

Damn. Yet another name to add to her list of people to question. Mitch, her brother, his best buddy. That list was growing more personal by the minute.

And more disturbing.

Chapter 11

From all reports, Amber Torrington had been a snotty, mean-spirited teen, liked only by her parents, because they had to, and by her boyfriend, because she put out.

Maybe because she was only missing, not officially dead, those who knew her felt free to speak badly about her. Her so-called friends, her boss at the clothing shop, the security guard who'd heard her shouting at her boss from five stores away—they'd all sung a familiar refrain. Spoiled brat, vicious temper. Not generally liked.

Dean tucked each bit of information away as he accompanied the local police conducting interviews Sunday. Each confirmation of what she'd been like convinced him that Amber's personality was significant to the investigation. The reason niggled at the back of his brain.

"Girl's address says the family's rich. Once again, he didn't make any effort to grab somebody who wouldn't be missed," Mulrooney commented as they walked toward the mall security office. Stokes strode on the other side of him, carrying an evidence bag containing the spent .22 shell casings they'd found in the tree line skirting the upscale shopping mecca. She would take them back to D.C. for analysis. None of them had any doubt they'd prove to be from the same rifle as the third case, when the cameras had also been shot out.

"No, he didn't," Dean muttered. "Or to even pick up her phone, or move her car."

"Either he was in a hurry, or he thought he was covered by shooting out the cameras and overhead lights." Out of shape, Mulrooney huffed a little as the three of them strode through the quiet mall, which was pretty empty on this summer Sunday afternoon. Well, empty except for the media crews busily sniffing for any dirt and broadcasting the slightest unconfirmed detail to the world.

"He couldn't count on having a lot of time for the guards to check out the department store alarm," Dean said. The one the unsub had, undoubtedly, caused.

Jackie finished his thought. "Or even that they'd all go. One of them might very well have done his damn job and stayed behind."

Funny how quickly the three of them had landed on the same page. They had fallen into an immediate rhythm on this, their first major case. Every idea was considered, its merits debated, all with professional respect it had taken years to earn in ViCAP. Blackstone's CATs were already becoming a team, right down to Lily and Brandon, whose phones had to be growing out of their ears by now with all the phone calls they'd shared.

Mulrooney said, "If one had stayed behind, maybe he'd have noticed the feeds from the other end of the mall going out one by one and come to investigate before the unsub had time to subdue Amber."

Possible. But the guy had worked fast. And he was an excellent shot.

Made him wonder if Stan Freed owned a rifle. Made him doubly wonder just what kind of weapons Warren Lee kept stockpiled out at his place.

"You notice how he picked a real piece of work this time?" Mulrooney asked.

"Uh-huh." He'd definitely noticed. And suddenly the detail that had been nagging at the back of his brain clicked in. He stopped suddenly, right in the middle of the mall. "In the other cases, Jackie, you said the interviews on the previous victims all hinted that they were difficult."

Jackie nodded. "Yeah. They were headstrong. Which I took to mean bitchy."

Just like Amber. There was the connection. "We've been thinking they were different from Lisa only because of their financial and social situations, not their personalities."

Mulrooney saw, too. "Meaning he must have known what each of them was like."

Dean nodded. "Yes. But how would he know that about them?"

"Unless he'd been studying them."

Bingo.

They knew that in another case a friend had come forward about a strange man watching the victim weeks before she'd disappeared. They'd already suspected he had to have picked out his victims in advance based on proximity and circumstance. Now they knew it was more than that.

He'd actually gotten to know them.

"He's been inside this mall." Dean started walking again, his gait quicker this time.

Mulrooney and Stokes matched his pace. "Probably even within the last few weeks," Jackie said, "since he knew she'd be working Friday night."

He'd followed Amber. Stalked her. He'd chosen her, made his plans, and then waited for the right moment, the right auction, to make her his next victim. He knew her schedule and her habits.

And he might very well be on a mall security tape from one of his previous visits.

"You think he believes he's doing the world a favor by killing mean girls?" Mulrooney asked as they passed a cluster of giddy young shoppers.

"Lisa wasn't a mean girl," Jackie murmured. "She was a lost girl."

A sad, abused lost girl whose father had died and whose mother might as well have, too, for all the care she took to protect her daughter.

"Right," Mulrooney said. "She was pathetic. He was experimenting. Then on to the main events. The challenges: successful women, attractive women, family women."

None of whom, apparently, had been nice women.

Reaching the mall office, they met up with the head of security, a guy named Baker, who'd been playing a game of cover-my-ass since the minute they'd arrived. With good reason.

He'd neglected to check out a surveillance camera covering the back of the mall, which had stopped working Friday around five. That camera might have revealed the unsub lurking near the Dumpsters, the loading dock, or the nearly hidden employees-only entrance of the store where Amber worked.

He'd left the video surveillance room unattended because of an alarm at one end of the mall, bringing his entire security team with him for what had turned out to be a broken glass door, shot through from a distance.

Finally, he hadn't bothered to check out the car left overnight in the parking lot, despite all the other unusual activities in the mall that night. The asshole had decided some kids were playing pranks, shooting off a BB gun. *Frigging moron.* He deserved to be fired.

But for now, they needed his cooperation.

"How long do you keep the mall security tapes?"

Dean asked the man the moment they strode into his office.

"They recycle every twenty-four hours."

Damn.

Seeing Dean's frustration, the man mumbled, "But there's a backup. The files dump to a server that holds on to them for a week before automatically purging them."

One week. Would the unsub have risked stalking his victim within a week of taking her?

Mulrooney had obviously had the same thought. Lowering his voice, he murmured, "The auction came up quicker than anybody expected."

Meaning he might have moved up his schedule. Accelerating could have made him sloppy. Made him take risks. "And he knew she'd be working," Dean muttered, figuring the store wouldn't have made up the schedule more than two weeks in advance.

It was worth a shot.

"We need those backups," he told the guard. "Right now."

He showed up at her house late that night.

Stacey had just gone to bed when she heard a car pull into her driveway. Two possibilities immediately came to mind: Dean. Or the bastard who'd killed Lady. One had her wishing she'd worn something at least a little attractive to bed, rather than a long Redskins T-shirt and gym shorts. The other had her reaching for her nine-millimeter, which was right beside her, on her bedside table.

Grabbing it just in case, she shifted her bedroom window blinds to the side, trying to make out the vehicle. And she realized there was a third alternative.

"What are you doing here?" she asked her brother a minute later when she yanked open her front door.

Tim stared at her, surprised that she'd answered before he'd knocked, which told her he hadn't been certain he was going to. Instead of answering her question, he mumbled, "You finally cut down those ugly bushes."

"Come in," she said, seeing a strange look in his eye, one she didn't like. He'd worn that expression quite a lot in the first few months after he'd been released from the military. It was vacant. Haunted. Traumatized. "Please."

"Sorry. I shouldn't have come here."

She took his arm, tugging him inside when it looked as though he might leave. At first worried he'd driven over here drunk, she grabbed his chin, studying his eyes, trying to smell anything on him.

He saw right through her. "I haven't been drinking," he muttered.

She believed him. Tim might have come home an angry stranger, but he had never tried to cover up his drinking. And he'd never been able to disguise his glassy-eyed, heavy-lidded reaction to too much alcohol. "Want some coffee?"

"It's not too late?" he asked, following her into her small house.

"It's not like I'll sleep tonight, anyway." Her head was too full for that. Full of Dean and what had happened the previous evening. Full of the case and questions about what was happening today.

She'd seen the news; it had only inspired more questions. The pictures of that pretty blond girl, however, would almost certainly inspire nightmares.

So, no, she wouldn't be sleeping much tonight.

Not entirely trusting him not to leave if she let him out of her sight, she said, "Let's go in the kitchen. I have junk food."

A ghost of a laugh emerged from his mouth, though he made a visible effort not to smile. He'd had several surgeries, but the scar tissue on his face meant any attempt at a smile would result in only a lopsided sneer.

It broke her heart whenever she looked at him. His left profile was perfect, about as handsome as any man could possibly be. His right wasn't.

She was the younger sibling, but was well used to being in charge. Taking his arm, she pulled him with her, then sat him down at her small table. Grabbing boxes of cookies and bags of chips, comfort food she generally tried to avoid but had really needed lately, she dumped them in front of him, then made coffee.

He twisted apart his cookie and ate the icing, just like he had when they were kids. Simple pleasures. How he must have missed them all those years.

"What's going on?" she asked as she sat down across from him.

"I heard about the dog," he said.

She waited, wondering how much he'd heard. She hoped her neighbors hadn't gossiped all over town.

"Dad's pretty broken up."

She nodded, glad he didn't know the rest. Tim might not be his old self, but her protective older brother still existed inside that scarred shell. He'd be just as furious and worried as their father if he knew the truth. "I know. Did he call you?"

"Yeah. I went out to see him this afternoon. Helped him plant some flowers on the grave. He wanted sunflowers; I guess Lady used to love to dig in them."

Her heart twisted, and Stacey made a mental note to plead with her neighbors to keep the questions she'd asked today to themselves. "I'm glad you were there for him, Tim."

Being needed by someone else was probably the best thing that could happen to her brother right now. It might keep him from dwelling too much on all the things that had gone wrong in his own life. "So," she asked, "did you come here tonight to talk about Dad's dog?"

He hesitated, then admitted, "I'm not doing so great."

No kidding. She didn't say it, hearing an unexpected vulnerability in his voice. "You didn't get your job back."

Shaking his head, he mumbled something, then cleared his throat and tried again. "No. And I won't be getting it back."

His defiant expression told her more than she wanted to know about Tim's involvement with some missing cash at his employer's used-car dealership. To think he could be reduced to stealing. It stunned her.

"It was fifty bucks and a couple of unauthorized joy-rides in some vehicles from the lot," he said flatly, reading her reaction. "I paid it back. He said he won't press charges. But I'm unemployed."

Her upstanding marine brother, a petty thief. *God.*

Forcing the law-abiding-sheriff part of herself away, she tried to transition into his little sister. "You'll get another job."

"I don't give a damn about a job."

"You obviously need money," she said, her tone pointed.

He ignored the sarcasm. "I'm working with Randy a little."

"Oh, great. Is he opening a beer-testing business?" When he stiffened and scooted his chair back as if to rise, Stacey reached for his arm. "I'm sorry."

He stayed seated. Barely. "I've just been riding along on a couple of his runs. No biggie—I give him a hand loading and unloading."

Stacey wanted to know the rest, sensing he had more to say, especially given the way his voice had trailed off. Knowing better than to push him, she made light of it.

"Come on, you're telling me Randy does anything more than back that semi up to the loading dock and watch the store employees roll out the big flat-screens?"

"Maybe I just go along for company; his kid isn't interested anymore," he admitted, still studying the stupid cookie as if it held the meaning of life. His tone turning bitter, he added, "I don't really need the bucks. You think Uncle Sam isn't compensating me?"

"So why did you take the fifty?"

He shrugged, at a loss. "I don't know. Boredom. Stupidity."

Anger. Tim had seemed to want to pick fights with everyone lately.

"Maybe I just want people to look at me instead of shifting their eyes."

And that was probably the truest thing he'd said so far.

"People look at you."

"Yeah, the circus freak."

"That's an exaggeration. You have beautiful eyes."

"Miraculously."

"Good features. Not exactly the stud you used to think you were, but there's nothing wrong with you, Tim, other than a few lines that people who know and love you don't even see anymore."

"And the people who don't know and love me?"

"Screw them."

Another of those sad laughs. "You always did tell it like it is."

The coffee was ready. Getting up, she fixed them each a cup, keeping her back to Tim so he wouldn't see the way her hands shook. She'd cried herself out last night, yet still suspected she had a tear or two left for her brother, who suddenly seemed so lost, so beaten. He'd been stateside for two and a half years, the first six months of it in a VA hospital, the rest here in Hope Valley. Yet this was the first time he'd reached out to her emotionally. The first time he'd admitted he was floundering, rather than just angrily demanding that everyone make way for him and give him whatever he wanted.

There was no way she was going to blow it.

"Angie asks about you all the time." Angie, a friend of Stacey's, owned the new Internet café. She'd been Tim's high school girlfriend, and he'd broken her heart when he joined the marines. Stacey sensed that the attractive divorcée still cared. But it was a little sticky; she'd been dating Randy a year ago, until Mama Covey had ruined things. Talk about best friends sharing and sharing alike.

"She pities me," Tim snapped.

"No, she doesn't."

"I don't want to talk about her."

Meaning he did still care. She knew it.

Forcing herself to let it go, she carried the coffee over. "So. If you don't need romantic advice, and don't need a job for money, what's the trouble?"

His head jerked. "Trouble?"

"Something landed you on my doorstep at eleven o'clock on a Sunday night. What can I do to help?"

"Help. You'll just help, no matter what?"

"Yes, I will," she murmured, wondering what, exactly, he'd gotten mixed up in. God, she hoped Randy hadn't involved her brother in any shady dealings that she wouldn't be able to help him with. Because she loved her brother, but she couldn't close her eyes if he were breaking the law.

"There's nothing wrong." He rubbed both hands over his face, visibly tired, but maybe covering his eyes so she wouldn't see the emotion in them. He seemed truly shocked that she'd offered her help so readily. Did he really think she would have refused him?

Maybe. She certainly hadn't been sympathetic the

other morning. Then again, he hadn't exactly been contrite and vulnerable, either.

"I'm sorry; I shouldn't have come. I just knew that if I stayed home, Randy would show up and I'd go out and do something stupid."

Something stupid with Randy. *Well, alert the media.* "He's trouble."

"He's my best friend."

"I know that."

"Look," Tim said, getting defensive, "I've known him all my life. We've been there for each other. Since his dad died, and our mom."

They seldom talked about their mother, primarily because Stacey had no memory of her. "I know. You think I don't remember him talking about how great it would be if Dad married Randy's mom and you two became brothers?"

Tim had just sipped his coffee, but he quickly spewed it back out into his cup. This time, a real smile appeared. It emphasized his scars. It also emphasized the beautiful color of his eyes. And broke her heart a little. "Jeez, I was petrified it might happen."

"Me, too! I thought you were all for it."

"You kidding? She's a barracuda. If a man could will himself to have a heart attack, I'd think Mr. Covey did just to get away from her."

"Lucky guy," she said with a laugh. Laughing. With her brother. How rare was that?

"Randy's had it tough," Tim insisted. "We're there for each other, thick and thin. Right and wrong."

That *right and wrong* part really stuck in her head. "Tim, I know there's something you're not telling me."

"You asking as the sheriff?" he snapped.

"No. I'm asking as your sister. Someone who loves you."

His green eyes locked with hers, and for a moment,

she thought he was going to open up. She braced herself to listen without reacting, knowing he was really worried about whatever was going on.

But he hedged, repeating, under his breath, "He's always been there for me."

"I know. But right now, he's not the kind of person you need to have 'there' for you. He's not helping you, and he could be hurting."

Tim's coffee sloshed over his cup as he lowered it to the table. Her brother was actually shaking.

"Tim, please, tell me what it is. Are you . . . Have you been taking something?"

He rose abruptly. "I'm not on drugs."

"I know Randy used to do them."

"Years ago," he snapped. "He's not anymore. End of story."

"I'm sorry." Stacey reached for him. "Please don't go."

He hesitated, then ducked away from her hand, as if he didn't want to be touched. But the anger left him and he quietly murmured, "You have to go to work tomorrow, keeping Hope Valley safe from the evils of the world. I've kept you up late enough."

Knowing it was useless and that he'd shut himself down for now, she rose to her feet as well. "Safe from the evils of the world, huh? Guess you haven't been following the local news."

"Oh, hell, I totally forgot. I heard about Lisa. That's rough."

"Her mother certainly thinks so."

Tim flushed. "Dick told you I was in the bar the night she disappeared."

"Yes, he did."

"Thanks for not calling me out all big, bad sheriff sister in front of everyone."

"I intended to stop by and see you tomorrow. Randy, too."

"He'll tell you the same thing I did. Lisa was drunk, like everybody else in the place."

"Did you talk to her?"

He shook his head, sneering now, for real. "Are you kidding? She couldn't even look me in the face. Oh, she never said anything; she might have been a little cock-tease, but she wasn't mean."

Stacey zoned in on the most surprising part of his statement, ignoring the self-pity in her brother's voice. "A cock-tease? I thought when she was using she gave it away left, right, and center."

"Maybe to a rich guy on the left, a well-hung guy on the right, and a drug-connected one in the center. Not with average dudes like Randy or ugly ones like me."

She rolled her eyes at the self-slam, too used to them to even argue with him about it anymore. Instead, she focused on this new aspect of Lisa's personality. Had the young woman had simply turned down the wrong man one too many times and drawn the Reaper's ire?

"How late did you and Randy stay?"

"I was there until closing. He left a little before that. I think he got antsy when your deputy came and hauled his brother out. I guess the punk used to run around with Seth or something, and Randy wanted to make sure his kid wasn't trying to score beer, too."

"You saw Mitch show up to get Mike?"

He nodded. "Oh, yeah. He grabbed Lisa and tried to get her to leave with them. Got ugly for a minute. Shame he didn't convince her; things might have ended up a lot differently."

Yes, they might have. They probably would have, in fact. Mitch was a good guy; he'd been trying to help Lisa Zimmerman; she felt sure of it.

But that surety still didn't erase the tiny hint of suspicion about why Mitch hadn't come clean about his relationship with the troubled young victim.

"Thanks. I appreciate the help."

Though she wanted Tim to stay and tell her the real reason he'd come over tonight, she didn't press her luck. This was the first time he'd reached out to her, and she wanted him to come back. She wanted him to want to come back. And hopefully, the next time he did, he'd be ready to reveal a little more.

Despite that, as she walked him to the door and kissed him good-bye on his poor, scarred cheek, she murmured, "You could go see the doctor down at the VA again."

He tensed.

"I'm not criticizing. Not judging. Just making the suggestion. If you can't talk to me or to Dad, maybe you could talk to him."

Tim stared down at her, saying nothing. But she knew him well enough to know he'd at least consider it, because she hadn't ordered, hadn't browbeaten him. She'd simply made a suggestion. It was the only way to deal with the man lately.

After her brother had left, Stacey locked the door behind him and returned to the kitchen. She'd barely touched her coffee, but it didn't matter. Caffeine couldn't jazz her up any more than she already was.

Too bad Dean wasn't here. Though, of course, it was better that he hadn't been when Tim showed up. Her brother would never have stayed. But now, facing the long night, she'd like the company. Her mind swam with details about the case, things she'd learned, things she'd speculated. Tidbits that seemed important, though why they should be remained just out of mental reach.

It was almost one o'clock. She needed to try to get some sleep. Still, she couldn't help eyeing the phone as she cleaned the kitchen.

As if by magic, it rang.

She grabbed it, laughing and about to ask him if he'd read her mind. "Dean?"

Silence.

"Hello?"

That ominous nothingness stretched on for several seconds. Unease made her throat tighten. Images of Lisa, memories of the vicious surprise someone had left on her porch, filled the recesses of her imagination. "Who the hell is this?"

No answer at first, then one single word.

"Bitch."

The call disconnected.

Chapter 12

Though he wanted to, Dean wasn't able to get back to
Hope Valley until early Tuesday evening.

Amber Torrington's brutal murder had debuted at
Satan's Playground Monday morning. And her body—in
two pieces—had been discovered later that afternoon.

The team had known someone was going to die. They
knew why. They'd had a rough idea who. A broad picture of where. And they'd regrettably known how.

Yet they hadn't been able to do a damn thing to stop
it from happening.

He had no business leaving D.C. Having spent most
of yesterday and today in the woods of southern Pennsylvania, where the body had been found, he'd returned
to the office to see whether Lily or Brandon was getting anywhere with the security tape. That they hadn't
had any luck provided him with a good reason to head
back to Hope Valley. If they were truly working under
the assumption that the man was at least familiar with
the area, they needed somebody who might recognize
him to watch the tape.

Stacey.

It was the only video he was going to ask her to watch.

Because what that sick fuck had done to Amber Torrington had made him puke for the first time since he'd been on this case.

Beheading, it seemed, was not as easy as it appeared on video games and movies. The fiend had had to work at it. Hard.

Arriving on the outskirts of town, he headed for the sheriff's office. Considering he hadn't spoken to Stacey at all since he'd left her place Saturday night, he wasn't sure what kind of reception he'd get. Not that he hadn't wanted to; he'd just been run ragged. He'd conducted interviews, overseen evidence collection from both scenes, talked to nearly every employee in the mall. Somewhere in there, he could have made a cell phone call to Stacey, but there was too much to say in a phone conversation.

She's a cop. She'll understand.

She was not like his ex, who'd wanted hourly reports on when he'd be home for dinner and had occasionally dumped said dinner onto his chair when he didn't make it. As if Dean should have been able to dictate when evidence could be discovered or violent criminals could be arrested.

When he reached the office, though, he learned Stacey wasn't there.

"Sorry, Agent Taggert," said the same older, big-haired receptionist. "She's out at the range doing some target shooting. Lots of them have been going out there the past couple of days."

Oh, great. If Stacey was brushing up on her marksmanship, that obviously meant she thought she might have to use a weapon sometime soon. Something he knew would not make her happy.

"Thanks," he said after getting directions.

After a quick drive, he arrived at the range. That was probably an exaggerated name for the actual facility, not much more than an old farm with a dirt berm bullet stop and some shot-out weathered plywood to hang targets on. The parking lot was choked with weeds, and potholed down to bare dirt in places, showing a general lack of use that confirmed what he'd figured: Stacey and her deputies didn't use this place very often. Until now, when he and his team had brought news of Lisa Zimmerman's murder to their quiet world.

He spotted her at once. Parking and cutting the engine, he sat in the driver's seat and watched. He leaned forward, dropping his crossed arms on the steering wheel, a slow smile widening his mouth.

Because, damn, she was hot.

Wearing hearing protection, she hadn't noticed his arrival. She stood alone, a few yards from his car, clothed in jeans and a bright pink tank top.

He'd seen her in her uniform. He'd seen her in her underwear. He'd seen her naked. He'd just never seen her dressed down. And the woman did some amazing things for a pair of jeans and a clingy top.

Her legs were slightly spread, arms extended straight out, shoulder height. The left hand cupped her other wrist, beneath the gun, for support, and the right flowed seamlessly into her Glock as if it were an extension of her own limb. As he exited the car, she grouped seventeen rounds through the center of a paper suspect's chest. From twenty-five yards. In under twenty seconds.

Repeat: hot.

Knowing better than to sneak up behind an armed person who wouldn't hear his approach, he leaned against the hood of his car, his arms crossed, watching. She was empty and had to change clips, which was when she caught sight of him. Her eyes widened in surprise, and a quick, spontaneous smile broadened her mouth.

Despite the past couple of days, and his own bone-deep weariness, he somehow found a smile of his own and returned it.

"Hi," she said as she walked over, holstering the nine-millimeter. "Didn't expect to see you here."

"I hope the target practice wasn't on my account," he said with an apologetic shrug. "I'm sorry I haven't called."

"Don't worry. I don't shoot guys who don't call back. Leave the toilet seat up, however, and all bets are off."

"Noted."

The smile flashed again, brilliant and honest and so good after all the darkness that he wanted to just lose himself in it. In her.

Yes, they had a lot to talk about regarding the case. He wanted to know if she was okay, if she'd gotten over the nightmare someone had left on her porch. But what he most wanted was to get her alone and make love to her the way he'd planned to Saturday night.

The urge to tug her against him and kiss her overwhelmed him, but he resisted. They were out in public, in a spot where her deputies came for target practice and could pull up at any time. No way would he put her in the position of being disrespected by one of her subordinates.

When he got her alone in private again, though . . . well, as she'd said, all bets were off.

"You okay?" she asked. "I saw on the news that the body had been found."

So much for a tender reunion. She was already back into the case. Exactly as he'd expect her to be. "Yeah. It was a rough scene."

"In Pennsylvania?"

"Right over the state line. Talk about jurisdictional nightmares. But you might be able to help."

She nodded immediately.

"We've got surveillance tape from the mall where the victim was snatched. There's a good chance the unsub was stalking her, memorizing her movements and her schedule."

"You want me to watch the tapes? See if there's anyone who might have had a connection with Lisa on there?"

"I know it's a lot to ask. We're talking hours and hours."

"Of course. I'll start right away."

He nodded in appreciation, though he'd had no doubt she would do it. Seeing her wipe a sheen of sweat off her brow, he said, "The car's still cool. Want to sit?"

She was one step ahead of him, already opening the door and sliding into the passenger seat. Before Dean had even started the engine, she reached for the air-conditioner controls, adjusting a vent to blow cold air directly on her face. She sighed in pleasure as the AC blew tendrils of her hair loose.

Since they were inside the closed car, he risked personal contact, knowing he had to touch her or lose his mind. He reached over, brushing his fingertips over the sensitive spot where her shoulder met her neck.

She turned into his hand, rubbing her cheek against his palm. That was all. The touch was simple, nonsexual, yet loaded with personal connection. It pleasured him the way even an embrace with any other woman wouldn't have.

Which said a lot about how much she'd been on his mind in the past few days. How much they'd been on his mind, as crazy and impossible as it was.

"Are you going to be in town for a while?"

He shook his head. "I have to be back in the office tomorrow morning. And tomorrow evening I get to spend time with my son."

She nodded.

"But D.C.'s not that far a drive," he said with a slight smile. "I could see myself commuting in the morning."

"Mm," she murmured, lightly kissing his palm, "and I am noble enough to save you from the bedbugs at the inn, if you'd like to stay at my place."

"Thought they didn't have them. Immaculately clean, you said."

"Maybe I exaggerated. My bed's nicer, isn't it?"

"Infinitely."

Staring into his eyes, she admitted, "I've been hoping you'd come back."

"I'm back." His voice was husky, the touch of his hand on her lips sizzling and electrifying. He wanted her again. Badly. "I don't know which I find more arousing, you kissing my hand, or shooting out that target in under twenty seconds."

Stacey laughed softly, sounding so sweet and feminine, such a fascinating mix of strength and softness. Wondering about that strength, and how she'd held up after he'd had to walk out on her the other night, he asked, "Are you okay? After what happened Saturday?"

She nodded, obviously realizing he was asking about the horror on her doorstep. "I don't know who did it, but I'm working on it. I helped my dad bury her on Sunday."

"Stacey, I don't want to worry you, but we have to at least consider the possibility that the guy we're looking for is afraid you're getting a little too close, and wants to scare you off."

"It occurred to me. And then I unoccurred it."

He didn't laugh. This wasn't funny in the least.

"Honestly, it's not me he'd be after; it's you guys. And he's not exactly the subtle type. If he did want me, I don't think he'd leave a message."

No, probably not.

"It's never been anything this bad before, but it's not the first time some redneck, beer-swilling asshole has decided to get even with me for writing him a ticket or hauling him in on a DUI. I'd lay money that's what we're talking about here." She opened her mouth, then closed it quickly, as if she had more to say but had thought better of it.

"What?"

Indecision washed across her features. But before she could continue, a car drove by, flying down the country road at an unsafe speed. She jerked away from him and leaned forward toward the windshield, glaring after it. "Damn. Missed the license plate number."

Soft woman to hard-edged cop in less than ten seconds. What an irresistible combination.

Clearing her throat, she spoke again, as if the subject of the dog, and whatever else she'd been about to tell him, had never come up. "You said you're having problems with jurisdiction in the case?"

He let her get away with it, knowing Stacey wasn't the type to hold back if something was really important. She said what needed to be said, when it needed to be said. He had no doubt that if she had something else on her mind, she'd tell him when she was ready. "Yes. Wyatt's jumping through hoops to keep on top of it. But at least it's made the BAU sit up and take notice. They've stopped stonewalling the agent working on the profile. We should have it in a couple of days."

"I bet we can make a couple of assumptions about this guy even without it."

"You know, *assume* is a very bad word in law enforcement."

"I know, I know. But come on, there are a few obvious points."

"Such as?"

"He was probably an abuser of animals."

Incredulous, given what they'd just discussed, he merely stared.

"I still don't think what happened to Lady is connected to this," she insisted.

Giving up, he merely replied, "Okay. Animal abuse is actually a strong commonality among serial killers.

Know anyone with a history of that kind of thing?" Frowning, he added, "Or two anyones?"

She shook her head. "Not that I know of. But I'll ask my dad."

"Good idea."

Leaning back in her seat, she thought quietly before continuing to speculate. "He hates women."

"Could be. Or he could want women and be unable to sexually perform with them, so he kills them instead." He paused before adding, "Three were violated with unidentified objects."

She shuddered. But not because of the air-conditioning.

"Okay," she said, "what about abuse?"

"Again, very possible. But not always."

"Abandonment?"

"Maybe. But it could come from so many angles—a wife who walked out, a mother who died."

She barked a quick, humorless laugh.

"What?"

"You just described both Randy and my brother."

He said nothing, just watching her until she scowled.

"That's not even funny."

"They were both at the bar that night."

"Back off, Agent Taggert."

"That Covey guy, you said he's a trucker, right? On the road a lot? He wouldn't be missed if he's gone overnight."

"This is ridiculous."

Treading carefully, he couldn't help adding, "And your brother, he seems like a very angry man."

"Angry, yes. Homicidal, no friggin' way." The heat in the car no longer came from the sun outside, but rather from her indignation. "Tim doesn't even own a computer, for God's sake. He lives in a crappy one-bedroom apartment in town and wants so much to retreat from the world that he seldom even answers his phone. I practically have to send up smoke signals when I want to see him."

He'd seen the guy. He understood and pitied the poor bastard. "Look, I'm not accusing either of them of anything," he insisted. "Just trying to make a point. Most times these profiles can be twisted to suit almost anyone, like that colossal screwup with the Atlanta Olympic bombing suspect. No doubt they can be very helpful. But they're by no means the only tool we use to catch guys like this."

She relaxed, at least a little, then grudgingly admitted, "Point taken. No more assumptions." Sighing audibly, she deliberately turned her head and stared out the window. "It's just . . . the waiting is killing me. All the possibilities, all the men who were at the tavern that night. We've got to narrow down the list."

Noting the way she'd looked away, not meeting his eye, he had a sudden suspicion. "You've been working on the case."

A slight nod.

"Damn it, Stacey."

She shifted in her seat to meet his stare directly. "I haven't done much. I talked to a couple of people, nobody dangerous. I certainly didn't go question Warren Lee or anything like that."

Small comfort. The idea that she might have confronted someone who could turn out to be the Reaper was enough to make him want to get her far away from here. Not that she'd ever run.

"I immediately thought of this latest kidnapping, wondering if Stan really had been working the late shift Friday night."

His curiosity outweighing his concern, he asked, "And?"

Her frown answered even before she did. "His boss backed him up. Furthermore, the hospital confirmed Winnie's story. Per their records, Stan brought her and signed her into the ER at two twenty a.m. the night Lisa died. And he was there to drive Winnie home when she was discharged at around six."

The stepfather would have had to grab Lisa, stash her somewhere, go home and beat his wife, and drive her to the hospital in the next town, all within a thirty-minute period. Impossible. "So he wasn't responsible for what happened to Lisa," he said.

Her green eyes darkened. "At least not for her murder."

The man was guilty of the rest; he didn't doubt that. He only hoped that someday he was made to pay for it.

"What else have you got?" he asked, no longer worrying about whether she'd done the right thing in investigating on her own. Stacey wasn't stupid. And what she'd told him already had helped a lot by ruling out a viable suspect.

"I tried to talk to Randy."

"Why?"

"My brother told me Randy left a little before closing that night. Lisa did, too. I thought it was worth asking if he noticed anything as he was leaving—a truck pulling in, or maybe one he passed on his way back to town."

"Did he?"

She shook her head. "I haven't met up with him yet. I stopped by his house, and his mother told me he's been doing a lot of overnight trips. He drives a big rig. She said she'd have him call me."

Noticing a half smile lurking on her lips, he asked, "What?"

"Nothing. Mrs. Covey hates that I'm sheriff, and tries hard not to even notice my uniform. I think she really believed I was there for personal reasons, that I'm another fast girl trying to corrupt her good boy."

He couldn't help saying, "I like that about you, fast girl."

She ignored him. "Randy's getting his girlfriend pregnant when he was in high school did not go over well in the Covey house. I think she's trying to scare away any other woman who might 'trap' him again."

"Why does he stay?"

"Who knows?"

Dean couldn't help thinking back to their earlier conversation about the profile. He had to say, "Abandoned by his wife, controlling mother. Do you think he was abused as a kid?"

Her eyes widened and she opened her mouth to hotly reply. But not a sound came out. Not a single sound.

"Don't tell me you haven't considered it," he said, knowing she was too good not to have. "He's a trucker, on the road all the time, traveling all over the place."

"I've considered it," she admitted, grudging but honest. "But he's a big, obnoxious teddy bear."

"John Wayne Gacy volunteered as a clown."

"Yeah, I know. But Randy? I've never heard an angry word come out of his mouth."

Before she could say anything further, another car swung into the gravel lot, parking beside his. She cast a quick glance toward the newcomer, murmuring, "I invited Mitch to meet me out here. Told him he should keep practicing with his good arm while his broken one heals."

He immediately remembered the guy who had burst into their meeting on Saturday. He'd had some kind of relationship with the victim, and his boss hadn't known a thing about it.

"You sure his arm's really broken?" he asked, immediately thinking of the video of Amber Torrington's brutal murder. Just because the Reaper had shown no sign of a cast didn't mean Mitch Flanagan could be ruled out.

For all he knew, the cast could be a perfect ruse, a visible disguise as well as a reason to miss work.

"Of course it's broken," Stacey snapped.

He didn't argue, knowing her well enough to know she'd get there on her own.

"According to witnesses, including my brother, he argued with Lisa in the bar the night she disappeared. I want to talk to him, but I need to handle it carefully. I don't want anyone putting the cart before the horse. If people think I'm questioning him, or that he's a suspect . . . well, given his family, they'll have him tried and convicted."

"Bad background?"

"His father's a nightmare."

"Abusive?" He could see her grit her teeth, but didn't back off. "Stacey, come on; you said yourself it's relevant."

Though she shook her head in denial, she admitted, "Yeah. He was pretty rough on Mitch, and I suspect he's still knocking his younger son, Mike, around."

"Do you think Mitch or the brother could be our guy?"

"Mike is probably capable of just about anything rotten, but I don't see a teenager being the Reaper."

"Just because most serial killers are at least in their mid-twenties doesn't mean it's a necessity. What about your deputy? Do you suspect him?"

"Of stupidity. Of being a sucker and falling for the wrong woman. But murder?" She shook her head slowly. "I can't picture it. But at this point I'm not ruling anything out." She reached for the door handle and sighed. "So I guess I'd better make a note to check on his broken arm."

A good-looking guy in his late twenties, Mitch Flanagan had a lot going for him. Starting with being able to break free of his family's no-good reputation and make something of himself, despite the odds against him.

Stacey had gone to school with him, though he'd been a few years behind her. But even as a senior, when she'd never spoken to him, she'd heard the snide comments and seen the condescending looks thrown his way. Girls were tempted by the bad-boy rumors, but warned away by their folks. Guys were threatened by his looks and smarts. He'd been a loner, keeping his head down, his nose clean, and his goal in sight.

Escape. That had been his goal. She'd known it then and she knew it now.

It had worked. He'd proved a whole lot of people wrong. He'd kept up his grades, never gotten into a day's worth of trouble. And by his senior year, most people were almost able to forget his last name.

As far as she knew, he'd left his parents' home the day after graduation and had never gone back. He'd pulled together enough money to go to college and get a degree. And her father had hired him right afterward. Stacey had promoted him to chief deputy a year ago. She'd never regretted her choice. Now, though, she had to wonder.

Because she needed her people to be honest with her. And he hadn't been.

"Hey, Mitch," she said as he stepped out of his car, careful with his broken arm. His cast, which Dean suddenly had her questioning, was scrawled with a few signatures and some graffiti, probably from the other deputies, all of whom looked up to him.

He was liked. He was sociable. He was smart.

So why on earth had he gotten himself mixed up with Lisa Zimmerman and then covered it up?

"Hi, Stace." He glanced toward the other side of the car, where Dean stood, watching in silence. "He's back?"

She nodded as Dean walked over to join them. "I

don't think you officially met the other day," she said, quickly introducing them.

Mitch flushed, then shook Dean's hand, obviously embarrassed by his unprofessional behavior. "Is there news?"

"No." Few people knew the FBI was investigating other murders in connection with Lisa's. She intended to keep it that way. If her subordinates wondered why the FBI was involving itself in a local case, they'd just have to keep wondering.

"You still haven't found her?"

She shook her head.

"But you're certain she's dead?"

Dean stepped in. "We're certain."

Seeing the dazed, empty look in Mitch's eyes, Stacey reached out and put a bracing hand on his shoulder. "We need to talk about this."

"I know." He glanced at Dean, as if wondering if the other man had to stay, but Stacey wasn't going to let Mitch off the hook just because he was her friend. The case was much too important for that. Realizing as much, Mitch shrugged. "Go ahead."

"How long had you been seeing her?"

"About six months," he admitted. "I pulled her over one night for speeding."

Wonderful.

"She was upset. Crying. She looked a little banged-up. I thought maybe one of those rough guys she went out with had knocked her around."

She knew what he was going to say before he said it.

"I found out later it was that bastard stepfather of hers. He . . ." Mitch's face turned red, and obvious rage tightened his entire body. "I really considered killing him."

"I didn't hear you say that," she muttered with a frown, even though she understood the sentiment.

Vilifying Stan wouldn't help, however. They already knew he hadn't murdered Lisa. Maybe her spirit, yes—he had probably killed that. But hell would have to deal with him. There was nothing she could do to the man now unless Winnie stepped forward to charge him with her own abuse.

"Tell me you're investigating him for Lisa's murder," Mitch said, still tense.

"He's been ruled out."

He pounded his fist against the hood of his car. "You're sure?"

"He's got a solid alibi, Mitch. He might be a twisted degenerate, but he didn't kill her."

His shoulders slumped, as if he'd wanted Stan to be guilty. Like Stacey, he had to want justice for the man who'd abused Lisa all those years.

"Go back to what you were saying. What happened with you and Lisa?"

"We started getting together. Not around here—we'd go up to Front Royal and grab some coffee or catch a movie. She was talking about cleaning herself up, maybe trying for her GED. Doing something with herself. I wanted to help, so we'd meet once in a while and go over some stuff."

The reformed bad kid tutoring the lost girl. There was something inherently sweet in that. If she'd known about it, she probably would have encouraged them both, even while urging Mitch not to get his hopes up too high.

She hadn't known, however. Mitch had kept his secrets well. "You fell for her?"

He nodded, defiant. "She wasn't what everyone thought she was. She was pretty and funny and smart."

"And an addict," Stacey said, not unkindly. "I suspect you were in over your head."

"Yeah." He rubbed a hand over his eyes, but held on to his control. "One day she said she wanted to stop seeing me. She'd hooked up with some ex-con, started using heavily again. I couldn't get her to quit." He frowned. "I thought for a long time she'd skipped town with him, until you mentioned that he was in jail down in Georgia at the time."

"Let's talk about the night she disappeared."

"I went out to Dick's to pick up my brother." He cast a quick, nervous glance between Stacey and Dean. "He's not really a bad kid."

"Yeah, he is," Stacey snapped. Seeing the sadness in Mitch's expression, she grudgingly added, "But maybe there's a chance for him."

"You gotta understand. I was the buffer when he was little."

A physical buffer. He'd been the wall between their father's fists and his younger brother.

Maybe that was what had drawn Mitch to Lisa. Had he felt some deep, intrinsic need to protect her from her own abusive situation, when he'd once been too young to protect himself and felt guilt over abandoning Mike?

"Once I left, I swore I'd never set foot in that house again." His face reddening, he muttered, "Our mom's not interested in anything that doesn't come out of a bottle. Mike has nobody."

Having nobody to stand up for him hadn't kept Mitch from breaking free. But she didn't point it out. The guy knew it already; he just didn't want to give up on his troubled sibling.

She got that. Wow, did she ever get that.

"I'm trying to reach out to him," he admitted. "Trying to get him to come stay with me once in a while. The old man's going to a NASCAR race later this week. I had been planning on picking Mike up, bringing him to the station. Letting him spend some time with some of the decent people around here . . ." Mitch's voice trailed off. "I guess that's not a good idea now, though."

With an active murder investigation? Definitely not.

"Let's get back to that night, Mitch."

"When I showed up at the bar that night, Mike was about to get his butt kicked. He doesn't like being laughed at. Mike was trying to pick a fight with a bunch of hard-drinking bikers who got a kick out of a kid thinking he could intrude on their turf."

The teen was lucky he hadn't gotten pulverized.

"I was hauling him out when I saw Lisa." He swallowed visibly and leaned back against his own car, as if his legs had weakened. "She was dancing on top of the pool table. Moving like . . . like she was, you know, wanting to have sex with any guy there. I asked her to leave and she just laughed at me. So I pulled her down."

"Bet that didn't make her happy."

"No. She scratched me, kicked me. Told me to mind my own business." His voice lowered, thickened. "Told me she was sick of being around somebody who didn't know how to have any fun and to leave her the hell alone." Closing his eyes, almost whispering now, he added, "It wasn't until after I left that I realized she was crying when she said it."

"But you did leave."

He nodded miserably. "Yeah. I took Mike home, then drove around for a while to try to get my thoughts together."

"By yourself?"

Another nod. Stacey hid a frown, wishing Mitch had gone somewhere with lots of witnesses who could give him an alibi.

Did she think he was the Reaper? No way. But she was standing beside an FBI agent who had to be building a case against the guy in his head with every word that came out of Mitch's mouth.

"I didn't want to give up on her, though, especially once I remembered those tears on her face. So I went back."

Oh, hell. "Back to Dick's? What time?"

"I dunno, around closing." He hunched forward, as if physically ill. "The place was crazy and packed. One of the waitresses said Lisa had just left, though she didn't see who she was with. I probably didn't miss her by more than minutes."

More information nobody at Dick's had bothered to volunteer. So much for doing one's civic duty. She could only again surmise that Mitch's position as her chief deputy had kept people's lips glued shut.

"If I'd been there earlier, maybe she wouldn't have left with him." He sounded on the verge of tears. "Maybe I could have stopped her from going with someone bad who wanted to hurt her."

"Going with him?" Dean asked, his tone sharp. "How do you know she voluntarily left with someone?"

Mitch slowly straightened. "Well, I just figured it. That was the last time anybody saw her, and Freed's car was there. She had to have left with someone. Obviously the wrong someone."

He didn't speculate that she'd been taken. Then again, Mitch didn't know anything about the Reaper, or the fact that he forcibly kidnapped his victims.

For all his intelligence and his background, he was still, at heart, a pretty innocent guy. She hoped, for his sake, that he never learned the true details of Lisa's murder. Because, having seen his eyes and heard his voice, she didn't doubt one thing.

He had loved her.

The Reaper had had direct, personalized requests before. He'd been offered bribes, had been accosted right in the middle of his playtime, had fielded personal e-mails filled with promises and pleas.

He'd never accepted.

The thrill of what he did was in the control it gave

him. Other than someone else deciding how he would
do what he did, the rest was in his hands. And the how
was incidental. Only the doing mattered. Only the blood.
The anguish. The terror. The pain.

All that was in his control. As was the identity of his
prey.

So when others had reached out, offering to pay him
to kill a man, or a brunette, or a specific person someone wanted out of the way, he had always refused. He
wouldn't be manipulated or controlled. He would never
sacrifice the pleasure he gained from killing his favored
victims to please anyone else.

At least, he thought he wouldn't. Now he wasn't so
sure. He'd never foreseen a situation like this one, where
he might actually be forced to do so.

He'd had enough of being forced. Enough of being
powerless. And the rage over Warren Lee trying to make
him that way again had him ready to erupt in ferocious
retribution.

He was a hand grenade with the pin pulled. Ready to
land right in Lee's lap.

"Calm. Control," he whispered, feeling his heart race
and his breath grow hot.

He counted to ten, forcing the helpless anger down
into his gut, where it had lived, seethed, and taken root
years and years ago. He could get through this. Even if
he had to, just once, go out of his way to accommodate
someone else's desires.

Possibly sick desires. One potential client, a big fan
from the start, had been particularly interested in choosing a very specific type of victim. He not only wanted to
name the age, sex, and physical description; he'd insisted
on seeing certain acts. Followed by the brand of death
he preferred.

And he'd offered an absolute fortune to see it done.

The very idea had repulsed the Reaper. He wasn't some sicko like that guy. Talk about weird.

The offers had been easy to refuse because, before, it hadn't mattered. The money hadn't mattered. He had certain needs. The auctions and drive-in ticket prices allowed him to meet them. All was well.

Now, though, with Warren Lee evading him, hiding out in his fenced fortress, almost certainly armed and watching every one of his security monitors around the clock, he wasn't going to be able to meet them much longer.

It was Wednesday night. He had three more days to come up with the cash to pay Lee's blackmail. And so far, his efforts to get at the man by lurking in the tree-studded forest along his property in the middle of the night had been useless.

Spotting Lee's security cameras hadn't proved a challenge. He'd easily avoided that danger. Hidden by the thick woods of the state park, he stayed out of visual range, only a shadow drifting through the softly blowing leaves. Sitting high in a tree overlooking Lee's land, he kept his night-vision binoculars close to his face, watching for any movement, any sign of life. Lee hadn't come out of his house on the previous two nights. That didn't mean he wouldn't tonight.

He only needed one shot. Just one.

But he doubted he'd get it. Warren Lee knew who he was. Lee also, therefore, knew he was up against someone who knew how to handle a gun. He couldn't be stupid enough to think he could threaten blackmail and not face retribution.

Then again, people were stupid.

He could have taken out the security cameras and gone in for a frontal assault. But Lee would be expecting that. The moment security went down, he would go on high alert. The vet supposedly had weapons that would make a terrorist jealous.

No, this was his only option, short of staking out Lee's driveway by day, following him, and forcing him off the road somewhere. But the potential to get caught was much too great. He had to control the situation. He had to be in charge of the where and when.

Here. And soon.

"You won't come out in the darkness. But I'll stay here until morning if I have to," he whispered, his lips barely moving.

In daylight, the risk of exposure would be great. With the coming of dawn, one of the park guards or some family on a campout could spot him or his truck, which he'd pulled off the road into a well-hidden clearing. They might hear a shot and come to investigate. Or they might just see him driving out of the park and remember his face or his vehicle.

The sheriff and the FBI had already been nosing around out here. If Lee turned up dead, they'd immediately connect the cases. Any chance sighting by a witness could screw him up. He needed to avoid being seen at all costs.

Still, he had to try.

It wasn't that he couldn't earn the money to pay Lee off, as disgusting as he found the idea. He just wanted the satisfaction of blowing away the man who'd blackmailed him. "Blowing away isn't good enough," he told the night. "What I wouldn't give to show you what drawing and quartering is like. Let you watch while your guts spill out."

Nice fantasy. But there was no time.

He had tonight, just this final night. Because if he was going to have to come up with the money, the wheels had to be set in motion by tomorrow. He needed to advertise, get things rolling. After that, things would be tight.

Thursday, the auction.

Friday, the kill.

Saturday, the payoff.

And he'd get his revenge on Warren Lee sometime afterward.

It could work. But he hoped it didn't have to go down that way. He'd much rather deal with the man right *now*.

Which was why he settled more comfortably into the crook of the limbs, unblinking, relentless, with the binoculars at his eyes and the scoped rifle in his hands.

Chapter 13

Lily had made a promise to her boss that she would remain focused on the Reaper case until the murderer was caught. And she meant to keep that promise.

That didn't mean she couldn't begin to pave the way toward catching the online sexual predator who haunted her dreams almost as much as the Reaper did. While she'd spent nearly every hour racking her brain, trying to figure out why there was no money trail from the several online auctions the unsub had held, she'd also made a few phone calls.

Including one to the special agent who'd investigated her nephew's murder.

Knowing her history, the head of the other CAT had tried to refuse her help. She'd remained calm, pointed out all the advantages. And finally, considering she was already hip-deep in the Playground and knew everything about the place, he'd relented.

She hoped they caught Lovesprettyboys soon. But if they didn't, if he was still out there once the Reaper had been stopped, she would be part of the team going after him.

It wasn't justice for little Zach. Or for her sister. But it was something.

"Oh, my God," she heard Brandon mutter from the desk beside hers on Thursday morning.

She immediately swung around in her chair, wondering what had instilled that note of shock in his voice. His usually exuberant mood had disappeared earlier this week, after what had probably been their fifth eighteen-hour workday in a row. Now they were both stretched to the breaking point, frazzled and desperate to help Blackstone and the others.

"What is it?"

"I don't believe this."

She slid her chair over next to his, looking at his monitor, not sure she wanted to see. Fortunately, there was no hideous video of a murder on display. Just a cyber sign in Satan's Playground. But it completely stopped her heart.

"Another one?" she whispered, utterly horrified. "Already?"

He nodded, speechless.

"My God. It hasn't even been a week."

"He's out of control. Accelerating wildly."

The Reaper was ready to kill again. His ostentatious sign outside the "town hall" where he held his auctions said he was hosting another one. In mere hours.

Lily's stomach tightened, and she pressed her fisted hand against it, trying to will away the emotion, the revulsion. The panic.

Taking a deep breath, she got her mind back into the game. She examined the screen again, focusing on the cyber billboard. Reading it closely, she leaned in to read the small print at the bottom.

"What does that mean? That line about it being special. About getting real?" Because if the monster hadn't been real enough already, she didn't even want to think about the further horrors he might conjure up.

Brandon frowned, obviously puzzled by it, too. "We'd better call Wyatt."

Lily reached for the phone on Brandon's desk, quickly dialing their boss, who was right down the hall.

He was in their office less than sixty seconds later, pale and tense, visibly exhausted. And equally as stunned. "Something's wrong. He's getting sloppy and far too ambitious. He's been careful until now; he must know we're onto him."

"Impossible," Brandon said. "Lily and I have covered our tracks; they don't know we're watching."

"Brandon's right," she said, meaning it. "We've been bouncing off servers all over the country, revolving IPs every single time either of us goes in. We're piggybacking on long-existing members, leaving no footprints that we were there. No way do they know we're as deep inside as we are."

That would be very deep. Brandon had been watching every move the cyber Reaper made, going back into the site's history to trace every interaction he had with other members: who he was "friends" with, who he'd purchased things from, who his victims had been, and where he lived in that incredibly detailed imaginary world.

Lily, meanwhile, was following the spiderweb-thin thread from each auction, which she hoped would lead her to the money and its final recipient.

"He knows," Wyatt explained, "because he knows we're looking for the first victim's body."

"Someone in that town . . ." Lily murmured.

"Yes."

The scrolling red line running across the bottom of the sign had been repeating itself over the past few minutes, the word *special* flashing out its message like a dark, evil heartbeat. Now, though, it changed.

All three of them leaned closer, reading the text. *New experience! Never before witnessed! All restraints are off!*

"Like the guy ever restrained himself before?" Brandon muttered.

You wanted more? You're going to get it. For the right price, you get the how and *the* who. *But be ready to pay; this one won't come cheap. Qualified bidders only.*

No credit.

"He's playing. Having a great time for himself," Brandon said. "Writing his own ads, like he's selling some damned piece of real estate. No credit, for God's sake."

No credit. Lily let the words replay in her head, trying to untwist those spiderwebs that led in so many different directions, and find a clear path to the unsub.

Wyatt, who'd been standing behind them, watching and deep in thought, suddenly spun around and thrust his hand against the door, sending it flying closed with a loud crack. His hard, lean form shook, and anger consumed his handsome face. "Damn him. Damn him."

She'd never seen him lose control. Never heard him raise his voice. Never witnessed a personal reaction from the man at all; he was always calm, reasonable, and in control. Now he looked ready to hurt someone.

"When?" he snapped.

Obviously just as shocked by their boss's out-of-character display, Brandon kept his voice low. "He posted it at around eight a.m. our time, and said within hours."

Lily had a thought. "We could . . ."

"What?"

Swallowing, still unused to this side of him, she said, "We could try to interfere with the auction, somehow disable the site temporarily to prevent it from happening."

"Without them knowing why?"

She exchanged a quick look with Brandon, who said

nothing. "We could try exploiting their security patches; they might be outdated. Or DNS poisoning."

"Oh, that's subtle," Brandon said.

"We can try," she insisted, then turned back to Wyatt, knowing he was the one who would have to be convinced. "There are ways to take it offline and make it look like just a random technical difficulty."

"Which, even if it worked," Brandon pointed out, "would merely postpone things."

"Giving us a little more time to find him," Lily argued.

Brandon nodded, conceding the point, then made another one. "He's never let anyone choose the victim before. If the Reaper means the winner can be specific about who he wants killed, maybe we could catch him by staking out the intended victim."

Wyatt's jaw clenched, and his dark blue eyes glistened with frustration. "We'd never find out who it is in time. We haven't been able to trace a single dollar to this guy going back a year and a half. You really think we're going to be able to intercept communications between the Reaper and the winner to get the name of the victim in a matter of hours?"

Lily glanced down, murmuring, "I'm sorry."

"Save it. We don't have time."

She took no offense. The man couldn't possibly be any more stressed. She found it amazing that he was still able to function, given everything this case had done to the team. They'd put in long days; he'd put in longer ones. They'd dug deep to find creative strategies for catching this guy; he'd dug deeper. Plus Wyatt had the added strain of being jerked around on the puppet strings held by supervisors who probably wouldn't even care that more victims would die, as long as Wyatt was humiliated.

Oh, yeah, everybody knew. And the more she worked

with the man and his team, the more she resented it. Wyatt was the kind of agent everybody wanted to be, and the kind everybody wanted to work for. Including Lily.

"So what are we going to do?" she asked, her heart racing as she remembered the team being in this position less than one week before.

Then, the consequences had proved horrific for a teenage girl.

Would they have to sit back and let this vicious psychopath take some other unsuspecting victim and extinguish her life?

Wyatt hesitated, considering. Then he yanked open the door, snapped, "Take it down. Take the whole goddamned site down," and stalked out.

Dean was on his way back to Hope Valley before noon on Thursday. Knowing the Reaper intended to host another auction so quickly had put the entire team on high alert. They were counting on Brandon and Lily to find a way to get the site offline for at least a day so they could try to find the man and stop him.

Their failure didn't bear thinking about. Especially because signs pointed to the unsub spinning out of control. "It's too soon," he muttered, alone in his car. Serial killers were never so deadly as when they began to melt down and decided they had nothing to lose by giving in to their darkest urges as many times as possible.

Something had spooked the unsub. Which just convinced Dean even more that the Reaper lived in Hope Valley and knew the FBI had been all over the town last weekend.

He dreaded telling Stacey. She had no idea the stakes had increased so dramatically, and he wanted to relay the news in person. Considering she had probably been making herself bleary-eyed watching the surveillance footage from the mall every waking hour since he'd left her yesterday morning, he didn't expect to find her in the mood to receive more bad news.

She can take it. She's a pro.

Yes, she was. A pro who was too good to be wasting herself in a job that would never fulfill her. He understood her original choices; he just thought it was time for her to reevaluate them. Not that he could say that to her. The lines on their sort-of relationship were carefully drawn. If he tried to go there, he had the feeling she'd shut him down completely.

Maybe later, when this was all over. *God, please let it be over.*

They had hours now, not days. So, not wanting to waste time tracking her down, he called her when he hit town. To his surprise, she told him she was at home.

One thing was sure: Their reunion at her door would not be as sensual as their good-bye had been yesterday morning. After spending Tuesday night in her bed, making love to her the way he'd wanted to Saturday, it had taken pure will to walk away again. With the exception of the two hours he'd spent with Jared last night, he'd wanted to be nowhere but back here.

Not that he was about to tell her that. Stacey had made it pretty clear Saturday night that they were having a fling. He didn't think she'd be happy if he told her that last night, before falling asleep, he'd mentally replayed every minute of the night before. That sounded like a little more than she was bargaining for. Hell, it was more than he was bargaining for.

"Hi," she said when she opened the door to him. She wore her uniform, though her blouse was unbuttoned to her collarbone. Her hair was piled loosely on her head, her face pale, as if she'd been dealing with a headache.

He meant to keep it cool and professional during work hours, but something within him demanded the right to touch her, to taste her. Stepping inside, he didn't even say hello before reaching for her. He tugged her close, wrapping his arms around her.

Their mouths met in a slow, warm kiss that demanded nothing yet promised the world. The kind only two people who'd shared incredible intimacies, and knew how good things could be, were able to fully savor. She tasted so sweet, and felt so right in his arms, that he couldn't even remember why he'd bargained for anything but the real deal with this amazing woman.

Though their lips finally parted, they stayed close, her forehead against his. In silence, they exchanged warm exhalations, and through their clothes he felt the pounding of her heart begin to slow. His, too.

They put off the world for one more moment, reconnecting before having to dive back into the nightmare. Dean allowed himself to enjoy the warmth of her skin and the curves and valleys of her body pressed so tightly against his before regretfully letting her go. "I've been wanting to do that since I left yesterday," he admitted.

She hesitated for a split second, then came clean, too. "So have I."

So much for just sex and nothing more. Because there was something else here, whether either one of them was ready to admit it out loud or not.

"How'd your evening with Jared go last night?"

He cracked his first real smile of the day. "Great. I took your suggestion and took him to one of those pizza places with the big dancing puppet dudes and the indoor play place. The kid loved it."

She rolled her eyes. "How have you lived thirty-four years of your life without ever hearing of Chuck E. Cheese?"

"Hard to believe, huh? Anyway, thanks. I was Dad of the Year last night."

"I'm glad," she said softly, her smile slowly fading.

His did, too. They'd finished with the personal stuff, the warmth. Now it was back to the cold darkness of the case both of them desperately wanted to solve.

"Working at home today?"

"I tried doing it at the office this morning, but couldn't get a moment's peace. Our esteemed mayor has finally heard about what's going on and has demanded to be part of the investigation into Lisa's murder."

Gawking, he could only stare at her.

"I know, it's ridiculous, and I told him so. He's an arrogant blowhard, and I guarantee you what he's most interested in is getting credit and attention once this thing is solved."

"Politicians."

"Yeah. Anyway, he informed me that the only reason he wasn't actively out there searching with 'his' deputies was because he and the first lady are going out of town for a day or two. Must be time for her latest face-lift."

That told him everything he needed to know about Hope Valley's mayor and his wife. "Hopefully by the time they get back, this will all be over with."

"Hear, hear." She quickly got serious again. "So tell me what's going on. I didn't expect you back here in the middle of the day. I could hear it in your voice that something else has happened."

Something had happened, all right. He filled her in quickly and concisely.

"Oh, my God," she whispered. "Already?"

"Yes. Have you gotten anywhere with the tapes?"

She ran a frustrated hand through her hair, sending it spilling from its loose bun to fall against her cheeks. *Beautiful.* "My eyes feel like they're about to fall out and my head is pounding. Considering all the different vantage points of the cameras, it took me all day and long into the night to get through one twelve-hour period at the mall."

They had a week's worth of video to go through. This would never work. "We don't have enough time to go through them all."

"You have a plan B?"

He had several, starting with conducting more interviews. But they could take one more shot at the surveillance video first. "I might. Show me."

"In here." She led him to the kitchen, where she'd set up her laptop. The picture on the screen had been paused in the middle of a shopping day, with harried, bag-laden shoppers and teenage mall rats armed with Daddy's credit cards filling the screen.

"Let's tackle this more effectively. I have the victim's work schedule. Assuming he had an idea of when she would be there and wanted to keep an eye on her, why don't we focus in on those times first. She worked only four shifts in the week before her death, ranging from four to six hours."

She scooted a chair around so they could both easily see the screen, then gestured for him to sit. "There are a dozen views of the mall in these files. We could narrow it further and focus on the ones closest to her store. If he went to the trouble of driving up there, he'd want to actually see her, wouldn't he?"

"One would think."

"From what I've figured out, you can select which camera views to watch and split the screen. Might be quicker if we include three views: the store, the closest mall entrance, and the nearest parking lot. I'll have a better shot at recognizing someone, obviously, but you can focus on the exteriors and let me know if a lone man is in the frame."

"You're good at this," he said. Too good to be wasting her time in a little town where the biggest crime she ever dealt with was an occasional red-light runner.

And the occasional serial killer.

Spying the half-empty pot of coffee, he rose and poured himself a cup, then topped off her nearly empty one. He had a feeling they were going to need it.

And over the next two hours, as they watched every second of the tapes, he was proved right.

The longer they watched, the more Dean's irritation built. He tapped his feet on the floor, his fingers on the table. Doing nothing but staring at a computer monitor while a psychopath was preparing to strike again filled him with impotent frustration. Stacey obviously sensed it; she'd grown very quiet, very intent, scooting closer to the screen so she wouldn't miss it if a mosquito had flown by one of the security cameras.

"Why don't we take a quick break?" he finally said. He wasn't used to this kind of inactivity. Sure, he'd conducted stakeouts that had proved boring and fruitless. But this... hell, it felt as if he were napping while a dragon was scooping up his own son.

"No problem. I'm starving.'

"Me, too."

"Cold leftover pizza okay?"

They'd ordered it Tuesday night. And had barely touched it, not wanting to consume anything but each other. Damn, it seemed like a lifetime ago.

"That's fine," he said. He opened his mouth again, about to say how much better he had liked it in bed the other night, when there was a knock on her front door.

Stacey tensed, her eyes shifting in that direction. "I wasn't expecting anyone."

It was the middle of a sunny afternoon in small-town America. Obviously the stress of this case was putting her on edge if the thought of an unexpected visitor had the woman tensing up as though she expected a home invasion. He wished like hell she'd never had to feel that way about the safe haven she'd been clinging to— burying herself in—for the past two years.

"Maybe some kid selling cookies."

She didn't relax. Instead, with quiet, measured steps, she approached the door, her head cocked to the side to peer out through the narrow window beside it.

That was when he realized something was really wrong, and remembered the dog. God, no wonder she was edgy. What an idiot he'd been not to think of it immediately. They hadn't discussed the incident since the other day in the car. With the insanity of the case, he'd let it leave his mind.

"Stacey, wait!" he insisted. "Let me get it."

She'd already reached for the knob. "It's okay," she said. "It's not for me, anyway. It's for you."

She opened the door. On the other side of it stood both Mulrooney and Stokes.

He didn't question how they'd tracked him to Stacey's home, or how they'd gotten the address. Because they both wore twin dark frowns. Nearly tangible tension caused Mulrooney's suit jacket to strain against his stiffened shoulders, and Stokes's jaw appeared carved of granite.

"What is it?"

Mulrooney answered, "They couldn't do it."

"Couldn't do . . ." The truth dawned. "Oh, hell."

Beside him, Stacey brought a shaking hand to her mouth as she figured it out, too.

Mulrooney explained anyway. "Lily and Brandon tried, but they couldn't bring down the site."

"No."

"It's worse."

He didn't ask how it could be worse. He already knew. "The auction?"

"Over."

Over. Mere hours after it had been announced. Not even one week since the last one. The unsub was either insane, desperate, or suicidal. "Meaning we have about twenty-four hours to find this guy and stop him from killing another woman," he said.

Jackie Stokes shook her head. For the first time in the several weeks he'd known her, she appeared less than entirely professional. Her mouth quivered the tiniest bit.

This was bad. Very bad.

"It's not just murder, and it's not a woman," she said. Her voice trailed off, as if she couldn't bring herself to finish.

So Mulrooney did.

"It's rape, torture, and murder. And this time, his target is a child."

Mulrooney and Stokes wanted to immediately go and question Warren Lee. The report they'd requested on registered American-made trucks in the area had given them a long list. Too long. But Warren's name was on it.

Then again, so was her own father's. Her brother's. And Randy's.

Dean was more interested in going back to Dick's and using the new information they had about Mitch's fight with Lisa, and the fact that nobody there had even thought to mention it, to try to get more people talking.

Stacey had other ideas. "You remember me saying my father was the sheriff of this town for twenty years? I want to go see him." She cast a quick glance at Dean. "His arthritis is bad, but his eyesight is very good. And he knows every person who's lived or died in this town since the day he took office."

She didn't really want to drag her father into this, but they needed the help. No way could she and Dean sit here and watch the surveillance videos for the rest of the day. Not if that monster really was going after a child.

Don't think about that.

She couldn't go there, not even in her imagination.

And knowing how Dean felt about his son, she knew he couldn't, either. Not while being so horrifyingly familiar with the kinds of atrocities the Reaper was capable of.

Right after Stokes and Mulrooney had arrived, Dean had excused himself for a minute. She'd lay money he'd called his ex-wife, telling her to keep a close eye on their son today. That was exactly what she would have done, anyway.

Dean saw where she was going. "You think your father would do it?"

"Do what?" Stokes asked.

"Look at the surveillance videos," she explained. "He can watch them. If anybody from Hope Valley shows up, he will spot him."

"Did you ever ask him about the animal abuse?" Dean asked.

Now it was Mulrooney's turn to appear confused. "What?"

Stacey debated on how much to say, how much to reveal without risking exposure of her affair with Dean. She also didn't want to reveal too much to Dean, at least not in front of the others. She hadn't yet told him about the phone calls that had followed up the bloody present on her porch. The one late Sunday, after Tim had left, had been followed by two more on subsequent nights.

She'd almost told Dean on Tuesday in the car, but something had held her back. Maybe because she didn't want to dilute his thinking on the Reaper case. She knew, deep down, that they weren't connected. The caller hadn't been trying to scare her off, or let her know that he was watching. No, this had felt different. Like he just wanted to throw some spite her way, as if she had done him some personal wrong.

As she had told Dean, there were a lot of men around here who disliked her intensely. Considering that the first call had come Sunday night, one day after their visit to Dick's Tavern, it had probably been one of those men who hadn't liked being questioned. Maybe Lester, the weasely little toady.

"Stacey and I were talking about some of the characteristics of known serial killers," Dean told Mulrooney.

"Which we wouldn't have to guess at if that damn profile had come through," Mulrooney said.

Dean crossed his arms. "Still nothing on that?"

"Nope. Get a load of this. Alec Lambert, the agent working on it for Wyatt? Turns out he's some kind of wild card. Got his ass shot in an undercover operation two days ago. The BAU just got around to letting us know."

What else could go wrong?

"They've given the case to somebody else, but the new guy is starting from square one. He won't have anything until at least Monday."

Monday would be too late. And they all knew it.

Stacey cleared her throat, knowing they couldn't waste precious minutes worrying about a profile that wouldn't do them any good, anyway. "I want to ask my dad if he remembers any cases of animal abuse from his years in office. Or even if he got calls about lots of missing pets in one particular neighborhood, that type of thing."

Stokes seemed to have finally regained her equilibrium. "Good idea," she said.

For the first few minutes since the agents had arrived, the other woman had said almost nothing, appearing completely lost in thought. Stacey didn't wonder what she was thinking about. Jackie wore a wedding ring on her left hand. And had proudly talked about her kids the other night.

How do they stand it? How do parents do it?

Stacey had wondered before. She'd probably wonder for the rest of her life.

"So you and I will take the surveillance files to your father and ask him about the animal abuse," Dean said.

"We'll have to bring the laptop and set everything up for him. He has a computer, though it's pretty old. I had wireless Internet hooked up for him, but I don't think he even knows how to sign on to it, and the network's not secured."

Stokes had apparently gotten her head back into the here and very desperate now. "Okay, while you and Dean go talk to the former sheriff, Kyle and I will head out to try to interview a few others, people who were a little friendlier with the victim than we thought?"

The woman exchanged a quick, private look with Dean, which Stacey interpreted immediately. "Deputy Flanagan's arm is really broken."

Dean coughed into his fist, and she nearly smiled. Did he really think she didn't understand the way he thought? Of course he'd continue to suspect Mitch until the other man was definitively ruled out. She would expect nothing less.

And would do nothing else herself.

"You're certain?" he asked.

"The local doctor's a nice old-timer. Realizing we probably suspected him, Mitch went to see him. Doc called me right before you arrived this morning, said he had copies of the X-rays if I wanted to see them. The left arm was broken in two places. He also said he always initials his patients' casts, and the one Mitch is wearing right now is the same one he put on the night the arm was broken. That was a few days before your last victim disappeared. I assume if the Reaper had been favoring one arm, or trying to hide it, you would have noticed something on the tape?"

Nobody answered. The three agents simply stared at one another, their moods growing even darker. Which told Stacey all she ever wanted to know about the details of that last videotaped murder.

"He used both arms," Dean said, his voice low.

Beheaded. God, that poor young girl.

"Thanks," he added. "It looks like you managed to get another suspect crossed off our list."

"So we go to this crazy commando guy's place," Mulrooney said.

Stacey groaned. "Oh, no, please don't go to Warren's. Let me handle him."

"We can't waste any time, Sheriff Rhodes." Mulrooney didn't sound unkind or unappreciative. "I know you've been very helpful, but—"

"This isn't about me not wanting you bigger kids to play in my sandbox," she insisted. "I just know this guy. He's not the Reaper. You'd be wasting your time."

Dean stepped in. "But we both saw the look on his face that day when he came out on his ATV. He knows something."

Yes. He might know something. Still, the last thing any of them could deal with now was an armed standoff with an unstable man who almost certainly was not the killer they sought.

"I agree; he might have information. But there's only one way we're going to get it, and that's if I can get him to come into the office. If a pair of FBI agents step onto his property, Warren will start screaming Waco. He'll threaten to kill anybody who gets too close, and you two will have to end up shooting him to protect yourselves."

"Jeez, and they say big cities have the crazies?" Mulrooney said with a rueful shake of his head. "What do they put in the water around this place? Crack? I mean, you've got serial killers, animal abusers, psycho commandos, abusive stepfathers. Sounds like everyone in Hope Valley is tripping."

It did sound that way, which broke Stacey's heart. Because it just wasn't true. Hope Valley was a good place. A safe place. It was a far cry from the rest of the world. "You're seeing the worst of the worst. There are many more good people here than bad. But we're not exactly out there looking for them, are we?"

"It's not like anybody in law enforcement spends their days tracking down the good guys," said Dean.

"Too bad." Mulrooney snorted. "If you ask me, going after Mr. Rogers beats chasing Jack-the-freakin'-Ripper any day." He and Stokes exchanged a look. "Okay, back to the bar we go."

Stacey thought for a long moment before she opened her mouth, considering what she and Dean had talked about the other night. About the possibilities, the profile. The chance that someone she knew very well might be a monster.

It didn't seem possible. But she couldn't deny it had to be checked out. And since she had to go to her father's, and the other agents needed to fill the time until she could meet back up with them to call Warren in, they were the obvious ones to do the checking. "I have something else you might want to look into," she murmured, not meeting Dean's eye. She bent down and scrawled a name and an address on a piece of paper, handing it to Special Agent Stokes.

"You think this guy could be involved?"

Did she? Did she really? It seemed impossible.

Then again, someone murdering innocent victims and charging people for the privilege of watching it done had seemed completely impossible to her a week ago, too.

"I don't know that I'd call him a suspect," she admitted. "But he was at the bar the night Lisa disappeared. And his background and lifestyle make it at least possible. He's worth a look, anyway."

Dean glanced over Stokes's shoulder at the piece of paper and read the name. He didn't respond with any more than a brief nod. But the gleam in his eyes said he agreed.

Her brother's best pal, Randy Covey, was worth checking out.

Wyatt had known it was a long shot. Brandon and Lily were brilliant at what they did, but knocking off an international Web site when they weren't even certain where it was hosted was a tall order.

But somehow, deep down, he'd expected them to pull it off.

Knowing he'd catch heat, knowing he'd be criticized for risking the whole operation, knowing he'd be blamed if this son of a bitch Reaper went underground and hid in anonymity for the rest of his days, knowing all that, he'd wanted them to succeed.

They hadn't.

They hadn't.

He didn't know who'd been more upset: Brandon because the failure was an insult to his abilities. Or Lily, because she was Lily.

Her reaction would haunt him in days to come. He didn't know if he would ever forgive himself for hiring her in the first place, knowing her vulnerabilities.

Lily had already become almost obsessed with that perverted character who called himself Lovesprettyboys. For the same deviant to win the auction and make his sick choice had almost pulled the legs completely out from under the young agent.

"A boy," he whispered, still not believing it. "He paid to watch someone rape and murder a little boy."

There could have been no worse words for Lily Fletcher to read on that screen. None that would stab straight through her heart as viciously as if she were pierced with one of the scythes the Reaper used so joyfully in Satan's Playground.

He'd tried to talk to her. She'd told him she didn't need to.

He'd tried to send her home. She'd refused to go.

Instead, she'd been in her office with Brandon, each working frantically on their assigned tasks. Brandon tried to monitor any private communication between the killer and his customer. And Lily was trying to find the money exchanged between them.

She'd had no luck before. That didn't mean she would give up. In fact, he now knew she wouldn't give up until both of the real monsters from that virtual world were behind bars.

"Wyatt? Wyatt!" Brandon called from out in the hallway.

He jumped up from behind his desk and hurried out of the office, seeing the younger man rushing toward him. "You've found something?"

Brandon shook his head, turning on his heel and hurrying back down the hallway. "No, it's Lily."

Oh, God. What had she done? What had he done to her? Had her fragile psyche finally cracked under the strain of her family's horror combined with this current one?

He skidded into the office Brandon and Lily shared. His heart pounding and his pulse roaring through his veins, he half expected to see her slumped at her desk.

She wasn't. Instead, she sat upright, her fingers clicking wildly, her nose almost touching the monitor.

"What happened?"

"Shh!"

He remained silent, and so did Brandon, for a long minute or two. Then Lily froze. Her mouth dropped and she jerked so hard her glasses fell off her face. Putting her hands on the edge of her desk, she launched herself backward with a shocked cry, as if she couldn't bear to see whatever it was she'd discovered.

"What?" Brandon knelt beside her. "Tiger Lily, what is it?"

She shook her head, looking up toward the ceiling, as if that held the answers. "I understand now. I see. I followed the spiderweb. Couldn't stop thinking of the way he'd worded it. 'Real.' 'No Credit.'"

"I don't understand, Lily." Wyatt walked over and put a hand on her slender shoulder, hoping the agent hadn't had some kind of mental breakdown. She'd been honest about the psychiatric therapy she'd undergone after her nephew's murder and her sister's suicide. Had today's horrifying discovery pushed her back over the edge?

"I couldn't track the money," she whispered. "Couldn't find it; the trail went nowhere, thin and fragile as a spiderweb."

She was starting to make sense. And his pulse gradually began to slow. "But now? What happened, Lily? Have you tracked it now?"

"No."

Brandon looked up at him, shaking his head. "Maybe we should call someone."

Brandon didn't know. Nobody knew, except Wyatt, that there was no one to call. Lily was completely alone in the world. Her sister and nephew had been her last two surviving family members. Now they were both gone and she had absolutely no one.

"Lily," he murmured, "tell me."

She finally tore her gaze off the ceiling and met his stare directly. "I can find him, Wyatt." The assurance returned. Steel oozed back into her posture, and the weak, haunted woman began to disappear right before his eyes.

"Good," he said, his tone soothing, though he was confused by her mood.

"I can track the auction payment as soon as it's made. Because this time, it will be made."

Brandon slowly rose, obviously realizing his office mate wasn't in the middle of a nervous breakdown. "What are you talking about? He's always gotten paid, except for that very first murder, Lisa Zimmerman's. Why is this one different?"

"Yes. Paid." She pulled her eyes from Wyatt's and looked back at the computer. The screen displayed a sequence of numbers, as well as some odd, coinlike symbols. "Paid in *Faida*."

Wyatt didn't follow.

"It's an old medieval term," she said, her voice growing hard. "It means blood money." She nearly spat the words.

"What are you saying?" Brandon asked, even as Wyatt felt the truth begin to slide into his brain like an ugly, awful black mist. It filled every pore, every cell, and he closed his eyes, not wanting to believe it.

"It's a game," she said with a laugh devoid of anything resembling humor. "All a game, with Faida as the currency, as real as the money on a Monopoly board."

Brandon still appeared confused. Any reasonable person would be. Because the horror, the awfulness of it, was almost beyond comprehension.

"The murders," Wyatt said quietly. "He never got cash for any of them."

"Not a penny." Obviously seeing the still-confused look on Brandon's face, she shook her head and laid it out with bald, horrific bluntness. "Don't you get it? None of the other auctions were payable in dollars or euro or yen or anything tangible. They were strictly Faida." She shook her head in utter disgust.

Brandon lowered himself into his chair, at last getting it. But Lily made it eminently clear anyway.

"He slaughtered those women for credits in this hell-hole of a game. He did it for play money."

Chapter 14

Transferring funds. Real funds. It made him very nervous.

But the Reaper had no choice. He needed the money by Saturday. Though he still hoped to get Warren Lee before the deadline, he had to be prepared for every possibility.

Which meant cash.

Maybe because he'd often wondered whether this day would come, whether he might someday need more money to survive in this, his unhappy life, he had already opened an online account using a stolen name and social. Amazing how easy it was to set up those offshore accounts without ever walking into a bank or having to produce ID. And so easy to find out how to do it on the information highway.

Once he proved he had the kid, his buyer would make a substantial deposit into the foreign account. A few clicks of the keys later, and he'd have it in his real one, ready to be used to pay off one filthy blackmailer.

It could be tracked. Eventually. But only if someone was looking for it.

Nobody was. Nobody knew about him. Because if the feds had infiltrated the Playground, the site would be long gone by now. The administrators were good, better than any dumb-ass FBI agents. They had security layers deeper than anything he'd ever seen, and Satan's Playground would have been nothing but a fond memory if there had been the slightest breach.

No, it wasn't because the Playground had been discovered that the FBI had come around looking for Lisa's body.

It was because of Warren Lee.

He couldn't believe he hadn't figured it out before. The blackmailer hadn't gotten curious about the cops searching the woods near his place. It had been the other way around. Lee must have called in an anonymous tip specifically to jack up the heat for his blackmail plan.

The realization had both comforted and infuriated him. He'd been happy to realize he wouldn't have to give up his playtime. And furious at the manipulation.

"I'm gonna get you, old man," he said, his hands tightening on the steering wheel of his truck.

Yes, discovery might come eventually. He'd deal with it at that time. If his secret activities ever did come to light, and he thought the police really knew anything about Satan's Playground and his alter ego, it wouldn't matter that they could trace it. Because he would never be taken, never tried.

No one would ever lay physical hands on him again.

But that was a long way off, hopefully to be worried about only in the distant future. Now he just had to get through these next few days, as difficult as they were going to be. He had to allow himself to be manipulated one last time.

"And then never again," he told himself as he trolled the playground. A mundane, boring real one. It was small, with just a few creaky swings and a jungle gym, in a small town between home and Leesburg.

He'd swung past it twice in the past hour. Only twice.

He couldn't afford to be remembered once a kid went missing. This was riskier than anything he'd ever done. He was much too close to home for his liking. But he had no time and no choice.

Funny how fate favored him. Because while he usually never had any peace unless he locked himself away and disappeared into his Playground, the house would be empty for at least the next few days. Meaning he could do what he had to do in private, with no chance of being caught. He'd snatch a boy, drug him, take him home, and spirit him down into the basement. Into his private rooms.

No one around to see. No one around to hear. No one around to stop him.

It was perfect. As if some entity were offering silent approval and support for what he did and wanted him to continue.

He just had to find the kid.

So far he'd seen no prospects. People weren't very trusting with their children these days. Mothers sat on benches overlooking the park, feeding slobbery babies and calling out, "Be careful," to their brats. Part of him wanted to move on to the next viable location for finding a vulnerable victim, an arcade or a public swimming pool or a park.

Another part wanted to drive right the fuck over to Warren Lee's house and put a bullet in the back of his head.

It was a flip of a coin. Whichever came first. Kill a kid. Kill a blackmailer.

No-brainer, really. But he couldn't risk failing. He had to cover both bases.

He'd swallowed his distaste for the whole thing, knowing it had to be done. That didn't mean he was going to enjoy it. Or even that he planned to do everything the buyer wanted. He wasn't raping a little boy. Only a sick weirdo would do something like that.

He'd make it look good for the camera, but he'd show mercy. He'd do something to the kid so he wouldn't feel too much pain. And he'd kill him quickly.

After all, he wasn't a monster.

Dean liked Stacey's father. The older man was only in his early sixties, with a youthful face and attitude. But the swelling of his joints and his slow movements told the entire story of his early retirement.

He'd been a lawman for many years, though—a deputy for his own father, then sheriff—and still thought like one. So not only did he immediately offer to watch every inch of footage from the mall surveillance cameras; he also proved able to help in another way.

Like any really good cop, the man had kept journals throughout his years in office. He still had them. "I can't promise anything," he told both Dean and Stacey as they set up her laptop on his kitchen table. "But I'll dig them out and glance through them, see if I noted any cases of animal abuse. Just because I can't remember it off the top of my head doesn't mean it didn't happen." He shook his head sadly and told Dean, "I recently lost my dog, you know. I can't imagine somebody hurting a defenseless animal on purpose."

Dean kept his mouth shut, understanding Stacey's reason for keeping the truth to herself. For her sake, and for Mr. Rhodes's, he hoped she never had to tell him.

Something else they didn't tell him: that a child's life was in danger. Neither of them wanted to add to the pressure. Though Mr. Rhodes was smart and capable, his daughter appeared to want to shield him, as if she'd assumed the role of protective parent because of his physical ailments.

The man's slight smile, and the occasional roll of his eyes, said he knew it. And that he put up with it.

Stacey might think she was fooling everyone with her

hard shell and swagger. But there was a nurturing, loving woman inside her. He'd felt it. He'd seen it.

He also knew why she tried to hide it.

It wasn't just her job, a woman as sheriff. Stacey's attitude was another means of self-protection, of getting over the emotional meltdown he suspected she'd experienced after Virginia Tech. She hadn't talked about it; she hadn't needed to. He'd watched the news coverage, seen the photographs, read the stories. The VSP hadn't been first responders, but they'd been on campus within hours of the attack.

She'd seen things that would haunt any sane person. And now, thanks to this Reaper case, she'd seen even more.

The campus shooting had prompted her decision to come back here. Her need to keep anyone from getting too close, her lone-wolf lifestyle, her refusal to think about having kids someday, all related to the way she boxed up her emotions and hid them away. That she'd finally begun to let them out with the crying jag in his arms Saturday night hinted she might be ready to deal with them.

He just wondered if she'd let him stick around long enough to be there when she let it all go and decided to move on with her life.

He hoped so. It was crazy to feel this way after only a week. But, God, he hoped so. Because he had the feeling that, with her, he could move on with his own, too.

"You really think I'll see somebody from Hope Valley on here?" Mr. Rhodes asked. Sitting at the table, he watched Stacey open the video file and cue it forward to the point where they'd left off.

"I don't know, sir. There's a chance."

"This is shopping mall footage," he said, nodding at the screen. His voice lowering, he asked, "Is this related to that little Maryland girl whose body they found in the woods Monday?"

Stacey had told him the bare bones, but she obviously hadn't told her father everything. Just as she'd promised.

Dean nodded once.

The older man shook his head in visible disgust. "I'll prop my eyes open with toothpicks if I have to. I promise I won't miss a face."

"Thanks, Dad," Stacey said, bending to kiss his cheek. "Normally I'd say to take it slow and easy and don't overdo it. But today . . ."

He patted her hand. "I'll overdo it as carefully as I can."

Thanking him as well, Dean said good-bye to the other man and walked out of the house, standing on the front porch. Stacey came out a moment later.

"So this is where you grew up, huh?" he asked, staring across the rolling green lawn. The huge trees, a pond at the base of a nearby hill, and the old red barn in the distance gave the whole place the feeling of an Americana painting.

Maybe it suited her father. Maybe it had once suited her. But not anymore.

"Yes. My grandparents built it." She walked down the stairs, tugging her keys out of her pocket. "I couldn't wait to live anywhere else when I was a kid."

"It's rustic," he said as they got into her squad car.

"That it is."

"You're not."

She had just put the key into the ignition, but paused and glanced over at him. "What?"

"This isn't you. You might have stepped right back into the lifestyle when you came back here, but here's not where you belong."

Her jaw flexed and she jerked her head forward. She pushed the ignition key a little too hard, grinding the engine, then thrust into reverse and backed up. "What do you know about where I belong?" she asked as she pulled out of the long driveway.

He didn't answer, instead countering with a question of his own. "Are you telling me that when this is all over you'll be perfectly happy going back to writing speeding tickets and reassuring old ladies who hear raccoons in their garbage cans at night?"

Her lips quirked the tiniest bit. But she was too stubborn to admit he was right. Not yet, at least. She was intuitive and bright, but never accepted anything at face value. She looked at every side of things before conceding a point. Which was, honestly, an asset in their profession.

He said nothing more. He didn't need to. She'd look at all sides and concede the point. Sooner or later.

Or else kick his ass to the curb for trying to force her to do so before she was ready.

Another voice interrupted the silence in the car. "All units."

She glanced at him, then grabbed her radio handset, fumbling it a little, as if unused to getting calls. Judging by what he'd seen of the town, he understood why.

"I'm here, Connie; come back."

"We've got reports of shots fired, Sheriff. Repeat, shots fired."

Any hint of a smile left her mouth, and the color drained out of her face as if someone had pulled a plug on it. *Shots fired. Damn.* He could only imagine when she had last heard that call.

"The address?" Stacey barked, immediately alert and ready. No more hesitating, no more fumbling; she was all business.

The dispatcher gave her the information. The street

name sounded a little familiar, though he couldn't immediately say why.

Stacey, however, obviously knew it. Her mouth dropped in shock. "Oh, my God," she whispered.

Then she floored it.

Since they'd been at her father's place, a couple of miles outside of town, they weren't the first to arrive. She spotted two other squad cars in the driveway, lights still flashing. From up the street came the sound of another siren: the volunteer ambulance crew. Per the last radio call, there was at least one known casualty.

Leaping out of the car immediately after she swung onto the lawn, she didn't even pause to shut the door. Nor did she wait for Dean, who came on her heels. Her fingers unsnapped her holster as she ran, her Glock in her hand as she darted toward the porch, her eyes shifting as she tried to spot her men.

No one was outside. The front door stood open. All was deadly silent, the late afternoon saturated in tension.

Then someone spoke. "Please just put it down. Put the gun down. You know you don't want to do this."

Mitch Flanagan. He stood right inside the open door, his own weapon drawn, his bad arm down at his side. He'd come back on duty a day early, and she thanked God for it. Other than herself, she couldn't imagine anyone better to have arrived first. Especially because right beside him was another deputy, a rookie named Joanie who'd been on the job for less than a year. Joanie's weapon was also drawn, but she looked a whole lot more nervous.

They both faced someone inside the house. Stacey strongly suspected she knew who that someone was.

Quietly stepping onto the porch, she caught Mitch's eye. He glanced back and forth between her and the armed perp, murmuring, "The sheriff's here. Why don't you let her come in? You can talk to her. See how we can fix this situation."

He was good. Calm and reasonable, he tried to soothe the shooter, gain his trust. Which immediately tipped her off more to what was going on. Whoever the perpetrator was, his weapon was not aimed at her deputies. Because Mitch wouldn't be trying to talk to him; he'd already have shot to kill. He was too damn good not to.

Suicide. She knew before she stepped into the door that whoever had fired the shots now had a gun to his own head. And she could imagine why.

Then she stepped inside, saw who it was, and realized she'd been wrong. Totally, horribly wrong.

The body lay on the floor a few feet from her deputies, inside the living room of the small, shuttered house. He was sprawled on his back, arms and legs splayed.

There could be no question he was dead. Half his face was gone. Blood and brain matter thickly coated the worn carpeting, splatters of it on the walls and on the small shepherd and shepherdess figurines on the nearby table. Not to mention the woman sitting beside it.

"Winnie?" she said softly, moving inside.

She fought to control her shock and mentally readjust to the situation. After hearing the address, she'd been sure that Stan had finally gone too far and killed his wife.

Not this.

Winnie Freed sat on her dingy sofa, motionless and silent. In one hand, she held the same framed picture of her daughter that Dean had commented on last weekend. In the other, a semiautomatic. It was aimed at her own head.

"Please put the gun down. Let's talk about it."

The woman appeared to be in shock. She didn't look up, simply staring at the face of her lost child. Her bottom lip was swollen and bloodied. One of her eyes had been recently blackened; Stacey had no doubt by whom. Streaks on her face indicated that she'd been crying, but now she was calm. Quiet. Looking at the little girl she'd lost, oblivious to the husband she'd killed.

"Winnie, please. Don't do this. Lisa wouldn't want it."

"He hurt her," the woman whispered. "He hurt her over and over and over."

Damn. "You didn't know."

The woman's hand shook, moving closer to her temple. "I didn't want to know."

"You tried to protect her. You told me you took her to the doctor all the time."

"I did." She laughed bitterly. "And I congratulated myself on having such good instincts, because she was physically healthy. But that was because he wasn't beating her with a strap, or was punching her kidneys so the bruises wouldn't show."

She said the words matter-of-factly, as if those occurrences were a regular part of life. For Winnie, they probably had been. At least since she'd married the guy whose head she'd just blown off.

"I went to see him this morning. Doc Taylor."

"After Stan did that to you?" she asked, easing further into the room.

"Yes." Winnie looked up, saw her moving closer, and stiffened.

Stacey froze, then spread her fingers wide on the grip of the Glock. She slowly lowered it, sliding it back in its holster, trying to calm the woman down, remain entirely unthreatening. No way was she going to be responsible for a suicide-by-cop. Not in her town. Not with this woman.

"Stacey . . ." Dean growled in warning.

"It's okay," she insisted. She did not, however, move into the line of sight between her two deputies, or Dean, and the armed woman on the couch. She was sympathetic, not stupid. If Winnie lowered the weapon and even came close to pointing it at her, either Dean or Mitch would take the other woman out without hesitation.

"What did the doc say?" she asked, staying a few feet away.

"He said my Lisa had gotten pregnant when she was fifteen. She came to see him."

Not news to Stacey. But obviously it had been to Lisa's mother.

"Then he told me Stan had been with her and had offered to pay for an abortion."

Son of a bitch.

"Doc thought Stan was being a concerned stepfather." The tears began to roll again. "I knew better right away. He wouldn't have paid for a gallon of water to douse Lisa if she had been on fire."

"What did you do?" She edged closer. One single step.

"I came home. Waited." Her lips curled into a sneer. "He's been off for a couple of days. People at work thought it was odd that he didn't seem to want to stay home with me after the news about Lisa got out."

Another step. Stacey nodded in sympathy, as if the two of them were having a normal conversation. As if Winnie weren't on the verge of taking her own life and Stacey weren't desperate to stop her. "What did he say when you confronted him?" she asked.

"He denied it at first. Then claimed she'd been coming on to him and he was just a poor, weak man."

They had reached critical mass here. Suddenly Stacey realized the implications. If Winnie survived this, anything she said now could prove very important.

"Winnie, I have no doubt Stan beat the daylights out of you and has been for a long time. We'll take pictures of your face. Doc will testify about the years of abuse I suspect you've undergone."

The woman looked at her as though she'd sprouted two heads. "Why should I care?"

Stacey pointed to Lisa's picture. "Because she would care. She loved you and she wouldn't want you doing this." Nor would Lisa want her mother going to prison for the rest of her life for killing the man who'd abused them both for more than a decade. Physically, sexually, emotionally.

Stacey didn't condone murder. But she could honestly see how someone in Winnie's position could snap. And she thought a jury would, too.

"She was my beautiful little girl," the woman whispered, again staring down at the photograph. "I should have been there for her. I didn't do right by her."

"Do right by her now. Live to see her killer caught and prosecuted. Stay alive and fight for justice."

The woman froze.

Sensing she was getting somewhere, Stacey continued. "We're getting closer to finding him, Winnie. I know you want to know who did it. See him put away to rot in a cell for the rest of his miserable life."

She doubted the Reaper would rot in jail for long. He'd killed in at least three states with the death penalty. But she wanted Winnie focused on life. Not death.

"Killing yourself means Stan wins and that he destroyed you both. You know that's the last thing Lisa would want to happen. And it's the last thing you want to happen. Don't give him one more piece of yourself; he took enough while he was alive."

A tear fell off Winnie's face, having ridden the deep lines of sorrow in her cheeks until it dropped onto Lisa's picture. The sadness rolling off the woman was a physical, tangible thing that filled the room, the house. For a long moment, Stacey thought she'd lost her. Because, really, how could Winnie go on? How had any of the parents of those poor college kids gone on?

But, mercifully, she was proved wrong. Finally, after what must have been an eternity of debate in her own head, Winnie slowly—ever so slowly—lowered the gun. And dropped it to the floor.

She was gonna kill that kid.

Having stood at the edge of the campsite and called for Nicholas for the past ten minutes, Tammy Logan was hanging on to her temper by its very last thread. Nicky had already practically ruined this camping trip by fighting with his future stepbrothers, and she'd had to take him to the parking lot and smack his butt. Was it too much to ask for him to keep his mouth shut and not annoy the older boys? Did he have to constantly tag after them, then complain when they rightfully got mad and shoved him away?

Now he'd gone to the park's public restroom, promising to be back within ten minutes for the start of their big soon-to-be-a-family cookout. He'd been gone twenty.

"You spoiled brat," she mumbled.

She'd worked hard to bring her long-term boyfriend, Jerry, around to marriage. They'd gotten engaged a few weeks ago and had decided to take the whole mixed crew on vacation for a trial run. And already, her difficult eight-year-old son had managed to annoy everyone. Including her. If he didn't get his scrawny tail back here soon, she was going to see to it that he couldn't sit down for a week.

"Everything okay?" Jerry asked, walking over to the edge of their campsite after he'd finished firing up the charcoal grill. "Nick's not back yet?"

She took his arm, rubbing against him. "He'll be here soon, babe. Just ran to the restroom."

"You sure you should have let him go alone?" He stared into the woods, frowning.

The cement building that housed the restrooms was

only a quarter mile away. Earlier, when it had been fully light, she'd been able to see its outline through the trees. When Nicky had left, it had been light enough for her to see that bright red ninja backpack he wore, which contained all his "guys," as he called his action figures.

So it was dark now, big honking deal. They were in a national park in western Virginia, for cripes' sake, not in inner-city D.C. "He ain't a baby."

Jerry rubbed his hand against his stubbled jaw. He might not be the handsomest guy in the world, but he was a nice one, and she was lucky to have him. Not every successful plumber would marry a single mom, a cocktail waitress with a son fathered by an ex-con. He'd been good to her, even trying to make friends with Nicky. And had gotten nothing but lip in response.

"Maybe I should send the boys after him."

Oh, perfect. His two sons, twelve and thirteen, already hated the kid. If they came back from their football toss down by the lake and found out they had to go hunting for Nicky because he had decided to throw a tantrum and hide, they weren't going to be very happy. They might complain loudly to their doting dad. Who might change his mind before the wedding.

"Forget it; he'll come back."

Jerry shook his head, not convinced. "It's gotten dark. I think one of us should go look for him."

"You really want to tromp around the woods when all three of the boys are out of sight?" She rubbed against him, trapping his arm against her full breasts. "You sure you don't want to make out a little, future hubby?"

Jerry's smile didn't quite reach his eyes. "Later. Humor me, okay? I'm worried about the boy."

Tammy almost bit her tongue, the desire to let loose an angry rant nearly overwhelming her good sense. For some reason, her fiancé had taken a real liking to Nick. Who the hell knew why. Did she really want him thinking she wasn't quality mother material for his own children?

"You're a good guy," she whispered, kissing his mouth. "I'll go find him."

"We can go together," he said, lifting her fingers to his mouth. Such a gentleman. And definitely a good guy. Way better than she deserved, and she knew it.

Jerry walked away to grab a flashlight and returned a moment later. Taking her hand again, he led her into the woods, which had been bright and cheerful when they'd set up camp several hours ago. Now they were dense and shadowy, the thick leaves overhead completely blocking out the stars that had begun to pop out in the sky.

Cripes. Maybe the kid really had gotten lost. She'd told him to take a flashlight, but hadn't actually checked to make sure he had done it. It had been more like dusk a half hour ago when he'd left. Now the day had quickly dropped straight into night.

"He's okay, right?" she said, feeling a tingle of concern for the first time.

"I'm sure he's fine." But Jerry didn't sound sure.

"There's, like, no grizzly bears around here, are there?"

"In Virginia?" He laughed at her. "Not likely."

Then they walked around the side of the small cement building, and his laughter faded. She followed his stare and saw Nicky's Orioles ball cap lying on the ground. Beside it was his still-lit flashlight, which was rolling an inch or two at a time, pushed by the nighttime breeze. Nearby was a dark circle, then another.

Oil? It took a second for her to process it. Not oil. As the flashlight rolled another inch, rustling across the dead leaves that had drifted onto the cement walk, it sent light across the stains.

Not black. Red.

Tammy started to scream.

Chapter 15

When she had returned to Hope Valley a little more than
two years ago, Stacey had felt sure she'd never have to
process a murder scene again. And she very much wished
she'd been right. Because dealing with the nightmare
that had taken place in the Freeds' drab little house was
something she would happily have forgone.

She had spent the entire evening here, accompanied
by the county medical examiner and a crime scene pro-
cessor from the state. Her own jurisdiction didn't have
the manpower for something like this.

Winnie had been taken to the hospital to be checked
out. She'd been making a strange wheezing sound as
she'd breathed, and Stacey suspected Stan had broken a
rib or two before she'd taken him out. Stacey would have
to head up there in the morning for formal questioning,
and to take the woman into custody. But she'd already
put a call in to the DA in Front Royal and explained
the situation. She doubted Winnie would face murder
charges. Maybe involuntary manslaughter, at most. And
with the extenuating circumstances, she didn't see the
woman actually serving hard time.

Dean and the other two special agents had offered

their assistance in any way possible. She'd refused. They had another job to do, one which she couldn't help them with right now. For all they knew, the Reaper was already out trolling for his victim.

Or worse, had found him.

They had no time to mess around with a local murder, especially one that had literally been solved as soon as it was reported. The proverbial smoking gun in the hand of the abused wife—it didn't get much more open-and-shut than that.

So, accompanied by random professionals who showed up as the evening wore on, she did her job, went through all the motions, as familiar with them as if she dealt with such things on a regular basis. What, she wondered, would Dean think about that?

The things he'd said to her at her dad's place hadn't left her thoughts, returning to echo in her head at odd times throughout the evening. And part of her, the part that resented the hell out of having to watch blood-spatter evidence being taken and Stan Freed's brains being scooped up off the floor, wanted to tell him he was wrong. *Wrong.*

Another part had to wonder. Because while she truly hated that this ugliness had come to the town she'd grown up in, she couldn't deny that it felt good to be doing real police work again. She was energized, her thoughts sharp and direct in a way they hadn't been for a long time. All the haziness, the lazy, laid-back attitude she'd had a little more than a week ago, had been eradicated.

That was a bad thing.

So why was she feeling so alive all of a sudden?

"Violent death," she muttered as she took one last walk through the Freeds' house late in the night. Such sudden, violent death would make anyone reassess what he was doing.

"I'm done here if you are," the young crime scene tech

said as he packed up his evidence kit. He looked around the room and shook his head. "Somebody's going to have a hell of a mess to clean up."

Stacey extended her hand and shook his. "Thanks for all your help."

"Don't mention it. Hope this works out the way it should."

He'd been around for hours and had heard enough to understand the situation. These kinds of things were hard even for law enforcement to deal with. Because while every cop she knew was committed to stopping, and solving, crimes, they were also human. And anyone with an ounce of humanity could look at the barely cognizant, badly beaten Winnie Freed and know she wasn't a cold-blooded murderer.

Desperately wanting to go home and shower, she checked her cell phone as she walked to the car. A blinking signal indicated a message. Dialing, she listened, figuring she'd hear Dean's voice. Instead, she heard her father's.

"Stacey, I heard about what happened and I know you're busy, but . . ." His voice broke, and she'd swear she heard him sniffling. He'd probably been thinking about poor Winnie and her poor daughter. "I need you to come over as soon as you get this."

She didn't like the sound of that.

"And I think you should come alone."

She definitely didn't like the sound of that.

"I've been watching the tapes and I found something. Please just come."

"God, what else?" she asked as she got in the car and drove. Had it really been just seven or eight hours since she'd left his place and come straight here, convinced she was about to find Winnie dead on her own floor?

Life. It was so precarious. So damned unpredictable. In big cities, big colleges, and here.

She shoved that realization away to deal with later.

When she arrived at her father's house, she saw him waiting for her on the porch. He'd stepped out as soon as she'd pulled up, obviously having watched for her.

"Saw your headlights coming up the drive," he called.

Stacey got out, tilting her head from side to side to stretch her aching neck. It was only after she'd reached the front steps and walked into the pool of light thrown off by the fixture by the door that she realized she had Stan's blood on her uniform. Her father looked at it, blanched a little, then beckoned her in.

"What is it?"

He led her into the kitchen. The laptop still sat there. Beside it was a half-eaten plate of spaghetti. Next to that, a nearly empty glass of whiskey.

Dad very rarely drank. And never alone. Fear making her voice rise, she asked again, "What is going on?"

He didn't say anything. Instead, he sat down, turned the computer so the screen faced her, and clicked the play button on the video player. "Watch."

She watched. The scene was like many others she'd witnessed in the hours of surveillance footage. A steady stream of people made their way through the mall, a woman stopping for a hot pretzel in the lower corner of the frame, a couple peering into the window of a jewelry shop on the top.

Then he came into view.

"Oh, my God."

"You see?"

She saw.

"It doesn't mean anything. Just that he was there. You can't think he . . ."

No. She didn't. She couldn't even begin to fathom that he'd had anything to do with the kidnapping and murder of that teenage salesclerk.

But her brother was on that tape. He had been in that mall, a few doors down from the store where the victim worked, only days before the last murder.

"Have you called him?"

Her father shook his head, though the agony in his eyes revealed just how much that had cost him. He loved his son. It must have taken every bit of willpower he had to remain the lawman and not the father.

"I need to call Dean."

"No!"

"Dad, look, neither of us believes for one minute that Tim had anything to do with this. And I am sure we can prove it. There's a lot you don't know about the case. A whole lot. One short search of his apartment and they'll see that he doesn't even own a computer." She hesitated. "Right?"

He shook his head. "Not while he lived here. And not as of the last time I visited him at his place a few weeks ago." More proof that would help her brother. Because whoever the Reaper was, he had a whole lot of Internet knowledge and the time and equipment to use it. Her brother didn't fit that description.

"What's a computer got to do with anything?" her father asked.

"It doesn't matter. The point is, he's not techno-savvy. He's not the man they're looking for. But his being at that mall might mean something, and the FBI needs to know about it. Maybe someone sent him there." She swallowed. "A friend. Maybe someone told him about this girl and asked him to look in on her. It could be just about anything, but we have to find out."

Her father's eyes filled. She'd only ever seen him really cry twice, once when telling Stacey how much she looked like her late mother, and when they'd first visited Tim at the vet hospital after he'd been shipped back from Iraq.

Now he was crying again. "Please. Just wait. Give your brother a day to figure out what this means before you bring in the FBI."

"You don't understand," she said as gently as she could, her own heart breaking as she realized what she had to do. "There's a little boy's life at stake. A child is going to die this weekend if this perpetrator isn't found."

He fell back into his chair, his gnarled hands rising to his face, wiping away his tears. "All right."

Stacey took his hand in hers carefully, lovingly. "He didn't do this. I have no doubt about it. Which makes it a lot easier for me to pick up that phone and call someone who is a very good agent. And a very good, decent man."

Dad looked up, hope in his expression. "You trust him?"

She nodded. "I do. Completely."

Maybe that was nuts, but it was true. She hadn't known Dean long, but she had already opened herself up to him more than she'd ever opened up to another person in her life. And hadn't regretted it for one moment.

"I'm going to make the call. Then you and I are going to back up and watch every second of every camera angle in that mall. There's more to find. Now let's try to find it."

With Stacey unavailable, Dean had hooked back up with Stokes and Mulrooney, who'd been unable to reach Randy Covey. The late afternoon and evening had proved frustratingly futile. They had gone down the list of registered trucks, cross-referencing it with men who'd been at the club, any who had a violent history, any who'd known Lisa.

The list had still been too damned long.

Despite knowing Stacey didn't want them to, they

tried to see Warren Lee. They'd pulled up to the gate at the end of his long driveway and had been greeted by the man's voice through a call box. He'd refused to let them enter. He'd refused to come out. They could do nothing more without a warrant, unless Stacey could talk the man into town, as she'd suggested.

By the end of the day, the frustration was wearing on all of them. He, Stokes, and Mulrooney shared that frustration equally and didn't take it out on one another. There were no egos here; he saw no competition, like he'd sometimes experienced in other agencies. They were completely united in their desire to save some unknown child's life.

Maybe they really were becoming a tight-knit team— something he hadn't been sure would happen when he'd first met his new coworkers a month and a half ago and had realized just how different they all were.

Even the CATs who weren't in town remained active in the investigation. Wyatt had been in constant contact. Lily had apparently discovered something about the way the money was moved and felt sure she'd have new information when the banks opened in the morning.

But they didn't even know that they had until morning.

There was one more interesting development involving Stacey's brother's friend, Mr. Covey. Not hard evidence, but something to keep in mind. Dean was anxious to share it with her. So when he got her call asking him to come alone to her father's house right away, he wasted no time.

She answered the door immediately. "We've got something."

Her voice sounded different. On the phone twenty minutes ago, she'd sounded exhausted, resigned even. Now, despite the paleness of her face and the circles under her eyes, she looked energetic. Keyed up. As though whatever she had, it was big.

"Come in here." She dashed down the short hallway into her father's kitchen, beckoning him to the laptop. Mr. Rhodes stood by the counter, nodding in welcome but saying nothing.

"You've spotted someone on the surveillance video?"

"It's my brother," Stacey explained.

She said it so matter-of-factly, he didn't really have time to process it at first. When the words did hit his brain and sink in, he felt an explosion of emotion. Elation that they might have found their unsub. Desolation at what this could mean for Stacey.

Stacey was clicking the keyboard. "See? There he is. He was in the mall, but he wasn't stalking her."

"Stacey, I know he's your brother . . ."

She threw a hand up, stopping him from speaking. "No, listen, please. Tim told me something a few days ago that explains this." She clicked a window on the surveillance video, splitting the screen to show two camera views. "We'd been looking at the interior, the closest entrance, and the parking lot. We weren't looking behind the store." She tapped the tip of her finger on one side of the screen. "Watch!"

He watched. A semi truck was backed up to a loading ramp, two young men wheeling big, TV-size boxes up it. While they made their second trip, a man rounded the cab from the passenger side.

It was Tim, the brother of the woman he'd come to care so much about. "I see."

"Shh."

Tim, easily identifiable because of his scars, walked to the driver's-side door and waited for the driver to hop down.

That driver was Randy Covey.

"Tim told me he'd been doing a couple of ride-alongs with Randy lately. That's why he was in that mall. He was just a passenger with no say in the destination."

She cued the video ahead a minute, fast-forwarding through the two men having a brief conversation, then Randy pointing toward the mall entrance. Tim went in, appearing a few moments later on the other side of the screen: the interior camera. Wandering to the food court, he ordered something from a fast-food shop. He appeared completely oblivious to everything except grabbing some takeout.

Dean focused on the other half of the screen.

While Tim conducted the errand Randy had sent him on, his good buddy watched the workers finish unloading. When they were done, he shoved a clipboard over to be signed, then waved at them as they disappeared inside. Once the rolling door was closed, he quietly stalked the rear parking lot, peeking into Dumpsters, easing closer to the back employees-only entrances of the stores closest to his rig.

She zoomed in until one sign was legible.

"That's the store where the vic worked," Dean snapped.

"I know."

He reached for his phone, wanting Covey picked up now, but she put a hand on his arm. "One more second."

Covey knocked on a door. A young guy opened it. He and Randy exchanged a few words, both looking around furtively. Cash exchanged hands. Then Covey beckoned the man over to the still-unlocked truck. Pulling a large box from it, he shoved it at the younger man, who dashed toward his store. A minute later, Tim walked out carrying a large fast-food bag. The two of them got into the truck and drove away.

The story the video told was perfectly clear. Randy Covey was stealing from his employer. Skimming off the top, selling electronics to some punk kid looking to pick up a stereo on the cheap. The kid had looked very familiar with the process; it hadn't been the first time.

"You saw, right? Tim was clueless about any of this. At least, as of then. I'm wondering if Randy tried to drag him into it, and that's what bothered him enough to come to my door the other night."

"Could be. And it adds one more piece to the puzzle. Randy could have been doing his side business and staking out his future victims at the same time. Amber might even have bought something off him before she died." It all made sense, especially with what he'd learned today. "Stokes and Mulrooney were able to get a look at the driving logs Covey has turned over to his employers," he told her. "He was on overnight runs on many of the nights the murders occurred, including the last one."

"I still can't believe it," Stacey admitted, "but everything you said the other night about the perpetrator, and what we've learned since, points to him as the Reaper. His background, his job, his history of abandonment, and his mommy issues. He delivers electronics, for heaven's sake. How hard would it be for him to swipe the latest computer or video equipment for his own use?"

From the other side of the kitchen, he heard Mr. Rhodes sigh deeply. "I've known him since he was a boy. He's not violent, sure isn't a genius. I never imagined him doing something like this."

Dean rubbed his jaw, feeling the rough stubble. It seemed like an eternity had passed since he'd shaved at his apartment this morning. Thank God this would be over soon.

Unable to take his eyes off the paused surveillance footage, Dean suddenly wondered about something. "He knew about the cameras," he murmured.

"What?"

"He obviously knew there was a camera positioned to cover that loading dock area and the back door of the store. It was shot out the night Amber was taken."

She followed. "So why would he conduct his side business in view of it?"

Good question. It made no sense.

Maybe Randy hadn't thought anybody would pay attention to his poking around near the Dumpsters, especially if no crime had been reported. But anybody would know the video would be examined after the last murder.

It was the only reason he could think of for Randy's initial carelessness. And he still wasn't one hundred percent convinced. But it was at least possible. They'd know a lot more when they brought the man in for questioning.

"His house is only two miles away," Stacey said.

Dean reached for his phone again. "I want backup." He punched in Mulrooney's number, gave him the information and Covey's address, and told him to bring Stokes and meet them there in fifteen minutes.

Stacey, meanwhile, had made a call of her own. "Mitch and two other deputies who will keep their heads will be en route shortly."

Good. If Randy Covey really was the Reaper, and he realized they were onto him, he could turn ruthlessly violent. With nothing left to lose, he'd have no reason not to.

A few minutes passed, and they both checked their weapons to make sure they were loaded. The tension in the Rhodes house was thick enough to swim in, but Stacey was about as calm and cool as he'd ever seen her. As if now that the end of the nightmare was in sight, she could stop worrying and just take care of business.

Finally, when it was time, they left the house and, by silent agreement, got into Stacey's squad car. They reached the main road and began to pull out onto it when Stacey's ancient, wheezing old radio came to life.

"Sheriff, if you're there, please respond. Over."

They exchanged a glance. "Mitch," she explained before answering.

Mitch said only a few words. But they were disappointing ones. "Randy Covey's not at his house. Over."

She barked a quick response. "Where is he?"

"Somebody called in a few minutes ago. A neighbor of Randy's saw a story on the news and wanted to see if we knew anything about it. I just got off the phone with the state police and they confirmed. Randy was involved in a serious wreck just before dawn somewhere down near Richmond. Over."

Before dawn. Before the Reaper's latest auction?

"He was in surgery for hours, but they think he's going to make it. Over."

Good for Randy. Not good for their case.

Stacey had obviously reached the same conclusion. Because as she slowly returned the radio handset to the dash, her hand shook. "I was so sure. . . ."

"Me, too. But it's not true. Covey's not the Reaper."

Really, he was doing the kid a favor.

Watching the unconscious boy as he lay on a cot the Reaper had set up in one of his secret rooms, he started to think that what he was going to do to him was for the best. His life was pure shit, his mother a bitch.

A blond bitch. A screeching, abusive, white-trash blond bitch.

He had heard what she'd said to the boy, Nicky, in the parking lot of the campground. He'd seen her hit him. Yeah, the kid was better off dead than growing up with that woman.

It had been easy to watch for his chance, sitting in his truck up on the ridge above the parking lot close to the family's campsite. Mothers like that never paid attention to their kids. When the boy had set off through the woods for the public restroom, he had simply looped around to the other side of it, made sure nobody else was in there, then waited for Nicky to skip back out.

He hadn't meant to hit him so hard—hard enough to draw blood. But he had needed to knock him unconscious. The kid hadn't been too badly hurt and had come around eventually. Not for long. Forcing Nicky to swallow a Coke with some crushed-up sleeping pills had taken care of that.

Now it was just a matter of waiting for the first half of the money to show up. Then he could finish this. He had plucked the boy from that hard life and, in the morning, would be delivering him from it.

This was merciful compared to what Nicky would experience if he remained with his dirty, filthy mother. So it was all good. What he was going to do was right for everyone.

"And don't you worry," he told the unconscious boy. "I'm not some fag child molester." He wouldn't do the deviant stuff; that was just sick.

Fortunately, the buyer couldn't expect him to actually rape the kid, risking his own exposure on the video. He snorted, wondering if somebody had invented dick identification.

Didn't matter. He wasn't pulling his out. This Lovesprettyboys scum would have to settle for whatever tools he had lying around that he could use on the kid.

But all of that was for the morning. After he had his cash.

"Maybe it won't come to that," he mumbled as he cleaned his rifle, one eye on the cot, watching for any sign of movement. Maybe he could just kill the boy and dump the body, without any of the extra stuff.

There was still the chance he could get Warren Lee. If he didn't have to pay the blackmail money, he would have no need for all that cash. He could waste the boy, offering a rebate or something to the buyer for not doing all the dirty shit, and everything could go back to normal.

After all, it wasn't as though he really needed the bucks for himself. Money in this world meant nothing. It was useless. It wouldn't add rooms to his beautiful dark mansion, which hovered over the Playground like a scavenging bird of prey. It wouldn't pay for more sharp and bloody toys with which to play. Wouldn't help in any way at all in his world.

How he wanted to disappear inside it. To step into the picture like some kind of fantasy movie. He would give just about anything to immerse himself in that life and never come out.

Just about anything.

Exhausted, defeated, and confused, Stacey realized she'd had enough for one day. It was nearly two in the morning; she had slept for no more than a few hours a night for the past week. And her brain didn't want to function anymore.

After they had heard about Randy, she and Dean sat in her squad care for a while, at the end of her dad's driveway. They both called off the reinforcements, then fell silent, not driving forward, not backing up. Before cutting the engines, she opened her window and he did the same. A night breeze washed through the car, floating across her skin, carrying a hint of coolness, a promise of relief from the never-ending summer heat.

The silence deepened. They were utterly still, both looking out the window into the night.

She knew in his mind he was picturing the same things she was. A little boy and a monster. Wishing for the dawn of a new day, when, please God, they could get the financial information they needed to track that monster and save that boy.

For him, it had to be a hundred times worse. Because

he was a father. He had a child to fear for, a child whose loss would surely crush his soul. For the first time, she wondered what the boy looked like. If he was dark haired and dark eyed like Dean. If he shared the stubborn jaw, the hidden sense of humor.

She wondered whether Dean had ever had to pick him up when he had fallen off a bike. If he had cleaned Jared's cuts and wiped his tears and tucked him into bed.

Of course he had. She'd been on one side of his sweet good-night conversation with his son. The love had been clear. There was nothing the amazing man beside her would not do to keep his child, or anyone he cared about, safe from harm.

Stacey could only wonder how, in his profession, he hadn't yet realized that was an impossible goal.

She sniffed.

"You okay?"

In the darkness, his hand reached out for hers. She clasped it, twining her soft fingers between his rougher ones.

She liked his hands. They were masculine and strong, yet, she knew from experience, capable of giving such pleasure. Such eroticism.

And, right now, such tenderness. That hand in the dark was like a lifeline she could cling to, a path through the tangled web of horror and memory and emotion that had buried itself inside her. As if as long as he was holding her hand, she could come out to the other side whole and unscathed.

"I feel like I've known you for a long time," she admitted softly.

"Me, too."

He leaned closer, and it was the most natural thing in the world for her to meet him halfway and rest her head on his shoulder. The feel of a soft kiss brushed on her temple soothed and warmed her. Offered safety and sanity.

Maybe because of that simple caress and the silence disturbed only by the cry of cicadas outside the open window, she was able to speak. Something made her want to try to make him see that her choice to come back here, to stay here, where he was so convinced she didn't belong, wasn't out of fear. But out of grief.

"I was on patrol when the first call came in," she whispered.

He said nothing, but his hand squeezed the tiniest bit.

"The radio traffic was insane. Reports that a student was shot in the dorm, then that the shooter was long gone, then that the school was under attack. Nobody knew what was happening."

He kissed her hair again. And the grip on her hand grew tighter as she kept speaking.

The words came fast now. They had been building for a long time. People knew the basic story, but she'd never shared what it had felt like being there, bearing witness. And once she started to speak, she felt almost unable to stop.

By the time she was finished, her face was wet with tears. No, she wasn't sobbing as she had Saturday night. This was low, deep-down, quiet grief straight from her soul.

At some point in the telling, he'd reached over and physically pulled her off her seat into his lap. Her arms were curled around his shoulders, his around her waist. Her mouth close to his throat, the whispers kept coming.

Until, at last, they were done. She was done.

He had murmured sweet, soothing sounds, holding her close, kissing her face, and wiping away her tears. He never interrupted, never asked unimportant questions.

He didn't offer trite words of comfort about how life went on or how bad he felt for the families.

Instead, between one brush of his lips on her cheek and the next, he whispered four others that were completely unexpected.

"You're not alone anymore."

They drifted into her consciousness, settling down deep inside. The certainty that he meant it filled her with possibility and with wonder. And brought her peace.

She drifted to sleep, her head nestled in the crook of his neck. Only for a few minutes, judging by the time on the clock when she awoke. Still, it was late—after three. And they had to be back on the job in a few hours.

Sitting up, she said, "I guess we should both go get some sleep."

He nodded.

"Do you want to go back to the inn?"

He shook his head.

She didn't realize she'd been holding her breath, waiting for his answer. It rushed out in a gush. "Is that going to be a problem? With Stokes and Mulrooney, I mean?"

"You know, right now, I don't give a damn."

She smiled. He smiled back. And their lips came together in a sweet, tender kiss that soon turned into a deeper, more intimate one. She shifted her head, parting her lips, licking at him with lazy hunger. Dean moved one hand to her back, tracing a slow path up and down her spine. The other moved down to her lap to stroke her with butterfly caresses that had her pulse pounding in anticipation.

"Let's go," she said when the kiss ended.

"Will I be breaking laws if I drive your car?" he asked. "You look so tired."

"I'm not too tired," she pointed out. Somehow, despite all the tension, emotion, and pressure, a low, sultry chuckle spilled from her mouth. "But yes, you drive. My legs are shaking all of a sudden."

He gently slid her off his lap and got out of the car to walk around to the driver's side. Stacey curled up, turning a little to watch him. When he started the car, the dashboard lights sent pools of soft yellow illumination onto him, highlighting the masculine angles of his face and the shapely mouth she'd just been kissing.

"Drive fast, okay?" she said. Because though she needed sleep, she needed him more.

"I don't want to get a ticket." He didn't look over, but she'd bet there was a twinkle in his eye.

True to his word, he drove quickly, not breaking any land records, but not exactly obeying the speed limit, either. She understood the urgency. The confession she'd made, the gentleness and then the sweet hint of passion they'd shared, had them both on edge, needing more, wanting more. Connection. They both hungered for it.

When they reached her house and walked hand in hand to the porch, however, she quickly realized she wouldn't be getting that connection. Not yet, anyway. Shards of broken glass glittered in the ruined window frame beside the front door, and the door was open a few inches.

Her house had been broken into.

God, would this nightmare of a day never end?

"Stace?" he asked, obviously realizing at the same moment that the slim front window had been smashed. Easy enough for someone to reach around and undo the lock. So much for safe, small-town living.

"Damn it," she muttered.

"Shh." He went immediately on alert, pulling his .40-caliber, pushing the unlocked door inward. It made a long, low squeak that seemed to demolish the silence, but probably couldn't be heard any farther than a few feet away. Putting a hand out to stop her from going in, Dean stepped in front of her. "Let me look."

She knew what he was looking for. Steeling herself for the possibility that the same sick, twisted bastard had left her another bloody surprise, inside her house this time, she allowed him to enter first. But she stayed close behind him.

There was no sign of anything wrong. Nothing else appeared broken except the window. As far as she could see in the dim lighting, the living room looked normal, everything in place.

But she suddenly wondered something. Why was there dim lighting?

Light shone down the hall from her bedroom. Not too bright, probably not from the overhead but maybe her bedside lamp. "I didn't leave it on," she whispered.

He nodded, putting a finger across his lips in a gesture for silence.

They crept down the short hallway, tense and alert, both with weapons in upraised hands, like two matching shadows. Honestly, Stacey wasn't sure what she was going to find. Someone lying in wait? Another dead animal? Her belongings scattered or destroyed? Anything was possible.

Anything except what she saw when they entered the bedroom.

A tall, lean man stood beside her bed. He had one hand up to his mouth, making low grunting noises into the small bit of pale pink fabric he held there. Judging by the jumble of items spilling out of the open top drawer of her dresser, she immediately suspected he held her panties.

Swallowing her disgust, she looked down. And almost gagged.

His pants were shoved to his knees and he stood directly above her bed, leaning against it. His other hand was wrapped around a fully erect penis, and he was pumping wildly, obviously intending to spew all over her bedspread.

"You motherfucker," Dean said, sounding not just disgusted but absolutely livid.

The man froze in shock and dropped the panties. Dean leaped, taking the guy down with two sharp blows to the face.

Stacey, meanwhile, couldn't even move. Or say a word. She was too racked with disgust and humiliation at having been violated, even when she hadn't even been at home.

With those emotions came pure shock. Because she'd caught a glimpse of the intruder's face before Dean had beaten him to the floor.

It was Rob Monroe.

Chapter 16

"He's a sick degenerate. Is it possible he's also the Reaper?"

Dean didn't really expect Stacey to answer; he'd been speaking more to himself. The two of them stood in her office back at the station, having hauled in the pervert who'd broken into her house. The guy had protested, screamed about his father the mayor, claimed it was all a mistake, then started crying.

Well, actually, he'd been crying all along. Ever since Dean's first punch had crunched into his cheekbone.

"Is it possible?" she asked. "Sure. Anything's possible, isn't it?" Stacey, who looked so bone-weary she appeared on the verge of dropping, rubbed an exhausted hand over her eyes. "Do I think so? No."

"You know he killed your dad's dog."

"He swears he hit her by accident when he was angry and out looking for me. That he did the rest only after Lady was dead."

"And you believe that?"

She didn't answer, looking as though she really didn't want to know the truth right now. Maybe it was easier to believe that version, and he supposed it was at least possible. Even if it was true, Monroe was one sick bastard.

"I do suspect he's the one who's made some late-night anonymous calls to me this week."

He gawked, not having heard that part before now. "He's obviously unstable."

Judging by the things Monroe said in the back of Stacey's squad car, he had been for a long time. He seemed to think he was in love with her because she'd had the really bad judgment to go out with him once when they were teenagers. He'd been obsessing about her since the day she'd come back to town.

The hateful act with the dog? All about punishing her for being with Dean at the diner.

Tonight's break-in? Simple, unrelenting lust. His parents had gone out of town, the leash was loosened, and he'd been unable to resist his depraved urges. Maybe he'd just come over to spy on her and had taken his shot at stealing her panties when he realized she wasn't home. Who knew what the sick creep had been thinking?

"If he was the Reaper, don't you think he would have just killed me when I pissed him off so much by being with you? Why the stupid, petty games? Why not grab me, take me somewhere, rape me, and slit my throat for his viewing audience?"

Jesus, did he hate hearing those tired, matter-of-fact words coming out of her mouth. "I want to hurt him," he growled, still feeling the black cloud of rage that had enveloped him when he'd seen the man in her room. The thought of what might have happened had he not accompanied Stacey home tonight haunted him. Yes, she could take care of herself. But she was exhausted and vulnerable. Any woman walking in on something like that might be slow to react. Even this incredibly competent one.

His whole body shook, and he clenched his fists,

pounding them on her desk, trying to force the fury away.

"I'm okay," she said softly, putting both her hands over his. "Dean, I'm all right."

Thank God. He couldn't even imagine what he'd do if something happened to her.

He hadn't realized it until now. Yes, he'd said the words to her, told her she wasn't alone. But he hadn't realized until he'd walked into her bedroom and seen the attempted mind-rape that prick Monroe was trying to inflict on her, that he had fallen in love with the woman. Fallen fast, but fallen hard. And he would do anything to keep her from harm.

"I don't think I can stand up straight anymore," she mumbled. Her beautiful face was haggard. Brown, half-moon smudges filled the hollows beneath her eyes.

"Go home," he said. He looked out the window, where dawn had begun to break. "It's almost six."

"You need me."

"I don't need you unconscious and collapsing from sheer exhaustion." Acknowledging that he was on the verge of the same thing, he added, "Come back with me to my room at the inn. We'll both crash for two hours, then get back here around eight and wait for Wyatt to call. He swears Lily's had a major break and should know something this morning. And if she doesn't, we won't waste time. We'll get a warrant and search Monroe's house."

No, he didn't really believe that weak, simpering prick was the Reaper. But it was something to go on, a thin lifeline to continue the investigation.

"I want to go home."

He frowned, hating the thought of her walking back into that house.

"Believe me, I'll be throwing my underwear and my bedding out, but I really need to be in my own place.

Besides, I don't think it would be good for your fellow agents to see me leave your room later."

She had a point. "Okay, I'll come with you, then."

"No, honestly, it's all right. I'm tired, but I'm also horny, and if you come home with me, I'll seduce you so neither one of us gets any sleep."

That didn't sound like such a bad thing. At least, not at any other time. But today, there was too much at stake. "All right, you win. But I do demand a rain check."

"You've got it, and I'll hold you to it."

Their stares met, and for an instant they were both back in the car, wrapped around each other, acknowledging in silence what he, at least, had already acknowledged in his head: They cared about each other. More than cared, on his part. Yet this wasn't the place and certainly wasn't the time to find out if she felt the same way.

"Let me make a couple of calls and then we'll go," she said. "I need to let the DA's office know about Rob so they can wake up a judge and get us a warrant."

He gave her fifteen minutes to make her calls. Then, as the sun rose and morning spilled through the windows, he took her by the arm and led her toward the exit.

"Sheriff?" the deputy at the front desk said.

"What is it, Frank?"

"I got a call a few minutes ago from Mrs. Covey."

Dean tensed. Hours ago, he'd been convinced Randy Covey was the brutal killer who stalked Satan's Playground. Now, even though he knew better, his head still pounded when he heard the name.

"Is there any word on Randy's condition?" she asked.

"He's unconscious, but it sounds like he'll pull through. She said she's been unable to reach Seth. I guess he was out when Mrs. Covey was notified, and she raced away, leaving him a note. He hasn't responded or shown up at the hospital. Now she's worrying herself into fits about him, too."

From the way she had talked about Randy's mother, Dean knew Stacey didn't like the woman. But sympathy for a mother's fear made her nod in understanding. "I'll swing by their place, make sure he's okay, then let him know about his dad."

"Now?" He glanced at his watch. "He's a twenty-year-old kid, and it's not even seven a.m. He's probably dead-to-the-world asleep."

"If the situation weren't urgent, I'd do it later. But Randy is in bad shape. If something had happened to my father, I'd want to know."

Being close to his own father, he completely understood the reasoning.

"Besides, I like Frank and would rather spare him any more frenzied calls from Mrs. Covey. And it's the least I can do, given what we thought."

He dropped a hand on her shoulder. "We thought that for very good reasons."

"I know."

They walked to the squad car, and Dean rode shotgun. He'd left his agency car at her father's house. Since Stacey was going right by it to visit the Coveys, he'd asked her to drop him off so he could retrieve it.

When they got there, he turned to her. "Go home and sleep."

"I'll try."

He reached for the door handle, then turned back with a frown. "Don't spend a lot of time at Covey's. You need to rest."

She put her hand up and made an old scout's-honor sign. "Promise."

Kissing her again, he got out and went to his car. As she turned around to drive straight out the long driveway and he followed, he couldn't tear his attention off the back of her head. He watched the weary droop and noted the tangle of her long hair.

He was worried. Well, he'd been worried for days, but this was something else. His cop's sixth sense tingled, telling him something was off. Something was happening that he didn't know about.

He almost followed her when she pulled into the next driveway, but didn't want to come off as nutty and over-protective. She'd proved more than once that she could handle herself. Could she ever.

Tapping the horn, he waved and kept driving toward town. "Thirty minutes," he told himself, watching in the rearview mirror as her car drove up the long, hilly drive-way to the Coveys'. He'd give her a half hour; then he'd call to make sure she was home.

Because he had the feeling he wouldn't be able to catch one minute of sleep until he knew she was okay.

Stacey watched Dean slow as she turned off the road, and waved him on. She knew he was worried; he'd been as shaken up by that filth Rob Monroe as she had. Later, when she had time, she looked forward to cleaning her home thoroughly, eradicating every trace of the vile man. But she had one more task to fulfill before she could, for at least a couple of hours, give in to her bone-deep weariness.

The Covey house sat at the top of the hill, and as she crested it, she saw Seth's truck parked outside. Wonder-ing if he had just missed his grandmother's note and gone to bed when he'd gotten back home last night, she found a last bit of energy to jog up the front steps of the two-story farmhouse and knock. And knock. And then to pound.

No answer.

Stepping across the creaky wooden planks of the porch, she reached a window, cupped her hands, and peered inside. The living room looked the same as it had since she was a kid. Plastic on the furniture. An old-fashioned upright piano, untouched and unplayed. Fussy and protected and cold, just like Alice Covey.

She returned to the door, knocked again, then walked to the opposite side and looked into the kitchen window. She'd just about decided to give up when she saw movement. A door inside the kitchen was pushed open a few inches, a skeletal hand appearing around the edge of it.

"Seth!" she called, rapping on the glass.

Seth stumbled out from behind that door, shock widening his eyes. His naturally pale face grew one shade paler, which emphasized the harsh red acne scars on his cheeks.

He met her stare through the glass, looking terrified. Jeez, if he was this startled, the kid must have been coming up from his room anyway, not having heard her knock.

"Sorry," she said, speaking loudly. "I need to talk to you. Open up."

His eyes shifted. He was thinking about it. Frozen with indecision.

Which was when she realized how wrong this whole situation felt.

She took a step back from the window. Staring straight ahead, she saw the smear her own face had made on the glass. Saw Seth's dark form move around the kitchen, heading past the window toward the front door. Saw that he was dressed in black from neck to toe, despite the earliness of the hour.

Her heart began to thud, tripping in an unexpected rhythm. Her pulse followed suit, surging through her, really waking her up for what felt like the first time in hours. Her body had gone into instant readiness even though her brain hadn't yet caught up and told her precisely why.

The front door opened a crack. Forcing herself to stay calm, she stepped over.

"What do you want?" Seth asked, his voice gravelly and filled with sleep.

"I need to talk to you. It's about your dad."

He stared, his eyes shifting. Glancing down, he spotted the blood on her khaki uniform pants, which she'd been wearing for twenty-four hours, and his mouth fell open.

"Oh, no, that's . . ." She almost said, *That's not his blood*, but caught herself in time. "Your dad was involved in an accident, but it looks like he's going to pull through."

Silence.

"Seth? Did you hear me?"

"My grandmother left me a note," he mumbled.

"Yes. She called the station this morning because she hadn't heard from you."

Another quick shift of the eyes. Then an explanation. "She didn't leave any number. I figured she wouldn't be able to answer her cell phone inside a hospital."

Plausible. Maybe. But still, how weird that Randy's only son wouldn't have gone right down to see his dad.

"Okay. Well, please do give your grandmother a call." She told the young man the name of the hospital, suggesting he write it down.

"I'll remember." He began to push the door closed.

Stacey reached out and touched him before he could shut it all the way. "Seth, is everything okay?"

His brow pulled down over his eyes and he glared at her hand, visible anger appearing, as quick as it was shocking. "Don't touch me." He swallowed, his Adam's apple bobbing in his thin neck. "You . . . you're dirty."

She let go immediately, seeing the stains on her blouse. Yes, she was a mess. But dirty? He'd said the word with such revulsion.

"I'd better go call Grandmother."

She nodded once, then watched as he shut the door in her face. The loud click of the lock cordially invited her to get the hell off his porch.

Shaking her head in pure confusion, she did so. For some reason, though, as she walked down the steps she found herself unable to face forward; she kept her head turned and edged down sideways.

Something in her didn't want to present her back to that closed door and all those windows. To Seth.

Her instincts screamed in her brain, demanding that she admit why.

And suddenly she did. The shocking possibility took shape and flashed in her head.

Ridiculous. But not impossible.

Her steps slowed as she walked down the driveway, to Seth's covered pickup. An American-made one. Late-model.

She didn't touch it, just peered through the driver's-side window into the cab. Nothing.

Walking to the back, she looked in that window. And saw something that turned her blood to a river of ice.

It was a backpack. A child's ninja-warrior backpack, the type a seven- or eight-year-old boy might like, lay on the floor of the truck. A few boyish toys spilled out of it.

"Oh, fuck," she whispered, slowly backing away from the window, her hand rising to her mouth.

It couldn't be, could it? Seth Covey? Quiet, unassuming, twenty-year-old Seth?

The wheels turned, the gears clicking into place in her head. That night at Dick's, his father had feared his son had been there and had left early. Had he, in truth, seen him or his truck lurking around the tavern?

The video and computer equipment—of course Randy would steal it for his son.

Tim had said Seth used to do the ride-alongs with Randy. Perhaps to the very mall where the last victim had been snatched?

He didn't seem to care about his father's accident, wanting to stay inside his dark, empty home. Quiet, secretive, secluded. Her father's house was the only other one for two miles. Nobody would hear anything while his grandmother and father were out.

The pieces continued to fall into place.

The mother who'd walked out. The grandmother who was so bitter, possibly even abusive. She had hated Randy's teenage wife, Seth's mom, had called her dirty even in the presence of others. Good God, how many times had Seth heard that growing up?

Dirty.

Quiet, soft-spoken Seth who had always been so incredibly bright as a kid. Smarter than anyone else his age, yet had shown no interest in going to college or doing anything with himself. He just wanted to play . . .

"Video games," she whispered.

She darted for her car, yanking the door open, grabbing her phone out of her pocket and the handset off her radio at the same time. She punched in Dean's number, getting his voice mail. "It's me. Get to the Covey house now. It's Seth. I think Seth's the Reaper. And I think he already has a little boy inside the house."

She cut the call, lifted the handset, and put out a call for backup. The deputy handling dispatch promised to get help out there right away, within fifteen minutes at the most.

Not good enough. Seth knew she was here; he was spooked. That child might not have fifteen minutes.

She checked her Glock, got out of the car, and ducked behind Seth's truck, trying to keep out of sight of the house. Front door? Back? Maybe even the Bilco access doors for the basement, just visible on the side of the house?

Before she could decide, she heard a car coming up the driveway. No way could her backup be here so fast.

Only it was. The best damn backup she'd ever seen in her life.

"Stacey!" Dean said as he jumped out of the sedan. Darting over, he joined her behind the truck, both of them instinctively taking cover. "I heard on the radio about a little boy who went missing fifty miles south of here last night. Local yokels tried to handle it themselves and didn't go public for hours."

"You came back to tell me?" she asked, knowing he had to have been almost here when she'd left the phone message.

"That, and I had a bad feeling. I was calling Wyatt to tell him about the report when you called. Couldn't click over in time. Jesus, I just heard your voice mail as I pulled into the driveway and almost had a heart attack until I saw you were okay."

Staying low, she gestured toward the rear window of the truck.

He glanced in and saw. Tension sizzled off his hard form as he growled, "The description of the kid mentioned that backpack."

"That's called probable cause."

"Damn right it is."

They both peered around the side of the truck at the house. "He came up from the basement. The window on the east side goes into the kitchen; basement door is about six feet from it, on the right."

"Got it."

With matched gaits, they darted toward the house, staying low. They certainly wouldn't fool Seth into a sense of security if he looked out the window and saw the vehicles. But he might not be expecting them to go on the offensive so soon. Especially not just the two of them.

If they were lucky, he hadn't looked outside. He might not even know Dean was here.

Reaching the end of the porch, they climbed up over the rails onto it, avoiding the steps. With weapons upraised, they positioned themselves on either side of the window. Dean silently counted down, then jabbed his elbow sharply toward the center pane just below the lock. Glass tinkled, but the blow was precise and only the one pane broke.

He reached in, unlocked the window, and slid it up, both of them watching the closed basement door. It remained closed.

Dean climbed in first; she followed. Slowly crossing the kitchen, they eased open the door, peering down into the dimly lit stairwell, which, as she recalled, ended outside the rec room Randy had finished. A sharp turn led down a short hallway to a series of other small, finished rooms, one of which was Seth's.

They crept down, covering each other. Dean faced the bottom, Stacey backing step by step with her weapon pointing up in case Seth had hidden upstairs, lying in wait for them.

Her feet had just hit the floor when she heard the slam. It came from down the narrow hallway, in one of the back rooms.

"The Bilco doors," she snapped, immediately recognizing the metallic clang and squeal.

They both hurried toward the sound, hoping to stop Seth from escaping. But as they skidded into the last room, with its low-hanging ceiling and uneven, damp cement floor, they realized they were too late. Sunlight poured from the open doors that led from the darkness up into the day.

Neither of them raced up the steps, however. Because they were both entirely focused on the small cot in the center of the room. And the nightmare that had been taking place down here in the hellish dark.

"Oh, my God, is he . . . ?"

Dean fell to his knees beside the cot, touching the boy who lay there, still, pale, silent. He listened to his chest, touched the tips of his fingers to his throat. It seemed like an eternity before he finally muttered, "He has a pulse. It's slow and thready, but he's alive."

So relieved she almost cried, Stacey knelt, too. Using her pocketknife, she cut through the duct tape binding the child's hands and feet. He remained utterly motionless, and she surmised that he had been drugged.

Seeing a towel on the floor, covered with a few tools and implements, she shook it empty and dragged it over the boy, trying to keep him warm and protected from the cold, damp air of the basement. "It's okay, honey. It's okay; you're going to be fine. We're not going to leave you."

He didn't groan or whimper; in fact he barely even breathed as she gently wiped the blood from the corner of his mouth. Now that they thought they'd saved him from certain death, she prayed that whatever Seth had given the child to knock him out didn't kill him anyway.

As Dean called 911, she looked around and immediately saw the tripod. It stood at the foot of the cot, set low to the ground. It was empty, but had a camera been attached, it would have been level with the boy.

At its base were wires that had been quickly disconnected. They ran to a state-of-the-art desktop computer, which was turned on. The screen was awash with odd, vivid colors. Toys, swings, grass, a blue sky.

Satan's Playground.

She looked away.

"I need to go after Seth," Dean said after he'd finished his call. "You okay staying here with him?"

She nodded. "Be careful. Call me and keep me posted. I'll catch up as soon as backup gets here; it shouldn't be more than a few minutes."

He leaned over the boy, brushing a tender hand across his pale, clammy forehead. Then, a muscle twitching in his jaw, he pointed toward the sharp tools on the floor. The ones that had been laid out neatly on the towel Stacey had grabbed. "Looks like he was setting everything up."

Stacey nodded. She'd realized the same thing. "We're fine. I won't let anything happen to him. Now go."

Pressing a quick kiss on her mouth, Dean went.

Seth had taken his truck, driving over the lawn to get around the two vehicles parked behind it. As Dean ran for his, he pulled his phone out and called Mulrooney. He explained in as few words as possible, not having time to give Kyle any more than the bare bones. That they'd found the Reaper. That he was Randy Covey's twenty-year-old son. And that he was on the run.

"I'm going after him," he snapped. Then he stopped short. "God damn it."

"What?" Mulrooney asked.

"He snipped the fucking valve stems on both cars." Both his car and Stacey's had two flat tires on the driver's side. He wasn't going anywhere.

"Get here fast," he told the other agent. "But first call Wyatt. Get an APB out on Seth Covey and his vehicle."

"Hold tight; we're on the way."

As he cut the call, he heard sirens, soft, in the distance. But no more than a couple of minutes away. He'd have to jump in with one of Stacey's deputies.

Hurrying back to let her know, he headed for the open metal doors and descended into the Reaper's personal hellhole.

"He won't get far," she said after he filled her in. "There are only a couple of roads that lead out of town."

"I know." Seeing the still-motionless child, he asked, "Any change?"

She shook her head.

A moment later, they heard voices from above. Dean darted back outside, seeing the ambulance, not a sheriff's car, and gestured for the paramedics. They followed him down, taking over the care of the Reaper's intended victim. Dean and Stacey watched in silence. Somehow, in the dark, their hands had twined together. She squeezed his, as if knowing that when he looked at that kid, all he saw was Jared's face. Jared lifeless and near death.

"Do you have any idea what he gave him?" one EMT asked after taking the boy's vitals.

Stacey hurried to the desk, grabbing a prescription bottle. She tossed it to the man, who read it and shook his head. "Who the hell would do this to a kid?"

If only he knew.

Stacey and Dean stayed out of the way, letting the professionals do their work. His impatience grew with every second that ticked by. The backup was taking too long; every mile that passed beneath Seth Covey's tires gave him an advantage.

"I know it seems like forever," she said, "but it hasn't been. The firehouse is a couple of miles closer, that's all. We're pretty secluded out . . ." Her voice trailed off.

"What's wrong?"

"You don't think he'd go to Dad's place, would he?"

He immediately shook his head. "No way. He's panicked and on the run."

She didn't look so sure. "You'd think if he was that panicked, he wouldn't have stopped to take his camera."

Not getting her at first, he followed her stare, noting that strangely empty tripod, the computer cables still tangled at the base, yanked free and dropped to the floor. Why would a serial killer lose precious minutes taking a damned video camera?

Unless he still intended to use it.

He swung around and stalked over to the desk, staring down at the desktop CPU. On the screen, nasty little people chattered and talked in excited gibberish. He clicked the mouse, running over the site, not wanting to go down the wrong vile rabbit hole, until he reached the drive-in movie theater he'd heard Lily and Brandon talking about.

"Oh, my God," he whispered when his instincts proved right.

"What?" Stacey asked, stepping behind him.

He pointed to the sign, the marquee outside the theater. One word appeared on it, bold and large, demanding attention.

Hanging.

She gasped. "The camera."

He'd taken it, and probably a laptop, for a reason.

"Where would he go?"

Dean had no idea. But it had to be somewhere close, in town, maybe. Someplace where Seth could quickly set up and hop online for his final performance.

The only question was, whom did he intend to hang? God, did he hope Stacey's fears about her father didn't bear fruit.

Desperate for more information, he clicked on the entrance to the drive-in. When asked to pay credits, he cursed the techno-psychos, then figured out how to spend some of the Reaper's own currency.

As soon as he'd done so, the screen faded to black. Then, very slowly, a picture began to emerge. Not a cartoon, not a phantasmic world of garish light and exaggerated color. This was the real world. And a real person.

"Seth," Stacey whispered, bending low to watch as the picture grew clearer.

When it did, he immediately realized it was already happening. All the excited people in the Playground were shelling out their gold.

The intended victim was the Reaper himself. He was going to commit suicide. Now. Right now, live on the Internet.

Utterly helpless, they watched as Seth Covey, dressed all in black, pulled a noose down from above, sliding it over his head. He stood on an old-fashioned wooden box; the walls surrounding him were rough-hewn and faded, the floor bare dirt.

Seth smiled at the camera. And, without hesitation, kicked the box.

Stacey flinched as the body dropped and began to writhe on the end of the rope. But rather than covering her eyes in horror at seeing her friend's son end his life, she smacked her hand flat on the desk.

"He's in Dad's old barn! It's within reach of the wireless."

They stared at each other for a split second, then rose and ran like hell up the stairs. He could see the barn in the distance. The EMTs were getting ready to bring the boy out and needed the ambulance. A siren was coming up the road, drawing closer, but still at least a minute or two away. More precious seconds would be lost to a trip up the driveway, back down, then two miles up the road.

Straight across the fields was shorter. A mile at most.

Neither of them hesitated. They both ran, flying across the ground, oblivious to the weeds and rocks covering the rough countryside. They reached the bottom of the hill, pounded through a small stream, up the other side.

How long? He didn't want to think about how many minutes it had been, whether Seth's body still twitched and spun. And how many sick fucks around the world were tuning in to watch.

God knew, if there was anybody who deserved the death penalty, it was probably the Reaper. But Dean wanted him to face justice. Not to escape by his own hand, his own way, on his own terms.

He found a reserve of speed and picked it up, covering the final quarter mile a few seconds ahead of Stacey. The barn door was closed, but he burst against it, shattering the old wood, splintering the planks into pieces as he stumbled inside.

He spied the killer immediately. The man hung still. Completely still. But still Dean charged forward, tripping over something—the infernal camera. He kicked it away, dove for Seth's dangling feet, lifting and trying to remove the pressure. Stacey was right behind him, shoving the wooden box back in place, and they both heaved up.

But even before they'd moved to cut him down, Dean knew they were too late. The body was deadweight. Covey's face was purple, his neck bent at an odd angle. It had broken in the fall. And then he'd suffocated.

It was over.

The Reaper was dead.

Chapter 17

Hope Valley had boasted a famous citizen or two in its day. Some World War II hero had hailed from the town, as had a semisuccessful country singer. Even a former Virginia congressman.

The Reaper, however, topped them all.

As soon as word about the case got out, the media descended upon Stacey's small hometown, covering every inch of it like fire ants on an anthill. She couldn't get away from them. She held formal press conferences right away, with Dean and his boss by her side, but the vultures still parked outside her house at night. She felt like a bug under a microscope as they all watched, hoping something new would happen to serve as the teaser for the next broadcast.

There was nothing new left to happen. Covey was dead. His last victim, little Nicholas Logan, would survive physically unscathed, though probably mentally scarred.

They'd even found the final piece of the puzzle they'd been looking for all along. While processing the scene at the barn, Dean had noticed a slightly sunken area in the ground in the back of one of the old stalls.

Lisa.

And that was the end of that.

Still, the reporters pried into all the angles, titillated beyond belief by word that the first victim's mother had killed her husband. And that the Reaper's father was hospitalized but facing charges for theft when he was released. Somehow Rob-the-Perv Monroe had even gotten tangled in there—*Sheriff Who Catches Killer Stalked in Her Own Home*. The mayor had quietly resigned, not stepping forward even once to take advantage of the spotlight. And his sick, miserable excuse for a son was sitting in a mental ward, hopefully being tormented with the memories of what he'd done to poor Lady.

The FBI tried to keep Satan's Playground out of it, but the media had wanted the full details of the Internet connection, and they'd found them. The site had gone black, for good this time, within twenty-four hours of Seth's suicide.

Sick bastards. She could only hope that the FBI would catch them when they inevitably resurfaced.

"Finally got a minute alone, huh?" a voice asked from the open doorway of her office late one weekday afternoon.

Spying Mitch there, she forced a weary smile. "I think it's my first in a week."

"How are you holding up?"

"I'm okay."

It was true. Not great, but she was holding up. She'd just be better if she didn't have to hold up alone. Oh, she was surrounded by friends, supported by her father and her brother, who'd finally gotten past his own situation to help his sister, his town, and his best friend through the ordeal. Her deputies had been rock-solid, the town residents sincerely grateful for a job well-done.

Even Warren Lee had done his civic duty, turning up at the station with some surveillance images from the night Lisa had been killed. He said he'd just discovered them, having gone looking after the case was blown open. She didn't know that she believed him. Still, all was good.

But she went to bed alone every night. She had for several nights, ever since Dean and the rest of the Black CATs, as even the media was now calling them, headed back to D.C.

He'd called. She'd called. But somehow, something had changed. He hadn't had to say it; she'd figured it out.

The case was over. He had no reason to be here. She'd been the one who had demanded a "meaningless," emotionless fling for as long as he was around. Now, the only reason he would have to be around was if she wanted him to be, if this thing they had became personal. Emotional. Real.

It was. Oh, God, it was. She just didn't know whether she could handle that.

A self-protective voice told her she was better off letting him drift away. It would be safer, less painful down the road. Another voice said it was time to let go of the fear and the regret, and take a chance on really living again.

Continue to hide in her small cocoon, playing it safe so she wouldn't get hurt? Or allow herself to rejoin the rest of the world and open herself up to loss? But also to such tremendous possibility. Excitement, passion. Love.

"Is there anything you need me to do?"

She shook her head. "I'm fine."

Mitch stepped inside the office, his hat, literally, in his hands. "Just wanted to say, uh, if you want my resignation, I'll understand."

Stacey merely stared, taken completely by surprise.

"I should have told you about me and Lisa when she first disappeared."

So much had happened, she hadn't given that another thought. "Yes, you should have. But Mitch, honestly, I couldn't do this job without you."

He laughed softly. "Yeah, you could. In fact, you could do this job anywhere. You are the best cop I've ever known, and I think your phone's gonna be ringing off the hook with offers." With a shy smile, he nodded, slipped his hat back on his head, and ducked out, leaving her to sit alone in silence.

She had fielded a few calls. But she hadn't given much thought to them. They'd lurked in the back of her mind, just as this whole thing with Dean lurked in the back of her mind. Something to think about. Something to ponder.

Something she had to decide. And soon.

Dean might have been the last person in the known universe to have discovered Chuck E. Cheese, but in the past couple of weeks, he had more than made up for it. He'd just come from his third Wednesday in a row there, and frankly, if he never saw that big singing rat again, he'd be very happy.

After dropping Jared off at his ex's, he made his way home, glad, at least, that it was late enough to avoid the unrelenting city traffic. It was dark by the time he pulled into the small parking lot beside the old school-turned–apartment building a few blocks from the Capitol. His place was small, but the location was convenient and the neighborhood had a lot of charm. It had an old-fashioned feel that wasn't often found in D.C. Not exactly Hope Valley standards, but quaint.

He wondered, not for the first time, what Stacey would think of it.

Then he saw the squad car parked in his reserved spot. And he realized he was about to find out.

His palms started to sweat as if he were some teenager about to get laid for the first time. And his heart did that crazy flippy thing it had done since he'd first met her.

He'd missed her. Had thought a thousand times about getting in the car and going to her, demanding that she admit what he'd known for quite a while: that she had done the crazy and unthinkable and fallen as much in love with him as he had with her.

It had taken every bit of his strength not to do it. She needed to be the one to figure things out. And he hoped her presence here meant that she had.

Parking beside her, he got out of the car and raised his brow. "You're in my spot."

"Sheriff on official business," she said as she stepped out to join him. "I can't be ticketed."

"You sure?"

A smile broadened her pretty mouth and, beneath the light cast by the lamppost, her eyes glittered with humor. And something more.

"I'll take my chances."

Four words. They could refer to her car, but he knew they didn't. The double meaning hit him dead center, and he smiled back.

She was ready to take her chances with him.

Without another word, he stepped over and grasped her shoulders, bending slightly to catch her mouth in a hot, openmouthed kiss. When they'd been together, Stacey had filled all the empty places, made him feel satisfied and whole for the first time in ages. He'd missed that feeling. Missed this. Missed her.

She arched against him, pressing her soft body against his in pure feminine welcome. Lifting her arms, she tangled her fingers in his hair, kissing him back with just as much hunger and, he hoped, just as much happiness as he was feeling.

When they finally broke apart and looked at each other, he saw she still had that smile on her beautiful face. "Official business, huh?"

She nodded. "I came to talk about my future. My career as sheriff."

He lifted a hand to her silky hair, loose and hanging in a curtain over her shoulders. She wasn't wearing her uniform tonight. Dressed in a soft yellow blouse and white jeans, she looked sunny and feminine. But he'd bet anything she had a backup piece strapped to her ankle.

He couldn't wait to get her inside and find out.

"You're a great sheriff," he said.

"I know." There was no conceit, just that irresistible confidence. "But I'm thinking maybe I'd be a better detective. Maybe somewhere around here."

He cupped her cheek. "Stacey, you don't have to change a thing for me. Hope Valley's not that far away."

"It's the other end of the earth," she replied. "And after my dad's term is up in a few months, I want to come back to this side of it. I'm thinking Sheriff Mitch Flanagan sounds really good." She leaned up and rubbed her soft cheek against his grizzled one. "I'm done. It's over. I'm finished hiding."

"I knew that the minute I saw your car," he said, covering her mouth with his again. This kiss was softer, gentler, infinitely more tender. And when their lips parted to exchange a warm breath of night air, he murmured, "I love you, Stacey."

Her soft sigh of happiness told him before she gave the words back. "I love you, too."

They stood there kissing for a while longer, then, in silence, moved toward the building. Her arm hooked in his, she stayed tucked by his side, fitting against him so perfectly it was as if she'd been made to be there.

"Dean?"

He paused at the door.

Her lip caught on her bottom teeth for a moment, and she looked up at him, her eyes swimming in indecision for the first time since she'd arrived. "I'm looking forward to meeting your son."

He knew what had put that indecision there, and knew he could offer no promises that everything would always be safe and she'd never experience pain or anguish. So he could only tell her what he told himself every single night when he hung up the phone after sharing the monsters-go-away poem with Jared.

"It's worth it. For as long as you have it, no matter what might happen down the road, loving like that is worth it."

She nodded once, not making any promises, not claiming to be ready to dive headfirst into all the things she'd been telling herself she didn't want. Kids, marriage.

They had love. That was the start. And for now, that was enough.

Read on for an excerpt from the next book
in Leslie Parrish's Black CATs series,

Pitch Black

Available now from Signet Eclipse.

*New team member Alec Lambert is trying hard to
reclaim his FBI career after being shot and nearly
fired from the BAU. His first case: to get inside the
head of the Professor, a diabolical killer luring his
victims via the latest Internet scams.
Teaming up with Samantha Dalton, a Web scam
expert, he begins to track down the wily killer.
Neither of them realizes the Professor has a new
victim in his sights: Samantha herself!*

Hello. I am the former finance minister for a once-great nation. I am writing to you about an issue of utmost urgency.

Recent upheavals in my country make it impossible for me to retrieve monies hidden by my government. I write to you begging for assistance. I am needing a partner to help me retrieve the monies. I can trace the funds but must work through a third party for my own safety and the safety of my family.

In exchange for your help you will be paid half of what is recovered, or ten million dollars. Please respond to me to arrange the transfer of money. Your Friend, Dr. Malik Waffi

"I still can't believe you fell for this bullshit."

Ignoring his passenger, Jason Todd clenched the steering wheel of his father's Buick, which he fought to keep on the dark, slippery road. His heart pounded furiously as he strained to see through the snow-streaked windshield. His short, jerky breaths punctuated his excitement.

"We coulda been at a party," Ryan added from the

other side of the car, where he'd been hunched since they'd left home an hour ago. "Instead we're in a blizzard, about to get scammed."

"Nobody forced you to come along."

"Shut up, loser. You know I wouldn't have let you go alone."

No, he wouldn't have. They'd been best friends since first grade, and Jason didn't know if he'd have had the stones to go through with this if Ryan didn't have his back.

"This snow sucks. I can't see shit." Ryan used a grimy Taco Bell napkin to try to clear away some steam from the windshield.

The light snow that had begun falling at sunset had spit down relentlessly for the past hour. The tires fought for every bit of traction they could get. The highway from Wilmington had been fine, but these back roads were untouched. Winter might have started late, with temperatures near fifty at Christmas a couple of weeks ago, but now that it had arrived, it was kicking ass and taking names.

"When's the last time your dad changed the wiper blades?"

"It's not like I could ask him, since he's in Florida." And by the time Jason's parents got back from vacation, he planned to be driving his own car. A nice one, not this crapmobile.

"You know this is all bogus, right? Internet Scam 101."

Man, the guy just wouldn't give up. "You saw the check."

Ryan nodded. He'd been as shocked as Jason when a check for a cool grand had arrived in Jason's mail, a down payment, according to this Waffi guy. "Yeah, yeah, the money," Ryan conceded. "But I still say that check could bounce."

"It's certified. They don't bounce."

"They do if they're fake," Ryan muttered, holding on to his skepticism harder than he'd held on to his belief in Santa Claus.

"It's not fake. Come on, dude, admit you were wrong. Nobody would part with that much money as part of an e-mail scam. Not even your cyber fantasy woman could deny that."

Ryan's lopsided grin made him look even younger than his sixteen years. "Bite me. You know she's a babe. You're just jealous because she never sent you a personalized e-mail."

Jason was happy to have been e-mailed by someone who wanted to make him a millionaire. But he had to admit, judging by the picture on her Web site, Sam the Spaminator was way hot.

"We shoulda waited for her to write me back," Ryan added. "I know she'll say this is all bogus."

"The mo-ney," Jason replied in a singsong voice.

The check in his pocket was all the proof Jason needed that this was legit. Waffi had sent it, saying he wanted to prove he was on the up-and-up. Jason could have cashed it and walked away. But by bringing it to meet the doctor in person tonight, he'd get to exchange it for another one containing a whole lot more zeroes. By tomorrow, he'd be so rich he could do whatever he wanted. Maybe he'd even buy Ryan a Hummer for being his backup.

Picturing it, he almost missed the turn Dr. Waffi had told him to look for. Nearly obscured by tangled brush, the gravel road would have been hard to spot even in good weather. He swerved onto it, maintaining control as the car fishtailed.

He hadn't gone fifty feet when Ryan yelled, "Watch out!"

Suddenly spying the huge truck parked across the entire lane, Jason jerked the wheel hard. They went into a skid, the car spinning wildly as it careened toward the trees. Gravel and snow spewed into the air, the clack of sharp limbs hitting the roof sounding like knives on bone. Ryan flew out of his seat, smashing against Jason, who was punched against the driver's-side window so hard he heard his cheekbone crunch.

As the Buick finally came to a halt a few yards above a slope dropping into a frozen pond, Jason felt sticky moisture dripping down his forehead. His face throbbed; salty fluid saturated his lips. His eyelids were heavy, his vision blurring. But just before he blacked out, he saw a dark shape approaching the car. Someone was out there. "S'okay, man," he mumbled. "Help's here."

They were the last words he managed before darkness washed over him.

And they were the first he thought of when he came to. *Help's here.*

He'd been unconscious for a few minutes. Or a few hours. As he moved from oblivion to awareness, Jason couldn't be sure. He knew only one thing: He was cold. Whatever warmth the car's heater had provided was gone. Sharp pricks of frigid air thrust needle-sharp into his face and body. Trying to force the murky clouds from his brain, he struggled to remember what had happened and where he was.

It didn't take long. They'd crashed. Violently.

But help is here. Right?

"Don't try to move, Jason."

The voice was strong and even, yet not comforting. It held a note of iron firmness that would stand for no disobedience.

It also wasn't the only sound. From nearby, he heard a loud creak, like a giant rocking chair set in motion. "Who—"

"Quiet."

He wondered if he was in a hospital, being tended to

by a stern doctor. If so, maybe his parents were there. They'd be mad at him for crashing, but so relieved he was all right they'd let it go. And Jason would tell them he was sorry. So sorry.

Though the fantasy enticed him, he didn't open his eyes. Partly because he was in so much pain. And partly because he already knew his parents were not there. That was a kid's dream. The nearly adult Jason knew he wasn't in a hospital. Not only was it dark; it was still snowing. The tiny drops of moisture landing on his skin and turning instantly to ice confirmed it. Plus, his lips were bloody. And every inch of him hurt.

"Jason, you were told to come alone."

"Who's there?" he whispered.

Bright light suddenly flashed on, thrusting like a spike through the fine skin of his eyelids and into his pupils. Jason turned away, instinctively trying to escape. His head, however, was the only part of his body he could move. Forcing himself to go slowly, he shifted his eyes down, then began to lift his lids, letting the light in bit by bit.

Definitely outside. His chest was bare. The skin he could see through the crystallized snow had turned gray with cold, possibly even frostbite. His legs, too, shone gray in the snow-whitened moonlight. And oddly, he was sitting upright in a chair.

"Jason?" More stern now.

He didn't look up, stalling as he tried to get his brain working. Icy snow, tinged pink with blood, covered his bare thighs. Seeing a solid strip of silver running across them, he realized why he couldn't move. *Duct tape. What the fuck?*

"What's happening?" he whispered. "Where's Ryan?"

"He's right behind you."

He jerked his head back. It banged against something with a thunk, garnering a moan in response. Ryan was alive. For now.

His eyes shifted frantically and he squinted against the brutal light. *Headlights.* "What's going on?" Another crack sounded nearby. His panic rose. Something in his brain told him he knew the sound and understood its meaning.

"You were told to come alone." The tone remained harsh, yet patient, as if he were some kid whose lesson had to be repeated.

He suddenly had a suspicion. "Dr. Waffi?"

"Ahh, it learns. Now, what have I been saying?"

"I was told to come alone," he admitted.

"You disobeyed. I would think you were being willful, but knowing what I do about you, I'll assume it was pure stupidity."

Tears oozed out of Jason's eyes, sliding an inch or so down each cheek before freezing hard. "Please let me go."

"Go where? To do what?"

"To go home to my parents." Oh, did he wish they hadn't gone away and that he hadn't answered that e-mail.

"Your parents should never have given you life."

Jason started crying like a baby. How could this be happening? He was only seventeen. He'd barely lived. He'd never even banged a girl, despite what he said in the locker room.

"Who is the other one? Is he as stupid as you?"

"Ryan." Hearing a groan, Jason regretted all the shit he'd ever gotten his best friend into. "He knew this was a scam."

"So, he's no fool. But he has poor taste in friends." The man's coldness was underscored by one of those maddening cracking noises. It was longer. Louder. "He'll pay for that now."

"Are you crazy?" Jason screamed. "Let us go!"

Another crack. Jason could now feel something crackling beneath his frozen feet. The hard ground felt uneven, rock-hard yet still unstable. So very cold.

Terrified, Jason suddenly realized what the sounds were. And what was about to happen. He jerked, fighting the tape, knowing he should remain still. "No, don't do this!"

He finally stared directly at the light—high beams from his dad's banged-up Buick. Facing him, it sat at the top of a small slope a few yards away. As he watched, a dark, shadowy figure, faintly visible in the snowy night, walked up the slope toward it.

For one brief moment, the figure passed in front of the headlights, casting a shadow so long it seemed to stretch for miles, enveloping Jason in its blackness. Then it moved on until reaching the open car door.

Jason knew what the man was going to do even before he bent into the car and flipped off the lights. The sudden darkness was almost as blinding, the terror infinitely more extreme. Because he didn't have to see the car being shifted into neutral or hear the emergency brake being released to know exactly what was happening. "God, no, please."

The vehicle began to roll down the slope, drawing irrevocably closer to the icy pond on which Jason and Ryan were trapped. "Why are you doing this?" he yelled, straining against the tape even as the front tires reached the frozen shoreline.

Behind him, he felt movement. Ryan was coming to.

"Good-bye, Jason," the voice called. "The world will be better off without you. Shame about your friend. You really should have come alone."

The shadowy figure moved, disappearing into the swirling snow. A moment later, an engine rumbled, then slowly faded away. He barely heard it as the car eased closer, sliding across the snow-slicked ice. Adding weight, so much weight.

Crack.

How deep is the water? How thick could the ice be? Will we freeze or will we drown?

"Jase?"

"Ryan, I'm sorry I got you into this," he sobbed.

Ryan's head moved, until his frozen hair touched Jason's face. "S'okay. Sidekick's always got the hero's back."

"Sorry!" Jason cried, trying not to move yet desperate to break away. But before he could do a thing, even say good-bye to his best friend, another crack came and the ice gave way beneath them. Freezing liquid rushed over his feet and ankles, bringing them back to life to experience the agony.

They plunged down until blackness covered their heads and ice seared his lungs. And as the water turned the world above him into an icy grave, Jason could think only of his parents.

God, how he wished he'd gone with them to Florida.

NATIONAL BESTSELLING AUTHOR
CARLA CASSIDY

EVERY MOVE YOU MAKE

On her thirtieth birthday, Annalise Blakely gets a strange package. Inside, along with one of her company's hand-crafted dolls, is a note: "I don't need this anymore. I have my own." Annalise puts the package aside—she has enough on her mind. Since her mother died, Annalise has been working nonstop to keep Blakely Dolls a success. Her deadbeat dad wants to be back in the picture. And she's dating again.

But the policeman she's seeing has chilling news: someone is murdering women, dressing them up as Blakely Dolls, and leaving them for the police to find. And, although no one knows it yet, the killer is stalking Annalise, the model for the original doll, for his final display...

<u>ALSO AVAILABLE</u>
Are You Afraid?
Paint it Red
Broken Pieces
Last Gasp

**Available wherever books are sold or at
penguin.com**